Ballet Orphans

Also by Terez Mertes Rose

Off Balance
Outside the Limelight
A Dancer's Guide to Africa

Ballet Orphans

Ballet Theatre Chronicles
A Prequel

Terez Mertes Rose

Published in the United States
Classical Girl Press - www.classicalgirlpress.com
Cover design by James T. Egan, BookFly Design, LLC
Formatting by Polgarus Studio

ISBN (softcover) 978-0-9860934-9-4
ISBN (ebook) 978-0-9860934-7-0

To my father, Tom Mertes, who passed away as I was finalizing this book. And to my mother, Mary Mertes, who waited 30 long years to welcome him Home.

"Call it a clan, call it a network, call it a tribe, call it a family. Whatever you call it, whoever you are, you need one."

— Jane Howard

October 1989
New York City

Chapter 1

Bad News from Omaha

The bad news arrived backstage at the New York State Theater, seconds before curtain. The timing couldn't have been worse. My partner Mick and I had already settled in our opening pose onstage, the orchestra cued, when the in-house phone next to the monitor rang. Everyone knew only emergency calls came through during a performance. Alarmed, I glanced over at the stage manager as he listened with a few terse "uh huh" replies. He looked up and met my gaze. His face was impassive, but I knew, right then.

It was bad. And it involved me.

There was no time to think. The curtain began to rise, giving me no choice but to freeze in our couple's pose, smile brightly, await our music cue, and dance. Which was fine in the end, because when something very bad is occurring in real life, it helps to switch over to performing life. My adrenaline had been triggered, because I knew, I *knew,* that something terrible had happened, and my biggest question at that point was, "Is my mother alive or dead?" I tried to tell myself it was simply a knee-jerk response after hearing of my dad's death in the same way, two and a half years earlier.

The opening section's lightning-fast pace, our arms moving as busily as our legs, required all my attention. A partnered arabesque en pointe flowed into a rapid pivot to the other direction, and a cartwheel-like lift that planted me on Mick's other side. The blinding lights from the side booms cast the stage manager in shadow, mercifully obscuring him and his news. Our downstage right exit, however, brought us right to him. As Mick, panting, loped over to the table that held his water bottle, I approached the stage manager. He'd swiveled away from his monitor to face me, headphones askew so he could hear both me and his crew.

"Just tell me this," I said. "Do I need to catch a flight to Omaha tonight?"

He hesitated. "You should."

Which meant my mom was still alive.

"How bad is she? It's my mom, right?"

He nodded reluctantly. "She's had a stroke. She's in intensive care. Your aunt called. She said your mother's condition is critical but stable, and for you to come when you can."

"Please, can someone find Vincent and tell him the news?" Vincent was my boyfriend and an ABT—American Ballet Theatre— company principal. I paused to steady my shaking voice. "Ask him to get me a seat on a flight departing from JFK any time after ten."

"All right," the stage manager said, and nodded to his assistant, who sped off.

Vincent arrived backstage while I was finishing my solo. He was in costume, performing in the night's third ballet with Natalia. Natalia, like me, was a soloist with the ABT although five years younger. Russian-bred and Bolshoi-trained, she was sublimely talented, eyeing the promotion to principal that all the female soloists wanted. More disconcerting, of late, she'd been eyeing Vincent with the same hungry expression. But now Natalia was the least of my concerns.

Vincent enveloped me in a smothering hug the instant I stepped offstage.

4

"Oh, April!" he exclaimed in a tragic, theatrical voice, over and over until I pushed him away. It was cloying. It seemed to be more about Vincent showing everyone how caring he was, rather than Vincent aching with genuine compassion.

"Did you get me a flight?" I asked.

"I did. There's a long layover; nothing gets you into Omaha until early morning."

"That's all right. I expected that. Thank you."

"How are you doing—" he began, but I held up a hand.

"I can't talk about the rest now. I'm sorry. I need to focus." I turned abruptly away from him and stepped to the upstage right wing, alone, to await the next cue. But by now, others knew about the news. One wing down, two male corps dancers were discussing it, unaware of my presence nearby.

"Didn't this already happen to her? Wasn't her mom dying a couple years ago?"

"That was her dad."

"Shit. Did he die?"

"Yeah."

"Shit. Now her mom?"

"Yeah."

"Is she dead?"

"Nah. But maybe dying."

"What a drag."

"Seriously. Hey, wanna go grab dinner tonight?"

"Sure. As long as I can ice my knee while we're eating."

"Antonio's will bring you an ice pack if you order a full meal."

"Sounds good to me. Where's my towel? I'm sweating like a pig tonight."

Mick appeared by my side. Unlike Vincent, he knew how to handle my news. He gave my hand a supportive squeeze and we stood without talking as the ensemble dancers waltzed off the stage and the music shifted from energetic to contemplative. Once onstage, we began our pas de deux. Midway, Mick lifted me high overhead. From this elevated view, I could see all the way out to the furthest tiers of the theater's seating. Little ovals of light punctuated the darkness throughout, reflections of people's eyeglasses, that right then seemed mystical. Like miniature celestial beings. Fairies. Spirits of the departed.

Spirits like my dad.

Please, God, not Mom, too.

Mick's grip on my hip tightened, letting me know I'd hesitated a millisecond too long. I lowered my gaze, straightened my body and slid down his, making up speed so that I ended en pointe, in arabesque, right in time with the music.

My focus returned. Mick's hands, sure and supportive, guided me through the trickier passages, and now I was able to remain in the zone, where only the dance mattered. Even my mom's situation faded to a different sphere of existence.

Oh, to stay in this place forever.

When my dad died, he'd been weak, the cancer winning after a protracted battle. My mom and I had seen his death coming, watched it grow closer, step by ominous step, and yet, when the end came, it managed to surprise us all. In retrospect, it was as if he'd harvested a burst of energy to offer me one last gift, an illusion of well-being, so that I'd remember that delightful day, his warm smile, his lucid, even witty banter, and not the memory of his decline, that gaunt, bony face, his body as light as a boy's, all bones and sinew and mottled skin. From Omaha, I'd flown back to New York City, confident I could finish the ABT's current performance run and return home four days later. But he'd gone into cardiac arrest and passed away the next evening, precisely at curtain time. He'd died at age 74; my mom currently was only 65. She was supposed to have been the one to last long, like her own mother, living into her nineties, and like her three older sisters, still going strong in their late 70s. She wasn't supposed to die. She hadn't yet, I reminded myself sternly, as my plane departed that evening from New York with a shuddering roar. Strokes could be managed.

Except that upon arrival at the hospital early the next morning, I learned a second, worse stroke had robbed my mother of most of her speech and right-side movements. Numbed by fatigue and the newest bad news, I pulled the chair close to my mom's bed and sat. It was dim in the room, weak morning light filtering through the half-closed shades. The cool, sterile air and mysterious noises of the ICU ward both soothed and jarred me.

My mom stirred finally. I reached over and took her thin, frail hand, its skin only now starting to speckle with age. Her golden-brown hair, its color and thickness in earlier years identical to my own, was now liberally laced with silver, but still long, in its customary braid. My mom had never been one to follow fashion trends, and her long braid remained eternal proof.

"I'm here, Mom." I tried to sound confident, matter of fact. "I love you."

In response, she clutched my hand. Her eyes transmitted all the feelings she couldn't express through words. Anxiety. Fear.

"Don't worry," I soothed. "It's okay. I'm here now. How about some more light in here?" Without waiting for her response, I adjusted the blinds. I spied a hospital toiletries bag that held the essentials—toothbrush and paste, comb and brush—and gestured to it. "Why don't I brush your hair? Redo the braid. That would be nice, I'm thinking."

The action of gently unbraiding and plowing the brush's plastic bristles through her hair seemed to relax us both. As I brushed, I told her about the latest goings on at the studios, the theater, light-hearted foibles and adventures in my life as a New York ballet professional. She always loved hearing my stories, first and foremost, before bringing the conversation around to how things were in Omaha. I described the challenging yet fun lifts Anders Gunst was incorporating into the new ballet he was setting on Vincent, Natalia and me. "Anders is the co-artistic director of Dance Theatre of Brussels, but he used to be our colleague at the ABT. A principal, like Vincent, except he's younger, only twenty-nine. Latest news, though, is that Anders has been selected to take over directorship of the West Coast Ballet Theatre in San Francisco. That's huge! Did I mention he's Danish? You can't tell when he talks—he speaks perfect English." I knew I was chattering and that she couldn't possibly follow everything, but I also knew it would upset her more if I treated her like the dangerously unwell patient she was. Best to converse as I always did. "The West Coast Ballet Theatre is a big company," I continued cheerily. "Nothing like New York, of course, but still. Anders is dynamite. I was so proud he picked me for his new ballet, alongside Vincent and Natalia. Those two are really good. It's going to be fantastic—I can't wait for you to see the performance in the spring."

My mom made a muffled groaning sound. I stopped brushing to look at her face. The slack nature of her right eyelid, the way her mouth drooped on the right side, seemed more pronounced now. She clearly wanted to speak, but was having trouble getting words out.

"Mmmgh. Rrrrg."

I studied her, mystified.

My mom's body tensed. "Sssss. *Sorry.*"

"You're sorry," I repeated, and the anxiety in my mother's eyes lessened.

"Mom, don't be sorry. About anything. Please."

What had I been thinking, bringing up the performance, the future?

"Ssss. Nnnn fmmm." My mom still wanted to speak. It became like a macabre game of charades.

Sorry? Sorry no foam? Okay. Sounds like film? No, like fan. Like fam. Family? Yes, family! Sorry no family.

After a minute of this, I finally figured it out. "You're sorry that I'll have no family once you're gone."

Bingo. Her straining body slumped back into the pillows.

"Oh, Mom. Whatever happens, I'll be okay. Please don't worry. I have the company—they're my family. I've known them, spent so much time with them. For eight years now.

"And there's Vincent," I continued. "Who knows? Dancers frequently marry dancers. They spend so much time together, and all, and understand the life of a performing professional. Maybe someday, Vincent and I..." I stopped. The words sounded absurd, even to my ears. My mother tried to speak again, and this time her words were clear and easy to understand.

"Nnnn. Not. Him."

Which hurt to hear. I'd brought Vincent home the previous summer, certain my mother would be as dazzled as everyone else. He was a star, after all, as an ABT principal. And even though he was a little too aware of his good looks, and, okay, a little too flashy, I firmly believed Vincent was a good person, deep down. He'd grown up in working-class Ohio, and although he scorned his roots and considered himself a New Yorker at heart, I saw that humbler, likeable boy in him from time to time. I would have thought my mom had seen that, too. But looking at her expression now, I could tell Vincent had not won her over.

A memory from last night reinserted itself back into my brain. Seeing, from across the stage, Natalia standing close to Vincent, all but pressing against him. Vincent not moving away. And while rehearsing Anders' new ballet the previous week: watching Vincent and Natalia as he flung her up, caught her, cradled her tenderly, reluctant to let go. The chemistry, the abandon the two of them had exhibited—I'd assumed it was simply great dancing by two brilliant dancers.

The instant the darker idea arose, I dismissed it. Vincent was not just my lover but my friend. He'd resist the advances of someone like Natalia, already notorious as a man-eater type who discarded as freely as she acquired. Vincent was smarter than that.

And yet.

Stop being paranoid, I commanded myself. "Why don't I read to you?" I asked my mom. "Remember all the years you did that to me when I was a kid? I loved that." I rummaged in my bag and pulled out the novel I'd brought for the plane. "I know *Jane Eyre* is pretty old fashioned, but for some reason, I've had an appetite for the classics of late."

She made a noise of assent and I began to read.

Disruptions abounded. Doctors made their rounds, offering prognoses that boiled down to a "wait and watch." Nurses and assistants bustled in and out. When a nurse returned to attend to my mother around eleven o'clock, I slipped away to the bathroom, to wash my face and comb my hair, apply moisturizer, niceties I hadn't considered since leaving the theater the night before. The nurse left and silence fell over the room. The peace was short-lived. I was applying lip gloss when I heard my aunts arrive.

Aunts Irma and Sally. Much older than my mother, they had grandchildren closer to my age than their own children. The extended family had been kind enough to me, the "caboose" niece, just as my own mom had been the caboose of four daughters, born twelve years after the other three. But she and I remained oddities within the family. My mom had been a spinster, a mild-mannered librarian who'd shocked all by courting and marrying my dad, an older physics professor, in scandalously short time. I was born ten months later, when she was a month shy of forty-one. Add my early signs of talent as a ballet dancer, my elite training far from home, my father's eccentric brilliance, and this completed the image of differentness for our little family of three. I made the effort to spend time with extended family whenever I visited Omaha, especially after my dad's death, but visits and events were more dutiful than pleasurable. Like an interrogation, albeit one with refreshments, everyone eyeing me warily.

I was about to call out a hello to my aunts through the closed door when Aunt Sally spoke.

"I see she hasn't arrived yet."

They were talking about me. I looked down at my travel bag, there in the bathroom with me. My coat and purse had been stowed away, out of view, to keep the hospital room neat.

"She was performing when I called," Aunt Irma replied. "It was late. She probably took the morning flight out."

"It's approaching noon, and still no sight of her."

"Maybe she took a later flight so she could sleep in," Aunt Irma suggested.

Silence. I could almost see them eyeing each other in mutual disapproval. They were Nebraska women, farm-raised, hard-working, plain-spoken. They thought what I did for a profession was all glamour and frivolity.

"Priorities." Aunt Sally allowed a note of scorn to creep into the lone word.

A snort from Aunt Irma seemed to echo the sentiment.

A wave of new weariness and sorrow came over me. My aunts were good people; they would be mortified once they realized I was in the room, overhearing them. But what they'd revealed couldn't be unheard.

I sucked in a slow breath, reached over, and flushed the toilet.

The conversation stopped.

I ran the water faucet, a pantomime of washing, pulling a paper towel as if to dry my hands. And now the conversation outside the bathroom took on a fake brightness, so that when I stepped out, we greeted each other with exclamations, awkward hugs and pecks on the cheek. We all marveled aloud at how good the other looked, and other polite falsehoods that you did to maintain pleasant family relations, but through it all, I felt the aching truth behind my mother's concern.

You'll have no family once I'm gone.

The three of us grew silent as we studied my mother. She looked worse; her cheeks had taken on a greyish pallor, casting doubt on any illusion of a positive end result. Terror flared up in me again, a breath-stealing child's fear at the prospect of losing my last parent.

Aunt Irma turned to me, her expression kinder. "You've been here a while?"

"Since eight o'clock."

"Poor dear," Aunt Sally said, her sympathy genuine. "That's early. You must be exhausted."

"I'm fine," I lied.

"Why don't you go get yourself something to eat?" Aunt Irma said. "There's that Denny's, less than a block away. It's much better than the cafeteria downstairs. We'll be here with your mom."

"Thanks, that's a good idea. I won't be long."

"Take your time. Your mom isn't going anywhere."

The brisk Omaha air made me wrap my coat more tightly around myself, but the walk to the restaurant served to ground me. All physical motion did. It always had, since my earliest memory of dancing in the living room, any time my dad put on one of his classical recordings, which was almost every evening. Leaping around in the backyard by day whenever my mom ordered me outside to "burn off that incessant energy of yours." One time I'd politely announced to the extended family that "my incessant energy exhausts my mother." I'd been three and a half at the time, and, according to my mom, everyone had stared at me as if the doll I'd been clutching had done the speaking.

"Those are some big words from such a little girl," Aunt Irma had managed, and my librarian mother had nodded with pride.

I was hungry; I'd had no time for dinner the previous night in my haste to catch my flight. I ordered a plate crowded with two kinds of breakfast meat, two kinds of carbs, a mass of eggs. It was dense, greasy and satisfying. Once I'd finished, I spied a payphone and glanced at my watch. Good time to call the ABT, to update them. I called and spoke with Ron, the associate artistic director, relayed the situation, and afterward asked about Vincent's whereabouts. Ron had someone pull him from his rehearsal and put him on the line.

"Sweetie, how are you?" Vincent exclaimed. "I've been thinking about you all day."

"I'm okay. My mom's hanging in there. Critical, but stable. My aunts are with her right now."

"How soon are you coming back?"

"I honestly don't know. If her condition deteriorates, that's a different scenario from if she stabilizes and improves. I told Ron I'd touch base as soon as I knew more."

"Good. Good. Stay as long as you need to."

Was it my imagination or did he sound relieved? Something about it rang false. Even when my father was dying, Vincent had cautioned me to "watch how much time you take off," because it came around to affect your reputation with the artistic director, the choreographers, the répétiteurs.

Vincent hesitated. He nervously cleared his throat before speaking again.

"There's something you should know. It's about Natalia."

My body grew still. *Please don't let this be that he's leaving me for her.* The possibility, indeed, the probability overwhelmed me, choked me of a reply. "What?" I managed.

"She got promoted to principal after last night's performance."

An instant of relief was eclipsed by a great roar of disappointment, even though I'd seen it coming. I knew the odds had favored Natalia. That they would always favor the Russian defector who dazzled audiences and made them clamor for more. The Bolshoi dancers were impossible to compete with. In spite of Natalia's youth—she'd just turned twenty—from the day of her arrival at the ABT the previous season, the writing had been on the proverbial wall.

It would always be this way at the ABT. I would forever remain soloist rank there, a prospect that would have filled me with happiness and comfort four years earlier, as a corps de ballet dancer starved for something bigger.

"Wow." I didn't know what else to say, how to best sum up this feeling of terrible news atop catastrophic news.

But this still didn't explain Vincent. He loved sharing thrilling, titillating news, even if it was painful for the listener to hear.

"Is that why you're relieved I'm not there?" I blurted out, surprising even myself.

"What are you talking about?" he stammered.

My suspicion built. "I can tell. I know you."

"That's a terrible thing to say! I'm worried about you. I'm worried about how you're coping, there in the hospital, with your dying mother."

"She's not dying." My voice shook.

Vincent fell silent, and in his silence came the painful truth.

Yes, she is. Your mother is dying.

I brushed away the terrifying thought. "Did you and Natalia go right out and celebrate her good news?"

"April! What is going on with you?"

How stupid of me, to have opened this Pandora's box, during this most vulnerable time. Had I kept my mouth shut, my suspicions unvoiced, I could have glossed right over this uncomfortable supposition and left it there, throbbing in the outer recesses of my mind. Instead, now, there it was. The chill of the hallway where the payphones were located made me start to shiver, spasms that increased in intensity until I wasn't sure how long I could remain there, holding onto the phone, staring at the tightly spiraled chrome cord that connected Vincent's voice to my ear.

"I am so worried about you," Vincent was saying. "You're not sounding like yourself. Should I come out? I'll tell them this is an emergency. Vasilio can take the final performance. You need me there."

I remained mute. To conjure up further dialogue, with its tricky twists and invisible side avenues seemed beyond my abilities.

"April?"

"I don't need you."

"Well, gee, thanks." He sounded hurt.

"I'm sorry. I mean, I don't need you to come here. But thank you for offering."

"You're welcome. I care."

"Thank you."

"By the way," he said, his usual buoyant tone instantly replacing the hurt one. "Anders came backstage last night after the show. He was looking for you."

Could anything worse happen on this terrible day? "I hope he's not planning to pull me from his ballet."

"Of course not, silly! Don't give that a second thought."

This time, at least, his words sounded truthful, unrehearsed.

"I wouldn't be surprised if it wasn't about trying to poach you," Vincent mused. "He already hit me with a request to join him in San Francisco." Here, he chuckled. "Don't go doing that, April. Sid Hauser was artistic director there for way too long, way past his prime. And since he left, the West Coast Ballet Theatre has been this sinking ship. They may have some strong dancers, but they've got issues far beyond what our young Anders Gunst can handle. They literally ran Sid's replacement out of town. The guy resigned, in the middle of last year's Nutcracker run, and the dancers themselves took over. So messed up. You can bet Anders wants dancers he knows and can trust. But if he fails, any dancer he brought over will go right down with him."

The thought made me wince. "I thought you liked Anders."

"I love the guy! He's amazing. His choreography is fresh and superlative. He and Sabine are doing great things with their Brussels company. He's young; if I were him, I'd stay put, right there, for another three to five years, and only then consider something like the West Coast Ballet Theatre. That is, if it hasn't gone under."

"Did you tell Anders where I was?"

"I did. He was very kind about it. Asked me to extend his condolences. Said not to worry, that he'd get in touch with you once you were back in New York."

The mention of New York, of Anders and his support, calmed me. I still had this—a soloist position with one of the best dance companies in the world. A choreographer and artistic director of rising power who believed in my talents. My art. My cloistered world in NYC.

Why did it all have to come with the price tag of losing my family?

"Look, I've got to run," Vincent said. "Rehearsal."

"Sure. I'm glad I caught you."

"Me too. Love you, sweetie. Talk soon."

"Love you, too. Bye."

I paid my bill and returned to the hospital. In the ICU, I trudged down the hushed, ghostly corridor to my mother's room. Aunt Sally was alone there with my mother, who, in her sleep, looked more dead than alive. Fear clutched at my heart and didn't let go.

Aunt Sally looked up as I approached. Her smile was less determinedly optimistic. It dawned on me that I'd never seen my aunt look discouraged before.

"Where's Aunt Irma?" I asked.

"She went for a coffee downstairs," Aunt Sally said.

We stood there, watching the slight rise and fall of my mother's chest as the machines nearby hissed and sucked. Atop the beige blanket, one frail hand rested, which I covered with my own. My mother didn't stir.

"Everything all right, back there in New York?" Aunt Sally asked finally.

I paused to consider the question. "Things will turn out as they should," I said, and was rewarded by an approving nod from my aunt.

"There you go. That's the attitude."

"What's going to happen next?"

It was a rhetorical question, one I didn't realize I'd vocalized until Aunt Sally nodded and pointed to me, as if my words had taken form and affixed themselves to my chest.

"Things will turn out as they should."

August 1990
San Francisco

Chapter 2

First Day

A noise outside woke me and for a moment I didn't know where I was. My eyes met white walls with high ceilings and elaborate cream moldings. A window delivered unfamiliar brightness and a half-dozen stacked cardboard boxes stood sentry by the door. Finally, it sank in.

San Francisco. My new life as a principal dancer with the West Coast Ballet Theatre. A place where, finally, I stood a real chance at being the best of the best.

Life took, and it gave.

I shimmied out of bed and padded into the kitchen. Today, without the blanket of fog, the sunshine spilled through the eastern windows onto the kitchen's wooden floors and made the whole place glow. The apartment was a coveted corner unit, with two bay windows that offered cozy nooks and views of the city street activity below. The building bordered a dodgy neighborhood but had the perk of being walking distance to the WCBT building and the adjacent California Civic Theater, where the company performed.

The ring of a phone made me jump. The phone company had estimated my service would start late in the day or the next. But there it was, my phone plugged into the wall, jingling away.

I hurried over and picked up the receiver. "Hello?"

"Your phone is working."

I recognized Anders' voice and smiled. "It is."

"Apparently your alarm clock is working too. You sound wide awake."

"The sun woke me."

"I told you the foggy mornings were temporary. Do you like the unit with this sunshine?"

"Love it."

"That had been my hunch."

One of the administrators had told Anders about the apartment availability, weeks earlier. Although small, it was adorable and had fit my budget constraints. After seeing it, Anders had been so sure I'd want it, he'd put down the deposit so the landlord wouldn't offer it to anyone else. He'd been a source of support and friendship like this since my arrival, five days earlier. Evening tours of the city; grabbing meals together; sharing with me his musings about challenges that lay ahead. He'd hosted a dinner on Saturday night in my honor so I could get to know the most senior dancers before rehearsals started. Although we'd been cordial and friendly in New York—we'd been dancers in the same company from '82 to '87, after all—I'd never been his peer or close friend, not in the way Vincent, his fellow principal, had been. But in this new setup, my status had risen.

"Are you ready for today?" he asked.

"I am. You?"

"Very. Except for a small, uncomfortable detail." He sighed. "My sources have shared that a mutiny is already being planned. Apparently I'm not as universally approved of as I'd hoped."

"What? How is this possible? The dancers met you last year and gave the green light on you. The ones I met on Saturday night seemed genuinely eager to work with you." My eyes fell on the cheat sheet I'd created, impressions from the dinner, which I'd taped to the refrigerator.

Curtis – principal. Good guy. Tall and well built. Anders plans to pair us a lot.
Carrie – principal. Pretty and blonde. Kind, gracious, but kept some distance.
Lexie – most senior of the soloists. Friendly and nice. Wants to choreograph someday.
Jacob – retired principal, now Anders' second in command. Seems nervous about it.
Kirill & Sonya – gorgeous Russian married couple. Aloof, very important dancers (and don't they know it). Talked only to Curtis, Carrie, Jacob. Anders not offended.
Dmitri – no show. Another Russian, also v. important. Anders thinks he'll be difficult.

"The company has forty dancers," Anders said, "ten to fifteen of whom I haven't been able to get a feel for. That's all it takes sometimes. A herd mentality takes over."

"What are you going to do?"

"Not change my strategy in the least. My hunch is that those looking to wreak havoc will be assessing me this week, but not acting just yet, except by not signing their contracts."

The contract business was a WCBT oddity. The dancers here, not yet unionized, had all been given a choice: to sign new contracts last spring for the upcoming year, or hold off till now, so as to decide whether they felt they could work with Anders.

"I saw a handful of dancers delivering their signed contracts when I was with Megann in Human Resources on Friday morning," I offered as I poured water into the tea kettle and set it on the stove to heat.

"And I know another dozen signed last spring. But that leaves over half still unsigned."

"What are those dancers thinking?" I protested. "A contract is protection. And frankly I'm a little surprised they aren't unionized."

"Sid Hauser apparently used to tell the dancers they didn't need that kind of protection," Anders mused. "Said they were a 'family' and that he'd look after them. Which he did. But he was lousy at working within the company's means. And while the arts world might have been flush with cash, sponsors and grants in the seventies, it isn't anymore. I've inherited a staggering budget deficit." He sighed. "Regardless, we move forward. Contracts, or what have you, there's always upheaval when a new artistic director takes over. By the way, did I tell you Loretta in Public Relations wants you to meet her at nine o'clock this morning?"

"You did. That'll be my first stop today."

"She's a good egg. We'll be fine with her on our side."

We talked until my tea kettle began to shriek. "Tea time," Anders observed.

"First cup of the day."

"Always the best one."

"Agreed."

"All right, I'll leave you to your tea. I'll plan to meet you before your meeting with Loretta. Shall we say 8:55, in the lobby, by the security desk?"

"Sounds great. See you soon."

I made my cup of tea and sipped as I wandered through the half-empty apartment. The second bedroom lay empty, waiting for my childhood ballet-buddy friend Fiona to claim it, once she moved from Omaha. The plan was within a month's time, to match her boyfriend's timetable. He'd been out twice to interview for a job. Fiona would be flying out the following Sunday to do some job hunting of her own. The living room held Omaha memorabilia, like my parents' old television, built into its own cabinet. It hunkered in the corner, a relic from my childhood. It had been bulky and expensive to transport, and, like my parents, I was more a reader than a TV watcher, but this was a piece of them I could keep forever. I caressed the wood now, feeling both sorrow and solace course through me.

Grief turned your life upside down. Losing your parents turned your life upside down. But paradoxically, it freed you in a way nothing else could. Once you survived the loss, being irrevocably separated from the two people who'd given you life, whom you'd loved most in life, big changes became possible in ways unconsidered. Had my mother not died, I might never have considered leaving New York and the ABT. It was all I'd ever known as a professional ballet dancer. But after my mother's death—she'd never left the hospital and had died there five days later—I'd felt as though I were floating. Back in New York, rehearsals and the ten-performance run of *Giselle* were a surreal experience. I'd broken up with Vincent upon my return, in spite of his stammered innocence of any wrongdoing (rendered less valid when he and Natalia became a couple a week later). When one of the corps dancers sprained her ankle, I'd asked to be her replacement—I'd begged, actually—even though I was a rank higher. It had been the only place I'd felt normal, in that unearthly second act, just one of twenty-four grieving, silent Wilis, jilted maidens dead before their wedding day. The lighting so pale and ghostly, the twenty-four of us in long, white tulle skirts, heads downcast, arms folded in, felt nothing short of transcendent. No wonder audiences loved ballets like this. They took the ugliness of death and regret and turned it into something unspeakably beautiful.

After I'd eaten, dressed and readied myself to go, I paused in the living room again to pick up a framed photo of my parents and me. I was fifteen, my first year away from home. I was in costume and heavily applied makeup, having just performed in the SAB—School of American Ballet—end-of-year recital. My parents were beaming, but plain-looking in their everyday clothes. It had embarrassed me at the time, made me feel ashamed of their Midwestern values, caring more about each other and their daughter than how they looked. How foolish I'd been.

I missed them. I would never stop missing them. When I slowed down enough to allow myself to visit that tender, unspeakable place of loss, the hole in my heart grew, big enough for me to fall into. But today felt brisk and can-do. With dry eyes, I tenderly drew a finger across the glass and planted a soft kiss on the frame. "Wish me luck, Mom and Dad. It's showtime again."

As I approached the WCBT front double doors, I noticed a cluster of girls ahead who were excitedly clamoring for an autograph from a beautiful, theatrical-looking man. He had the body language, sleek build and assertive stance of a star principal dancer. Since I'd met Curtis and Kirill at dinner on Saturday night, I surmised this was the third male principal, the night's no-show, Dmitri Petrenko.

Two older women approached from a different direction once the girls had dashed off, waving their paper prizes. I stood back and watched in amusement. Dmitri was taking it all in with pleasure. He smiled at all of them, not without affecting a faux-weary demeanor that portrayed the depth of his commitment to his adoring fans.

"Oh, Mr. Petrenko," I heard one of the older women speak in a breathless tone. "It *is* you!"

"It is," Dmitri replied. "Please. Call me Dmitri."

"I love you!" the woman gushed, and her two friends laughed out loud. "I mean," she hastily added, "I love your work. Everything you do. Albrecht in *Giselle*. Basilio in *Don Quixote*."

"And the lead you had in that contemporary one," another of the women added. "The one last February, where you carried off your dead beloved and made the whole audience cry."

Her friends nodded vigorously in agreement.

"May we have your autograph?" the first woman asked.

"Of course, of course!" He accepted the scraps of paper each of the women pulled from their purses. I studied my new colleague. He had a magnetic presence, there was no denying it. An intense, dark-eyed gaze. Thick, glossy black hair and full, pouty lips. All of which seemed exaggerated in person. Up close, famous people tended to have these curious flaws you never saw in print or on film. He was shorter than I'd realized. Leaner. It was hard to believe he was so strong, but I'd seen videos of his performances where he'd made the partnered lifts look effortless.

The women exclaimed over their autographs, Dmitri's kindness, the thrill of seeing him. He politely inclined his head in the direction of the front double doors.

"Of course, you have to go," the oldest one said, catching the hint. "We're sorry to hold you up!"

"Not a problem."

Only after they walked away, clearing the area in front of the doors, did I approach. Dmitri eyed me in interest and flashed me the same professional smile.

"Um, hello, Dmitri," I stuttered, suddenly shy. "It's nice to meet you. I was—"

"Please. Call me Dmitri," he said, clearly on autopilot. "Would you like an autograph? I saw you standing there earlier, too shy to approach. Don't worry, I don't bite!"

"No, actually, it's that—"

"You don't have a piece of paper on you? That's no problem. I carry spares for this very reason." He reached behind him to a side pocket of his dance bag in a practiced gesture and withdrew a blank index card. As he fished around for a pen, I tried again to explain myself, with increasing chagrin.

"Dmitri," I tried again, but something behind me distracted him, made the movie-star smile lessen. He straightened, and a haughty look came over his face.

"I see you've met," a familiar voice said. I swung around and saw Anders approach. I'd never been so grateful to see him. He was slightly taller than Dmitri, but less flamboyantly attractive. Anders was a thinking-woman's attractive, Danish-born, with refined yet neutral features, an alert stillness in his demeanor. He had intelligent grey eyes that lit with animation whenever he laughed, transforming his face into something dazzling, except that he didn't laugh often. I wondered if it were a Scandinavian thing, to appear so somber.

"Dmitri and I haven't actually met yet," I told Anders. I turned back to Dmitri, feeling the warmth of embarrassment creep up my neck. "I'm April Manning. I'm your new colleague."

"Of course, you are," he said, not missing a beat. "Which is why I'm giving you my phone number so that if you ever need my advice or support outside the workplace, you have it." He scrawled it out on the index card and handed it to me with a regal flourish. "Trust me, I only offer these to colleagues. My female fans would kill for this information, you know."

His gaze was calm, inscrutable, leaving me with the eerie impression that I'd been the one misinterpreting the situation, that he'd known all along who I was.

The three of us proceeded up the steps.

"I'm available to advise you right now, if you wish," Dmitri told Anders. "As part of last year's acting-director team, I imagine I'll be a great source of support to you."

"Thank you," Anders said. "Your support and advice last season, when I spent time here, was indeed helpful. But I have things covered now."

"You'll want a slow transition, from the company's way of doing things, to your own," Dmitri said.

"Thank you, again," Anders said, only this time he didn't sound particularly thankful. "I plan to implement my style from the first day, the first company class."

Dmitri stopped in his tracks. "That's a bad idea."

Anders turned and regarded him coolly. "Oh?"

"I know this company and you don't."

"I am now its artistic director."

We'd reached the double doors, which Dmitri held open. "Young Mr. Gunst," a warm voice boomed out once we'd entered the lobby. "Welcome, welcome!" A man strode over from where he'd been standing, at the security desk.

A smile spread across Anders' face. "Charlie! So nice of you to meet me down here. I am honored."

"I'd call this perfect timing," the man said. He appeared to be in his late thirties, eyes twinkling from a tanned face, his brown hair cut close. He sported a suit and tie. "I just now came down to check and see if you'd arrived."

"Perfect timing, indeed." Anders gestured to me. "Charlie, I'd like you to meet the company's newest principal dancer. April, this is Charlie Stanton, the West Coast Ballet Theatre's executive director."

"April Manning," he exclaimed. "Welcome, my dear." He clasped my cold hand within his warmer one and vigorously shook it.

"Thank you. It's good to be here."

He greeted Dmitri as well, before turning back to Anders. "Do you have a bit of time? I'm meeting Roger Gilmore for a coffee. He's on our board of trustees—maybe you remember meeting him?"

"I do. Friendly, a little heavy-set, has a prodigious collection of classical music records?"

Charlie's eyes lit with delight. "You told me you had a photographic memory for people. I believe you now."

"I'd love to join you." Anders glanced at his watch. "I have ninety minutes before I teach company class."

"Excuse me," Dmitri said. "You shouldn't worry about making it to teach company class. Bob and Jacob covered all the company classes last year, and it worked for everyone. Why fix what isn't broken?"

Anders smiled at Dmitri with a bemused tilt of his head. "Thank you for sharing that," was all he said. He glanced over at me and back to Dmitri. "I'd be indebted if you could show April to the Public Relations office. Loretta is expecting her at nine o'clock."

"Of course I can do that," Dmitri said.

"Thank you. And I'll see you both at 10:30 in the main studio."

Dmitri didn't speak again until he and I were in the elevator, side by side, watching the doors slide shut. "My apologies for missing Saturday night's dinner," he said. "I had plans I couldn't change."

"It's quite all right. There were plenty of other new faces and names to memorize."

"Not to brag, but my name and face are rather unforgettable."

And I thought Vincent had a big ego. "I believe you're right," I said.

He glanced my way. "You'll want to guard that phone number I gave you. You'll come to see—you both will—that I am still the de-facto artistic director in the eyes of many of the dancers."

"Enough to instigate a mutiny?" The words just slipped out.

"What a curious thing to say." He looked genuinely perplexed and again I had the sense of not knowing whether I was a babbling fool or he was just a very good actor.

"A figure of speech, of course," I said.

"Of course."

A musical ping announced our arrival on the executive level. The doors slid open. Dmitri directed me down the hallway and to a reception area on the right. "There you are. Loretta's office is the second one."

"Thank you. I'll see you in the studio later."

Company class started at 10:30 a.m., but the main studio was curiously empty at 10:15 when I entered. After claiming a spot at the barre, I dropped to the floor to stretch and warm up, feeling edgy and awkward and vulnerable. Others walked in: Lexie, the friendly soloist from Saturday night; Carrie, a principal I'd also met that night. Today her long blond hair was pinned into a bun, and she seemed younger, more down-to-earth in workout clothes, face scrubbed clean of makeup. Anders liked her, and had encouraged me to get to know her better, even though at thirty-six, she was ten years my senior. It seemed, too, that Carrie had her own best friend already: Jana, a soloist whose own makeup—heavy black eyeliner, blue eyeshadow and thick Pan-Cake foundation—seemed excessive for morning. She was heavy set for a ballet dancer, with a surly demeanor. As I stretched, I overheard them talking. Jana seemed unaware, or uncaring, that her voice carried across the room.

"Did you sign your contract?" Jana was asking Carrie.

"Jana, I did it last spring. I've told you that."

"I still haven't." Jana sounded proud.

"Why not?" Dismay was evident in Carrie's voice.

"Because I don't trust this new artistic director. What if he makes bad choices? He shouldn't be able to just come in here and take over!"

"Of course he should. He's the artistic director. Period."

"Dmitri hasn't signed his contract," Jana retorted.

"Dmitri's a risk taker. Please don't go following him on this."

"Hey, what do you think of that new girl?"

"Shh." Carrie lowered her voice. "She can hear you."

"No she can't," Jana said. "And even if she did, so what? I don't trust her either. She came with him. And no way she can dance as well as you. She should have come in as a soloist and earned her promotion. She's not as pretty as you, either."

Her words made my ears burn. I used the adrenaline rush to stretch my leg further, the hamstring aching in protest. The pain felt good.

More and more dancers strolled in. I watched their eyes eagerly scan the room and seek me out, the expressions on some of their faces cooling the instant they spotted me. I saw myself through Jana's filter: an unwelcome newcomer, the dancer who'd never even had to audition for the company. Someone who'd never known Sid Hauser and the former greatness of the WCBT. The younger dancers, at least, seemed to react to me more kindly, offering me shy smiles, which I gratefully returned.

The accompanist entered, a heavy-set man with a stack of music scores tucked under one arm, his reading glasses perched atop his frizzy grey hair like a tiara. "Chess, my man, good to see you!" Lexie exclaimed, as others called out greetings too. He gave everyone a good-natured wave and shuffled over to the piano.

Anders arrived, and looked around. "I don't like this. Only half of you are here. Starting at 10:30 does not mean arriving 'sometime around then.' It means you're warmed and ready to move." As he spoke, three more dancers hurried in and, behind them, Dmitri, taking his time.

Anders made a great show of consulting his watch. "Ten-thirty. That's it. We start."

"Don't you want to wait for more of your dancers to show?" Chess called out from his place at the piano. He sounded amused.

Anders frowned. "I don't think so. What kind of artistic director caters to the whims of each dancer's timetable?"

"Sid did," an older male dancer called out.

"Yeah. Sid really knew us," Jana added. "He understood us."

"Boy, I miss him," another dancer chimed in.

"Just not the same without him," Dmitri agreed, trying to look sorrowful, but I saw the grin he was trying to hide.

Anders ignored the comments. "First position," he called out. "Two demi, one grand plié, port de bras front and back, relevé and hold, arms in high fifth." He demonstrated in brief, truncated movements what he wanted for the other positions as well. "Take it slow," he told Chess. "We'll let their bodies wake up."

Chess began to play a number that sounded suspiciously like a Broadway tune. A half dozen dancers scurried in as we began. They continued arriving through the tendu exercise that followed (another Broadway tune). Some even ambled in during dégagés, taking their time to warm up. This wasn't unheard of; the ABT had a "suit yourself" attitude about company class. But never on the first day of the season, before rehearsing and casting had been decided. And never when you were meeting a new artistic director and eager to make a good first impression.

The same relaxed policy seemed to apply to conversing, as well. During the rond de jamb exercise, two dancers nearby began to chat, prompting others to do the same. I heard Jana ask Dmitri if he had plans that night, to which he replied yes, and she told him that was too bad because she wanted to cook him dinner. It was all unspeakably poor etiquette for a ballet class.

Anders finally signaled for Chess to stop playing, but everyone was slow to stop talking.

They were doing it on purpose. I saw the gleeful looks some of them exchanged, their mock-surprise over Anders' tight-lipped disapproval.

Anders waited till everyone fell silent before speaking. He looked around at all of us. "Don't do this." He sounded more sorrowful than irritated. "Have a little more respect for your craft. Give this your all. If you're not up to that today, if you can't give me what I ask, you're free to leave, take conversations into the hallway, the café next door. I'm not here to babysit you. You make your own choices. But do consider the consequences."

No one spoke. Some of the dancers looked confused.

"We'll continue," Anders said.

Following barre, in the center of the room, Anders demonstrated a smooth-flowing adagio (slow Broadway tune). He still had the pristine technique of a principal dancer, tight fifth positions, beautiful feet with powerful arches. His arms were effortlessly artful. Everything was neat and clean. Very Danish, very Bournonville, with its understated elegance. The adagio was long, mentally taxing as well as physical. Everyone now took their work seriously.

I felt eyes on my back, like I had during barre. Everyone was assessing me, and not in a friendly way. But I kept my focus on my work. Since the steps and movements of ballet were the same whether you were taking a class in New York, Paris, Moscow, Johannesburg or San Francisco, it was uncomplicated, and soothing, to immerse myself in the movements. At the same time, I found myself watching the others just as critically. Carrie was a beautiful dancer. Observing her extensions, the poetic nature of her arm movements, I felt the sharp bite of competition, understanding that Carrie would be the dancer to beat.

After the adagio came petit allegro, those quick, fast jumps that helped sharpen footwork. "Jeté, assemblé, jeté, assemblé, brisé, brisé, brisé, entrechat quatre," Anders called out, demonstrating with his hands. "From the left, same thing. Then repeat, adding beats onto the assemblé, and try for an entrechat huit. Keep it light, clean."

It was hard work. No one was gloating anymore, or chatting. We were now united, all of us trying to keep up with the challenge.

Class always culminated in a grand allegro across the floor and from the diagonal. (Yet another Broadway tune!) We launched ourselves across in groups of four with sautés, chassés and big space-hogging leaps. It was exhilarating. Grand allegro was my favorite part of company class, and I could tell I wasn't alone in that sentiment. I saw the way everyone smiled and seemed to relax into their work.

But Anders wasn't looking to relax us. After the traditional end-of-class révérence and our applause, he raised a finger for our attention. "Starting tomorrow, we will begin at 10:15, not 10:30. Note that beginning at 10:15 means arriving in advance, warming up on your own, and having found your place at the barre."

This created a stir. "That's too early!" Jana cried over the buzz of voices.

"Company class is only intended to be an hour." Dmitri squared his shoulders to regard Anders haughtily. "Sometimes only fifty minutes. That suits this group fine."

"Class will be an hour and fifteen minutes. This is not negotiable."

"That's ridiculous!" Dmitri fumed.

Anders looked around the room, his expression grave. "My goal right now is to give all of you a comprehensive class. Not just a warm-up. Your bodies need more than a surface readjustment. Last year I guest-taught, I watched you. It's my opinion that, for many of you, your technique has grown sloppy. There are moments of extraordinary skill and talent among you. I see that. But your work is inconsistent. I want seventy-five minutes of company class and I want you to work hard, reconsider old, ingrained habits."

I glanced at the other dancers. Some were nodding. Others were directing angry looks in Anders' direction. I noticed that Jana had left Carrie's side to edge closer to Dmitri. Except that every time she stepped closer, he stepped away. I felt a flash of sympathy for Jana. She was one of the lesser dancers; she hadn't been able to make it through the class, but instead had hung back by the barre through the grand allegro, one leg slung up on the barre, massaging her hamstring, her chin a stubborn tilt as if to defy any suggestion of weakness.

"And get those contracts signed by the end of this week," Anders added.

"We don't have to," Jana said in a petulant voice.

"HR said we had until the end of next week," another dancer added.

"Fine," Anders said. "You don't 'have to' sign until then. Just keep this in mind. I don't have to rehearse you. I don't have to cast you. We all have our choices here. And they carry consequences."

It was easy to tell who'd signed versus who was balking: private smiles from the former, scowls from the latter, which included Dmitri and a dozen of his friends. Unsurprisingly, the ones who'd given me cool, assessing looks in lieu of a welcoming smile. They would not be my friends, ever. A glare shot my way from one of the older males, just then, confirmed it.

Anders' assistant, a cowed-looking young woman with wispy hair and glasses entered the room and hesitantly approached him with a note. "It's something for you to consider," he said to us, glancing distractedly at the note she handed him. "And it appears Jacob just posted today's and tomorrow's rehearsal schedule in the hallway."

The other dancers stampeded out to see what chances they were being given for the fall's West Coast tour and the spring repertory season, but I hung back, uneasy. Today's class had shown me that just because I'd been made principal didn't mean I could relax. The battle over who was the best had only begun. And Vincent had been right: this company was not without its strong dancers. Dmitri, Curtis and Carrie were amazingly good dancers. Sonya and Kirill, the Russian star couple, were apparently even better. They hadn't even bothered to show up for the first day of company class. When you were deemed that superior, you could call your own shots.

I slipped booties on over my tight-fitting pointe shoes, even though my toes were throbbing and stinging from the weeks of being off pointe. The first two weeks back would bring blisters, aching calves and quads, and a host of other physical issues.

You couldn't avoid the pain, the process, in your journey to get back to good shape.

Kind of like life itself.

Chapter 3

The Outsider

I'd had every reason to be concerned.

The rehearsal sheets were tacked onto adjacent bulletin boards, one for each of the four studios. On each sheet, the lead roles and names for the ballets being rehearsed were typed in bold on the top, with a longer list of ensemble names below. Like everyone else, I quickly scanned the sheets to find my name. Unlike everyone else, my name didn't show up a whole lot. Only one time, over the next two days. In the half-dozen spaces for lead couples, over and over, it was Carrie and Dmitri, Sonya and Kirill, Curtis and a soloist named Marilyn.

Jacob saw the dismay on my face. "The ballet masters and I talked with Anders," he said. "We convinced him of the wisdom of keeping casting for the two touring programs largely intact. Everyone knows their parts already—we performed everything last spring. Rehearsals will be a breeze. We understand Anders wants to make big changes, but the less he changes for those two programs, the more rehearsal time it frees up to consider new casting for the ballets in the spring."

"So I won't be cast for anything on the tour?" I asked, hearing a quaver rise in my voice.

Jacob looked apologetic. "That could change, of course. The tour's not for two months." He was a nice enough guy, in his early forties, warmth in his eyes when he wasn't looking nervous, a state he slipped into whenever he was around Anders. "But we thought it easiest to start off here with what the dancers—well, the other dancers—already know. But don't worry, by Wednesday, we'll start up rehearsals and auditions for the spring's repertory season."

"And what if the same philosophy applies?"

"What philosophy?" He sounded wary.

"This sense of 'let's change as little as possible.'"

Now he looked nervous and I knew I was on to something.

"We'll make sure you're on the rehearsal sheet for Wednesday," he assured me. "And Thursday, too. We'll have a stager there for *Ten Ways*, and Anders wants to jump right in to look at *The Sleeping Beauty*. Don't worry," he repeated.

Jacob was true to his word, and after company class on Wednesday, two dozen of us remained in the big studio to audition for the stager in charge of *Ten Ways of Looking at Love*, a ballet from the 1980's already in the company's repertory. He eyed the two dozen of us over the next hour, murmuring to his assistant, as we performed segments of the ballet. He stopped to arrange different configurations of partners. He frowned at the dancers one minute and came alive when someone danced a passage in the way he liked. He paced back and forth, watching. He had Curtis and me dance the lead roles, but I could tell we didn't hit the sweet spot. But it was clear who would.

Sonya and Kirill.

Sonya was a leggy, beautiful brunette with a gravity-defying extension. With her elegance, knockout technique and cold eyes, she was like an older Natalia. It was uncanny. Or maybe not, since both of them were Russian-born, Bolshoi-trained dancers. They all were: Dmitri, Natalia, Sonya and Kirill. The latter were better dancers than I'd expected. They were sensational; they could have been ABT principals, and I wondered why they'd stayed here in San Francisco. Likely because here, they were the undisputed stars.

"This is what I want," the stager said, and gestured to Sonya and Kirill. "Again, please."

The two launched back into the passage with easy confidence. Everyone fell silent and watched in awe. Despair washed over me. To think that I'd hightailed it out of New York to have a chance to shine, away from the show-stealer allure of Natalia, only to find the same thing here.

Once they'd finished the passage, everyone burst into applause. The stager looked at them with an expression that hovered between reverence and bliss. "Yes," he said in a hushed voice. "Once again, you have found the choreographer's intention and put it into motion." He turned and pointed to Dmitri and Carrie. "And you, and you."

And so the next rehearsal went. And the next day's rehearsals.

Late Thursday afternoon, the first rehearsal sheets for *The Sleeping Beauty* went up, which sent everyone scurrying to look for their names. The tense silence was broken by coos of delight, *tsks* of disappointment, murmured conversations among the dancers over Anders' choices.

I waited my turn behind the others, trying to affect a neutral expression, but inside, I was whining and hopping up and down like a little girl, frantic to see what chances I'd be given.

Aurora. That was all I wanted. The exuberant, lovable princess who, on her sixteenth birthday, pricks her finger with a spindle, falls asleep for a hundred years, and is woken by the kiss of a prince, after which they marry and dance an iconic grand pas de deux in the final scene. It was the role all females wanted to dance, right there alongside Giselle, Odette/Odile, Kitri and Cinderella.

Finally a space cleared. I stepped forward and hastily scanned the sheet, heart thumping.

Sonya—first cast Aurora. Carrie, second cast. My heart twisted. Finally, my name, in the humble third cast. *At least you're on the rehearsal sheet,* I consoled myself. *You are still officially rehearsing Aurora.*

After perusing the rest—I was first cast as one of the solo fairies in the Prologue, and Act III's sapphire fairy—I took a step back so others could look over the list. The bravado I'd worn all week evaporated, a *poof* of confidence and good spirits. I felt everything in me sag.

"Yeah, I know," a voice said behind me, and I turned to see Jana's gaze fixed on me. She was wearing her trademark heavy eyeliner and blue eyeshadow, but the chilly judgment usually in her eyes had been replaced by something more like sympathy. "I was hoping for better news on the Aurora front too."

This stopped me short. Was she joking? Testing my knowledge of company hierarchy, like the young corps dancer who'd grandly announced to me on Tuesday that he was a senior soloist, as his friends snickered into their hands? "Is that so?" I replied politely.

Jana took note of my skepticism. "Hey, Dmitri," she called over to where he stood, a few feet away. "Come here!"

Dmitri glanced our way and hesitated. For an instant, he looked uneasy, almost nervous, which I dismissed as preposterous as he glided over in that princely, confident way of his. "What is it?" he asked curtly.

Jana reached out to caress his arm, which he tolerated for a millisecond before taking a step away, leaving Jana's hand momentarily suspended in air. "Aurora," she continued, undaunted. "Wasn't I the greatest?"

Instead of the sneer I was expecting, Dmitri smiled, a genuine one, and his eyes took on a softness I wouldn't have thought him capable of. "You were. You were something else, back then."

"See?" Jana said to me, her face alight with pleasure. "I can tell what you were thinking—that there's no way sloppy old me, now, could be Aurora. But I was young and new once, too." She sized me up. "So don't go thinking you have something over the rest of us."

"I don't think that," I stammered, but the truth was, I did. I was proud of my SAB training, my ABT years, my principal rank. It gave me an unmistakable advantage over most of the dancers. But the rehearsal sheets were telling a different, more humbling story.

Dmitri turned to leave but Jana grabbed his arm. "So, I'll see you tonight, right?" she asked him in a coy, conspiratorial voice.

The annoyed look returned to Dmitri's face as he shook off her hand. "I told you not to discuss that here."

"Oh!" Jana's hand flew to her mouth. "You did! I'm so sorry. Anyway, see you later," she added in a stage whisper. "You wouldn't... drive me there, would you?" Hope filled her voice.

Dmitri shook his head. "Stick with Carrie. She's good for you."

"She is. But so are you!"

They left and I returned my attention to the disappointment of the rehearsal sheets. *Don't go thinking you have something over the rest of us,* Jana had said, and I felt a dull sinking of spirits that I hadn't expected to feel here.

Alone in my apartment that night, my sense of gloom continued. Fiona would be arriving on Sunday afternoon, but that was little comfort for me tonight. I debated calling one of the dancers I'd gotten to know. Lexie had given me his home number, but I decided it was too soon to share my vulnerability with someone I still wasn't positive was a friend. Too restless to escape into one of my books, I decided to make myself a nice dinner. My dad had been the creative cook of the family, employing his imagination and love for chemistry in the kitchen. Like him, I'd stock up on filet mignon when it was on sale, freezing the extra in chunk-sized pieces. I pulled out several chunks now, which I pan seared along with chopped onions and garlic. I combined ingredients for Dad's specialty, a Dijon-marsala sauce that I allowed to slowly reduce while I sipped a glass of wine. Alongside a baked potato and steamed broccoli, the beef tenderloin tips made for a good dinner, and I felt myself relax into the familiarity of it. *Hey,* I found myself thinking, *let's call Mom to tell her I'm making Dad food tonight!*

The thought flashed through me, improbable and damaging, followed by a dreadful pang of loss, as if it were new all over again, this shock, that I couldn't pick up the phone and call my mom ever again. Even now, ten months later, it stunned me.

The room blurred. I set my fork down and drew a slow, shaky breath. I dabbed at my eyes, finished my meal, and considered calling Fiona. But the local time in Omaha was approaching 11:00 p.m. and she was living at home with her parents. *Vincent,* I thought. Midnight in New York was rarely too late for a performing dancer; they were just winding down, post-performance, post-dinner.

The call would surprise him. It hadn't been a good breakup. Last winter and spring, I'd avoided him, rebuffed his efforts to remain friends. Ironically, we'd continued to dance beautifully together, and I'd found a certain tacit comfort in performing with him. I found myself missing that Vincent, more and more. Being alone, in the end, was a lonely business.

Decision made, I strode over to the phone, well aware that it had "bad idea" written all over it. Before I could talk myself out of it, I punched in his number and waited.

The worst thing that could happen, did. Natalia answered.

"Hello, and this is the surprise!" she said after I'd announced myself, already regretting the call. "How are you?"

"Wonderful," I replied, feeling horribly awkward. "Never better. And you?"

"So excellent, thank you!"

"Is Vincent there?"

"I am so sorry. Vincent, he is not yet here at the home."

"Oh. All right." Disappointment mingled with shame.

"How is San Francisco, I should add?" she asked.

"It's fine, thank you. Very pretty."

"And the West Coast Ballet Theatre?"

"Oh, it's great!" I lied.

"You know that I am the good friend with Sonya, yes? She and Kirill. We made the training with each other in Moscow, in Bolshoi. There, we are close friends. Very close. How nice, that you are now the very close, yes?"

Yeah, right. I was spared a reply when a click on my line announced a second caller. "Excuse me, I need to take this call."

"Would you like I should give my boyfriend message from you?"

My boyfriend. She just had to add that in.

"No, that's all right." I hoped I didn't sound pathetic. "In fact, don't even bother to tell Vincent I called."

"Is good idea. Is better for you."

I heard amused pity in her voice and it made me hate her all the more. "Good bye," I blurted out and hung up without waiting for her reply.

It was Anders on the other line. "Hello there," I said. My hands were shaking; so was my voice. I commanded myself to relax. "Good to hear from you."

"Do you know what your colleagues were doing this evening?" he asked without preamble.

"I don't have a clue," I said, trying to shake off my bad feelings from the last call. "No... wait. I overheard Jana tell Dmitri she would see him tonight."

"Dmitri held a meeting in the back room of Giovanni's Pizzeria.

Apparently a majority of the dancers were there. I am not privy to all that was discussed, but suffice to say, it's likely some plan for disruption."

"What?!" I clutched the phone. "Maybe you got it wrong. Maybe it was someone's birthday and they all went out together. They're so clannish, I could see them doing that for every last person's birthday."

"It's a nice thought, but, no."

"How can you be sure?"

"One of the dancers told me in confidence. He thought I should know."

"This is awful," I said. "What are you going to do about it? Play dumb about knowing they met up?"

"Not in the least." He chuckled. "I footed the bill for their pizzas. I called, told the staff to put the meal on my credit card, and had the restaurant manager go out there and tell them."

A cackle of laughter escaped me. "Oh, wouldn't you have loved to see Dmitri's face when the manager announced it?"

"It brings me tremendous pleasure to consider it all. Apparently they all clapped, because it meant they'd gotten a free meal. Then it sank in that the 'enemy' not only knew about the event, but had, for all intents and purposes, hosted it. Lexie told me everyone was a little unnerved by it all."

"Whoops, you just gave me the name of your confidential source."

"So I did. I owe him an apology."

"I would have guessed Lexie anyway. Him, or Jacob."

"Yes, one would have thought my second in command would be the one to share such news. That was not the case." He didn't sound happy.

"So. A plan was being formed. Any idea what it is?"

"Lexie has his loyalties to both sides. I see this, so I didn't press him. And, in turn, I didn't share my own plans with him."

"Will you share them with me?"

"It depends. Are you going to call Dmitri after we hang up?"

I chuckled. "My good friend, Dmitri? I do have his phone number on that index card, don't I? But I think it's safe to say my loyalties rest solidly with you."

"All right. I'm thinking that first thing tomorrow morning, Jacob and I will do a little rearranging of the rehearsal schedules. Not just for tomorrow's, but through next week. I'm done with this unsigned contract business. I won't sit back, helpless, as they toy with me. No signed contract, no rehearsing. On the positive side, for you, I think you'll enjoy looking at the revised rehearsal sheets."

A flutter of child's delight passed through me. "Sonya and Kirill. …they haven't signed?"

"Regrettably, not yet. I'll have a word with them before company class. I need them, desperately, but I can't go creating two sets of rules. They need to sign."

Anxiety battled with excitement. This meant unprecedented opportunity.

It also spelled out potential chaos and destruction.

"I'll let you go," Anders said. "Get good rest. You'll likely need it for tomorrow."

Chapter 4

Friday Drama

Anders wasn't there to start company class at 10:15 on Friday morning. Neither was Jacob. Some of the dancers around me, the Dmitri groupies, found this incredibly amusing.

"I say we start," Dmitri called out. "We all heard him on Monday. Class begins at 10:15 promptly. His rules." His eyes gleamed. "Unless one of you has an objection, I teach."

"Dmitri…" Carrie began, and stopped. She met Curtis' eyes, and they both reluctantly nodded.

"Good," Dmitri said. "No objections. We'll begin."

There were no objections from Chess, the day's accompanist, either, who grinned broadly back at Dmitri.

But while Dmitri was demonstrating the pliés, Anders and Jacob walked in, carrying two oversized poster boards each, all with multiple rehearsal schedules pasted on. Jacob set his poster boards down and looked inquiringly at Anders.

"You can go now," Anders said to him, but Jacob hesitated. He seemed torn, gaze flickering to Dmitri, to the other principals, and back to Anders.

"You can go," Anders repeated. Jacob nodded reluctantly and left.

Anders turned to Dmitri. "Thank you for starting barre. It's good to know I can count on you in a pinch. But I'll take over now."

"What are those?" Dmitri gestured to the four poster boards.

"Rehearsal schedules. But there's no need to deal with this now. Company class first."

Dmitri gave Anders one of his haughty looks. "I don't think so."

"There was a rehearsal schedule up for today already," Jana said.

"This one takes its place," Anders said.

"What's different?" one of the dancers called out.

"Rather uncomplicated, actually," Anders said. "I discussed this on Monday morning. I mentioned it on Wednesday morning as well. And yesterday morning. I will only rehearse those with signed contracts. Starting now."

I watched everyone's expressions as they processed what Anders was saying. Jaws dropped. Panic flared in the eyes of those who hadn't signed. I couldn't deny a certain satisfaction in watching how Dmitri's core group of followers—ten of the older, less talented dancers—reacted with outrage. None of them had been kind or welcoming to me.

Everyone tried to talk at once.

"You can't do that to us!"

"Don't worry, he's just bluffing."

"Do *not* sign that contract yet. It'll ruin everything."

"But what if he isn't?"

"I can't do this. I'm signing."

"You're not going to tell us when we can or can't sign our contracts," Dmitri burst out. "We are our own agents and we were told we had till next Friday. You have no right to threaten us. We won't take it."

"I don't see that you have a lot of options here," Anders said.

"We do!" Jana blurted out. "Dmitri has enough dancers for a boutique company. And enough places that want to see us perform, places you pulled from our touring schedule."

A collective groan arose from a dozen dancers around the room. The wrathful looks they cast at Jana should have made her shrink with embarrassment, but she only smiled hopefully at Dmitri, whose eyes had flickered shut at her announcement.

"This is your big plan?" Anders asked. There was a note of laughter in his voice, which made Dmitri's eyes fly open.

"Don't you dare mock the works of Sid Hauser and the venues he was faithful to."

"Stop being a drama queen and answer the question."

Dmitri looked around at his supporters, who gave him a "go ahead" nod. "Our plan is still in progress," he said with great dignity. "But this is our intention. We want our contracts revised to reflect extra performing, as the Sid Hauser Dance Theatre. You see, not one but two places have contacted me. *Me* and not you. They want us back. Meaning, Sid's original dancers. A dozen of us can tour his smaller ballets in the venues you rejected. You add that clause, and we'll sign our contracts." The dancers behind him smiled and nodded in agreement, as if this were some sort of win-win situation.

"Ah. Fascinating," Anders said. "Excuse me for asking silly, tiresome logistics questions, but who are you thinking is going to foot the bill for this?"

Dmitri hesitated. "The plans, still in the works, mind you, are that a subsidiary of the WCBT will pay."

"Is that right? A subsidiary. And here's what I'm thinking that means. That ultimately the WCBT will foot the bill."

"In a matter of speaking." Dmitri looked less confident. "Yes."

"Absolutely not." Anders smiled pleasantly. "I pulled those smaller venues from touring to save costs. What on earth made you think I would allow such a thing?"

No one spoke. I looked down at my hand, still gripping the barre. My knuckles were white. I saw that Lexie's hand, near mine, was the same.

"You will allow such a thing," Dmitri said, "because if you don't"—here he drew a deep breath—"the group of us will walk out of here and you will only have half a company."

The tension in the room had grown toxic, almost violent. But Anders only shook his head, slowly, deliberately. "No. I don't believe I will allow such a thing. And it was incredibly naïve of you to think, even for an instant, that I would comply."

"I think you'll want to reconsider my offer," Dmitri said.

"No. You're wrong."

"Then you've given us no choice." Dmitri's voice was low and cold.

Anders' eyes narrowed. "There's the door."

Anders' mousy assistant appeared at the door. She looked terrified as she approached Anders. "Not now," he snapped at her. "Can't you see I'm busy?"

She jumped and skittered back a few feet.

Several of the dancers had congregated around Dmitri, dance bags in hand, all prepared to leave. "You are not striking," Anders warned them. "You are refusing to sign a contract."

"We have until next Friday!" Jana cried. "Are you stupid?" Her eyes had taken on a wild, unhinged look, and I saw a few dancers exchange uneasy looks before edging away from her.

Anders ignored Jana. "Any of you who leave today without signing your contract should be aware. I will not change that rehearsal sheet. I will not rehearse you; I will not cast you. I will instruct other choreographers and stagers to not cast you. Yes, you have until next Friday to sign your contracts. Delay signing at your own peril."

He beckoned his cowering assistant closer. "Get that in writing. Now," he barked, when she only stared at him in confusion. She scrabbled around in terror for a fresh sheet of paper. He repeated the words for her, glaring at the dancers periodically. Conversation had halted. Comically so, because you couldn't argue with someone who was trying to transcribe important words, which Anders had to feed the assistant two at a time because she was so rattled. So much that she dropped her pen not once but twice. Even the angry dancers tsked with annoyance when it happened the second time. I would have laughed, had the situation not been so deadly serious.

I had a flashback to Vincent's words from last October. *The West Coast Ballet Theatre is a sinking ship, April. They've got issues far beyond what Anders can handle. If he fails, any dancer he brought over will go right down with him.*

I felt sick. What had I gotten myself into? What if I'd put my own career at risk? This goal of mine, to be the best of the best, garner opening-night lead roles in a big company, could be derailed in one day's time. One hour's time.

Once Anders' assistant had finished writing, he grabbed the clipboard from her, scrawled out his signature, and thrust it back at her. "That goes to HR the minute we're done here."

Carrie had been watching the proceedings with wide eyes, her hand over her mouth. "Jana," she said now. "*Don't.* Please come back here."

Jana didn't budge. "Don't you see? Dmitri's the one really in charge."

She wasn't the only one to think so. Sonya and Kirill had been standing off to the side, expressions unreadable, watching the argument. Now they looked at each other, exchanged a small nod and walked over to Dmitri.

Anders had lost his star couple.

He was in big trouble.

"This is your last chance," Dmitri told Anders. "You cannot run this company without us."

If Anders was in a panic over how things were going, he didn't show it. "I can, and I will."

"You'll beg us to return."

"I will not." Anders solemnly assessed the dancers behind Dmitri. "This is your choice," he said to them. "Think very carefully here."

No one moved. Dmitri glanced around behind him and smiled. "It looks like we've all made our choice."

"Fine." Anders gave a flick of his hand, as if now impatient with it all. "Please leave the studio if you don't intend to join us for class. And if you do not have a signed contract and you leave the building, I'll say my goodbye to you now. Because I won't be considering you for anything." He turned to his assistant. "Get their names down."

She stood there, frozen in terror. "I don't know all their names."

Anders' patience gave out. "*Gottverdammt!*" he shouted. "Someone help her with names."

One of the more sympathetic dancers hurried over to the girl, who'd begun to gasp, frantic little animal noises. She sniffled as she wrote down the names the dancer murmured to her. In all, there were fourteen.

All fourteen of them walked out the door. "Jana!" Carrie screamed. "Stop! It's a mistake!"

Jana ignored her. Carrie turned to Curtis and buried her face against his neck. His arms went around her and I saw she was crying, which struck me as extreme.

Anders' assistant had begun to cry as well. "I don't think I can do this job," she sniffed.

"Then go with them, dammit!" Anders roared. "I can't bear your sniveling any longer. Leave. Just leave. Go to HR and have them reassign you. Go!"

With a sob, she tore out of the room.

Now I wanted to cry, too. I wanted to shrink into a ball and self-soothe until the toxic energy had passed. It seemed impossible that we could proceed forward from such destruction. But Anders, when he spoke a moment later, sounded perfectly composed. "All right, pliés," he said to us. He glanced over to Chess at the piano, who'd been watching the drama with a smirk. "Please give me something smooth and flowing," he called out.

Chess promptly plonked out the same utilitarian-sounding music he might use for tendus.

"Just stop right there," Anders said, no longer sounding so composed. "Enough of this oom-pah-pah sound. And what's this Broadway tunes diet you're so enamored with? Are you not classically trained?"

Chess seemed affronted by the question. "I am conservatory-trained, thank you very much. I have a master's degree."

"Then show it. Give me classical music. That should be your default, not that fluff."

Chess assessed Anders coolly. "Do *you* have a master's degree in music? Care to demonstrate for me what you'd prefer?" His smile grew self-righteous when Anders didn't reply. "No. I didn't think you could."

"Give me plié music. That means something classical and smooth flowing. Do your job and if you can't, feel free to follow Dmitri and his group out the door."

No, no, please, I silently begged Anders. *Not the musician, too. We need our live music.*

Fortunately, Chess lacked Dmitri's defiant spirit. A sour look crossed his face, but he gave Anders the music he'd asked for. Anders demonstrated pliés, and the group of us did precisely as he'd shown. There was no dialogue or analysis, no struggling to maintain focus over others' noisy inattention. Right side followed the left. Anders demonstrated the next exercise and it, too, was quietly and efficiently executed. And suddenly it all seemed rather uncomplicated: if we followed his lead and worked hard, the rest would sort itself out. Even the mood among the dancers had lightened. No wonder. All the negativity had left the studio. During one exercise toward the end of barre, I realized, to my surprise, that three dancers from Dmitri's group had crept back into the room and were doing barre with the rest of us.

When class ended, we clapped, like always, but this time, the clapping went on and on. We were all punchy and unhinged, cheering and hollering in lieu of quietly freaking out. It seemed like the best option. The minute the clapping stopped, Megann from HR charged in, followed by Loretta from PR. Jacob was behind them, moving slower, looking anguished.

We'd done it.

All that remained to tackle was the fallout.

Rehearsals were an entirely different game with the revised schedules. It felt oddly dream-like, the change in favor, or maybe it was the previous days of anxious misery that receded into dream status. By day's end, I was exhausted, my brain spinning with all the changes and new choreography absorbed. My quads felt wobbly. My arms and calves ached. I loved it all.

Once I'd changed into street clothes, I met Anders at L'Orange, the same restaurant as last Saturday's dinner. He'd arranged for a post-mortem with his remaining highly ranked dancers. I was the first of the dancers to arrive; it gave us the chance to speak candidly.

"I lost my temper," he mourned. "I'd sworn I wasn't going to let that happen." He raked his fingers through his hair. "Worst of all, I discharged my personal assistant. Why the hell did I do that? I desperately need someone in that job at all times. Now I'm going to have to suffer through the purgatory of interviewing and testing out applicants. I can't think of a worse fate."

An idea came to me, so inspired it made me gasp out loud. "Anders! My friend, Fiona, the one I'm holding the second bedroom for, is coming out this weekend. To job hunt! We danced together as kids, but she never went professional. I know for a fact she'd love to work behind the scenes in this capacity."

"Really?" He eyed me with interest. "What's her background?"

"College graduate, just completed two years with the Peace Corps in Africa. She was a high school teacher. She told me the first year was brutal and the second year was great. Apparently she learned the art of being adaptable."

"An indispensable art to learn," he commented, but before he could ask me anything more, Curtis, Carrie and Jacob arrived, followed by Bob, one of the ballet masters. He was an old-timer, a principal dancer back in his prime. He'd been around the WCBT since even before Sid, a total of thirty years. He was the most unlikely former dancer I'd ever met. In his T-shirt and unbuttoned flannel shirt with rolled-up sleeves, he looked and sounded like a truck driver. I sensed it was a coup for Anders that Bob had shown up tonight; he'd told Anders from the start that he and Yelena, the ballet mistress, never took sides.

"I value your honest opinion here," Anders said to him. "I need it."

Bob motioned to the waitress for a beer before replying. "Push hard but not too hard. You don't want to lose one more person."

"Did I make a mistake with Dmitri?" Anders asked him.

Bob had placed a cigarette into his mouth. He let it sit there, unlit, as he considered. "No. He needed to have his bluff called. He needs to know who's boss." The cigarette bobbed up and down as he spoke. "Dmitri gave Sid's replacement a dose of this. The guy caved early on. After that, it was battle after battle, no one winning, everyone losing, until he resigned and left everything in a worse mess."

Lexie showed up with news. "Dmitri didn't leave the building when we thought he did." He took a seat, his eyes rich with amusement. "He signed his contract after all, around two o'clock. Only then did he leave."

We all stared at Lexie, who beamed back at us.

"Why did he do that?" I asked.

"That's Dmitri for you," Lexie said. "Loves to keep people guessing."

The others smothered chuckles as Anders sighed and shook his head. "Dmitri Petrenko is going to be a thorn in my side forever."

"But he couldn't make you back down," Bob said. "That's big."

"The Russians," Anders murmured to himself. He turned to Lexie, eyes lit with hope. "Tell me Sonya and Kirill did the same."

A helpless look came over Lexie's face. "No. They're gone."

I glanced over at Anders. Misery hung over his face like a damp towel.

"*Merde*. Fuck. *Av for fanden*." He took a long slug of his beer.

"This situation is a mess," Jacob said, looking equally miserable.

Curtis snorted. "As if you didn't see this coming, Jacob. You were there last night." An uncharacteristic edge had come over his voice. "Having a private exchange with Dmitri."

An awkward silence fell over the table. Mystified, I looked around at the faces. Bob folded his arms and regarded the others with a serene *I'm not getting involved in this* look.

"Do tell, Jacob," Anders said coolly. "Because surely you're aware that your boss might be interested in how you plan to divert your loyalties."

"My loyalties are entirely with you," Jacob told Anders.

"Oh, come on, Jacob," Curtis said. "We were there too. He was going to use you as much as possible in an administrative capacity.

You were planning to play both sides."

"I was not! I mean, okay, I was going to advise him, serve as a consultant, but I told him it couldn't interfere with my salaried job. He was willing to go forward under those conditions."

Anders paled. He was slow to draw his next breath. "I should have known," he said. "You and Dmitri, working together, once the other artistic director had been run off. That I should trust you now, simply because you were assigned as my second in command? I'm not sure who I'm more disappointed in right now—you, or myself."

"It's not that way," Jacob said. "Of course you can trust me! Did you hear me say a word in protest this morning when you told me of your plan? I dropped all loyalties to help you make those new rehearsal schedules, even though I knew my former colleagues, my friends—some of them for twenty years!—would pay the price. I could have called Dmitri to tell him what we were doing. I didn't. I'm on your team. You can trust me."

"Easy to say now, isn't it?" Anders shot him a chilly glare. "Meanwhile, look at the risks these other dancers have been taking, demonstrating from the first hour which side they were on." He gestured to Curtis, Carrie, Lexie.

Abruptly, he turned to face me. "Your friend. Can she be trusted?"

"I can be trusted!" Jacob exclaimed, but Anders ignored him.

"Absolutely," I assured Anders.

"When did you say she's arriving?"

"Sunday afternoon."

"If she's so inclined, bring her in with you, first thing Monday. Make it eight o'clock."

"I will. She'll be thrilled. She's always wanted an insider's view of the ballet world."

"Let's see how thrilled she is when reality intrudes on her illusions."

He turned back to Jacob and regarded him stonily. When Jacob, eyes full of abject apology, tried to speak, Anders held up his hand.

"I don't want to hear it. But take this as a warning. You go behind my back again to support someone whose intention it is to compete with me, I'll fire you. No matter how much I need you. Do I make myself perfectly clear?"

An unfamiliar awkwardness had descended over the table. Anders may have been younger than everyone in the group besides me, but right then he radiated a terrifying authority that made everyone shrink a little in their seats. All except Bob who was leaning back, a benign smile on his face, nodding at Anders' words.

"Yes," Jacob told Anders. "You made yourself clear."

"Good."

Amid the stillness, Anders turned to Lexie. "You have a story to tell. I see that look on your face. Please share."

Lexie grinned. "All right. The three dancers who came back into the studio during barre? Apparently, after the group's grand walkout, they overheard the Russians talking. Fortunately, in English. Sonya and Kirill were telling Dmitri they had no interest, after all, with his boutique troupe plan. They'd found gigs already, lucrative ones. So, they betrayed the betrayer—can you believe it?" Lexie shook his head and chuckled. We all regarded him with varying degrees of disbelief and fascination. "The three other dancers, hearing this, realized how wrong it could all go, without the star couple. That's why they went right back into the studio."

"They're strong dancers," Anders said. "We're infinitely better off with their return. Some of those others who left with Dmitri, good riddance, I say. What on earth was Jana still doing with a contract?" Anders turned to Curtis and Carrie. "You two know her the best. What was that about?"

Their reaction surprised me. Curtis flushed a dull red and Carrie's mouth soundlessly gaped open and shut, like a fish. "Sid liked her," Lexie said, rescuing them, although from what, I didn't have a clue.

"He did." Curtis recovered first. "She was amazing in her first years with the company. But she had... health issues." He looked over at Carrie, who took the cue.

"You know how it is," she told Anders. "A really good dancer, you want to give them the benefit of the doubt after they're sidelined for a long spell, then struggling to get back into peak performing condition. It's a toss-up for an artistic director. How long is too long to wait? What if all the dancer needed was a few more months of recuperation time?"

"I understand," said Anders. "But an artistic director isn't a father. Sid lost money by making decisions that were gentle on the dancers. Three years ago, there were forty-five of you. He dropped no one; he let you all dance till you retired. Keeping an increasing number of dancers is costly, in more ways than one. If he'd made better choices in his last few years, the West Coast Ballet Theatre wouldn't be in the dire situation it is now. Costumes are old and tired, as are the sets. No money for new commissions. No money to take the orchestra on tour. Why did he allow this?"

For a long moment, no one spoke.

"That's what you haven't yet come to understand," Jacob said finally. "We're family. We may disagree and bicker among ourselves, but our bonds run deep. We've been through a lot together, through the years. The decades. Ten years for Lexie here. Twenty years for Curtis and Dmitri. Twenty-two for me. Eighteen years for Carrie. Sid was there through it all, and we were there for him. Through highs and lows. I'm not sure it's possible for outsiders to understand."

I could tell Jacob was speaking for the others, too. The bond between the four dancers present was palpable. A spasm of envy shot through me. I'd been close enough to my peers at the ABT; I'd called them "family." But it was nothing like this.

The waitress reappeared to see who wanted a second drink. All our hands shot up. "Would you like appetizers with them?" she asked, and everyone glanced over at Anders.

"Why not?" Anders shrugged. "At least tonight I get to foot the bill *and* eat the food."

"Thank you for last night," Carrie said, as the others laughed. "It was good."

"My pleasure. I think."

As the others pored over the menu, I touched Anders' arm. "What is Charlie Stanton going to say about what happened today?"

"Actually, he and I have already spoken."

"And?"

"I told him that I had every confidence that this smaller group will rise to this newest challenge. All total, we lost ten dancers. I told him the six dancers I plan to add to the company roster, combined with the increased motivation of the current dancers, would produce a leaner, better, more polished company. Without spending an extra dime. In fact, with thirty-six dancers, we'll come out ahead, budget-wise."

"And his reaction?"

"He wanted to know more about the six dancers. Whether they'd match the quality of what we lost. That was trickier. Couples like Sonya and Kirill don't come around just like that. There are freelancing dance stars out there, like the ones who land at the ABT as guest artists. But we could never afford that kind of dancer." A despairing look had crept into Anders' eyes.

"Six new dancers." My throat had gone dry. "That's a tall order."

"Fortunately, I've got two good leads. The first is a very promising young man, Royal Ballet-trained, newly returned to the U.S and the West Coast. When we spoke in July, I told him I had no space on the roster, but that the minute I did, I'd call him. Which literally is what I did, right after today's drama. He's interested—I invited him to come try out a company class next week. I know he's a winner, someone who could be fast-tracked."

"Good, good!"

"And then there's Renata, a former principal here who retired two years ago. Amazing dancer. A gem. Jacob keeps in touch with her, and said she sounds hungry to dance again. She retired for personal reasons, apparently, and not injury-related ones. She and I are going to meet up on Sunday."

A flutter of competitive unease erupted in my chest. Would this Renata prove to be another Sonya or Natalia, slotting me right back into third place?

"Well done!" I made sure my voice sounded just as hearty. "Both sound promising."

"I agree. I'll promote Lexie to principal; he's ready for that challenge. That'll make up for Kirill's loss on the roster, at least on paper. Otherwise, it's a terrible time of the year to be seeking out top-tier dancers." His worried expression eased. "Fortunately, I have Sabine."

At the mention of his wife, something in me relaxed too. I adored Sabine. She was smart, warm and engaging. Still running the Brussels company she and Anders had co-directed, she was closely connected to the European ballet scene, and would know who was available or just completing their elite training. I secretly hoped it would be the latter. Young, talented newcomers would offer great promise to the WCBT, without stealing the lead roles right away.

"And this, too, is what I know," he continued, that determined glint back in his eyes. "I am not about to let today's prank get in the way of my job. This company will shape up, well before the repertory season starts in January. Mark my word, I will not fail here."

He couldn't afford to fail.

Neither of us could.

Chapter 5

Fiona Arrives

Fiona got the job within thirty minutes of meeting Anders. What clinched it, she told me on Monday evening when we met back at the apartment, was her outspoken bluntness, the very thing that had always gotten her into trouble in younger years. "There we were, chatting," Fiona said, "and I told him to drop the hypothetical 'what would you do?' scenarios. 'You're in desperate need of support and I'm here,' I said to him. 'I have no other place to be today. If you want, I'll trail you as long as you can tolerate me, help you where I can, educate myself on what I don't know, and we'll take it from there.' He gave me this long, assessing look. All of a sudden, he stands, gestures to the door, and says, 'Why don't we start at HR? You're hired. I'll walk you in to Megann's office.'"

Fiona grinned at my astonishment and nudged a cold champagne bottle on the kitchen counter toward me. "I figured it all merited a celebration."

"Without a doubt!" I peeled off the top wrapper as she grabbed two glasses.

"And did you know he speaks fluent French? We kept switching back from English to French—it was fun! Like being back in Africa, except, obviously not. Anyway, I am now an official employee of the West Coast Ballet Theatre."

"Omigod, I'm so happy for you. For all of us." The cork I was jimmying out of the champagne bottle released itself with a loud *pop*.

Fiona handed me the glasses. "Anders wanted me to start work tomorrow, not fly back to Omaha at all, and just have my things shipped out. No way could I do that. My mom would freak if I disappeared on her so fast again, after two years away."

I finished pouring. "Here's to your success today. Brava. I'm bowled over."

We clinked our glasses together.

"I am so glad you're here," I told her. "Last week was chaos. Unsustainable."

Fiona smiled. "I'm glad to be here, too. And, hey. That chaos resulted in a job for me."

When I'd seen Fiona striding toward me at the SFO arrivals gate the previous afternoon, that familiar pretty face dusted with freckles, her wavy, red-gold-blonde hair loose and flowing, I'd felt something tight in me give a great crack. Familiarity. Almost family. Fiona's brother, Russell, had moved to the Bay Area too. It hardly got better than this.

The Garveys had been the family I'd wanted to belong to. Did everyone have one of those, I wondered? A family and home environment that was everything yours was not? Fiona's house was always full of people and noise. Granted, it wasn't always cheerful noise, not when Fiona was quarrelling with her siblings, which was often. I got along fine with Fiona's sister, Alison, who was my grade at school, with Fiona one year behind us. How I'd hungered for a sister, so close in age, a built-in friend. I wasn't so sure about the brother business. Russell, short and scrawny, seemed to be perpetually scowling, annoyed by our girl-ness, our giggles, the way Fiona and I were always stepping into arabesques, attitudes derriere, chaîné turns. One time, I rounded a corner while dancing and nearly slammed into him. He regarded me in fury behind oversized glasses that dominated his face. "Watch it," he cried, his mouth a hardware store of braces, until he realized he'd just shouted not at his sister, but a different girl, one who was nearly his height.

He was fifteen to my twelve, with honey-blond hair that poked up in untidy tufts. He shared the same eyes as Fiona, a pale blue under brows that cut a straight line across, like two decisive slashes. It always made Fiona look like she was being stubborn. It made Russell look both studious and cross. Fiona came around the corner, crashing into us both, and this time Russell shouted for real. Fiona grabbed my hand and the two of us reversed course and ran back to the family room, giggling.

"When will you fly back to Omaha?" I asked Fiona now.

"I'll go in to do orientation stuff tomorrow morning in H.R. I told Anders I'd help him the rest of the day. I'll fly to Omaha on Wednesday, return here on Monday. One last chance to enjoy Mom's Sunday night's roasts. Do you know how to make roasts?"

"I do. It's not complicated."

"Good. At least one of us knows how to cook."

My eyes settled on WCBT paperwork Fiona had left on the counter. On top was a glossy PR photo of Dmitri. It was signed.

"Oh, good Lord, what is this?" I exclaimed. "Did he give this to you?"

"Sure! He even autographed it. I'm thrilled! I've read *Dance Magazine* articles about him for years. It's too cool that I get to be around the real deal."

"I hate to burst your bubble, but he's not a nice person. I told you what he did to those dancers who followed him out on Friday."

It still shocked me, how despicable it had been for Dmitri to stage a walkout, only to change his mind and sign his own contract. Those eight dancers, out of a job, just like that. And throughout the day today, Dmitri had acted as though the walkout had never happened. He was even smiling. His ruthlessness, against people he'd called friends, chilled me.

Fiona gave a dismissive wave of her hand. "So he's the company's Bad Boy. Bet it gets him good press. And I have to say, for all the chaos you said last week was, I didn't notice anything. I mean, it was my first day there, but I didn't catch a whiff of conflict."

"You're right," I admitted. "It's a hundred times better now. Just… don't trust Dmitri. He's not a nice guy at the core. Not like Lexie."

Fiona's face lit up. "Oh, Lexie's *fun*! I felt so comfortable talking to him. He said the three of us should meet up and do a dinner together some night. I told him, sure!"

"Speaking of meet-ups, don't forget, we made plans with your brother for tomorrow night."

Fiona groaned out loud. "I forgot. Can't we move that forward a week?"

"What makes you think next week is going to be any easier? You'll be starting a demanding new job. Besides, I'm looking forward to it."

"But *why?* It's just Russell. Trust me, we'll end up doing our bickering thing."

"Oh, come on, you're adults. That was kid stuff. Besides, he's here, which surprises me. He didn't seem like the California type."

"That was in the days before Silicon Valley. I guess it's no surprise that he moved out here." Fiona reached over and poured more champagne into each of our glasses. "All these tech companies and startups and math geeks. He'll fit right in. Remember that computer he had assembled in his room, when we were kids?"

"That was pretty forward-thinking of him."

"I know, it was like science fiction! I always thought he was a little touched in the head, the way he'd start rambling about how it worked and the future of computers, and so on. But turns out he was right. Right now, he's part of a tech startup that's going gangbusters. Crazy. Then again, we'll see how it all turns out. Maybe this technology explosion is just a phase."

"So, we're set? Still meeting him in Palo Alto tomorrow evening?"

"Seriously?" Fiona asked. "You're going to dig in your heels?"

I gave a small shrug. "Kinda, yeah."

Fiona released a heavy sigh. "Okay, fine. I'm doing this for you. Not for myself or him."

"Thank you. The gesture is much appreciated. And tonight, let me take you out to dinner to celebrate *you*. You won big today."

On Tuesday after work, we took the train from San Francisco to Palo Alto and walked down University Avenue to the brewery-restaurant Russell had proposed. The sky had turned a darker blue, with pink clouds catching the golden rays of the sinking sun. A mild breeze stirred the leaves in the nearby trees. Downtown Palo Alto vibrated with energy, with its restaurants, bookstores, cinemas, shops and throngs of people. Inside our meeting place, we had to thread our way through crowds congregating on the bar side. I caught a glimpse of a good-looking guy further inside, who reminded me of Vincent. It sent a surprising flutter of electricity through me. Suddenly an urge overtook me, to fill my world, or even just an evening, with something carnal and sensual and physically satisfying. I took it as a good sign, that I was finally starting to heal from my mom's death.

Fiona turned to me and gestured toward the restaurant section. "I see him," she called out over the noise. "By the reception stand."

"I'll follow you," I said, as we made our way through the cheerful, beery revelers.

"Russell!" Fiona shouted, and he turned around.

The good-looking guy. It was Russell.

I stopped short.

The teenager's short, scrawny body was gone, replaced by something wondrous, with broad shoulders to match his medium-tall height. His blue eyes were exactly the same, the only reason I knew, without a doubt, it was Fiona's brother.

He didn't recognize me. I watched his gaze sweep past me and turn back to his sister. A moment later, he glanced at me again, with the same non-recognition. A pause. A frown. Disbelief washed over his face.

"Big brother!" Fiona exclaimed as we drew closer, in a way that managed to sound both familial and combative.

"Little sister! How are you?" They exchanged stiff hugs.

"I'm good, thanks."

"Welcome to the Bay Area."

"Thanks. It's great to be here. And guess what? I got a job already."

"Really?" He looked skeptical. "One that pays?"

"Of course," Fiona sputtered. "What are you thinking? It's a fulltime, salaried job."

"All right, don't have a cow. Congratulations." His gaze shifted to me and the elder brother assurance left his face. His mouth worked but no words came out. "April," he said finally. "I'm… I'm speechless."

"I'll say." Fiona's voice was rich with amusement.

"Russell." I smiled at him. "It's been a long time."

We reached out at the same time, fumbling through a clumsy hug, which made us both laugh. Behind Russell stood a short, generously-built young woman with tortoise-shell glasses and wavy black hair, regarding us with a smile that held a trace of impatience. She cleared her throat noisily, and Russell swung around to regard her in surprise.

"Oh, right. Sorry! Fiona, April, this is Nicola."

"Who is…" Fiona prompted with a mischievous grin.

"Sorry! Nicola is my girlfriend."

"Nice to meet you," Nicola said, and shook my hand firmly. She had a pretty face behind her oversized frames, but the smile she flashed me seemed more competitive than warm. I watched in bemusement as Fiona and Nicola next tried to shake hands, only Russell kept stepping the wrong way to get out of the way. When Fiona took him by the shoulders and deliberately moved him to the left, Nicola laughed.

"I love watching brother-sister interactions," she told Fiona.

"Someone has to be allowed to push him around, am I right?"

"You're right," Nicola agreed.

"I'm *so* glad to meet you," Fiona said. She glanced from Nicola to Russell, her expression suffused with delight. "Really. Russell, a girlfriend! Wow, you've become so civilized."

This made all of us laugh. Nicola hooked her arm into his and pressed herself closer. "He's a diamond in the rough," she told Fiona.

"I don't know about the diamond," Fiona said, "but I agree about the rough part. Russell, you lucky dog, someone so gorgeous is giving you a chance."

Nicola's eyes went droopy with affection for Fiona.

The hostess signaled to us that our table was ready. We followed her to a table in the center, where Nicola claimed the seat next to Russell and patted the chair on her other side with a "sit here!" gesture to Fiona. I sat in the fourth spot, quiet like Russell, as Nicola and Fiona chatted on. Nicola gave an absentminded shake of her hair, which truly was a marvel, like something out of a shampoo commercial. It was glossy, thick and luxuriously wavy in a way mine, so straight and fine, could never be. I envied her hair; I envied her confidence. She didn't seem to care that she was short and busty. She looked like the kind of girl who'd found everything she'd wanted in life, all by age twenty-four, which she'd apparently just turned the previous week, complete with big birthday party and a necklace from Russell.

I studied the place, its distressed wood walls and high ceilings that exposed the rafters and sent the noise upward. Ambient lighting cast Russell in shadow as he read the menu, his familiar brow creased in concentration. Absurd that he'd reminded me of Vincent; the two looked nothing alike, save for the blond hair and a similar build. Vincent was flamboyant and never failed to draw attention, whereas Russell seemed as studious and introverted as he'd been as a boy. I knew he'd found his way to the top of his own craft—he was an MIT graduate, like my dad, and now part of a successful tech startup. It held a certain exotic allure; I hadn't been around brainy overachievers in a long time. Which clearly defined Nicola, too. I overheard her tell Fiona she was a UC Berkeley graduate, with a degree in mechanical engineering, another exciting talking point for them as Fiona's boyfriend was a UC Berkeley graduate from the engineering school, too. They stopped talking in order to study their menus, and I could feel Nicola furtively eyeing me. Once the waitress took our orders and departed, Nicola addressed me directly.

"So, you're a ballerina."

"Yes, I am."

"That must be exciting!"

"Yeah, I guess it is!" I tried to echo her enthusiasm, although I thought of my job as "exciting" approximately two percent of the time. Mostly, it was sweaty, hard work. "Did you ever take ballet as a kid?" I inquired politely, always a safe question to ask a female, since half of them either had or had harbored an interest.

Bad call. Nicola's eyes seemed to light with fire from within. You'd think I'd asked her thoughts about child pornography. "Oh, no, no, no," she exclaimed. "You know how they say all little girls want to be ballerinas? Not me. Couldn't have been further from the truth. I loved horses. Did you ever love horses?"

It sounded more like a challenge than a question. "No," I replied. "I was that little girl who wanted only to be a ballerina."

"Did you go to college?"

It was growing harder to smile. "No. I left home early to train at the School of American Ballet. I finished high school the same year I finished my training and won a position with the American Ballet Theatre right after that."

Nicola turned to Fiona. "You danced too, right?"

"I did."

"And yet you managed to earn a college degree at the same time."

"I did." Fiona glanced my way. "But April is on an entirely different plane of existence in the ballet world. She's amazing. One of the best. Very few dancers make it to principal rank."

"I suppose." Nicola gave a dismissive wave of her hand. "Tell me about *your* studies, Fiona. I must confess, I can relate better to achievements in the academic world."

As Fiona and Nicola talked, Russell glanced at me. "This is probably boring to you. All this talk about academics."

"I'm fine with it," I told him. "You knew my dad and how he was."

He nodded. Russell had been a protégé of my father's, whom he'd met when Fiona's family had invited mine over for dinner one night, early in our friendship. My dad had spied the prodigy in the eighth-grade Russell and offered to tutor him in more advanced math and physics curriculum.

Nicola seemed to have a radar trained on Russell's attention, and now leaned in toward him. "What are you guys talking about?" she asked.

"April's dad," Russell said. "He was my mentor through high school years. I was so young, and he made learning the advanced concepts feel effortless."

"He had all these college students seeking help during his office hours," I said, "and then there was Russell, this high school freshman, clamoring for harder stuff."

Russell touched my hand. "I was sad to learn he'd passed away," he said. "You must miss him."

"I do," I said, and steeled myself for the inevitable "I heard about your mom, too—I'm so sorry." But it never came, and I realized he might not know that my mom had died. The thought horrified me. I didn't want to go there tonight. As soon as people heard I'd lost both parents within three years, it changed the dynamics, never in a good way. I'd told no one at the WCBT and intended to keep it that way.

To my relief, Nicola steered the conversation to memories of her own favorite mentor from high school days. I silently thanked her and made a mental note to have Fiona break the news about my mom to Russell later.

Our food arrived: cheeseburgers for Fiona, Russell and me, and a grilled chicken salad for Nicola. Russell seemed amazed that I ate "real" food like he did. "I'd heard all ballet dancers have to starve themselves," he said, reaching for a napkin to wipe his oily fingers.

"Yeah, I'd heard that too," Nicola said, her lips in a tight smile. She stabbed at her grilled chicken salad with her fork as if she resented the choice her body type had dictated.

"Don't believe everything you hear," I told them.

"Yes," Fiona said, "but now tell Russell and Nicola how many hours a day you dance."

I set down my burger. "I dance roughly seven hours a day during rehearsal periods, and when we're performing, that's another two hours. But I eat salads a lot." I gestured to Nicola's food. "That's my lunch every day."

"You're so thin." Russell sized me up. "You're like, Olympic-runner thin."

"It's kind of the same thing. Training is everything, with food consumption being more 'eat to live' than 'live to eat.' Although I like to cook as a way to relax."

Russell took my wrist and encircled it with his thumb and first finger. There was ample room to spare. "Look at this," he said in wonder. "You're delicate as a bird."

This made me laugh. "I'm not delicate. I'm pretty kick-ass actually."

"You can let her go now, Russ," Fiona said with a sideways glance at Nicola.

"Oh!" Russell dropped my wrist as if it had scalded him. He looked flustered until he addressed Fiona. "So, sis, tell me about your new job."

"I'll be the assistant to the artistic director at the West Coast Ballet Theatre."

"So, like, the associate artistic director?"

Fiona and I both began to laugh at the thought. "No, not that," Fiona said.

"That would be a very big job," I added. "Huge. A career position for someone who's been in the ballet world for some time."

"Then what?" Russell pressed.

"The artistic director's personal assistant," Fiona said, but she sounded less confident.

"Like, take messages for him and get his coffee, handle his appointment book?"

He seemed genuinely baffled. I could see something in Fiona hardening, growing defensive.

"The job is crucial," I told Russell. "The timing, in getting Fiona on board ASAP, is crucial. My boss—now *our* boss—is incredibly demanding. This is a big company, and the artistic director has to be everywhere at once."

"And while we're on the subject of work, how's that startup of yours going?" Fiona asked. She sounded combative.

Russell shrugged modestly.

"He's not going to brag, so I will." Nicola sat up taller. "His company, Pegasus Systems, got second-round VC funding last spring. *That's* how gangbusters it's going. They're already talking about an IPO, maybe as early as next spring. And, well, we all *know* the Internet is going to explode, once Berners-Lee's project moves from theory to reality. Perfect time to be developing a full-text retrieval system for the Internet, wouldn't you say?" Her eyes glowed.

Who was this Berners-Lee, and what project? What the hell was a full-text retrieval system? And an IPO? I couldn't decide if Nicola was testing us to see what we knew about the high-tech sector, or that she assumed everyone knew the terms she was throwing around so casually. But I only nodded, as if digesting it all, before turning to Russell. "Tell me what it is you do, exactly."

He smiled. "Easy version is that I'm an engineering manager. I supervise the programmers, which is the job I had myself for the first year. Programming code."

"You got that promotion recently," Nicola said, and turned to us. "He's now at the director level."

"Same work, fancier title," Russell said with a shrug.

"No more working from your boss's barn?" Fiona asked.

"A *barn?*" I repeated.

"It was actually a great working space," Russell told me. "Wired for electricity, plumbing installed, plenty of room for desks and a lab. But to answer your question," he said to Fiona, "no more barn.

We've got a real office now."

"What are your hours like?" I inquired.

"I get up by six and I'm into work before seven." He rubbed his hair absent-mindedly; it stood up in tufts like it had when he was a kid. "Basically, I'll work till I need dinner or sleep."

"We're talking a lot of nine o'clock dinners." Nicola gave Fiona and me a wry look.

"I lighten the load on Saturdays and Sundays," Russell added. "Sometimes I don't go in till ten and I rarely work past five. And sometimes I'll sleep in on a weekend morning and not show up till noon."

"Oh, the decadence," Fiona drawled. "How do you live with yourself?"

Russell looked startled. "It's not really being decadent," he began, as the rest of us laughed.

"I think it was intended as a joke," I said.

"He is *so* serious," Nicola said. "Takes everything so literally!"

"And you're dating him by choice?" Fiona teased her.

"I am!" Nicola's eyes glowed as she reached over and touched his shoulder possessively.

The waiter cleared our table. I looked down at my watch. "Whoops," I told Fiona. "We just missed the train. And the next one isn't for an hour."

"Don't even bother with the train," Russell said. "I'm happy to drive you two to the city."

"Seriously?" I asked, and Russell nodded. "That would be wonderful. Thank you."

"No problem." He smiled at me. Out of the corner of my eye, I could see Nicola's eyes dart from Russell to me and back to Russell.

"I'll go with you guys," she said. "I just love that view of the city, when you're driving up Highway 101 and there it is, the city skyline."

He looked at her, perplexed. "Wouldn't you prefer to get home and into bed early? Tomorrow's a work day."

"Oh, I'll deal with tomorrow later. It'll be fun to drive with you to the city! Get to know your sister better. And April," she added as an afterthought, a concept as disingenuous as it sounded.

The drive in the car was much more relaxing than the train, and I grew sleepy. Nicola had twisted around in the front passenger seat to chat with Fiona. In my spot behind Nicola, I was happy to remain silent and simply bask in the presence of these two Garvey siblings, this precious link to my past.

Nicola stopped talking and a peaceful silence fell over the car. Russell met my eyes in the rearview mirror. "Do you know what this strangely reminds me of, seeing the two of you in back? That trip to Chicago the three of us took with my dad. The math contest for me, some big ballet class for you two."

The memory flowed over me. "Oh, wow," I said to Fiona, "do you remember?"

"How could anyone forget?" She sounded sad. "That was the day I realized you were bound for the top ranks. And that we would have to separate. For life."

"But look at us now," I said softly, and the two of us smiled at each other.

"Damn," Fiona said. "Here we are."

"Welcome to the world of professional ballet, Fi. You're in for a wild ride."

Chapter 6

The Master Class

It was no surprise I dreamed about childhood years that night. I woke before daylight, too early to get up but too late to fall back asleep, and thought back to that dizzying, life-changing Chicago trip Russell had mentioned.

In short, Fiona and I shouldn't have been there. I was twelve and thought I was hot stuff; Fiona was eleven. The master class, which I'd overheard the most advanced students at our ballet studio talking about, had been intended for pre-professional students and above. It was taught by one of ABT's ballet masters while the company was performing in Chicago. The class was far too advanced for Fiona and me. The barre exercises were long and involved, and half the time the teacher marked the moves with his fingers, not his body. He spoke and proceeded rapidly.

The jump combinations in the center all had beats attached to the entrechats and assemblés. Pirouettes were expected to be doubles and triples. Some of the boys got in turns with eight revolutions. The grand allegro, long and involved, felt like a ballet in itself, a terrifying, ill-rehearsed one.

By this time, Fiona had moved to the very back of the room, lodged herself there, as she stonily regarded the other dancers. She refused to budge when I pleaded with her to join me across the floor for grand allegro. I felt dizzy with panic; grand allegro was intended for groups of three or four. I couldn't go alone, and we were the last two dancers remaining. I stood there, in preparation pose, my knees knocking together in fear. The teacher glanced my way and his strict expression softened. "Someone come join this poor girl. I told you I wanted groups of three and four. Why was the previous group five?"

Two of the more advanced dancers bounded over from the left side with good-natured smiles, even looks of encouragement. Relief washed over me, and something more. A quivering adrenaline rush came over me, to dance as well as them, dance exactly like them, from the tilt of their heads as the three of us commenced the waltz turns, the elegance of their arms, their fingers, and the way they leapt so powerfully, jumped so high, their pointed toes the last thing to leave the floor and the first thing to return, with whisper-soft landings. I'd never worked my feet and calves so hard, pushed my quads this much to jump higher. Most of all, I felt the thrill of dancing with a pair of extraordinary dancers. I could tell they were paying attention to me as I danced, so that all three of us leapt at the same time, angled our heads for the second set of waltz turns in precisely the same way. It was a performance. It thrilled me beyond words. I could feel everyone else's eyes on us, and something took form in me right then, germinating and flowering. This hunger to excel, to perform flawlessly.

This baptism. When you discover that you value achievement over pain, over shyness, over nerves, over resistance from your parents. Going across the floor once wasn't this "happily ever after" feeling, either. It ignited a dare, to do as well again. Posed by myself, by the other students, all of them older, many of them performance-level. A dare posed by the teacher, a former principal dancer himself, handsome and toned, thick brown hair and intent eyes, on me, now that I'd detached myself from the "please don't look at me" pack of younger and less talented dancers who'd comprised the last two groups. I forgot about Fiona, still sulking in the back of the room with other too-intimidated students, and focused all my energy, my attention, on dancing.

After we'd done the combination on the left, we repeated it, both sides. I watched the first set of dancers closely, the true "best of the best." They were sublime. They didn't just dance the steps, they inhabited them, adding nuance with their hands, their heads, ensuring a sense of originality and theatricality.

The awe and respect for their beauty was so powerful inside me, it felt like a knife thrust. I was so bowled over by it all, I wanted to cry afterward, when the teacher finally signaled for everyone to return to center. We followed his moves in an elegant, grace-laden révérence, curtseyed in courtly thanks. Then everyone clapped and, like that, the magic ended. Just beyond my euphoria hovered a grey, soggy despair. I didn't want it to be over. I wasn't ready to go back to that earlier, complacent me. I trudged toward Fiona, standing by the shelves in the front corner of the room where we'd all stowed our dance bags. As Fiona scrabbled around for her jacket, which had gotten lost in the adjacent coat pile, I glanced longingly back at the teacher, surrounded by clamoring dancers. He looked up and around. He spied me, and to my shocked surprise, he gestured for me to approach.

I walked over to him uncertainly, worried he was going to realize I wasn't the person he thought I was, and that he'd dismiss me with a wave and a scornful laugh. "What is your name?" he asked.

"April Manning."

"Are you auditioning?"

It dawned on me he was genuinely interested in me and that this wasn't a mistake.

"You mean for New York summer intensives?" I stammered. The

issue was the newest battle with my parents, who kept wanting me to be content with what I could find, there in Omaha. Even this master class in Chicago wouldn't have happened if Fiona's dad hadn't planned on driving to Chicago that weekend anyway, for Russell's math competition.

"That, and the winter term."

His words made the breath whoosh out of me. The best dancers from summer intensives were invited, some even given scholarships, to study during the school year as well. But it meant moving away from your family, to live with a host family or in some housing setup with other students. My mother's response at the mere proposal of that in the future had been a flat out "No."

"Not yet," I told him.

"How old are you?"

"Twelve and a half."

"This is the time to be thinking about it. Don't wait too long." He eyed me closer. "Where do you live?"

"Omaha."

"Who are you training with?"

"Kathryn Pulaski. And her daughter, Rochelle."

His face scrunched up, as if in confusion. "Never heard of them."

I wanted to shrink in shame. I knew, right then, that if I stayed there with Miss Kathy and her daughter, in that comfortable, easy environment, I'd never rise to the this level.

This. Everything in me lunged toward it—the ballet master, his glamour and aura of stardom, the world I'd just caught a glimpse of. I had to have it. I had to. No matter how much my parents resisted it. This was my destiny.

"Think about what you want your next step to be," he said. He spoke to me like I was an adult. Which made me realize that, in the ballet world, if you were training in New York, away from family, no matter what your age, you sort of *were* an adult. Your career was your life, your business. Not your parents' life. The thought exploded in my mind, sparkling with allure.

A trio of older dancers, waiting to speak with him, shifted impatiently. "Don't wait too long," he repeated to me, before the other dancers commanded his attention.

And that was that, I thought, as I rejoined Fiona. Already I could feel dreary acceptance settling in. I had no idea how to proceed further in Omaha. Miss Kathy wouldn't either. A master class like this was the pinnacle for most of her students. But as Fiona and I left the building ten minutes later, I heard someone call out my name. I turned and saw one of the older male dancers from the class hurrying toward me.

"Mr. Keefe wanted you to have this." He handed me a card, which I studied. It had the teacher's name, title and phone number on the front. I turned it over. On the back, he'd written two names and phone numbers.

"He said for you to use his name as reference, when you call these two and explain your situation. And that you should try and call them in the next month or two."

Prickles rushed over my arms.

It was all going to happen. I knew it right then.

On the return drive to Omaha, I sagged into the back seat, utterly depleted from the overexertion of the class. So much extra energy had roared through me and now was I paying the price. I felt physically ill. Fiona was quiet as well. Russell, in the front seat alongside their father, never spoke to the two of us if he could help it, so his silence went unnoticed. Fiona's dad glanced quizzically at us through the rear-view mirror.

"Why are you two so quiet? I expected you'd be talking a mile a minute about the class."

Fiona and I looked at each other. "It was a hard class," I said, and Fiona nodded.

"Did you enjoy yourself?" He addressed this question to Fiona directly.

"It was too hard," Fiona mumbled. "I couldn't finish it."

I didn't know what to say. Hard or not, I'd never felt more alive, more connected to what I wanted most in the world, than I had, launching myself across the floor with the other dancers.

"April finished it, though," Fiona added.

"It was hard for me, too." I spoke softly.

Fiona met my eyes for the first time since the class. "You were so beautiful to watch." Her blue eyes grew shinier and she burst into tears.

Fiona's dad looked over his shoulder in surprise. "Fiona! What's the matter with you? Why aren't you happy for your friend, that she enjoyed it?"

"I'm losing my friend," she sobbed.

"Don't be silly. She's right there beside you."

But I got it, and I didn't know what to say. Fiona was right; nothing would be the same after today.

I must have fallen back asleep, because when I opened my eyes again in my apartment, the room was brighter, and I had the most delicious sense of having dreamed of my mom's presence. The memory of the dream itself was hazy, already dissipating, but the good feeling remained.

Fiona was back in my life. So was Russell Garvey. As if my mom had reached out and made it so.

Chapter 7

Yelena and Jana

The week Renata, esteemed former principal, rejoined the company—and she was indeed a gem—I approached the rehearsal boards with queasy trepidation. *Please, don't let her be another Sonya,* I thought. *Please let me keep Aurora.* Since Sonya's departure, Carrie had been moved up to first cast, myself to second, and Marilyn, a senior soloist, to third. Heart thumping, I studied the list for the morning rehearsals, which included the six Fairy solos from baby Aurora's christening scene, which opened the ballet.

Lilac Fairy was a lead role, a recent acquisition for me, and I saw with dismay that I'd been demoted to third cast. Renata had taken my place in first cast. Before I could process the disappointing implications of that, however, I caught sight of the next sheet, the afternoon's rehearsals. In the Act III wedding pas de deux, featuring Aurora and her prince, my name had been moved to first cast.

I blinked, twice.

First-cast Aurora. The hugeness of this, those simple three words, *Aurora: A. Manning,* stole my breath. It meant I was now in the running to prove I could be the best of the best.

My heart sang. *Mom! Dad! Look at this! It's all paying off!*

I walked away, expression neutral, trying to act nonchalant, which was hard to do when you were floating, high on euphoria and the prospect of fulfilling a lifelong dream.

Aurora—first cast!

But even the most thrilling pieces of news came with a downside. Being first-cast Aurora meant I'd be on the front line now, for rehearsals. Yelena ran *Beauty* rehearsals. And Yelena didn't like me.

Yelena was the ageless, imperious, longtime WCBT ballet mistress, Bob's female counterpart in rehearsing the dancers. She'd been with the company since before Sid. She was ancient, born in 1916, before the Russian Revolution, a concept nearly impossible to wrap my brain around. She'd trained in Leningrad—once known as St. Petersburg—and danced with the Kirov Ballet for a dozen years before emigrating to Paris, then to New York, and finally San Francisco. Although she was younger than George Balanchine (who was dead now, anyway), you saw, in her craggy, formidable bulk, the kind of Imperial-era teacher who'd instructed him, back when he was Georgiy Balanchivadze at The Imperial Ballet School. She still wore chiffon dance skirts and a leotard, neither of which complemented her stocky build, her sagging flesh. She had a bulbous nose and jutting chin and looked like a witch when she was scowling, which was most of the time except when she was coaching her favorites. (No surprise: Dmitri. Curtis and Carrie. And now, Renata.)

As a former Kirov dancer, Yelena was, admittedly, an outstanding repository of information and wisdom about the story ballets by Marius Petipa, the 19th century ballet master and principal choreographer of the Imperial Ballet, which included *The Sleeping Beauty,* that most classical of the classical ballets. It was hard to ask for a better source of knowledge, and the WCBT's reputation for their evening-length story ballets was surprisingly excellent.

But she was mean. Old school mean.

Throughout my professional training—those four terrifying, overwhelming, exhilarating years at the School of American Ballet—

there'd been a few similar teachers, Russian-trained émigrés, holdovers from a bygone era. I'd been disciplined, even hit with a cane, by teachers like Yelena. They singled you out, picked on you, humiliated you, sometimes because you were indeed worthless, but other times, in some sort of Zen logic, they did it because they felt you had great potential. It was impossible to discern the difference, until roles for the end-of-year recital were doled out and you saw where you were on the pyramid. Another way you found out was by being called in to learn why you weren't, in the end, the perfect fit they'd thought you were, for the School of American Ballet. I'd lost my two closest friends to those meetings. Training years were a period of such high anxiety, such breath-stealing insecurity, that I could only shake my head now, wonder what kind of madness gripped its young students, except I knew the answer to that. It was a siren call we couldn't resist. Our burning loyalty to the muse defied explanation. We thought nothing of giving up our families, our home life, to follow her.

Today Yelena was rehearsing us in *The Sleeping Beauty*'s Act III wedding-scene pas de deux. Curtis was my partner, Prince Desiré to my Aurora. Dmitri and Carrie were the second cast. Dmitri watched in amusement now as Yelena lit into me for not acting "100 years older" than the Act I Aurora. Never mind that Aurora and the royal household slept through 100 years and woke up precisely the same age. I'd danced Aurora on tour with the ABT (small-town midweek matinee, but hey, it was Aurora). I fully understood that, as Aurora, I was expected to present three different moods: a 16-year-old princess on her birthday; a sleeping "dream" figure, ethereal and elusive; and for the wedding scene, I was supposed to be more mature, stately, as if sleeping 100 years lent one perspective and gravitas.

The latest clash with Yelena was over the stupidest of things, the angle of my head as I took Curtis' hand. "Not like that," Yelena screeched, and stopped us for the fifth time. She strode over, gripped my head in her beefy fingers and violently angled it to an absurdly cocked position. I looked possessed, not regal. Curtis and I took the pose again. And again. Still wrong. I wanted to scream in frustration. Apparently Yelena felt the same.

"Either you are difficult on purpose or you are idiot girl! You stomp around and make head move like robot. There is no art in you! Why you are here, with these other fine dancers, I do not know. Marilyn should dance with Curtis, not you." Marilyn, the third-cast Aurora, looked up hopefully. I ignored her, as well as Dmitri's snickers, and tried again.

Yelena slapped her hand down on the fold-up chair so hard it rang. "No more! We stop with you!"

I wanted to shout back, but I'd been too well trained. I stood there, eyes to the floor, fuming.

"You have watched the company's archived tapes of the production?" Yelena demanded.

"No," I admitted.

"No?" Yelena sounded incredulous.

"Anders told me the production was faithful to the Petipa original. The American Ballet Theatre danced the Petipa staging, too. I know it all."

Yelena let her jaw drop in exaggerated shock. "You are a member of this company and yet you haven't watched the archive tape of this company, these dancers? We have a gem, caught on tape. Januschka, who understood all three Auroras, each with its own personality."

Januschka?

"You mean Sonya?" I asked.

"Not her! The other!"

"Jana," Curtis murmured to me. "*Januschka* was the nickname Yelena gave her."

"Do it, now," Yelena commanded. "Go and watch that tape where Januschka dances. Leave this rehearsal. I am through rehearsing you. I want to see my other cast. Dima." She gestured to Dmitri. "Come with your partner and show me your talent, beautiful boy."

My face and neck burned with shame as I vacated the center of the room. In silence I retrieved my dance bag, traded pointe shoes for sandals, and made my way out.

The archival library was across the street, in the lower level of the California Civic Theater, where the company performed. It was a quiet, cavernous place, dimly lit and soothing to my jangled nerves. I followed directions down the stairs and to the right. At the library, I looked around. Half reference library and half museum, the long, open room featured archived material that pertained to the city's performing arts scene, dating from the 1920's. Newspapers, ancient tutus, swaths of fabric from earlier theatre drapes shared space with microfiche projectors and a newer video annex to watch taped performances. The curator, a silver-haired, smiling woman, came out from a back room and greeted me. She helped me set up in an annex, dim and cave-like, that held three chairs and a television on a rolling cart with a VCR player beneath. After inserting the videotape and checking to see that it worked, she handed me the remote and I settled into my seat.

Yelena had instructed me to watch the Act III wedding pas de deux. Instead I forwarded the tape to the second act, Aurora's entrance on her sixteenth birthday party. I felt a surprising pang to see a beautiful, long-legged coltish girl hurrying down the grand staircase. Jana, a mere seven years ago.

Jana did an amazing job of looking like an excited sixteen-year-old princess. She was younger than I'd presumed, not Carrie's age. I thought back to the fleshy, aging dancer I'd been around that first week in August. This videotaped Jana was positively adorable. She was so lit from within, all full of energy and enthusiasm. I marveled over how airborne Jana's pas de chat jumps were, how clean her grand jeté leaps. What she seemed to lack in pure classical refinement—she was young, after all, and not New York-trained—she made up for in other ways.

One of the most famous parts of *The Sleeping Beauty* is the Rose Adagio, which Aurora dances with four suitors. Few greater challenges existed in the classical repertoire for the ballerina, who had to find an iron balance as four different partners took their turn promenading her in a full circle, en point, her back leg in arabesque, later repeated in an attitude. Post-promenade, she had to let go of one suitor's hand and remain unsupported, balancing, before taking the next suitor's hand. The tip of a pointe shoe was roughly the size of an Oreo cookie; this was the space on which she had to find balance. On top of having been promenaded in a circle, which meant she couldn't focus on one, single, unmoving object. Not to mention fatigue, blinding stage lights, and the uncertain grip of a partner planning to withdraw his hand.

Jana triumphed through it all with a bright smile. To Tchaikovsky's sumptuous crescendoing music, she locked all her pirouettes in place, and through the final, grueling, back-attitude promenades, she maintained her balance. Nor did she look nervous or wobbly in the least. It was mesmerizing to watch. Jana danced Aurora as well as any of the ABT dancers.

What had happened to *this* Jana?

I tried asking Carrie about it the next day. She took a long time to reply, her eyes fixed on the pointe shoes she was breaking in. "Like we told Anders," she said, giving the stiff shoes a few good smacks against the nearby wall. "Her health. You know. One of those things."

"Oh, sure," I said, even though I didn't know.

But her message was clear: *Back off. I don't plan on discussing Jana with you.*

We smiled insincerely at each other, and I let the subject drop. I would get no answers from this polite stranger and colleague that I was supposed to be getting to know better.

In the way life could present bizarre coincidences, it was Jana herself I encountered, a week later. I'd gone to Marshall's to buy cheap T-shirts and lounge attire. As I approached the line to pay, an agitated voice at the front of the line claimed my attention. The realization that it was Jana made me dizzy, as if the power of my curiosity had physically conjured her.

Right then, however, Jana didn't look like someone I wanted to interact with. She was arguing with the clerk in one of those excruciating yet fascinating situations to watch from the sidelines. Her voice grew strident as she told the clerk it must be a mistake that her credit card had declined.

"I tried twice," the clerk said, sounding both apologetic and defensive.

"Fine," Jana said in exasperation. "I'll pay cash."

But this, too, raised problems. Jana sifted fruitlessly through her bag. As the delay stretched into an awkward eternity, the customers in line exchanged impatient yet amused glances.

"It was in here somewhere." Jana sounded shrill. "A hundred-dollar bill!"

The clerk said nothing, her lips compressed in a tight smile.

I didn't think; I just acted.

I strode right up next to Jana. "There you are! Why didn't you wait for me? I told you I planned to pay for everything with my card." I dumped my items on the counter, slapped down my credit card and flashed the clerk a smile that relayed both confidence and chagrin. "Sorry to do this to you, but could you maybe delete that transaction and add these things?"

The clerk smiled back, clearly relieved to de-escalate the conflict.

Jana met my eyes for a bewildered instant, but swiftly assumed the role I was silently urging on her. "You're so sweet," she said. "It's just that I didn't want to burden you."

"No, it was my turn. You paid for dinner last night. In fact, we should go by L'Orange and see if they were the source of the problem with your credit card. Remember that time I got charged 3200 dollars on my card instead of 32? Imagine the same thing happening with that 200-dollar dinner bill. That would max out a person's card!"

Everyone laughed at this—the clerk, Jana, the supervisor who'd edged closer to make sure there was no problem. The supervisor sized us both up.

"Pardon me, but are you two ballet dancers?"

Jana hesitated.

"We are!" I said. "Principal and senior soloist, right here with the WCBT."

This set voices abuzz with pleasure.

"I thought so!" the supervisor exclaimed. "Except I wasn't sure, because I didn't recognize you, the way I recognize Carrie Bryson, say, or Dmitri Petrenko."

"I'm new!" I trilled. "But Jana here started with the company several years back. When was that, Jana?"

"Gosh, I joined back in 1981. I was a bitty thing, just turned eighteen."

In 1981, I'd turned seventeen. Which meant Jana was only a year older than I. How was that possible? But I only smiled indulgently as if I knew this about this "close" friend of mine. "You might have seen Jana dance Aurora in *The Sleeping Beauty*, seven years ago," I said to them. "She was the star of the show."

"Oh my gosh," the woman behind us in line exclaimed. "I do recognize you! You were the youngest Aurora that year. You were amazing!"

As Jana turned to thank the woman, I looked pointedly at the clerk. "Separate bags for our purchases, please. And is that receipt ready for me to sign? We have an important rehearsal to get to."

"Super important," Jana broke in. "Dmitri will be furious if we're late."

"Oh, *Dmitri*," the clerk breathed. "He is such a hunk."

The two of us sailed out together, arm in arm. I could feel Jana trembling. We kept up the charade by unspoken agreement until we'd walked a half-block and turned right at the next corner. Our arms dropped and we swiftly stepped apart.

"Why did you do that?" Jana asked in a low voice as we continued to walk.

"Because you looked like you needed help out of a difficult situation."

Jana exhaled heavily. Her steps slowed, as though, with each one, a weight was being added to her shoulders. "Fuck," she muttered. "How did I max out that card?"

"Did you have the cash?"

Jana glared at me. "No, I didn't. Wasn't that obvious?"

"Frankly, no. You were giving an excellent performance of someone who regularly carried hundred-dollar bills."

Jana studied me suspiciously. "Are you funning me?"

"No, I'm being perfectly serious. You look posh," I lied. "Refined."

It was worth the lie. A relieved expression came over Jana's face. It bloomed into a happiness that made her look lovely, much younger, like the buoyant Aurora I'd seen on tape. The expression disappeared a moment later.

"I can pay you back," she said.

A hunch arose in me that Jana couldn't, that she was dead broke. "Please don't bother," I said. "It was nothing."

Which made things awkward, because what was "nothing" to me was a big deal to her, and now we both knew it.

"Please," I repeated.

As Jana studied me, I could see something in her eyes relent. "Thanks," she mumbled.

"No problem."

We walked. "They really bought our story," I said, and began to laugh, which made Jana laugh, too.

"Your line about the 200-dollar dinner. Boy, did they look at me differently after that!"

"Let's go march over to L'Orange *right now*." I affected a prim, self-righteous tone.

We laughed as we darted across the street.

"So, how are things at the studios?" Jana asked once we'd resumed our regular pace.

I had so many questions for her. What had happened to the dancer she'd been? Why had she been so determined to march out of signing a contract that would have protected her from the uncertain fate she seemed to be living out now? But I liked the easy conversation we were having now. "Things are busy. I've got a lot of catching up to do on learning choreography that the rest of the dancers know, especially for the fall tour."

Jana nodded. "That's how it is for the newcomer. We haven't had too many new commissions in the past few years, just Anders' ballet and a pair of short ballets from local choreographers. Which means most of us know all the ballets by heart."

I noticed the "we" and "us" references and how, with each one,

Jana's shoulders seemed to straighten.

"That's it," I said. "For the fall tour, only two of us are newcomers. And did you know that Renata has come out of retirement to dance with the company again?"

I held my breath, unsure if the mention would only make Jana more keenly aware of what she'd lost. But to my relief, her eyes widened in pleasure. "That's good news. She's wonderful, one of our best dancers. Everyone was sad to see her go, two years ago."

We'd stopped at the corner. I was going one way and she was going the other, but we kept chatting. I could tell Jana needed it; there was something desperate behind her eyes that sent a wave of sympathy through me. "Hey, I meant to tell you," I said. "I watched the archived performance of *The Sleeping Beauty* the other day. Your Aurora performance—wow. Just amazing."

Jana regarded me in surprise. "Seriously?"

I nodded. "There was something gorgeous and… transcendent about it. Your musicality, the way you wholly embodied the role. It's like you really *were* Aurora. I wanted to watch it over and over."

Jana stared down at the sidewalk. "Boy. It's been a long time since someone raved about my dancing." She gave a sniff, dabbed at her eyes, and looked up. "Thank you. That means everything to me."

"Yelena had sent me to watch it," I admitted. "She was shouting at me in front of everyone because my interpretation wasn't good enough. She kicked me out of rehearsal and told me to watch your Aurora, that it was 'a gem, caught on tape' and that you'd captured the essence of all three Auroras."

"She said all that? Really?" Jana began to laugh. "That's hilarious. All she did, it seemed, was shout at me when I was rehearsing it. I was only a corps dancer at the time, and she scared me to death."

"Has she always been like that?"

"Sure." Jana grinned. "That's why her name is Yell-ena."

This made us both burst into peals of laughter. For a long, delicious moment, it was the closest I'd felt to any of the WCBT females. How ironic that it had to be a dancer no longer with the company.

Jana hesitated. "You probably have to get going, huh?"

"Actually, yeah." I gestured in the direction of the studios.

"All right." Jana said. "But listen, do me a favor. Don't... don't tell Carrie about this. Or the others. It's awkward, is all." She held up the bag in her hand. "And I owe you. I really, really owe you for helping me out. I'll make it up to you."

"You don't have to do that. It was nothing."

"No, I insist." A bullish look came over Jana's face, carrying with it a glimpse of the aggressively unpleasant dancer she'd been at the studios.

I didn't want to talk to that Jana. "Okay," I said brightly. "Just... no pressure."

"Okay." Her face relaxed back into a smile. "See you around."

"See you."

Chapter 8

Housewarming

Anders and Sabine had bought a house together in August, and now she'd flown back to San Francisco for the signing. On Thursday afternoon, with a flurry of signatures, they became homeowners. Anders was all smiles as he informed me of this on Friday. "Come over on Sunday afternoon," he urged. "You and Fiona. We're having a small, informal open house. Particularly informal since we won't have furniture yet." We were in his office and he turned to Fiona, who was filing papers nearby. "Did you take care of the stacking-chairs rental?"

"I did," she replied. "And am I correct in assuming you wanted a few tables as well? I took the liberty of ordering three."

"Tables. Yes, we'll need them. I hadn't thought of that."

"That's why you hired me," she teased.

He smiled. "I am very glad I did."

"Me too." She grinned back at him. The happy factor in the room was off the charts.

"Four o'clock," Anders told us as he reached for a now-ringing phone.

"We'll be there," I promised.

But what Fiona and I encountered on Sunday afternoon at the Russian Hill home seemed anything but informal. The house, a beautiful, cream, two-story Edwardian with expensive-looking gold fixtures, appeared to be crowded with people inside. Fiona and I stood on the sidewalk, bearing gifts of wine and cheese, and gazed about at the profusion of shiny, expensive cars crowding the driveway. "Did you get the correct address?" I asked Fiona. "We're not crashing someone else's party, are we?"

Fiona consulted the folded paper onto which she'd jotted down the address. "Nope, this is it. Oh, and look." She gestured to the front window, through which we could see at least two dozen people socializing, some sitting, some standing, drinks in hand. "Those are stacking chairs they're sitting on. Yay, my chairs made it!"

We approached the door and rang the bell. A moment later the door swung open to reveal a flushed, smiling Anders.

"What's going on?" I asked him. "On Friday you made it sound like this would be small."

"Ah, but on Saturday, Sabine got us an invitation to a Sunday brunch."

I took in his attire: expensive-looking dress slacks, a royal-blue dress shirt, a tie. A high-end brunch, I guessed. With San Francisco high rollers—a coup for any artistic director.

"She went on to invite people back here, and everyone took her up on the offer." His grin widened, his grey eyes animated in a way that melted my heart. I knew it was just the way his eyes were shaped, like a hopeful boy's, but their charm was undeniable.

Once inside, we encountered Curtis and Carrie, en route to the kitchen. "Welcome," Curtis said, and held up his empty wine glass. "We're getting refills. Who needs a glass?"

Fiona and I raised our hands.

"Red or white?"

"White, please," I said.

"I'll join you two," Fiona told Curtis. "We've got these things for the fridge."

Alone with Anders, I sized him up again. He returned my gaze with a blissed-out smile. "I am so happy right now," he said.

"You look very… relaxed." What he looked was drunk, but it seemed imprudent to point this out. Besides, if it made him more open and chatty, all the better for me. I missed this Anders, the camaraderie of our early days here. "I like seeing you this way. Happy housewarming."

"Thank you."

"I like your house, too."

He looked around, as if taking in the contours of the place for the first time. "I am crazy about this place. You've got to see the view from upstairs," he said, and beckoned me to follow. I followed him up the stairs and into a vacant side room with an enormous window.

He was right. The view was amazing. Through leafy trees lining the block, I saw the San Francisco Bay. The water's aquamarine color was punctuated by white dots that must have been sailboats. A ferry, miniaturized by the distance, churned across the bay. The sky was a dazzling, popsicle blue. There was even a glimpse of the Golden Gate Bridge to the far left. I stood there, agog, taking it all in.

He smiled at my reaction. "I felt exactly the same way, the first time I saw this view."

We stood there in silence, gazing at it all. A soft breeze from the open window stirred the air, a lemongrass freshness. "For the first time in my life, it all feels within reach," Anders said in a hushed voice. "Everything I've wanted. Everything I've worked my entire life for. Directing a company with world-class potential. Living in this amazing city. Moving into the perfect house with the perfect partner."

"How much time is Sabine going to be able to spend out here?" I asked. "Based in Brussels, and all."

"Quarterly visits, hopefully long ones."

I thought of Fiona and her boyfriend. "You could make that work."

"We could. And between you and me," he added in a more conspiratorial tone, "if I get things moving in the right direction, get the budget where it should be, with a surplus for another administrator, I'd love, more than anything, to have Sabine join me at the West Coast Ballet Theatre. She wouldn't accept anything less than co-artistic director, of course, so I'd have to sell it that way to the board of trustees."

"Oh, Anders." I gazed at him in delight. "That would be amazing."

"Agreed."

"Have you brought up your idea to Sabine?"

"No. I'll have to bring it up to her at the right time. She loves Brussels and the troupe there. Fiercely."

In silence we mulled over this. Sabine was highly independent; Anders might have bitten off more than he could chew on this issue.

"But we just bought a house together," Anders said, as if reading my mind.

"You did. That's a very permanent thing to do."

"I agree."

He hesitated. "Don't you breathe a word of what I just told you to anyone."

"Don't worry, I won't."

"I shouldn't have said all that to you. My personal aspirations, and such." He frowned, and the confidential mood evaporated.

"I like it," I protested. "I want to hear your thoughts and hopes."

He shook his head. "It's not professional."

"But… we're friends. Former colleagues. I mean, yes, you're my boss now, and you were the boss last year as our choreographer," I continued on, uncertain now. "But do you remember the cast party last spring, after opening night? You, me and Vincent, hanging onto each other, singing that Danish drinking song you taught us?" I'd even set aside my grudge toward Vincent for the night, and it had been warm, congenial, like old times.

"I do." A smile softened Anders' expression. "That was memorable. Except that Vincent's a terrible singer."

"But a very enthusiastic one."

"Very." He chuckled.

"That was a great night."

"It was."

We smiled at each other, camaraderie restored. The front doorbell chimed, followed by the voices of new arrivals.

Anders cocked his head in the direction of the sound. "Renata!" He looked pleased. "She made it. She wasn't sure if she could. Excuse me. And you still don't have a drink. Go get yourself a glass of wine."

Not waiting for my reply, he bounded down the stairs. A moment later I heard his exclamations of welcome and Renata's response, his "let me introduce you to Sabine" and her smooth "I've been looking forward to that." My hands balled into fists.

Upstaged. By the newcomer.

Correction: I was the newcomer. She was the old-timer, the ultimate insider. Anders had been thoroughly won over by her. How long, I wondered, before he shared his personal thoughts and aspirations with *her?*

Stop it, I told myself fiercely. *Drop the attitude.*

My fists uncurled; I sighed.

No matter how I felt personally, I knew Renata was a huge asset for Anders and the company. I myself had yet to figure out where I stood with her. Her first day back in company class, she'd greeted me kindly enough before the others claimed her attention. German-born, she was tall and thin, in her late thirties, with cropped raven hair and alert eyes. Everyone in the company liked her. She and Dmitri were close, which made me wonder just where she would have stood on the contract-signing issue. She wasn't chatty; during breaks she seemed more inclined to listen and observe the others, preserving her energy, massaging her various aching joints. But in class and rehearsal, she came alive, with an astonishing attack and relentless energy. None of Anders' tricky combinations in class ever fazed her. Petit allegro, adagio, grand allegro—she managed them all with the same display of effortless precision and grace.

Probably the most comforting thing to me was that Renata didn't want to dance Aurora. She'd told me so, laughing out loud when I'd raised the question. "I had my time, years back," she said. "I'm looking forward to a few more runs as Giselle and Odette-Odile, but I'll let you and Carrie keep Aurora. Anders knows that."

She and Carrie got along well. The conversations between the two of them always seemed warm and personal, heads close as they murmured together, abbreviated sentences that alluded to a long relationship. One time I overheard Renata tell Carrie, "I know, it's hard. But it's better that she's gone. She's not your obligation anymore." Which could have only meant Jana, and struck me as hurtful, even if Jana wasn't there to hear it. Poor Jana—broke, forgotten and unmissed, all because she'd trusted Dmitri.

"April?" Fiona's voice came from the foot of the stairs. "You up there?"

"I am. Come up here."

Fiona trudged up the stairs with two glasses of white wine. "Check out this view," I told her as she handed me a glass. Fiona looked out and gasped in delight.

"San Francisco is amazing," she said in a reverent voice that made me smile.

"Lucky us, we get to live in this city."

"We are *so* lucky."

We clinked glasses, sipped our wine, and I felt better.

By the time Fiona and I rejoined the group downstairs, Lexie and Jacob had arrived, and were chatting with Sabine. Even Dmitri was there, a friendly, respectful look on his face as he listened to her. No surprise; Sabine's vivacious personality drew people to her. Even though she'd just turned forty, she still looked youthful and beautiful as a model. She saw me finally, and a smile spread across her face. She excused herself and hurried over.

"My beautiful April. How much better you look, from last year! California suits you!" She gave me three kisses on alternating cheeks, Belgian-style, and afterward enveloped me in a warm hug. She was shorter than I, just shy of being petite, but her personality, the fire in her beautiful brown eyes, made her seem tall, indomitable.

"How *are* you?" she asked. Before I could reply, she took my hand and led me through the crowd to the back of the house, a quiet, empty room that looked out onto the enclosed garden. "There," she said. "Now we can talk."

I loved that she'd done that; it made up for Anders' earlier snub. I told her how things had gotten better with each passing week, admitting how scary it had been, that first week, when I wasn't sure Anders could hold up against the force of Dmitri and the hostile dancers. I shared the more recent changes in the aftermath of the drama and Renata's arrival. Sabine took it all in, nodding thoughtfully.

It felt like old times, when she'd been a principal at ABT, Vincent's friend and, by extension, mine. She'd put on no airs over her higher rank, but instead had welcomed my contributions to the conversations as if I were one of them. I'd been agog with respect when, after her lead roles began to dwindle in favor of younger dancers, she'd boldly decided she wouldn't wait for administration to drop her from the roster, that she would go out and recreate herself as an artistic director. And when it had worked against her that she was a single female in a traditionally male job, she'd turned to Anders and they'd eloped—no one had even known they were *that* kind of partners—marketing themselves thereafter as an artistic directorship team.

"It seems he's got a more solid hold on the situation now," Sabine mused once I'd finished.

"I agree. I don't think he ever sleeps or takes time off. His energy and drive are relentless."

She chuckled as she relaxed against the empty room's wall. "That sounds like my Anders."

"Where's Sabine?" I heard someone call out, over the buzz of voices. "We need her."

"Oh, look at me," I exclaimed. "I'm monopolizing your time!"

"Nonsense. You and I needed this. But let's go back now so I can entertain all these wonderful new friends with their delightfully deep pockets." She examined her half-full wine glass and gave a happy sigh. "I do like San Francisco. I do like this part of the job. People can be so *lovely.*"

As the afternoon shadows lengthened, the guests began to leave. Finally, it was just the WCBT group minus Dmitri and Renata, who'd left together. The house in its quiet state felt even more inviting. High ceilings and the lack of furniture lent a sense of tremendous spaciousness. From a bank of south and west-facing windows, the last of the sunlight tinted the kitchen area gold. A sitting room held, curiously, a grand piano, a bench and a packing box, and nothing else. We regrouped in the kitchen, where Sabine informed us she'd found the perfect fit for the company, two young dancers.

How young? I wondered, and felt something in me clench. *Please not Natalia's age.*

"Students still," she added, and I breathed easier.

"The girl is Paris Opera Ballet," she said. "And the boy is Cuban-trained, all the way to the top. He took a year before accepting the Cubans' contract at Ballet Nacional to refine his skills in Spain. Which is where I found him."

I met Anders' eyes. His were lit with barely contained excitement.

"She's green," Sabine warned. "So's he. They're both children still. He's approaching eighteen, but she just turned sixteen."

Good, I thought. *Perfect.*

"When will they be available?" Anders asked.

"Possibly four weeks' time. Realistically, I'm going to say mid-October."

"The company tours in mid-October," he reminded Sabine.

"We'll call it the last week in October, then. It's good timing for me; I'll accompany them."

"Excellent." Anders released a pleased sigh.

"How were their audition tapes?" Carrie asked him.

"Outstanding. I feel very fortunate that Sabine got to them before anyone else."

"Paris Opera Ballet," I said in a hushed voice. "That's huge."

"And a Cuban dancer," Curtis sounded equally reverent. "Just as big."

"This is all amazingly good news," Jacob said.

"It is," Anders agreed. "News that calls for champagne."

Lexie opened the refrigerator. "Will you look at that? There's three bottles remaining."

The pop of the champagne cork brought the big-party mood right back. We shared toast after toast and drank until Sabine announced it was time for music. Specifically, piano music.

"What's with the grand piano in its own room?" I asked.

"Our second big acquisition," Anders replied. "We always said, first the house, then the piano. It was delivered yesterday."

"Do you both play?" Curtis inquired.

Sabine shook her head. "Only Anders. He loves to make music and I love to listen to him. He's quite good."

"Do we get to hear you play it?" Carrie asked.

"You do," Sabine replied. "Right now."

We made our way into the piano room, bringing along stacking chairs that we arranged in a semicircle around the piano. Anders's fingers skimmed across the keys softly, producing a charming, nuanced melody. I knew he played the piano, but his sense of authority and familiarity surprised me.

He reached into the nearby packing box and drew out a worn book of piano music selections. "Which one shall I play for you, my beautiful wife?" he asked Sabine as he settled himself on the cushioned bench.

"Chopin, I'm thinking. Maybe the Waltz in C sharp minor." She joined him on the bench.

"From *Les Sylphides* as well. Excellent." Anders paged through the music book. He found what he was looking for, set the book on the piano's stand and began to play.

It commenced with a tender, thoughtful waltz tempo, the notes slow and deliberate, before gliding into a passage of softer, much faster notes. They reminded me of petite allegro from the best of dancers: speedy, dense, but cleanly articulated, never losing its refinement nor its energy. I watched his fingers move, mesmerized, astonished. The softness of the quieter notes made us lean in to catch them, followed by jaunty, robust chords that filled the room and beyond. All of it was so compelling, once he finished, I wanted to hear it all again right away. I wasn't the only one. There was a chorus of breath intake by everyone, before Fiona cried out, "Again, again!" in a childlike voice, which made us all laugh.

"Anders!" Carrie exclaimed. "How is it you can *play* like that?"

"I had training before ballet took over," Anders said. "In truth, I'd wanted to become a concert pianist."

"How did I not know this about you?" I protested.

He offered me a mischievous look. "I'm full of secrets."

"Sabine doesn't look surprised," I retorted.

"I keep no secrets from my wife."

"Out with the piano story," Lexie said. "We all want to know."

Anders considered this. "I've always loved the piano and its repertoire. One of my earliest memories is attending music conservatory concerts not far from where we lived. My mother would take my sister and me to watch these student concerts. They were free, which fit the family budget. My sister was two years older. She was the one offered piano lessons when she was eight. I remember watching while she practiced, and later trying to imitate what she did. The lessons bored her—she had neither aptitude nor interest, and three months later, I was allowed to take her place with the teacher, someone affiliated with the conservatory, actually. We adored each other. There was no challenge she threw at me that I didn't devour, or work endlessly to figure out before the next lesson. Meanwhile, my sister had set her heart on ballet."

He hesitated and his eyes took on a faraway look. "We needed these things, you see. Artful things. My mother saw that. Ours wasn't a happy home. My father was a harsh man, a tradesman who'd never finished high school. He drank too much, communicated with his fists, and treated my mother, my sister and myself egregiously. No, I take that back. He had a soft spot in his heart for my sister. He decided she could be the artful one of the family. I was to learn a trade by age sixteen, high school be damned. He did recognize my aptitude for the piano and allowed me to take a few years of lessons. By age ten, I was proficient enough to find local work as an accompanist, earning enough for me to continue lessons with my teacher. When my father insisted on taking fifty percent of my earnings, to pay back the investment of lessons, my teacher accepted a pittance, so that we could continue to work together one afternoon a week. And for the rest of the week, I was an accompanist—at my sister's dance studio, no less."

The mention of his father jarred a memory in me. His father had died the same year as my dad. I knew, because he'd told me so, after my own dad had died. Anders had been a real comfort, amid all the awkwardness from the other dancers, who hadn't known what to say to me, so they'd said nothing. The compassion and pain in his eyes when he'd told me he understood my loss, had made tears rush to my own. "It's an enormous relationship, a piece of your life, gone," he'd said. "It's a very complicated loss." I'd nodded, too touched to speak, and it had created that first, important bond between us.

Anders was still talking. "The sad truth was that my sister lacked talent in ballet, as well. She had no turnout, little musicality. There were sixteen girls in her class, and while she wasn't the worst, the best that could be said for her was that she was enthusiastic and obedient. The music I was playing was the same for every class, thumping and repetitive—I could do it in my sleep. It gave me the opportunity to analyze what made a good ballet dancer good, the importance of good turnout, leading a tendu with the heel, a solid demi-plié before a turn. After a year of watching, I started experimenting on my own.

"I tried to show her one day, before class, what she was doing wrong with pirouettes. I was demonstrating how to bring up the passé knee fast, to the side, so it could serve as a counterweight while turning, and Madame walked in on us. My sister and I were both horrified. Madame looked angry, or at least that was what my eleven-year-old mind told me. She ignored my sister and asked me who'd taught me to do a pirouette. When I told her that her own instructions had, she looked baffled. She asked me to demonstrate and I did. My first double."

"How was your sister taking this?" Fiona asked.

Anders made a wry face. "Not well, I suppose. I was preoccupied, still mortified over being caught. Madame ordered me to the barre, told me to tendu, do a ronde de jambe. She had me développé to the side and she took my leg, twisting it around in its socket, pushing it to a full turnout, raising it high, seeing how far I could extend. I was tight, my body unused to this kind of stretch, but the leg went further than I'd realized it could. Madame was very quiet about it all, and after that class, we didn't speak of it again. But a month later, she began selecting students to audition for a place at the Royal Danish Ballet School. She paid a visit to our house, where she told our parents she wanted me to audition. Which stunned us all. My sister was beyond furious. She considered it all a personal betrayal, and as for my father, he was enraged at the thought of his son even considering becoming 'one of those pansy dancers.' But my mother and I saw it for what it was—a chance for me to safely leave the home and get a quality education. The Royal Danish School of Ballet has a very comprehensive academic program alongside the ballet. I never saw it as an opportunity to become a professional ballet dancer—I was going to be a concert pianist. But it was an escape, a free education infinitely superior to what could be found in our neighborhood. I could continue with my piano training through the curriculum, in fact. And a shared room in the dormitory meant I could leave a home that was becoming ever more toxic.

"So I auditioned, and, as Madame had promised, it didn't even matter that I'd had no training. I had the right body type, the musicality, the potential, and I was male. There were two dozen boys to three hundred girls auditioning. Twenty girls and five boys were offered places—I was one of them. My sister never forgave me. Ever. My father, the bastard, tried to beat me one last time into compliance, and I fought back—the only time I ever physically retaliated. My mother, forced to choose sides, chose the only one she could. She still had to live with my father, after all. I never held that against her. But, suffice to say, my family life ended with my departure to the training school."

He abruptly cut off his story, and in the silence that followed, I tried to realign my own memories with this shocking new information.

Last September, a month before my mother's death, we'd been in rehearsal with Anders, for his ABT-commissioned ballet. Just Vincent, Natalia and me. Anders was elaborating on the intention he wanted Vincent to have when he held Natalia in his arms, which wasn't supposed to be romantic (too bad that hadn't proved to be the case) but instead protective.

"I get it," Vincent had said, "Like a dad with his kid?" He wore a hopeful smile, like a schoolboy who's sure he knows the right answer, but wants to keep it humble.

Anders grew still. I saw him grip his clipboard as if it had become a life rope. The silence stretched out so that even Vincent caught on to the awkwardness.

Anders lost his father, I wanted to scold him. *I've lost mine. You are so insensitive.*

But when Anders spoke again, it was in his usual calm voice. "No. That's not at all what I was thinking. Fathers are strong but not vulnerable. Fathers are clumsy. Think of a mother, where the strength is internal, at odds with the vulnerability. Or, say, an older brother. Think Hansel and Gretel. You are Hansel and you must protect her even as you struggle to protect yourself."

Vincent's eyes lit up as he bobbed his head. "Got it. Thanks!"

I'd gotten it so wrong. Anders hadn't been grieving a beloved father in the least. Quite possibly he'd been grieving that he'd never had a beloved father, one who had carried or held his son. Instead, he'd had a father who'd beaten him.

Anders was now answering the questions the others were throwing at him, as I sat there, mind still whirling. How foolish of me to have assumed I knew him, deep down. Or maybe now, only now, could I begin to understand what made him tick. Which put me on the same footing as these colleagues of mine. This made me feel lesser, somehow. Less special.

"Play something more for us!" Fiona was saying, as the others clamored their agreement.

"Twist my arm," Anders said, once again genial and relaxed. He turned back to the piano and leafed back through his music book.

"Anders, why haven't you told Chess you could play the piano?" I asked, feeling wary, as if he were about to spring something else new on me. "The way he likes to challenge you, asking you if you can play any better. The truth is, you can."

"I don't need to be the winner there," Anders said. "Let him think he has something over me. He seems to need it." He turned another page and nodded.

"Here we are. Chopin's Opus 25, number 1." He commenced, a passage with a cascade of notes, like a stream of golden liquid, the music instantly recognizable as the piece playing at the end of the 1977 film, *The Turning Point*. Through the closing credits, Leslie Browne danced a solo on a half-lit stage, hair unbound, her expression ecstatic as she spun and bourréed and piqué arabesqued. We all knew the film; every ballet dancer surely had it all committed to memory. I'd been thirteen, locked in conflict with my parents over my single-minded desire to study at the School of American Ballet and become as good a ballet dancer as Leslie Browne. I'd wanted it more than life itself. Every time I saw the film, or heard the music, I'd bawled.

All of my colleagues here were older than I, most by at least ten years. Curtis, Carrie and Jacob were already well established in their dance careers in 1977 when the movie came out. Did it conjure up in them the same unspeakably tender, vulnerable feelings? Joy, euphoria, but also a sense of bittersweet sorrow, of deep longing? Their expressions offered no clues.

We remained silent, everyone absorbed in Anders' performance. Even after he'd played the last note, no one spoke. "Just as it should be," Sabine said finally, her voice rich with satisfaction.

It was an obscure comment, one that likely held different meaning for each of us.

This time I didn't try to guess. I'd learned my lesson. People were walking puzzles.

Particularly the people in this room.

Chapter 9

One Year Orphaned

The first weekend in October, Fiona's boyfriend flew out for a weekend visit. Training for his own San Francisco job was taking place, ironically, in Denver; he wouldn't move here until after the holidays. I had the hour free from rehearsal, so I joined Fiona in the lobby on Friday to meet him. "There he is," she cried the instant we stepped out of the elevator into the WCBT lobby, and she burst into a run toward a guy who could only be William. Not just that he matched Fiona's description—nice-looking, sandy-blond hair, height just over six feet. It was the expression on his face, all soft with adoration, focused on the approaching Fiona. I watched them hug, the way they held onto each other, laughing, kissing, rocking back and forth. A pang of sorrow cut through me, even while I was happy as anything for my friend.

I wanted what they'd found. What Anders and Sabine had found. After the Vincent breakup, I'd told myself that no romantic relationship was worth the price you paid when it ended—always poorly, painfully, for me. Flying solo, devoting oneself to work, was safer.

There was a lot to be said for choosing safety. Or so I sternly told myself at times like this.

Eventually Fiona disentangled herself long enough to introduce

William. He and I shook hands. His smile was genuine, his handshake firm.

"You two are going to Napa Valley for the weekend?" I asked.

"We are indeed," Fiona said. "Anders is letting me off early so we can avoid rush hour."

"Lucky you!" I forced a brightness I didn't feel. "But you deserve it. You've been working so hard."

Fiona laughed. "You weren't kidding when you told me this job would be a challenge."

I nodded. Through September we'd prepared furiously for the fall's twelve-day West Coast tour. The shifts in casting had meant a steep learning curve for me, but a productive one. And yet, now that we were into October, a different challenge arose within me.

October was a tricky month. October was when I lost my mom. A year ago this weekend, in fact.

Fiona had been living in Africa at the time; she didn't know the date of my mom's passing, and I'd declined to mention it. I wasn't about to dampen her high spirits with my sorrow. The three of us chatted, about William's flight, about wineries they planned to visit. They left a few minutes later, in their own cloud of happiness and laughter. I stood there, watching their figures recede, feeling my personal ache settle back in.

On Saturday morning I rose early, before my mind could start working, and took a long, brisk walk through the city. I went to a coffee shop afterward, where I splurged on a sugary, decadent muffin to go with my coffee. From my table in the corner, I observed a mother and preteen daughter enter the shop. The daughter looked to be on the cusp of rebellious adolescence, with her black eyeliner, a tight-fitting, low-cut top showing off budding breasts. She stood apart, as if determined to establish her independence. The mother reached out to stroke her daughter's hair. The girl, gazing away from her mother, nonetheless allowed this. In fact, she took a step closer, and soon was leaning into her mother, eyes dreamily half-shut as her mother stroked. Clearly, in spite of raging hormones, her need for maternal love hadn't abated.

It never did.

A wave of grief crested over me and burst. I scrambled to my feet, cup clattering in its saucer, thrust the second half of my muffin into a napkin, moving fast so no one would see my tears. Vacating the coffee shop, I strode down the street and let the emotions pour out.

I'd lost my mom.

I'd lost her, years before she'd died, because I'd valued ballet over family.

I'd lost big.

Back at my apartment, I made a proactive decision. Even with Fiona gone, I still had a surrogate family member in the area. "Come visit anytime," Russell had said when he'd dropped us off in the city. "Our new office, I mean," he'd hastily added. "I'm very proud of it."

Fiona had laughed dismissively, but I'd taken Russell's business card and thanked him.

The card was still where I'd put it, tucked into the mirror portion of my chest of drawers. I picked up the phone and punched in the number for his office. He'd said he worked Saturdays; I wasn't ready to call the home number he'd scrawled below.

He answered, and I nervously announced myself. "Remember how you said I should call if I wanted to check out your new office?" My heart drummed against my ribcage so loudly I worried it was audible.

"Yes! I'm so glad you called."

"I was thinking of taking the train down the Peninsula today. To explore, and such."

"Perfect. Our office complex is walking distance from the Belmont train station."

I turned down his offer to meet me at the train station. "You keep working. I've got your directions, so I'll see you in a few hours' time. What's good for you?"

"Around two o'clock?"

"Great. See you then."

At two o'clock I arrived at the address he'd given me. A small one-story building crouched beside a newer, gleaming multistory one. Russell had told me he worked in the smaller one. It looked humble yet prosperous, just the kind of place I'd visualized for a startup that was moving up in the world, with ample space for a dozen employees, maybe even more.

Entering the building, I found no one in the dimly lit reception area. "Hello?" I called out. Four puzzled faces popped up from four different cubicles in the adjacent room's center. To my relief, Russell appeared from out of a back office.

"You made it!" he exclaimed as he approached.

"I did!" This time I greeted him with an easy hug. In truth, I clung. I sensed his surprise, but when I pulled back, he smiled at me like the old friend he was.

"The sign for your company was a little misleading," I said. "Good thing you told me Pegasus was the smaller of the two buildings. I might have gone into the wrong building." I expected him to laugh, but he only shook his head.

"This is where programming stayed. My guys like it. We call it The Cave."

I hesitated; what did he mean by 'stayed'? I was further flustered by the way the four guys—all young, similar-looking in their T-shirts, facial scruff and startled eyes—continued to gape at me.

"April's here for a tour," Russell announced.

They nodded without speaking.

Russell leaned in. "We don't get many ballerinas here," he murmured.

"Sure. All right."

"I thought I'd show you the new office space first," Russell said.

"Okay," I said, but to my confusion, he led me out the door I'd just come in. "Weren't we going to tour the new space?" I asked, feeling even more awkward and displaced.

"Exactly." And yet he continued his purposeful stride away from the office. "Those were my coders, in there," he said, gesturing behind us. "They're brilliant, each and every one of them. As a team, they make magic. Anything we can do to keep them happy is good for us. That's why we're in that building and not the new one. They prefer to work where it's quiet, dimly lit, kind of homey. One of the old offices is now a dorm room with four beds, and the conference room is now a rec room, equipped with a fridge, snacks, foosball and a ping-pong table. We got them covered."

I stopped short. "Russell. I'm so confused. Isn't that other building *the* new building?"

He cocked his head at me. "Whatever gave you that idea?"

"Didn't you tell Fiona you went from a barn to an office?"

"Sure, but that happened eighteen months ago, when we got our first round of funding." He gestured to the gleaming new building. "This is the building we moved into when we got second-round funding. All of us had grown too big for The Cave, anyway."

"How many employees do you have?" I sputtered.

"A hundred, and growing."

I could feel my jaw drop. "That's *huge.* Why didn't you tell me it was so huge?"

He shrugged, bemused. "Why should the number of employees matter?"

"Because…" My thoughts were in a scramble. Because it gave him bragging rights. And he didn't see it that way. I hadn't been around someone so modest in a long time. "Never mind. But, congratulations. Growth is great."

"It is. We're very happy."

Russell opened one of the double glass doors and ushered me in. A security guard greeted us and as he and Russell chatted, I looked around. The lobby had a high ceiling and tinted glass walls that allowed ample daylight in. There was a profusion of plants and the sound of burbling water from a tile lagoon that stretched along one entire wall. It enchanted me. None of it was anything like I'd expected.

We took the elevator to the second level, where two dozen cubicle spaces dominated the room's center, with offices along the sides. There were a few people working, others conversing, and the sound of someone's radio. Those who glanced our way gave Russell a respectful nod, which he returned with an easy wave. After Russell pointed out in a low voice who worked where, what they did, we took the stairs up one level. Here, the broad expanse of mint-green patterned carpet looked and smelled new, as did the ivory walls. When I commented on this, he nodded. "The building is only four years old, and this carpet is brand new. I feel like a king, walking down these corridors." He glanced around furtively. "Don't tell anyone this, but sometimes I'll do this on a Saturday or Sunday. Just walk down the hallways, taking it all in."

"Good exercise," I observed.

"That's exactly what I tell myself."

We walked down the quiet hallway past a dozen closed office doors, most of them darkened and unoccupied. No cubicles on this level, Russell informed me. It was the floor that housed accounting, HR, sales and marketing. Most of them weren't big Saturday workers, he added, with a touch of disdain in his voice. In the central reception area by the bank of elevators, he gestured to the floor above us. "Executive level is the fourth floor. The carpet and décor are even nicer—you'd think you were in a luxury hotel. Devon, Nate and Mike have their offices up there, and the big, fancy conference room is up there, but the guys are doing number crunching today in advance of a shareholder meeting, so we won't interrupt them."

"This is all amazing." I looked out at the floor-to-ceiling window that revealed the glimmer of highway traffic to the east and beyond that, a smudge of blue that was the San Francisco Bay.

"I know. It blows my mind, still. From the days in Mike's barn, to this."

"I saw on your card that your title is programming manager, but Nicola said you were a director now."

He pressed the button for the elevator. "Yeah, that's an old card. Since the second round of funding and the hiring of another thirty employees, I am now a senior director. Crazy, huh? Devon is now chief technical officer and Mike is the CEO."

"A senior director, wow."

He looked abashed. "It's just a title. I was the company's first dedicated programmer and only moved up when it became clear we needed a team of programmers, not just one. My job was to hunt them down and hire them. Two are Stanford dropouts. One only has a high school degree. But they are amazingly good. They work fast and their code runs circles around mine. I'll give one of them a thorny, intractable problem the rest of us can't solve, and twenty-four hours later, he's back, having figured it out through code."

The elevator doors opened and we stepped in. "I hate to sound stupid," I said, "but I'm still not sure what your product is."

"You sound honest, not stupid. So, our first product was a full-text retrieval system for the Internet called SearchX. With it, users can search for electronic information based on concepts or ideas, as opposed to more limited keyword searching. Using that older method of retrieval technology is incredibly slow and difficult. SearchX users can rank searches by assigning weights to keywords and subtopics and find what they want in minutes, not hours."

It all sounded like Greek to me. The elevator doors opened on the ground floor and Russell directed me through the lobby. "I gather it was a big hit," I said, a bland but safe reply. I could almost hear the spectral echo of Nicola's laughter at how high-tech clueless I was.

"Huge. It was a great start, and gave birth to two more products that we'll be rolling out in the next nine months. Busy times, but crazy exciting."

We returned to The Cave and I meekly followed Russell to his office. Inside, a desktop computer and scattered industry magazines dominated his desk surface. One of them, I realized with shock, featured Pegasus Systems on the cover, the very building we'd just toured. An oversized pile of papers flowed from an adjacent in-box. He gestured for me to take one of the seats across from his desk as he neatened things up.

"Can I pose another stupid question?" I asked as I settled in the chair.

"Go for it."

"Okay. I've heard about the Internet. I get that scientists and academics are posting their scholarly articles and such, somewhere out there, which allows others to access it. But I can't draw a picture beyond that, what's going to make the Internet relevant to someone like me."

His face lit up. "Oh, it's going to be relevant to everyone, trust me. Sooner than you or I can imagine. The biggest player to watch right now is a guy named Tim Berners-Lee, a scientist at CERN, near Geneva, a European research lab." He paused. "CERN stands for...

Hmm. Something in French."

"Actually, I know about CERN. My physics dad, after all. He loved staying up to date with their particle physics research and programs."

"That's right! Good, I don't have to explain."

"That part, you do not."

"Anyway. There's a growing need to be able to access articles and research reports more easily, regardless of what kind of computer or operating system you use. Back in 1980, Berners-Lee created a hypertext database system, and now he plans to take information management further, using hypertext as a way to link and access each article as a web of nodes that the user can browse. It's a project he calls 'WorldWideWeb.'

"The idea's pretty elementary, actually. You take the hypertext idea and connect it to the TCP—the Transmission Control Protocol—and then utilize a domain name system, and it comes together like... like a symphony!" His eyes were bright with excitement. "His thought is to use it just at CERN, but we at Pegasus, and scores of other Silicon Valley businesses, see what potential it holds. If everyone could easily access information, simply by having a personal computer and a modem, it would be the opening of a giant new frontier of information retrieval. It would allow the Internet to be a treasure trove of information, as big as the ocean."

He continued on, utterly caught up in his world. It was so reminiscent of the way my dad used to be when he got lost in his musings about astrophysical phenomenon. A pang cut through me. Another. It felt like the emotional equivalent of nausea, the way you tried to not move, not think, in the hopes of lessening the onslaught.

No go. The tears sprang up with a vengeance. I'd cried about my mom's loss all day through the three-year anniversary of my dad's death, last spring. It was only fair that today I should grieve his loss.

Eventually Russell caught on and fell silent. I could feel his concerned gaze settle on me as I kept my gaze down, sniffed and brushed the rogue tears from my face. "You know," he began, "I've bored people plenty with my talk. I've made them yawn, even fall asleep, but I don't think I've ever made them cry."

Which made me laugh through my tears. I steadied myself to speak. "It's that you remind me so much of my dad."

"Oh, April." He sounded helpless. "And Fiona told me your mom had died, too."

I made a mental note to thank Fiona for saving me from more awkwardness. "Yeah. Bad luck in the parent longevity department."

He pondered this. "She said it was around this time last year."

"It was."

"What date?"

"October sixth."

"But that's today," he exclaimed.

"Yes."

"Why did you pick today to come down here and see my office?"

Chagrin crept over me. Had I miscalculated our closeness? "I wanted to be with someone I've known for a while. Someone who knew my parents. Fiona's gone with her boyfriend this weekend. So that meant you." I kept my eyes fixed to the corner of his desk, unwilling to look up and see another perplexed expression on his face. Or, worse, unease.

The silence stretched on. I suddenly wanted to be back on the train, northbound to San Francisco, where, even alone, I'd be on safer terrain.

I heard Russell rise from his seat behind the desk and come around to my side. He squatted down in front of me and took my hands. To my relief, he didn't look uneasy or awkward.

"Thank you for turning to me," he said. "Thank you for coming down here. I'm so glad you did, for a half-dozen reasons. Mostly, I'm glad I can be here for you."

He rose and pulled me to standing. "Let's go walk. There's a footpath close by. That's the right place for us to be, not this dumb office."

"It's not a dumb office." I managed a smile. "It looks like a very smart office. Full of very smart people."

"Maybe not always so smart. But we're very curious, and very driven."

On our way out, he paused, glanced down at my shoes. "Do you want to do some real walking? As in, a hiking trail? There's a great one that's a short drive from here. The views of the Bay Area are fantastic."

I arched and flexed a foot. "Will these sneakers do the trick?"

"They will."

I smiled at him. "Then let's do it."

His choice was perfect, a regional park with trails that led us up through shaded tree groves and grassy plateaus with vista views.

"This is nice," I said. "Great call."

"And you're keeping up with me."

I found this amusing. "Did you expect me to slow you down?"

"I get told constantly that I walk too fast."

"Not by a dancer."

"Why would a dancer be able to keep up? Isn't that just about flexibility and moving gracefully?"

"Are you kidding? Dance is cardiovascular, too. Some ballets, especially the Balanchine ones, it's like a nonstop sprint."

"No way!"

"Yes!"

He looked so disbelieving, I began to laugh. "Race you," I said, and took off running. For the next sixty seconds I dashed up the trail, darting to avoid branches, roots poking up from the earth. I could hear him behind me, trying to keep up. "What's taking you so long?" I taunted over my shoulder. "Is that you breathing so heavily? You're letting a ballet dancer, a *girl*, beat you?" Laughing, I increased my speed, never mind that by this time my own lungs were burning.

Finally I made it to the top of the hill. I watched him huff his way through the last steps, before he collapsed onto a wooden bench that overlooked the vista. I sat beside him, grinning.

The hole in my heart. It was gone. I hadn't felt this free, this secure and happy, since before my mother died. I wanted to reach over and hug Russell.

"Well, I learned my lesson," he said once he'd caught his breath. "Never underestimate the physical fitness of a ballet dancer. Or are you in particularly good shape for a dancer?"

"Nope," I said cheerfully. "We're all this way."

"Well, who knew?"

"Truly. And who knew tech geeks were such good hikers?"

"It just goes to show you."

Together we regarded the vista view. "My mom would have loved this," I said. "She was the walker in the family. She kept trying to get my dad to join her on her morning walks, but he'd always come up with an excuse."

"Want to hear a story about your mom?"

I glanced over at him. "I'd love to."

"When I was thirteen, I'd go to her library every Thursday after school and consult with her about what books to read. I was bored with the school library—everything seemed geared to the younger kids. So your mom would hunt down these fiction books about boy scientists, or anything that was boy-related. The following week, she'd ask my opinion, both about the fiction books she'd chosen, and the math and physics books I'd picked out for myself. I loved the way she treated me like an adult, even though I was only in eighth grade at the time."

"She loved connecting with motivated young readers. She told me that was her favorite part of the job."

We rose and began walking again, slower, more reflective now. "You know what makes me sad to think of right now?" I said. "How much of a hurry I was in to leave home. The first year I got a scholarship for the School of American Ballet's winter term, a huge deal, I was a month shy of fourteen. My mom said nope, you're too young. She and my dad flat out rejected the offer, told me I had to wait a year. When, for all I knew, the SAB might bypass me in favor of someone younger. I was so angry with my parents, I hardly spoke to them for the next month. I spent that whole school year sulking, dreaming of being out of Omaha, away from my parents' influence."

I stopped and looked around at the golden hills, the San Francisco Bay, and the East Bay hills beyond that. "Professional ballet robs parents of their kids. They tried to hold on to me, and in my hostility, I stole that year from them, too."

"Hey," Russell said gently. "They understood that, April. That when you raise a kid with an extraordinary talent, you have to let them go earlier than you'd like."

I turned his way but the wind whipped my hair up and around, laying a swath of long brown hair across my face, right into my mouth. He chuckled and plucked it from my face and tucked it behind my ear.

"I saw your dad weekly, that first year you were away," he said. "He was mentoring me through the college application process. He'd give me news about you, talk to me about the East Coast, the weather, his own undergrad days at MIT. He loved talking about you. He'd glow with pride. And he got it, that someone with your talent couldn't stay put in Omaha. He told me so. In fact, he told *me* to get the hell out of Omaha. My parents wanted me to choose a school in the Midwest, not Massachusetts."

"Dad loved that you chose his alma mater."

"My dad did *not* love the price tag. Even with scholarship money, it was expensive."

"Money well spent, I imagine he's saying now."

"Oh, yes. Dad's pretty happy with me now. My sisters, not so happy. Why is it that sisters are so complicated and hard to talk to?"

"You're asking the wrong person, Russell."

"You're Fiona's friend," he grumbled. "You'll always take her side."

"Tell you what. I'll take turns."

"Thank you."

"And you are my hero today. Just saying."

"Thank you."

Relaxed and windblown, we returned to Russell's car. The sun had begun its descent in the sky, creating a golden hue, like something out of a portrait. "Back to my office?" he asked as he started the car.

"Sure. I'd like to use the restroom before I catch the train."

'You know, I could drive you back to the city."

"You don't want to do that. It would eat up your evening."

"The weekend schedule for trains is lousy. Let me drive you. Do you have dinner plans?"

"I don't."

"So let's make an event of it. Celebrate this day, this anniversary."

Relief washed over me. This was turning out to be all I'd hoped.

"I'd love that," I admitted.

In no time, we were back at his office. "Let me shut down my computer, check a few things, and I'll be good to go," he told me as he turned off the ignition.

"Sure. No problem."

But as soon as we walked in, one of his programmers called out. "Hey Russ, your girlfriend's been phoning. You're supposed to call her back."

"Okay, thanks." In his office, he gestured for me to take a seat, as he made the call to Nicola. "I'm driving April to the city," he told her. "We're going to grab some dinner, too." He listened, and when he spoke again, he sounded less enthused. "Well, sure, you can join us, if you really want to." He looked over at me. "You don't mind, do you?"

Dismay filled me. I wasn't feeling that kind of sociable. And of course Nicola wanted to join us; she thought I was out to poach her boyfriend. Which was laughable. It should have been clear from the start that I wanted the family connection, not some budding romance.

Russell hadn't even cupped his hand over the receiver, leaving me with little choice. "Of course it's all right," I said. "She's your girlfriend. It's Saturday night."

Russell grinned. "Those were her exact words." He returned to the phone call, where they agreed on a meet-up time, whether she could be waiting outside or not, as my enthusiasm for the evening began to wane.

Nicola was waiting outside her apartment. I quickly switched to the back seat. "You didn't need to do that!" Nicola exclaimed. "But thanks." Russell, for his part, looked disappointed, which, I decided, was not the way to act around a girlfriend. But that was for Russell and Nicola to figure out. I leaned back against the headrest in back, suddenly tired and depleted.

The feeling only increased as Nicola chattered on and on.

Without Fiona around, Nicola had decided to befriend me. In truth, I would have preferred silence. As we crested a hill that revealed the city skyline in all its glory, Nicola gave a crow of pleasure, eliciting a new burst of manic chatter, and I decided I was done.

I touched Russell's shoulder. "Forgive me, but I'm exhausted. Would you mind just dropping me off at my apartment?"

Russell looked stricken. "But… why?"

"It's been a weird day. A weird week. I just need to quietly recharge."

"Oh, I get it," Nicola said. She twisted around from the passenger seat and flashed me a smile. "I feel that way too, at the end of every work week. I'm no good if I can't recharge."

Nicola had clearly gotten her recharge time in.

Russell didn't seem happy about my change in thought, but he obediently took the Civic Center exit, Van Ness to Hayes, to my apartment. "You can just drop me off at the next red light," I said.

"No, I see someone leaving ahead." He gestured to his right as a car edged its way out of a parking space. He slid into the spot and put the car into park.

I reached over and gave his shoulder a squeeze. "Thank you for today. I so appreciated your company." I gave Nicola a polite smile. "Have fun tonight."

"Thank you!" Nicola trilled. "I will!"

I was walking toward the apartment when, over my shoulder, I heard a "wait!" I turned and saw Russell hurrying toward me.

"Uh, oh. Did I forget something?" I asked.

"No. It's just that… Did I do something wrong?" His light-blue eyes seemed brighter than usual, lit with concern. He seemed to genuinely not understand.

"I thought you wanted to be with me tonight." He sounded as woeful as a child.

"I did. I mean, I do want to be with someone who feels like family. But not… other people."

"You don't like Nicola?"

"It's not that. It's…" I made swirling motions with my hands, as if that might conjure up the correct phrasing. No words came.

"Whoops," he said. "If Fiona got along with her, I figured any female would."

"Fiona has a college degree and spent the last two years teaching high school in a foreign country. I'm a dancer. I have a high school degree. This is what Nicola sees. You don't see this?" I asked in impatience when he still seemed confused.

"No. I was thinking that girls liked to do things in twos. Like you and Fiona both coming down to meet me last time. I thought you'd enjoy another female around tonight." Sorrow washed over his face and his shoulders sagged. "I am so sorry. This was supposed to be for you, tonight. What an idiot I am." He smacked his palm against the side of his head.

Pity stirred in me. "You don't have a lot of experience with women, do you?"

"Not girlfriends," he admitted. "Colleagues, I'm better with."

"And friends of your little sister, whom you knew when you were both younger."

"Yes." His gaze grew intent. "My hope is that she would give me and my lack of expertise the benefit of the doubt here and join us tonight anyway."

I looked over his shoulder at Nicola, twisting around in impatience in the passenger seat. "I think you need to take care of business at hand. You can't do that to a girlfriend. You can, however, do that to a friend. So, good night, and treat Nicola right." I laid a hand on his chest, leaned in and kissed him on the cheek. It was bristly, but warm, and for the briefest second, I hovered there, breathing in his warmth, his male scent, before I pulled back.

He looked at me sorrowfully.

"Good night," I repeated more firmly. Without waiting for a reply, I turned and walked to my apartment.

Chapter 10

Touring

Four days before we left to go on our twelve-day tour up the West Coast, Dmitri tried to present a case that I wasn't ready for opening night in *Jeux d'Enfants*, the ballet Anders had set on the WCBT dancers two years earlier. A dozen of us had assembled onstage for a run-through, and all I could do about it was silently fret and maintain a neutral expression.

Anders was the decision-maker; *Jeux* was his ballet, after all. "I'm here to observe," he told Dmitri. "I'll keep your issue in mind. Which section would you like us to watch?"

Dmitri considered this. "The fourth section, just the two of us, where the tempo speeds up."

Anders nodded. Without a word to me, he left the stage for the auditorium, where a group had congregated in the tenth row to watch us: Jimbo, the production manager; Phil and Larry, backstage manager and director of lighting, respectively; Yelena, Bob and Jacob. All there to judge whether Dmitri's griping that I wasn't ready for opening night held any truth.

The other ten dancers moved to the wings. Phil's assistant cued the music and Dmitri and I waltzed onstage. I didn't know where Dmitri was finding fault, so it was hard to give him what he was seeking. Was it the blink-and-you've-missed-it acrobatic movement that had me curving beneath him and then taking the movement in reverse? Or the super-fast shifts from the chaîné series into the leaps we took in tandem? Too decisive in my pas de chats, or not decisive enough? Dmitri was impossible to please. This carried a certain edgy benefit; he'd so jittered and pissed me off that I stopped worrying about pleasing him and poured my energy into working it out my way, a solid effort that drew applause.

When we finished the section, Phil's assistant cut the sound. I bent to catch my breath and await the verdict. Dmitri and I didn't look at each other as Anders and the others murmured among themselves. Finally Anders broke from the group and returned to us. My heart began pounding, equal parts from nerves and the exertion of the pas de deux. I curled my hands into fists to keep them from shaking.

"She stays in." Anders addressed Dmitri directly. "Which means that you stay in. Opening night is yours." He cocked his head as if in confusion. "I have no idea why you wanted to risk that."

"I could have done opening night with Carrie," Dmitri said.

"Carrie is pairing quite nicely with Curtis on this one. I wouldn't have separated them."

"Renata, then," Dmitri said.

Anders shook his head. "No Renata. She's never danced this ballet."

"She's a lightning-fast study. She'd have it down by tomorrow."

"No Renata," Anders repeated. "I cast you with April for a reason." He glanced at his watch. "I'm late for a meeting. Carry on with your rehearsal. Casting stays as is."

Dmitri scowled but nodded, as the ten dancers joined us onstage. I released the breath I'd been holding, and allowed my squelched spirits to rise again.

Opening night!

Seattle, Portland, Ashland, Redding, Sacramento, Santa Rosa. Twelve days, on and off a bus, in and out of hotel rooms.

Finally. Time to perform again.

Jeux d'Enfants began with the simplest of music. A piano and, curiously, a xylophone. A celesta, bells, a gong, before a cello joined them, a rich, soothing sound. The curtain rose to reveal Dmitri and me, standing center stage, heads down, in matching, multicolor unitards. Gel lights had turned the stage and the backdrop a royal blue. For eight counts we kept our gazes down. Next eight, our eyes slowly rose, followed by our hands, descriptive and articulated as a mime's. I stepped into a piqué arabesque, as Dmitri balanced me by the hips. A dip, an arch back, a pivot so that I faced him, my back to the audience, as I delivered a développé a la second, arms to high fifth, leg high to the side.

Anders had been clever with *Jeux d'Enfants*. While the ABT ballet he'd set on Vincent, Natalia and me last year had been solemn and classical with contemporary touches, *Jeux* incorporated lots of room for play, all within a classical framework. The WCBT dancers loved its charm and whimsy. No wonder they'd been dismayed by his more conservative, traditional approach to company class.

Two ensemble dancers joined us onstage. Four more. The eight of us danced in unison, filling the stage with leaps, pirouettes and chaîné turns. Dmitri supported me in a grand jeté leap, after which the two of us ran offstage.

Dmitri strode right to his water bottle and a towel that he used to mop at his sweaty skin. He met me by the upstage right wing. "You lagged at that one spot, just before the second lift."

I'd been right on time with the music, but this was no time to argue. "I'll keep that in mind for next time," I replied.

"And you need to be more at an angle on the big lift if you want me to get you higher. We could have done better, there, you know."

"I thought it went well."

"You could have done better," he insisted.

"Okay. I get it." Prickles of irritation rose on my neck.

At our next cue, we leapt back onstage. My energy grew, fueled by euphoria. It felt so incredibly good to be performing again. As though my soul had been squeezed into a cage for the past four months, brought out periodically to rehearse, but only now did it feel completely liberated, wildly free. Oxygen coursed through me, along with the determination to do better, dance better and prove myself.

Dmitri seemed to be responding to a similar inner call, his energy high, his hands firm during the partnered movements. During an arabesque promenade, he met my eyes, his beautiful face made even more so by stage makeup, eyes outlined, cheekbones enhanced. His focus on me was absolute as he set me up for the inside pirouette that I whipped into from the arabesque.

"That wasn't as bad," he grudgingly admitted, once we were backstage again.

"Thank you."

"And just so you understand," he added in a more conciliatory voice, "this isn't personal. I just think you're an inferior dancer."

Which was such a typical, half-insulting Dmitri thing to say, I couldn't help but laugh.

He kept his eyes trained to center stage, awaiting our cue even though we still had a full sixty seconds. "Watch Renata perform White Swan. You'll see what I mean. You'll see what it is you yourself are missing."

"Thank you. I'll keep that in mind."

I discovered more about my colleagues while on tour. Carrie and Curtis were partners offstage as well as on. Holt, a soloist, had been

SAB-trained like myself, two years ahead of me; we'd known—and disliked—the same teachers. Alice, a young corps dancer and San Francisco native, shared the same book-reading hunger as I. We swapped the books we'd brought on tour: *The Joy Luck Club* and Jane Austen's *Emma* in return for *Like Water for Chocolate* and Kazuo Ishiguro's *Remains of the Day.*

The female principals shared a dressing room, and through the process of preparing each night, I grew to know Renata and Carrie better. Mostly by listening—an eavesdropper but not. Carrie would glance my way from time to time as they chatted. Renata, meanwhile, would only give an airy wave. "So my marriage didn't work out. April can know that. And returning to Germany and trying to live a 'normal' life there didn't work out. April can know that."

Tonight, Renata brought up Sid. "I got a card from him just before we left," she told Carrie.

Carrie smiled. "That was sweet of him. What did it say?"

"That he was happy to learn about my return to the company. But I haven't been in touch for ages. How did he find out?"

"Curtis, probably. He calls Sid every few weeks."

"How's he doing?"

"Pretty good, it sounds. Says he's liking Florida well enough. Misses us."

"Does he know that Jana walked out of her contract?" Renata asked.

Carrie hesitated. "No."

"That she's gone, at least?"

"No."

"Carrie! Why not?"

"Curtis and I discussed it. It would only worry him, and there's nothing he can do for her anymore. Let him relax, enjoy his retirement."

"But..." Renata sounded perplexed. "Okay. All right."

I kept silent as I roped my hair into a bun. The story of what had happened to Sid was a lot like inquiring about what had happened to Jana. No answers beyond "a stumble, a concussion that made him realize he was getting old and clumsy, so eventually he retired." I sensed there were more details, ones no one planned to share with the outsider.

"Retirement." Renata snorted, and when she spoke again, her voice had taken on an edge. "So much more work than I ever expected."

Her tone had caught my interest. "How so?" I asked.

Renata met my eye in the mirror before she picked up a long hairpiece, one of two that she'd clip into her short hair, which would allow her to gather up the hair and pin it into a bun for that quintessential ballerina look. "I couldn't do it. I failed as an ex-dancer. I hadn't anticipated how awful it would be, to pull the plug on this biggest thing in my life. So I ignored the feeling and got married." Her expression was bleak. "Until that became worse than the not-dancing."

Renata's words shocked me; I'd assumed she was the type of highly accomplished person to call her own shots, and succeed wherever she went, never looking back. Not so, apparently.

"We are so very glad you returned," Carrie told her gently. "I never would have wished a failed marriage onto you, but if we are the consolation prize, I'm so grateful."

Renata gave Carrie's hand a squeeze, and when she turned back to me, the sorrow had left her face. "Never marry an actor," she told me. "Or a chef. It's all about them. There's just no room for you in the equation."

"Pets are good companions," Carrie offered.

"Pets are excellent companions," Renata agreed.

That night I watched Renata and Dmitri perform the White Swan Act II pas de deux from *Swan Lake*. My skepticism—surely what

Dmitri had wanted was for me to simply admire him and how he made Renata look good—lasted only a few seconds. Renata stepped onstage as Odette, instantly transfigured. Gone, the performer, the thin, aging dancer who complained about aching bones and a failed marriage. She'd become a vulnerable, sorrowful Odette, bewitched by the evil sorcerer, Von Rothbart, into a fate of swan by day, young woman by night. Here she was now, a delicate, light-footed creature, daring to hope. Dmitri, as Siegfried, wore a look of pure longing as he paced the stage, looking for her, unaware that she'd come to him. He, too, had become his character, a tormented prince, desperate to find and embrace the mysteriously elusive Odette.

At this part in *Swan Lake,* Odette is fearful of, yet intrigued by Siegfried; you saw this in the way her body trembled, her arms pressed against her chest, her eyes registering both wariness and a dawning awareness of a new fluttery feeling inside of her. Siegfried is dazzled yet anxious, afraid she's going to fly off. When she leaves him at one point, he slumps with dejection, all the light leaving his eyes. Then she returns, like a shy wild creature, softly bumping his arm with hers, inviting him, with her movements, to come closer. You could see the battle within Odette—to trust or not?—and when she finally did, allowing Siegfried to wrap his arms around her, I felt the experience like a visceral jolt inside me. Renata melted into Dmitri's embrace and her eyes flickered shut for the briefest moment, an expression on both their faces like religious ecstasy. A lump arose in my throat, surprising me.

Dmitri had instructed me to watch Renata's performance in order to learn, but watching him dance was equally telling. Renata's presence had transformed him into someone entirely different. Her vulnerability elicited the same in him. Her longing, the sorrow she hid beneath the surface, made something bigger, more noble and heroic, arise in Dmitri. Her power as a performer, in the end, was greater than his. But she never took advantage of this.

Oh, those adorable bird-like quivers, one foot in a front coupé that beat against Odette's ankle as Siegfried promenaded her in a circle en pointe. The joy in her eyes, a smile so sweet and hopeful, and his endearing solicitude. It was the kind of performance you watched and everything in you went still. The kind where you didn't realize you were crying until the wetness rolled down your face.

Dmitri had been right. I had so much to learn.

The tour, like all tours, gradually assumed a shape and texture of its own. Some of the stops were one performance only, the original one-night stand. Venues were smaller and less professional than what I was used to. Seedy, even. After Portland came a college auditorium with mildew-ridden dressing rooms. A delay en route had us arriving late to our fourth town. The backstage crew set to work hastily, as I followed the other dancers hurrying backstage through the maze of hallways and unfamiliar (to me alone) rooms.

Unpack, dress, rehearse. Rest, dress, perform.

Lather, rinse, repeat.

In Redding, the company was greeted by an enthusiastic but coarser crowd that liked to hoot and holler when their favorite dancers—predictably, the old-timers—danced. They roared with approval over Renata. I received a cooler treatment. I'd had a grueling performance where I had to fight for every solid turn, every airborne moment, my core and limbs trembling with the exertion. During the curtain call, there was a pulse of unfamiliar energy, a murmur, from the audience. Sometimes girls squealed over Dmitri, but this was different. And when Dmitri extended his arm for me to take my solo bow, the sound was unmistakable.

They were booing me.

Hisses. Even a shouted, "Go back to New York!"

Dmitri looked furious; for once he was on my side, as my partner. But for the audience, he was all princely smiles, taking a second bow, extending his arm for me to take a second curtsy. Then it was the whole ensemble, and the applause became unequivocally positive.

After the curtain had come down for the final time, Anders saw my expression. He shook his head with a smile that seemed to say, *don't take it so seriously,* but someone else claimed his attention before he and I could speak. I dully made my way through the chattering dancers to the dressing room, to change and take off makeup.

Back at the hotel, Fiona tried to convince me to go out to the cast party, hosted by a local friend of the company. "Lexie and Holt said they'd be our dates and make sure we felt comfortable," she told me.

I shook my head. I felt depleted on too many levels.

"You'll regret it if you don't go," Fiona said.

"No, I won't."

Fiona eyed me sympathetically. "You okay?"

"Sure. Just tired."

"You do look beat. Stay and relax. Want me to bring you back food?"

"Thanks, I'll be fine. Go have fun."

Fiona didn't need any further encouragement. When Lexie and Holt knocked on our hotel room, she greeted them happily and bounded right out.

I sighed and looked around the room. The carpet was green shag and looked thirty years old, as did the bedspreads. The walls were thin, the windows poorly insulated and through them, I heard the sound of laughter outside.

I felt so alone. My body hurt. The memory of the boos stung.

I had a sudden urge to call Vincent. I missed him right then, and the way tours had been such fun in our dating days. And before then, when he'd befriended me and dispensed wisdom, humor, whatever I needed. He'd talk pragmatically about the fact that I'd screwed up, saying, "That's how these things go, April, move on." Or commiserating with me. So I'd gotten booed? Fuck them. They lived in Redding, after all. What did they know about culture?

But I wasn't about to call Vincent again.

Then Russell.

No, I told myself sternly. *Do not call him.* Nicola mistrusted me enough already.

I sighed and trudged over to my suitcase. From my "too tired to go out for dinner" travel stash, I pulled out a fifth of brandy, a bag of almonds, apricots, wrapped cheeses and crackers.

I could take care of myself.

Which was good, because there weren't a lot of other options.

Santa Rosa was our last stop, so close to home that after the performance, we would board the bus and return to San Francisco and our own beds. And yet, no one in our dressing room was prepared for Jana to show up at our door, a plate of fresh-baked cookies in hand.

Carrie looked shocked, even upset. I glanced sideways at Renata, and was surprised to see wariness on her face, as well. Even her body language seemed tense, although she continued to stitch away at the pink satin ribbon she was sewing onto a new pair of pointe shoes.

"It's only this one time," Jana told Carrie. She looked next at Renata, offered a respectful "hello," and glanced over at me. "Besides, I owed April something."

I watched as Carrie grew rigid, in what could only be called fear. "What?" she shrilled. "What 'something' do you owe April?"

Jana glared at Carrie. "Stop looking at me that way. I'm cool. I meant the cookies. As a way to thank her, for back in September, when she bailed me out at Marshall's."

"What are you talking about?" Carrie exclaimed. Renata, too, had hastily set down her pointe-shoe sewing to catch Jana's response.

Jana and I exchanged guilty glances. "You see," I began, "Jana and I were both shopping at Marshalls. She realized at the checkout counter that she'd forgotten her wallet and I walked right up and insisted on buying the items for her. They were cheap; it was no biggie."

Carrie looked from Jana, to me, and back to Jana. "Really? So you encountered each other by chance?"

We both nodded.

"All right," Renata said to Carrie. "That's no big deal."

They exchanged a look, and Carrie nodded. "That was a nice coincidence for you, Jana."

"It sure was!"

Carrie's shoulders relaxed but she still looked wary as she studied Jana. "You look… thinner. Are you all right?"

"Sure. I'm fine. Stop being a mother hen."

The air in the room crackled with a tension I didn't understand.

"Here you go." Jana handed me the plate. "I told you I'd find a way to thank you."

I hesitated before taking them. The cookies' buttery sweetness wafted up from the paper plate. "Thank you," I said to Jana. "This was really sweet of you. Chocolate chip cookies are my favorite."

Jana smiled back at me. "Mine too." Then she looked at Carrie and her lip curled. "Thanks for your show of support, old friend."

"Jana… Don't be that way," Carrie said.

"Do we all get to eat the cookies?" Renata asked.

"Sure!" Jana and I said at the same time, which lessened the tension and made us laugh.

A knock sounded at the door, and Fiona poked her head in. "Just checking to see... what do I smell? Yum!"

She eyed Jana uncertainly.

With reason. Anders had been rabid about not allowing ex-company members to visit in the studios and backstage. He'd justified his position by stating there were some vindictive types among the dancers who'd walked out, and he wanted us all kept safe.

"Fiona, this is Jana," I said, keeping my voice bright and casual. "She's... an old friend of Carrie and Renata's, come to say hi and bring us goodies."

Fiona, I could tell, didn't buy for a minute that Jana was simply a friend, but she played along. A faux-easy conversation followed, and we all shared the cookies. I reached for Fiona's arm as she was leaving. "Look. Don't tell Anders Jana showed up. Okay?"

There was a moment of hesitation, and for the first time, I felt as though Carrie and Renata liked me, or at least they liked what I'd said.

"Okay," Fiona said, with a look in her eyes to me that said, *please explain this later.*

I nodded, although Fiona was going to be disappointed by how little I knew.

"I should go, too," said Jana, once Fiona had left.

"I think so, too," Carrie said, and at least this time, she sounded more solicitous than accusing.

"Thank you again for the cookies," I said.

"Yes, thank you," Renata chimed in. "Good to see you, Jana. Take care."

Our dresser arrived to hook up our costumes, right after Jana's departure. Carrie and Renata seemed to relax into her amiable chatter. Meanwhile my brain was whirling in confusion over what had just transpired.

Yet again, I didn't have a clue.

Chapter 11

The New Arrivals

Sabine's two young dancers had arrived. Monday, following our return from touring, there they were, warming up in the main studio before class. Katrina, Dutch-born and Paris Opera Ballet-trained, was blonde, pale, ultra-slender, sporting pink leotard, pink leg warmers over pink tights, a pink knit sweater tied around her tiny waist. One might have thought "bland" until she moved. Those long, long arms and legs. The delicate wrists and ankles. A small hand clasped a heel and she gracefully lifted her leg up, up, à la seconde, so the leg was parallel to her torso, her foot above her head. *Fine,* you could almost hear the other dancers say to themselves, *I can do that.* But when Katrina let the leg descend and did a second développé à la seconde, this time without hand to heel, the leg lifted to exactly the same hyperextended perfection. The room fell silent as thirty jaws dropped in astonishment. Katrina, absorbed in recalibrating her dancer's body to this new continent, this new time zone, probably didn't notice. The rest of us closed our jaws, resumed our own business of pre-class stretching, but it was there, in the room. This gauntlet thrown. No matter that Katrina was only sixteen and fresh out of training; even I felt the primal tug from within, a competitive contraction.

If Katrina was all pale and pastels, Javier was her photo negative. He was tall, his curly black hair cut close, his skin an appealing golden brown. His face was still that of a boy, big eyes and stark angles, even as his legs were powerfully built like an adult's. Born and raised in Cuba, he spoke only a smattering of English. Katrina spoke English, French, Dutch and German. Likely she'd speak Spanish by the end of the month, I mused, observing the way she and Javier had bonded, choosing spots side by side during barre and during work in the center. Their chemistry, too, was palpable. Their heights were complementary, their status as newcomers identical, but it was something more. A moment of clasped hands before they split up for grand allegro made me think of Hansel and Gretel, setting off through the dark forest with only each other as protection and comfort.

A pang cut through me. They looked so young, so vulnerable, almost like orphans.

Ballet orphans.

Which, then again, described us all.

Javier was a marvel to watch throughout class. A powerful presence emanated from his core, which made him seem calmer in his center than the other male dancers, and concurrently, more masterly in his movements. During the pause between barre and center work, he demi-pliéd in fourth position and shot up into a pirouette, passé leg locked into place, knee high, toe right at the knee of his turning leg. Everyone who was watching—which was to say everyone—silently counted the number of rotations of his turn. Four, no, five. No, six. Six clean, impeccable rotations, finishing in fifth position neatly, casually, as if all he'd done was gone up into a passé relevé. You could almost hear an exhale of defeat from the other males in the room.

The new arrivals proved all week long that their talent and technical prowess hadn't been a temporary display. They were slotted into rehearsals and picked up the choreography quickly. It woke up the rest of us, galvanized us, made us work harder. Everyone profited from the increased challenge. Or maybe not. Because late one day, when the others had gone home, I heard muffled weeping as I entered the women's changing room. Quietly, I rerouted myself away from my own locker. I made my way three rows over, to where Alice, my book-exchange buddy, sat on a bench, shoulders sagging, biting on her fist.

"Hi," I said softly, and Alice shot to her feet in alarm. I raised both hands. "I'm sorry. I didn't mean to startle you. Sit down. Here, I'll join you."

Alice made furtive swipes to brush the tears from her face and kept her gaze down, as if ashamed of how she might look. I wanted to tell her not to worry, that she was beautiful, tears or not, blooming with youth and fine features.

"What's up?" I asked.

Alice sighed and studied the wadded Kleenex in her fist. "It's nothing, really. Just the kind of stuff that builds up. Anxiety. Fear that my job is at risk."

"But why would you think that? You're doing great. You're paying attention, listening, giving Anders what he's asking for, not being a squeaky wheel. Not to mention that you're a beautiful dancer."

"Here's the thing." Alice clasped her hands and gave them an anguished twist. "That Katrina girl? She's never seen Anders' choreography before, and did you see how she instantly picked it up? Not just the steps, but the nuances. She didn't mark the steps, she danced them. Instantly."

I nodded sympathetically. "Paris Opera Ballet does an amazing job of mixing classical and contemporary. She's seen it, been trained on it. Anders' style bears the influence of Paris Opera Ballet. His wife,

Sabine, was POB trained. Their choreography has a lot of the same energy and innovation. It's exciting stuff." I observed how Alice's shoulders had sagged. "But it's learnable, Alice."

I glanced at my watch. "I have time to kill. The small studio is still unlocked—I just came from there. If you've got thirty minutes, I can teach you a few tricks."

A hopeful light came into Alice's eyes. "I'd love that."

"Let's go."

In the rehearsal studio, Alice showed me the passage troubling her the most. "There's something about it I'm missing," she said afterward in frustration. "They're not challenging steps. But it's the speed, and something more." Her hands fell to her side.

"I get it," I said. "Now watch."

Alice stood watching intently as I demonstrated not just that one, but similar passages that Anders favored in his choreography, all of which bore the same trademark pacing. Anders had a way of interspersing lightning-quick movements like chaîné turns with a sudden halt in a pose—arabesque, or attitude—held in a way that seemed to defy gravity and time.

I explained all of this as I demonstrated. "It's like you lift up, up, in your core, while you're holding that extra count. Just when the audience expects you to come down, you lift an extra millisecond."

Alice considered these words, nodded to herself, and tried the movements on her own.

"Close, but not enough," I said.

Alice tried again and again. We spent a full twenty minutes on just that delayed movement, the way it melted into the next movement, which sped right back up. Finally, I told her to stop thinking, to drop all the analysis and counting, and let her body run the show.

She aced it.

As I clapped, Alice returned to my side. She looked stunned. "I get it. I really get it! Omigod, I'm so happy!" Impulsively she hugged me.

I hugged her back. "Okay, now, I have a request for you."

"Sure, anything."

"I'm so new to this company's repertoire and I need to learn a ton, in as little time as possible. *Nutcracker* rehearsing is starting, and I'll bet I'm the only dancer who doesn't know all the Act II variations by heart."

"Oh, I know lots of those! I've memorized all of Sugar Plum Fairy and the Rosebud soloist in Waltz of the Flowers just from watching it so many times."

"Perfect. Anders told me I'd be learning both those. What about Snow Queen?"

"I know most of that, too."

"What luck, to have found you."

She smiled, her cheeks pinkening. She sat to unlace her pointe shoes. "Hey. Listen. Please don't tell anyone you saw me crying," she said.

I joined her on the floor. "All of us break down and cry from time to time. There's no shame in that."

Alice shook her head. "My mom was merciless about it, when she'd catch me crying in public, when I was little."

"That's harsh."

"She was harsh," Alice admitted. "Unafraid of tough love."

"I promise I will never tell your mom what I saw."

"Easy enough done. She's dead."

It was like the silence that follows in a restaurant right after a server drops a tray of dishes. I was speechless, but not for the reasons Alice assumed.

"You weren't supposed to hear that," she said to me in a small voice.

I found my own voice. "Why?"

"Because I don't talk about it."

"I'd ask 'why not?' except that I think I know."

"How would you know?" Alice sounded guarded.

"My mom's dead, too." It made me curiously lightheaded to say the words out loud.

I heard Alice suck in her breath.

"My dad's dead, too," I added recklessly.

"Oh, God. At the same time?"

"No. Two and a half years apart. He went first. He had cancer."

"My mom died of cancer when I was ten."

This time I was the one to suck in my breath. The poor girl had been robbed.

"One of the worst things was the way people treated me when she was sick," Alice said. "And later, after she'd died."

We regarded each other in new awareness.

"I get it," I said. "Everyone says the wrong thing. And the people who don't say anything, that's even more awkward."

"Yes," Alice breathed.

"Easiest to bury it in the past and not bring it up."

Alice nodded.

"What year did you lose her?"

"1982."

"That was the year I joined the American Ballet Theatre as a corps dancer," I mused. "When did you join the ballet school here?"

"The next year. I was eleven."

"That's early."

"The advantages of a local home base and a dead mother," she quipped dryly, before she caught herself and looked at me in apology.

A bark of sharp laughter came out of me. "Who knew you had a dark, clever, sassy side?" I exclaimed.

"It was kind of horrible of me to joke about that."

"Nonsense. If *we* can't joke about dead mothers, who can?"

We relaxed further and talked more about Sid's *Nutcracker*, which, Alice told me, had premiered in 1983. Renata had been the Sugar Plum Fairy with Jacob as her cavalier; Carrie and Dmitri had been the Snow Queen and King.

"Which role in his production do you like the most?" I asked.

"I think Rosebud. Sid set it on Jana, you know," Alice said.

"No, I didn't. How interesting."

"It was the same year she danced Aurora, the previous spring. She was like this rising star."

"Tell me more. Please."

"Okay, so I knew Sid loved all his dancers—that's kind of legend around here—but they say Jana was his favorite, the underdog he saw merit in, and went on to champion. The story has it that after she auditioned for the school, and they awarded her a place but not a scholarship, she went back to plead her case. Even though she was just fifteen, she was living on her own means, no family support. They told her, 'sorry, no scholarship for you.' But then Sid encountered her outside the building, crying, all out of hope and one step away from being evicted. He brought her back inside, set up a second impromptu audition, just him and Yelena judging. Afterward he walked Jana back to the school's administration office and told them something like, 'I believe in this girl. Give her a scholarship.' They did. He and Yelena made sure she found a safe place to live, and Sid kept his eye on her through the next few years, as caring as a father. And it paid off for them both. I guess within two years, she'd surpassed all the teachers' expectations. When she turned eighteen, Sid put her right in the corps, not even as an apprentice first."

"Do you know what happened to her in later years?" I asked. "Because it's clear something hijacked a very promising career."

Alice considered this. "What's that condition where you gain weight and have to take medication for it?"

"Hypothyroidism?"

"Yeah. Maybe that. Because she was so slim and lively and unstoppable those first few years. I remember her being a big sensation when she danced Aurora. I was new at the training school and it made such a big impression on me. I begged my dad to let me go see it three times, in fact. Jana was so young and pretty, like a fairy-tale princess come to life. Watching her, knowing how Mr. Hauser had singled her out, believed in her. From all of that to being this dream Aurora, made everything feel more possible for me, too."

Here Alice's face grew somber. "Imagine my surprise when I arrived here as an apprentice last year, all thrilled to work alongside this dancer who'd so dazzled me. And she was unrecognizable as that Aurora. I mean, I get that she'd been sidelined due to health issues, more than once, and that it can be really hard to get back up to speed when your body's been down. She looked heavy, and everything about her seemed sluggish. Almost sedated. There were periods where she seemed to be improving, slimming down and dancing with the energy and fire that I remembered. It was really great to see. Only then she'd have a relapse, be out for a month and return as that less exciting dancer. I felt so bad for her. She was close with the principals, at least. Carrie and Jana had been roommates for a few years, and even after that, Carrie seemed to be on the lookout for her. And everyone knew Jana had a crush on Dmitri. He never encouraged it, or her. If anything, he seemed uncomfortable with all her adoration."

"Yeah, I noticed that."

"I kept hoping the medication her doctors were giving her would turn her around once and for all, and I'd get to see that amazing dancer again. But it never happened."

We both considered this. "How cruel," I said softly. "To know you have it in you to be a rising star, and then your body betrays you."

"The thought petrifies me," Alice admitted. "Something like that could happen to anyone."

"Except not us," I said briskly. "And what I'd love right now is for you to show me the main Rosebud solo."

"Happily." Alice grinned at me and trotted over to center stage, the opening position. I joined her and imitated her movements, as we hummed out the music, both of us laughing when we got it wrong.

So now I knew. Sympathy welled up in me.

Poor Jana. It could have happened to anybody.

Chapter 12

Rehearsal Mishap

A trio of mishaps occurred while we were deep in preparation for the November gala.

"Regarding the backdrop you were considering reusing," Jimbo, the production manager, called out to Anders as he and I were discussing placement on the empty stage. "It's got some problems." He gestured with his head to the backdrop storage area in the very back. Anders sighed and walked toward him. Curious, I followed.

With a flashlight, Jimbo pointed out the spot, high up on the scenery backdrop. The flashlight beam swept over the backdrop and settled in the center to reveal bucolic green hills which had clearly seen better days. The green had faded to grey in places, and there were stains on the peaks of the two central hills.

"Dear Lord," Anders said in a hushed, horrified voice. "They look like a pair of breasts. Complete with nipples."

"Leaking nipples," Jimbo said.

Phil, the backstage manager, approached and looked up to where Jimbo was shining the light. He gave a great whoop of laughter. "I say you choreograph a new subplot into your newest ballet, Anders," he sputtered. "Or maybe reconsider the theme? Red gels and this. A brothel ballet."

"What the hell happened?"

"Exposure," Jimbo said. "Poor storage, years ago. Or, who knows—maybe the choreographer's set designer was going for this look. Maybe it's been in storage for twenty years for a reason."

Anders' shoulders sagged. "Back to the drawing board, as they say."

"We say that a lot here," Jimbo said cheerfully.

The second mishap occurred when a rogue fire sprinkler burst over the weekend, soaking two wardrobe containers, which might have been airtight but weren't waterproof, as was discovered Monday morning. Half the company's *Cinderella* costumes, as well as costumes from two smaller ballets, were all stained now. Ruined. "If it's any consolation," the wardrobe mistress told Anders, "they were in poor condition anyway."

The very next day, the staircase for the Romeo and Juliet balcony split into two. This problem was more dire; I would be standing on the upper level of the balcony as part of the pas de deux that Curtis and I were performing for the gala. And yet, Anders and I seemed to be the only ones shocked and distraught about it. Everyone else just sighed and shrugged.

"Better at rehearsal than performance," Phil said as he assessed the damage with Anders and me.

"What the hell?" Anders exclaimed. "Why weren't preventative checks on this done months earlier?"

"As it so happens, that's when we caught the problems with sets for *The Sleeping Beauty*," Phil said. "The set design crew has been working miracles right and left. The problem is always the same. The sets are old. Everything has seen better days."

"We need more money," Anders said.

Phil rubbed his temples wearily. "Of course we do. That's the story of this company."

"I'll find more." Anders' expression looked steely.

"That's what they all say."

"Who, like Sid? And his replacement, who bailed after five months?"

Phil nodded.

"Which is why they're now gone, and I'm here. And I'm hungry, Phil. I'm hungry for success for this company. I'm a different kind of animal."

Phil cocked his head and studied Anders. "You know, for some crazy reason, I'm starting to trust you. But I'm here to tell you. All of this is just the tip of the iceberg. You've got a hell of a job in front of you."

The bad luck continued. On Thursday, Bob was rehearsing Curtis and me for a ballet we'd be performing in January. Dmitri and Carrie, the other lead couple, stood behind us, shadowing our moves. It was the last hour of rehearsal, the last rehearsal of the day, and we were all exhausted. Curtis had just lifted me overhead and next would come a midair flip, from which he'd catch me before I descended downward. But during the hoist to midair, he gave a cry of pain and I felt his arms go boneless beneath me.

A blind moment of panic morphed into an eternity as I frantically clawed at the air to anchor myself to something, anything, finally catching onto Curtis' wrist as the rest of me slammed into the ground. My hold on him slipped as I lay there, too stunned to rise.

Everyone moved at once. Bob rushed over to me. Carrie, with a cry of fear, leapt over to Curtis, who'd clamped his right hand over his left shoulder and was rocking back and forth in pain. He regarded me in anguish. "I'm sorry. I am so sorry."

I took Bob's proffered hand and hauled myself to standing. "It's okay," I told Curtis in a shaky voice, even though it felt anything but okay. I tested my body, shifted my weight around. Even though my right hip was killing me from having landed on it, I sensed I wasn't injured.

Dmitri, unfathomably, seemed entertained by it all. "I trust that Carrie and I won't be expected to duplicate that move?" he called out.

"Dmitri?" Bob spoke casually, the way he always did. "You know those times where a perceptive person might choose to keep their trap shut?"

"I do. This is not one of them."

"Maybe let your peers be the judge of that."

Even as Bob spoke, he kept his eyes on Curtis. He reached over and patted the damaged shoulder, gently rotating Curtis' arm back and forth. "Is this what was dogging you last year?" he asked Curtis, who nodded, wincing when Bob found the trouble spot.

"What happened?" Anders' voice, sharp with concern, came from the doorway. "I saw the fall." He strode in. "April, are you all right?"

"I am," I mumbled, rubbing my hip.

"Curtis." Anders sized him up. "Don't you try to tell me you're all right."

"It's my shoulder," Curtis said. "This happens sometimes. But I'm good. It just needs a few days' rest."

Anders said nothing, but I could tell he didn't believe Curtis. Neither did I. He wouldn't have dropped me unless the pain were so bad it superseded his determination to not show any sign of infirmity. This was something big.

The gala. *The gala.* The thought froze my blood.

We were screwed.

"Let's go over to see Sheila in physical therapy," he said to Curtis. "That shoulder will need ice, for starters." He turned to me. "Come with us. You say you're fine, but you took quite a fall. I want to play it safe." He scanned the room and the other dancers waiting expectantly. "Carry on with the second cast," he told Bob, who nodded.

The three of us walked in silence to the therapy room, where Sheila, the physical therapist, looked at Curtis holding his shoulder and shook her head. "Not this again," she said.

"I'd hoped it was gone for good," he said mournfully.

She offered him a sympathetic look. "We'd all hoped that."

No one spoke as she gave his body a once-over on her worktable, prodding at various spots on his shoulders, his collarbone and neck. "Could be better, could be worse," she admitted. She set him up with an ice pack and a wrap, nestling it all into a shoulder sling. She sized me up and agreed with me that I was fine, aside from the sore hip.

"Let's go offsite," Anders proposed to Curtis and me. "The three of us need to talk."

Of course we did. Because there could be no Romeo and Juliet pas de deux with Curtis as my partner anymore. His injury wouldn't magically heal itself in two weeks, no matter how much we all wanted it to be otherwise.

Anders took us to Murphy's, a cool, gloomy dive a block from the studios that was the complete opposite of the lounge at L'Orange. It did, however, have its own dive-bar charm. A wooden floor was strewn with peanut shells beneath wooden tables. A half-dozen men hunched on bar stools around the bar. There was a pool table and a juke box that was playing a song from the '60s, tinny but cheerful. Two scruffy-looking guys, too young to be barflies, too old to be students, were taking turns at a dart board on the wall.

Anders bought the three of us a beer and we settled at a table to talk.

Curtis took my hand and squeezed. "I am so sorry," he said, and his voice was so heavy with regret, I knew right then that this was it for us. He might rebound temporarily, but this would not be the sure-thing partnership we'd all banked on.

"I'm sorry too. How's your pain?"

"The ibuprofen is kicking in."

"It would appear this is a recurring issue." Anders gestured to the sling.

Curtis nodded reluctantly.

"What do the doctors say?"

"What you'd expect. Time off is good, the more the better. Surgery would go a long way in repairing the deltoid injury once and for all, but a surgery would require four to six months of recuperation and rehab."

Here he stopped and miserably regarded his beer.

"I turned forty last spring. I don't have six months to lay off dance. I'd lose my edge. We both know that."

"You can ignore a chronic injury for only so long." Anders' voice was gentle. "And right now, you're playing with fire. What if that had happened during a performance?"

"I would have pushed through."

"Through a torn ligament?"

"Adrenaline goes a long way in disguising an injury," Curtis said.

"True. But there's payback involved. Ultimately it's our bodies that call the shots."

We sat there gloomily, sipping our beer. The dart-board players were cawing with laughter as each one seemed to be outdoing the other in lousy throws. The jukebox played a new song about how hard it was to be humble, when you were perfect in every way.

"Injury or not," Anders said to Curtis, "I need you. You bring value to the company. I'm particularly grateful for your cooperation and support. But you have to modify. If that means you don't get a lead role, you have to be honest with what your body will allow you to do."

"I understand."

"You have twenty months on your contract as a principal dancer. Don't rush this recuperation. If you're sidelined for months, you still have another year for lead roles. But here's what I could use your help on in the meantime. We've got a very talented but very young company developing here, with a terrifyingly steep ramp-up time. There's James, fresh from Royal Ballet, as well as our young Javier. There's Holt, who's ready for bigger things. I want these young men to start learning the lead roles. During the times you need to let your body heal, I'd greatly appreciate it if you worked privately with them. In a ballet-master capacity."

"Of course, I can do that," Curtis said. Some of the gloom lifted from his expression.

"Thank you."

We were finishing our beers when Dmitri and Carrie showed up. "We guessed it was a 'Murphy's' issue and not a 'L'Orange' one," Carrie called out. "Did you know this was Sid's spot for the same reason?"

"I did not," Anders said.

Carrie sat next to Curtis with a worried look, as Dmitri went to the bar. He returned with two beers, one of which he set down in front of Carrie. He smiled confidently at Anders as he sat across from him. "Fear not. I have a solution to the gala casting problem," he said.

"Do tell," Anders said.

Dmitri took a sip of his beer, slow and deliberate. Afterwards, he stretched back, lifted his arms high to clasp his hands behind his head. "Kirill," he said finally.

Anders said nothing, but his focus became intent, like an animal having sighted a particularly delectable prey in the distance.

"Well?" Dmitri said. "No interest in the details?"

"Of course I'm interested. Talk."

"I spoke with him over the phone just before coming over here. He's free. He and Sonya are doing back-to-back performances with ABT. Our gala falls right between their productions."

I sensed Anders was trying to play it cool, but it was impossible for him to disguise the relief in his eyes. As for me, I felt queasy. There was more to this bargain, I sensed.

"Can he accept our budget constraints?" Anders asked.

"He's willing to. Because he still harbors a deep respect for the West Coast Ballet Theatre."

Anders expelled a long breath. "If that would work, it would be ideal." He turned to me. "It would work. You two are the right height, the right aesthetic."

"There's a catch," Dmitri said.

I knew there was a catch. Dmitri was too self-serving for there not to be one.

"He wants to dance it with Sonya," Dmitri said.

I sat there, trying to regain the breath knocked out of me. Curtis and Carrie exchanged a private look. Anders remained silent.

"My interest in this company's welfare runs deep, as you can see," Dmitri said. "And what you need for the gala is not a pair of junior principals. You need a star in the equation, and you know it."

"But what about my role in the gala?" I burst out. "Like that, I'm out?"

Dmitri cast me a lofty look. "Maybe you need to think about the big picture, April. A gala isn't set up to offer the limelight to one young newcomer. It's to show off the company in its entirety. This year's goal is to represent the West Coast Ballet Theatre in an exciting way that makes people want to flock to see us."

"He's right," Anders admitted.

"Wait!" I could hear the panic rising in my voice. "Can we please discuss this?"

"We just did." Dmitri eyed me critically. "The fact of the matter is, you're green. There's no denying that you are a beautiful dancer with great potential, but you're a youngster."

Anders responded before I could sputter out my own protest. "On the other hand, this is why the Romeo and Juliet balcony pas de deux is perfect for April. Juliet is young, a mere girl, in love for the first time." He paused, lost in thought. "The audiences were so impressed, years back, when April debuted as Juliet to Vincent Neumann's Romeo. It was—"

"Vincent!" I cried out in excitement, interrupting Anders. "Vincent! That's who we should contact." I sat up taller. "It makes such sense. It would be a seamless transfer of partners for me."

Dmitri frowned. "He might not be free."

"You just said yourself that Sonya and Kirill are between productions with the ABT," Anders pointed out. "The same would apply to Vincent."

"Vincent doesn't know our stage." Dmitri dismissed the idea with a flick of his fingers.

"Oh, come on," Anders said. "A seasoned ABT principal has danced on over a hundred stages. They are masters of adaptation."

I waited, heart thumping. Vincent was my only chance.

Anders nodded to himself. He looked at all of us. "Thank you both for these excellent suggestions. I'll speak to both parties and make a decision tomorrow."

"I know what's best for the company," Dmitri insisted.

Anders' expression grew cooler. "Oh, really? Might I add that the dancers you're proposing walked out of a contract offer here and left us in a terrible bind? And *you* were the drive behind that grand walkout."

"Untrue! I was merely the group spokesperson."

Anders rolled his eyes. Even Curtis and Carrie chuckled over this.

"Fine," Dmitri admitted. "So I was being an obstructionist. That was August. My concern now is that we produce the best gala possible."

"That's my concern as well," Anders said. He glanced at his watch and rose. "I need to take my leave. I'll think about it all and make a decision tomorrow."

He called me at the apartment, two hours later. I was with Fiona, making dinner.

"Vincent is interested," he said. "And available."

"Anders! That's such good news!" I swung around to Fiona and flashed her a thumb's up.

"He's holding off on a yes, however."

I gripped the phone tighter. "Why?"

"He thinks you'll be hostile toward him. Says you gave him the cold shoulder all last spring and have repeatedly rejected his attempts at friendship."

"Yes, but that was because we had a bad breakup. That's not *now*." How ironic, that my directive to Natalia not to let him know I called, back in August, should backfire on me now. "Tell him I will not be hostile, and that I'd welcome his presence as my partner." My voice shook, because now I genuinely felt afraid. Anders had a star couple waiting to claim the role for the gala. Dmitri was right—they would be very welcome, back in San Francisco.

"I imagine he's there right now. Call him."

"Why me? Can't you take care of it?"

Anders chuckled. "You don't sound like someone eager to embark on a decidedly romantic pas de deux with him. Should I be concerned?"

"No! Absolutely not. I'll call him."

Fiona looked up from her onion chopping and regarded me with amusement. She'd heard bits and pieces of the Vincent story, through letters exchanged while she was in Africa. It had been mere snippets, a "we're an item!" once, and "well, we're not an item and it sucks" six months later, and my final lofty pronouncement last spring that "I'm off men—I'm sticking to ballet for the next decade."

I hung up and gazed at her in dismay.

"Seriously?" Fiona said. "You don't want to call Vincent Neumann? Omigod, he's such a hottie. I still can't believe you were lucky enough to date the guy. I can't imagine calling such a god 'my boyfriend.'"

"Yeah. Almost as much fun as what came after, calling such a 'god' my ex-boyfriend and watching him flirt with his new girlfriend during our rehearsals together. That was a great time."

Fiona eyed me curiously. "Yes, but isn't it worth it here? You don't want that Russian couple stepping in to steal your role, do you?"

"You're absolutely right."

I grabbed the phone before I could lose my nerve and punched in Vincent's number.

He answered on the second ring. At the sound of his voice, I felt myself slip back into that dizzy, ungrounded state, that had felt so sublime for months, and so devastating after my mom's death.

"Vincent." I cleared my throat nervously. "It's April."

"April," he said, genuine affection in his voice. "Sweetie. How are you?"

"I'm fine," I said tersely. "You already know the situation. I know Anders and you spoke. Will you do this pas de deux with me?"

"Do you want me to?"

"Of course." I thought of Dmitri. Of Sonya and Kirill. "I very much want you to."

"I'm onstage through the last week of October, and I have an event in Los Angeles right before your gala, but Anders was thinking we could make rehearsals happen even with those constraints."

"Yes, I agree."

"You sound all business." A teasing note entered his voice.

"That's because this *is* business."

"So, you need this, do you? You need *me*."

I rolled my eyes. He was going to milk this for all it was worth. "I do."

"Say it. 'I need you, Vincent.'"

"I need you, Vincent," I parroted back. I saw Fiona snicker and shake her head.

"No, no, that won't do. Say it like you mean it."

Good Lord, his ego. I injected a note of craven desperation that, in truth, wasn't far from what I was actually feeling. "Vincent. I need you."

This time Fiona laughed out loud.

"Done deal, my angel." I could tell Vincent was smiling broadly.

"Will you call Anders right back? I just hung up from talking to him. He'll want to know as soon as possible."

"I will."

"Do you promise?"

"April. My love. Of course I will."

"All right. I'll be seeing you soon, then."

"Yes. I look forward to it."

"Me too," I lied.

After I hung up, I stared at the phone in its receiver.

"Did I just make my life easier or harder?" I asked Fiona.

"Easier. Don't be silly!"

Vincent, bursting into this shaky new life I'd carved for myself.

I couldn't wait to see Dmitri's face when he heard.

Chapter 13

Vincent and Dinner

Vincent was an instant hit at the West Coast Ballet Theatre. The morning after his arrival, he strode into the studio like a lord viewing his lands, his minions, greeting people right and left. He was like a politician, the way he wielded his charisma, his classic good looks—thick blond hair, megawatt smile and chiseled jaw—without alienating a single person in the room. He introduced himself to principals and corps dancers alike. The female corps dancers were all agog afterwards, clapping their hand over their hearts as they swiveled around to murmur excitedly to their friends. It was all surface glitter, I thought in annoyance. He was shallow, and his lone saving grace was that he knew it and cheerfully exploited it. And everyone loved him for it.

He knew many more of the dancers than I'd realized. Renata. Curtis and Carrie. He and Dmitri exchanged hugs, laughter, words tumbling out, about mutual friends and long-ago events they'd both been a part of. Finally he spied me, where I was warming up at the barre on the far side of the room, and his eyes took on a theatrical glow.

"April! My sweet, lovely April!" He strode over as I tried to collect myself, maintain a cool reserve, which fell flat when he reached me and gathered me up in a bear hug, his body instantly familiar to mine.

"It's so good to see you again!" He stepped back and sized me up. "Look at you," he exclaimed, as though it had been five years instead of five months. "You look fabulous." Aware of his audience—all eyes were on him, watching his every move—he pulled me close again and pressed his lips against my cheek in a smacking kiss. Before I could process all the intensity, off he bounded, to greet more people he knew, and those he'd like to know. Judging by the way a dozen females hungrily followed him with their eyes, he'd get to know them all sooner than later.

Over twenty people had gathered to watch our first rehearsal. No surprise, with so much at stake. In addition to Anders, who was personally running our rehearsal, with Curtis there to advise, there was Charlie Stanton, looking out of place in his suit and tie. Loretta from PR. Yelena, casting us both dark, suspicious looks. Phil, Larry, Jimbo. Fiona snuck in, as did a half-dozen of the dancers, who should have been in their own rehearsals, but there you had it. Everyone wanted to see Vincent dance Romeo. Even Dmitri and Renata stood by the door to watch.

"Let's just do an initial run-through, from where Juliet has spotted him, has come down the stairs and now joins him center stage," Anders told us. "Go ahead and mark the trickier lifts and turns—this is just to get a sense of what kind of work we want to focus on."

If I'd harbored any unease over partnering with Vincent again, it faded in seconds, from the first partnered steps, the feeling of his sure hands on my waist, the way he knew my timing, my innate ways of moving. When you got down to it, he'd trained me to dance well with him. He'd selected me from the corps, told the artistic director, "There, that girl. She's someone to watch. Pair us up."

With everyone watching, we made an unspoken decision to dance full out. Vincent loved to perform for an audience and, as for me, I was tired of being seen as the junior principal who'd almost gotten bumped from the gala. We danced everything right to the end, where I hesitated, because the last thirty-two counts were pure romance and romantic energy. For a full eight counts Romeo and Juliet stare helplessly into each other's eyes, lips growing closer, closer, until Romeo kisses Juliet, not just a peck, but a long kiss. I held up a hand like a traffic officer, stepping out of character to announce, "okay, we're marking this part today," which made everyone laugh. It was unprofessional of me, but it was too soon for me to switch from cool, betrayed ex-girlfriend to besotted, "please, please kiss me" Juliet.

Everyone clapped and cheered at the end. Anders approached us, beaming. "Excellent. Excellent. This will work." Even Dmitri, arms crossed, gave a grudging nod.

"Five-minute break," Anders said, "and we'll run it again, you two, more slowly this time. The rest of you dancers, what are you doing here? Get to your own rehearsal." He was trying to sound gruff, but I saw relief, practically giddiness, on his face. As the others in the room began to disperse, Anders beckoned to me. Vincent had turned to his new fans, accepting invitations for drinks that night, for dinner another night, for plans straight through his time in San Francisco.

"Congratulations, you pulled it off," Anders said, once we were out of earshot.

"Thank you. I think."

He nodded at my hesitation. "Yes. It was fine for a rehearsal, a run-through. But what I want from you is the starry-eyed girl in love with her Romeo. It's clear your feelings toward Vincent have changed. Don't let that get in the way of delivering a performance that will dazzle the audience. Not just your own dancing, but the way you dance together. Your chemistry."

"This was just our first rehearsal," I started, but his skeptical expression made my words wilt. "It's hard," I said in a less confident voice. "Last year cost me a lot."

He studied me. "Can you do this?"

"Of course I can! I'm a professional."

"Find some time together. A glass of wine. Or have him over to your place."

"I think he's booked." I gestured to the women still surrounding him.

He didn't release his gaze on me. "I know what kind of performance you're capable of. It's that dancer I want to see onstage a week from now at the gala."

"You will. I promise."

"He and I are meeting for dinner tonight. I want to try and woo him for two more productions. If Curtis can't rebound fast enough, that puts *The Sleeping Beauty* and your Aurora at risk. Lexie's not ready for first or second cast. Vincent would be a perfect fit with you."

Fiona entered the studio. Spying Anders, she made her way over to us. She handed him two messages that he glanced at, even as he continued addressing me.

"We want him to like the West Coast Ballet Theatre. We want him to be eager to come back."

"Got it." My smile was growing more brittle.

"What about dinner with him, tomorrow night?" Anders persisted.

"I have plans. Fiona can vouch for that."

"We're having my brother over for dinner," Fiona told Anders. She gave an exaggerated roll of her eyes. "He's a pain. We'll end up arguing and the evening will be a chore. It's why I insisted Lexie join us."

Anders pointed at Fiona. "Perfect. You girls invite Vincent over, too."

Fiona's eyes lit with pleasure. "Oh, April, let's do it! It'll be so much more fun for me."

"But it's supposed to be a dinner for your brother," I protested. "Lexie is fine because that makes an even quartet. He's easy going and won't try to dominate the conversation."

"April," Anders said, and now he sounded annoyed, "stop acting like I'm mandating you go out on a date with him. Just be a hostess. Get comfortable with him again. I'm saying this as your artistic director. We have a gala to dance in six nights' time. I backed your choice of him over Sonya and Kirill. Now you do your share."

Vincent was delighted with the invite and Lexie was pleased by the addition. Russell, to my relief, didn't seem to mind. In fact, it seemed as though I was the only one feeling out of sorts at dinner the following night. I'd dressed nicely for the occasion, designer jeans and a blue silk blouse that matched my eyes. Whether it was for myself, Vincent or Russell, I wasn't sure. Vincent and Lexie both wore dress button-down shirts. Russell alone was dressed casually, in a stretched-out black T-shirt and jeans. His hair was mussed and it looked as though he'd forgotten to shave that morning. He had a reason, as it turned out.

"I was up for the better part of the past forty-eight hours, working with the team to meet a deadline. Good news is that we met it. Once everything was a go, I went home and thought, fine, I can sleep for three, four hours and have plenty of time to get ready. Instead I slept six hours." He rubbed at the scruff on his chin ruefully. "I guess you other guys found time to shave."

Lexie and Vincent nodded. Vincent sized up Russell in something akin to pity.

In truth, it made Russell seem even more attractive. His hair was thick and the color of ripe wheat. The matching golden stubble on his chin made me want to touch it and see if it felt bristly or soft. I met his eyes with an encouraging smile. His smile back warmed my heart.

I'd made Italian food for dinner. I loved making pasta dishes. Russell and Fiona had never heard of spaghetti *puttanesca* but when I learned Russell liked ultra-savory foods like olives and anchovies, I knew this was what I had to serve.

Everyone loved it. "How did you make it?" Lexie asked as he helped himself to a generous second serving.

"It's ridiculously simple," I said, nudging the dish of grated Reggiano parmesan his way. "You buy the Italian imported canned tomatoes, from San Marzano, if you can find them. Minced garlic and anchovies simmer in the olive oil—it makes the house smell so good. I tossed in the tomatoes, cooked about fifteen minutes. In went the olives, capers and red pepper flakes. The whole thing was an investment of thirty minutes."

Russell prodded the spaghetti with his fork. "I don't speak Italian. What's a puttanesca? Maybe Italian for anchovies?"

Vincent spluttered with laughter. "Hardly! A 'putana' is a whore. Spaghetti puttanesca is 'whore's spaghetti'."

Fiona snickered too, which I considered disloyal of her. I should have guessed it, though. Another reason I hadn't wanted Vincent here: he had to be the king and win over the others. Fiona was an easy conquest. Lexie, too.

"Remind me, Vincent." I said coolly. "What *is* the word for anchovies in Italian?"

He looked at me blankly. "I don't know."

"Oh. That's right. You don't speak Italian beyond that." Without waiting for his reply, I turned to Russell. "The name evolved from the story that Italian whores made this sauce because all the ingredients could be found in the pantry, and that it could be made quickly, late at night, when they were hungry."

"Actually," Vincent interrupted, "it's called 'puttanesca' because the smell of the sauce cooking lured prospective clients."

"I never heard that part," I said.

"Sweetie, of course you have! When we were in Italy. Do you forget who taught you to appreciate real Italian food from Italy?" Vincent reached over and patted my hand affectionately. "You were so cute, this Omaha girl on her first trip to Italy." A faraway smile spread over his face. "I think I had more fun on our Italy tour than any other."

"It was a good trip," I admitted.

"You two danced together?" Russell asked.

"Yes. And now I am happy to once again be April's partner," Vincent said.

I scowled at the proprietary tone in his voice, which made him chuckle. "That is to say, April's onstage partner. Look at that expression of yours, sweetie. You'd think, judging by it, that an offstage partnership with me had been the worst thing imaginable. Was it so bad?"

"I'm just setting the record straight."

"Oh." The idea seemed to pierce Russell's mind finally. "So, you were once the other kind of partners?"

"We were," Vincent replied. "But April left New York to come out here. Alone."

A dozen accusations sprang to mind, starting with the easy way he made it all sound. Even though I'd been the one to break up, to leave New York, it was because he'd hurt me terribly. Watching him and Natalia cozy up all winter and spring had been agony. Calling him in August, only to speak to Natalia, had been shame atop agony. But he only smiled at me now, his brown eyes free of guilt.

"We were one of ABT's hot Romeo and Juliet couples in 1987,"

Vincent told the others. "The critics adored us. There were four casts that year, but only three taken on tour. And *we* were the ones chosen to perform it in Verona. Romeo and Juliet's own city! April, do you remember?"

In spite of myself, I laughed. "Who could forget?"

"The rain squalls," he said.

"The sound production."

"The wind that kept blowing your dress up over your head."

I turned to the others. "It should have been incredible. It wasn't just that it was the setting of Shakespeare's play, the venue was a Roman amphitheater, where they do these amazing operas. The arena dates from the first century—it was ancient even back in Shakespeare's time!"

"It was the coolest place I've ever performed," Vincent admitted.

"And our final dress rehearsal went so well!"

"You know what they say," Lexie offered. "Bad final dress, good performance."

Everyone besides Russell nodded.

"Are you serious that it *rained* on you guys?" Fiona asked.

"It did," Vincent said. "Not too bad to cancel, but enough to get rained on in two scenes."

"It got slick onstage," I said. "The production crew was ready to call a stop, not once but twice, but each time the rain let up first."

"And then there was the music," Vincent said. "The musicians from the local orchestra the ABT had hired went on strike the week we arrived, so everyone was scrambling to make it work with canned music. But the sound system was awful, and sound kept dropping out. You had to keep going—sometimes as long as twenty seconds without music which, trust me, feels like twenty minutes when you're out there trying to maintain character, not to mention count. The lighting, too, would just flicker for no reason. So like Italy. The most beautiful, charming sites in the world, the most malfunctioning place otherwise."

"But we did it," I said to him. We smiled at each other and for a moment, it felt like Vincent-and-April again, this great mix of partnership and passion and romance, so charmed and golden. He was right; I'd been this besotted, impressionable girl, and in Italy, with Vincent, I'd been living out my dreams.

"Has April told you about our balcony for your pas de deux?" Lexie asked, and he, Fiona and I smothered our chuckles.

"Do tell," Vincent said.

"It's this old, rickety structure that has already split in two," I said. "It's as stable and secure as a tightrope."

"Excellent!" Vincent exclaimed. "It'll feel like Italy again." He reached over and gave my hand a squeeze that became a caress, which I couldn't interpret, nor did I want to. He and Natalia were still a couple, I'd heard him tell Dmitri. I myself hadn't brought up her name, nor had Vincent offered. The April-and-Vincent glow evaporated and I pulled my hand from his.

"That's not the worst thing that's happened on the WCBT stage, unfortunately," Lexie said. "Last year, the stage's fire alarm water sprinklers went off during the performance. We had to stop the performance because it's in our contracts that we stop dancing if it's raining, and honey, it kept raining. Took them five minutes to stop all the sprinklers."

I stared at him, horrified, but Vincent and Fiona only laughed merrily.

"You know, the West Coast Ballet Theatre sort of has a reputation for things falling apart," Vincent told Lexie.

"My dear Vincent, we are the Italy of North American ballet." Lexie sighed. "I don't know where to begin."

"Try me. We've got all night!"

169

As Lexie launched into a new story, I realized, with a pang, that Russell had been largely silent and could contribute in no way to the conversation. I fell silent too, as the stories continued, but the others didn't even notice. Fiona was the perfect audience. No detail about the ballet world, the performing world, was too small, and her eyes were worshipful as they moved from Lexie to Vincent, depending on who was telling the story.

Finally, though, I'd had enough.

"Can we talk about something else?" I interrupted. Fiona, Lexie and Vincent looked at me, startled and perplexed, as if I'd proposed we skip dessert and instead study algebra together.

But Vincent prided himself on his conversational skills and, in truth, could be very kind about coaxing stories out of the quietest person in a group, although, no surprise, he preferred it if the quiet person were female. As we finished our dinner, he got Russell to explain what he did, what Pegasus Systems manufactured and sold, although I got the sense nothing Russell was saying in response was sticking in Vincent's head. Not until the predictions.

"Tell me what part high technology will play in the future," Vincent proposed.

"Oh, it's going to change the world," Russell said, and the authoritative ring in his voice, the fire in his eyes, made everyone sit up to listen. "With the Internet and its accessibility evolving, high tech as a field will explode, and its products will serve everyone."

"Not us," Vincent said. "Dancers don't do technology."

"Oh, but you will," Russell said. "And mark my word, there will even come a day when technology and your ballet audiences meet."

"How?" Vincent challenged.

"My hunch is, there's going to be entertainment, just like television except online, that will allow everyone who has a computer—which will be everyone, eventually—to log onto a site and click on a link and watch videos. With an archive as big as the sky. A video of a past dance performance could be seen by anyone, if the company wanted to allow it. Your kids will have access to watching dancers from around the world that they'd never see performing live."

"They have that in video form already. That's what video stores are for," Fiona pointed out.

"The VHS format won't last as technology evolves. Neither will video stores."

"No *way!*" Fiona cried.

Russell continued, undaunted. "They'll be replaced by companies that offer electronic products, movies that you order by computer and have delivered. Maybe someday they'll skip the physical delivery entirely and it'll be delivered straight to your television or computer. A project being implemented in Europe, a global hyper-linked information system, is going to someday make it all possible. People all around the world will exchange information—and so much more."

His eyes had taken on that mad scientist glow, and I tensed. While I saw my brilliant dad in him, I knew the others just saw a tech geek, geeking out.

"Digital things," he was saying. "Like these new digital cameras. They'll take over in popularity, and we'll find a way to upload photos to the Internet. Not just photographers, but anyone. Celebrities. Famous ballerinas, posting photos that everyone will want to see, pictures of their everyday lives, in rehearsal, in their dressing rooms. It will be like our media now—newspapers, magazines, books, films—except through the Internet, which will allow everyone to engage socially, no matter where you live. Which is going to change everyone's life. Everyone's. And it won't just be a desktop computer that's powering the revolution. We'll have electronic notebooks, even smaller devices, maybe even the size of your wallet, and you'll walk around, with this device connecting you to the entire world, there in your pocket, reachable by a mere swipe of your finger."

A long, electric pause followed. My heart was thumping with excitement because I could visualize it happening, all that Russell said, no matter how farfetched it sounded. I took the silence from the others as proof that they, too, saw his extraordinary prescience. Then Vincent began to cackle. Not just cackle: he burst into howls of laughter. Laughter that went on and on. And because Vincent was the king, Fiona and Lexie followed his lead and laughed with him. Even Russell began to laugh. I alone wasn't laughing. Instead I sat there, thinking, *Vincent, you prick, you're mocking him.*

"Wow," Vincent finally said between wheezes of laughter, "you really had me going there. Except I'm still waiting for the line about our spaceships waiting to whisk us over to Mars for dinner."

Russell stopped laughing. I willed him to meet my eyes so I could telegraph my disgust at Vincent's jeering, but he ducked his head, suddenly interested in his wine glass, in the swirling motions he produced by tilting it around.

"This isn't science fiction, Vincent," I said. "This is technology. And this is Silicon Valley. You don't have a clue what's being generated here, all these creative tech minds. You're sort of stuck in New York performing-arts land, like all of life begins and ends there."

"April!" A stricken look came over him, one of those wounded expressions he excelled at, as if I'd been causing the harm. "You're so hard on me. Russell was having his fun with us. He got me. Why am I the villain?"

"Don't you see that what he's saying might very well actualize?"

"Not in our lifetime," he said with a chuckle. "I mean, remember how there was all this talk about how we were going to use telephones that had built in cameras so you could see the person you were talking to? What happened to that grand idea? Computers for everyone? What would I do with a computer?! I'll wait for the flying car, thanks."

I rose. "I'm going to start some dessert assembly. No, sit," I told the others, who half-rose to help clear the dishes, all except for Vincent, who smiled at me expectantly as if I were his waitress.

I'd planned a decadent dessert: warm, dense chocolate brownie beneath a scoop of vanilla ice cream, topped with a drizzling of raspberry sauce. Russell wandered over to help.

"I'm sorry about Vincent," I said. "This wasn't how the evening was supposed to be."

"Don't give it a second thought. I'm just glad to be here with you."

I glanced at him out of the corner of my eye as he dug at the ice cream with a scooper. He was so cute. It wasn't just his looks, either. I spent most of my waking hours with beautiful men who had beautiful bodies and moved beautifully. What so drew me to Russell was his lack of agenda. In his intent gaze was the math geek who'd been unable to find a date for the prom, the guy who'd been seen for his brain first, looks second. Looks that, when they arrived, had likely baffled him as much as they'd pleased others. He didn't know how to flirt. He didn't know how to play those cards to his advantage. He was the most honest person, outside my parents, I'd ever known.

I placed a generous brownie square in each of the five bowls and handed them one by one to Russell. "Hey, can you give me some female advice?" he asked. "I'm in a bind."

"Of course."

Russell dropped a scoop of ice cream onto the first brownie and sighed. "So, you and Vincent, you broke things off, and remained friends?"

"I suppose you could say that. I've always maintained my respect for him as a dancer. We had to work together, last year. And we need to work together, closely, now."

"How does one break things off and remain friends?"

"Uh, oh." I eyed him in concern. "This is about Nicola?"

"Yeah."

Fiona came over. "You two are chatting away. Are these ready?"

I drizzled raspberry sauce on the first two desserts. "They are now."

Fiona took the two bowls to the table. I glanced at Russell. "Back to Nicola. Why do you want to break things off? She seemed very devoted to you. Crazy about you."

He shook his head gloomily. "She wants too much. The thing is, I don't have time to date. I don't want the burden. The guilt, when I have to put the entire weekend into work, and she gets all huffy because she wanted to do something fun. And weeknights, too. I want to be free to work past ten and not feel guilty. I'm starting to dread phone calls from her."

"Oh, poor you," I said softly. "Poor Nicola." Because I remembered precisely how it had felt, knowing I was losing Vincent's loyalties, his romantic interest. "Just be honest with her, Russell. Try not to hurt her."

"That's why I'm afraid to say anything, frankly. It's going to hurt her. But I can't keep going on with this façade."

I regarded him curiously. "How long have you felt this way?"

"Since I met you." He stopped, flustered. "What I mean to say is, since that night we met you and Fiona out. I'd invited her because I always do better with Fiona when I bring a human cushion along. Nicola was flattered, but in the wrong way. She told me how glad she was that we were on to the 'meeting family' point in our relationship. To her, meeting Fiona was proof that we were meant to get more serious. There's been this snowballing effect ever since."

"You can't string her along. It's just going to get worse, for both of you."

"You're right."

Fiona returned and sized us up in disapproval. "You still haven't finished? Your guests are waiting, you know." She gestured to the table, where Vincent and Lexie were deep in conversation.

"Um, your brother *is* our guest," I said in the same reproving tone. "The original one."

"That's fine," Russell said. "We're done talking. Thank you for your advice, April."

I smiled at him as I drizzled raspberry sauce on the last two desserts. "Any time."

Conversation grew easier as we ate dessert. Lexie talked about the ways in which being promoted to principal had changed his life. Russell shared his relief over his team's having achieved the important deadline at work. He explained how he'd been buried in work the past month and only now could he come up for air, but the good news was that he'd be free to attend the gala next week, like I'd proposed. I had two free tickets, one for Fiona and one for Russell.

Hearing this, happiness welled up in me. With Fiona and him, I'd have old friends in the audience. It made so much difference in how you performed, knowing a loved one was watching. "I'm so glad you're able to make it," I told him.

"Me too."

"Of course you shouldn't plan on spending actual time with April," Vincent said. "As my partner, she'll be considered one of the celebrities at the post-performance party. Everyone will want to talk to us after our performance. Well, and they'll want to talk to me because, you know, an ABT principal at a WCBT event is a big deal, if I don't say so myself."

My fists clenched under the table. I turned to Russell and smiled sweetly at him. "Russell, would you be my date for the party?"

I relished the surprise on everyone's faces, particularly Russell's and Vincent's. Russell looked like he'd just won the lottery. Different emotions crisscrossed Vincent's face: confusion, woe, annoyance.

"Are you sure, April?" he asked. "I think Anders has something else in mind. A 'golden couple' look, to replace what Sonya and Kirill were."

"Oh, we can pose for the cameras," I said. "We don't have to be each other's date for that."

"I still don't think it's a good idea," Vincent said.

I reached over and patted his hand. "I still don't think this is your choice for the making." I turned to Russell. "Would you be my date?"

"Of course," he stuttered. "My pleasure."

"It had better be," Vincent muttered.

I met Russell's eyes and we exchanged a moment of private mirth. Our gaze lingered as Fiona, laughing, offered to be Vincent's date. As Lexie gallantly replied that he'd be a much better date for Fiona, Russell's eyes, still on my face, lost their mirth. They grew darker, which sent a bolt of sensation through my solar plexus that settled deep in my pelvis. I broke the gaze, feeling heat suffuse my face, and took a gulp from my glass of water, keenly aware that his gaze still hadn't dropped. Those Garvey blue eyes, fixed on me alone.

Gala night had just become much more interesting.

Chapter 14

Gala

The night of the gala, Vincent drew applause when he ran onstage as Romeo, cape fluttering behind him. He cut an admittedly impressive figure, boyish yet princely, thick hair slicked back, makeup accentuating his good looks. I stood above him, stage left, on the balcony, having pantomimed my euphoria of a newfound infatuation, a teen girl's amazement over this new emotion filling me. Right behind me, invisible to the audience, two of the stagehands crouched, gripping the attaching parts of the set that had continued to come apart during rehearsals.

Having dashed elegantly across the stage, Vincent now turned and caught sight of me. Our eyes locked. He walked slowly toward me as I pantomimed excited indecision, before holding up a "wait" finger. I stepped away from the balcony, descending the rickety steps (during which time both stagehands and I held our breath) to the wing below the balcony.

I burst onstage like a caged animal set free, chest forward, my thin chiffon dress billowing behind me. Vincent and I met center stage and clasped hands, the two of us now bashful, awestruck by our daring, meeting up like this after dark. *See how you're making my heart pound?* I pantomimed, and took his hand, laying it on my chest. Sixty seconds in, our partnering grew energetic, a stage-filling, sensuous, uninhibited expression of young love. I ran, leapt, turned. He spun me in partnered pirouettes, four effortless rotations. He lifted me and I draped myself over his shoulder with wanton abandon, every move imparting a feeling of joyous euphoria, absolute infatuation.

You always perform better when there are people you know in the audience watching. But this time was different, a hyper-awareness that comes when you're in the throes of—face it—a crush.

Russell Garvey was out there watching me.

I felt the thrill of a performance going well, an unexpected turbo charge that ratcheted up the quality of each movement. Each leg extension higher, each arch back exquisitely curved. I threw myself into every extravagant move and Vincent, equally galvanized, responded.

Another leap. He caught me in a twist and I held the pose upside-down, frozen like a statue, gravity disregarded, this precarious inverted pose, one of Macmillan's distinctive touches that, I knew, enthralled the audience. Vincent, too, enthralled the audience—I could almost feel the way they were leaning forward in their seats.

Tonight, I threw all grudges of the past aside and became his Juliet once again. I ran to where he was kneeling, center stage, and stepped into a piqué arabesque over him, chest and arms high. He lifted me overhead and dipped me, still kneeling, as if I weighed nothing.

Our communication now seemed telepathic as we rode the same wave of power. Or maybe not telepathic. Because in that final, romantic thirty-two counts, where he cradled my face in his hands, as choreographed, and kissed me, as choreographed, he caught me by surprise with a real kiss. His tongue slid inside my mouth, now agape with surprise, which allowed him to hungrily probe at my tonsils before releasing my face.

It wasn't erotic. It was, in truth, disturbing, robbing me in an instant of the confident space I'd created between us. That the kiss made me tremble with confused desire surely made my performance as Juliet all the more real. I used my shock to pantomime bedazzlement, a *he kissed me* daze, as I backed away from him and skittered back up to my place on the rickety balcony, where I bade him a good night. The audience began clapping, cheering. Once the curtain came down, I descended the steps indignantly, determined to give him a piece of my mind.

But Vincent was preoccupied by something else. "Shit," he said as he limped off center stage into the stage-right wings. He was laughing, in a wry, self-effacing way. "That passage with the double turns always messes with me. Bad landing."

"You covered it well," Phil said, eyes on his monitor. "Nobody noticed a thing."

"That's because I'm very good," Vincent said with a satisfied smile.

"And humble," I added.

We had mere seconds before the curtain rose for our bows. The dancers' code of etiquette was that if someone got injured or was valiantly trying to brush off an injury-but-not, you supported them. You were teammates, comrades in the trenches. Earlier onstage clashing didn't matter. A stage kiss, tongue or not, didn't matter.

The audience didn't want to stop clapping. Vincent and I were called back onstage for two more bows. The house manager, clad in a suit, came out and presented me with a dozen roses. I pulled one out and gave it to Vincent, who kissed my hand. The audience roared their approval.

The explosion of triumph within me blotted out any last indignation over the kiss. A lot had been at stake tonight. I'd almost stopped believing I was capable of something huge and dazzling within the WCBT.

Vincent met my eyes and smiled broadly. He was a star, and he knew it.

Together, tonight, we both were.

We talked en route to the gala after-party, across the street, and agreed the performance had been extraordinary. Even his ankle had stopped hurting, he announced.

"You've gotten so strong, so solid," he said. "Lifting you has never felt so effortless."

"You were amazing," I said. "In everything."

"I agree. Damn, it was great dancing with you again. We have a history. A longtime relationship. It all felt so right. Even that kiss."

"Right," I said in a more chilly tone. "About that kiss."

"Now don't be mad. I was just so into the role, the familiarity of dancing with you again. And, okay, remembering two years ago."

"Funny, because what I remember is a year ago."

He didn't reply to this. Instead, he stopped walking and turned to regard me. "Are you happy out here?" he asked.

The question surprised me. So did the answer. "I am. I really like San Francisco."

"You don't miss me." He sounded mournful.

I stared at him. "Vincent. Are you going to keep playing blind to what happened between us?"

"We were friends. We were partners. Before we were the other kind of partners."

I began walking again. "Well, it so happens the 'other kind of partners' is trickier, and you mishandled it. You hurt me." I increased my pace. He hurried to catch up.

"Didn't this make up for it? Didn't I get you and Anders out of a bind here?"

"You did," I admitted.

"Did we or did we not have kick-ass onstage chemistry tonight?"

"We did."

"So, I just went with it. That kiss—are you serious that it bothered you? Because, don't attack me here, but you were acting like someone with a massive crush."

"That's just it. I was acting."

He shook his head and regarded me fondly. "I know the real deal when I see it. Face it, you've still got the hots for me."

I didn't know whether to splutter with indignation or laugh. He raised his hands before I could speak. "It's okay. It's just me, Vincent. You don't have to deny it or make excuses."

Laughter trumped indignation. "Good Lord. Who has the bigger ego, you or Dmitri?"

"Answer me this. Who's the better partner to Miss April Manning?"

"You are."

"Yes. I thought so."

He offered me his arm, in that gallant way no one did in real life anymore except in theatrical moments like this. We'd arrived at the front double doors of the gala venue. I linked my arm with his, and together we sailed in.

The gala after-party took place in the elegant, soaring City Hall rotunda with a sweeping grand staircase. Patrons had paid $1000 a couple to eat inferior banquet food prior, and during the performance, the space had been transformed into a nightclub. Music boomed from strategically placed speakers. The gel lighting delivered purple and blue hues mixed in with pink. Enormous fabric swaths, diaphanous and ghostly, hung from the second level's balcony railings. Balloons, clustered together like multicolor grapes, bobbed against the ceiling. Colorful abstract designs were projected onto two-story marble beams. All the dancers had been invited and the corps dancers, the girls so pretty in their ballgowns, long shiny hair flowing down their backs, clustered together in a pack with the suit-clad boys, all of them exempted from the higher-ranked dancers' mandate to mingle, make friends with the donors and the city's high rollers. I recognized more than one face from Anders and Sabine's open house, which went to show you how adept Anders had been, early on, at meeting the right people. He himself strode easily through the room, shaking hands, accepting congratulations, working the crowd with a confident smile that made him seem years older and more experienced than he actually was.

I looked around for Russell, who'd come over with Fiona. Before I could find him, strangers swooped in to speak with Vincent and me.

Vincent had been right; people seemed to enjoy seeing us together. Photographers snapped our picture, as patrons clamored to be included in on a photo with their own camera. I smiled and posed and smiled more and small-talked for fifteen minutes until I spied Fiona, who gestured from a distance that she was keeping Russell company.

We chatted with board of trustee members, important donors, unimportant donors, friendly strangers, and posed for picture after picture. It began to feel like torture, to beam and pose for the camera, Vincent's arm around my waist, when all I wanted was to see Russell, let him see me in my glittery ballgown.

Then I saw him. He, too, was in dress attire. He looked stunning. We stared at each other, both momentarily taken aback, followed by laughter, because, in the end, it was still just Russell from my childhood. I excused myself to Vincent and went over to where Russell stood.

In dress suit and tie, he acted different. Patrician, Ivy League. I complimented him on the suit—I knew quality tailoring when I saw it—and he shared, wryly, that his business partners had insisted he invest in at least one top quality suit, back when they were looking for more funding, and he had to look the part of a business executive. "A suit," he complained. "I blew my meager savings on clothes."

"Was it worth it?" I asked.

"Yes," he admitted.

I'd been concerned he might feel intimidated by the crowd, my job of continuing to mingle and chat with important guests, but he fared impressively, and I was more surprised than anyone when one member of the WCBT board of trustees, a portly, smiling man named Roger recognized Russell. "Why, Russell Garvey," he said after he'd introduced himself to me, "you do operate in refined circles."

Russell laughed and shook Roger's hand. "Roger is one of the venture capitalists who took a chance on our company," he explained to me.

"An extremely good decision," Roger added.

The two of them chatted about the state of Russell's company, in that unfamiliar tech-speak that had me grasping to figure out what they were talking about. No matter. They both looked happy and eager to discuss what the future held for Russell's company. Russell's hand had fallen to my waist in that distracted way of his, caressing my back as he searched for the words to describe something to Roger, and giving my waist a squeeze when he found them. It felt oddly natural.

"Well!" Roger said afterward, and scrutinized the two of us, as if trying to decide whether we were a couple or not. Russell's hand abruptly dropped from my waist, and I knew by his flustered pause that he'd been unaware of the intimacy he'd just created.

Roger leaned in toward me, speaking over the rock band that had just started up. "My dear, you were amazing. A fine contribution to the West Coast Ballet Theatre. You know, more than one of us felt concern in August about the goings on, the departures, but I've a feeling young Mr. Gunst knows what he's doing. He's off to a good start."

"Thank you, sir."

"Roger, please."

"Thank you, Roger. I'll be sure and share your comments with him. He'll be happy to hear. He's been working hard."

"It shows."

He excused himself a minute later to go find his wife. Russell and I watched him walk away. "He seems really nice," I commented.

"He's the greatest. Most times with venture capitalists, it's all business, I meet them once or twice, and that's it. But Roger's been a friend and a mentor since I met him. We meet for lunch in the city quarterly. He seems genuinely interested in what and how we're doing. He'll ask my advice on things I know and offer advice on things he knows better."

We wandered over to the drinks station for more champagne. "So," he said, eyeing me over his champagne glass, "you and Vincent. Your performance blew me away."

I felt my cheeks grow warm. "Thank you."

"It was like I was watching something real take place between you. Everyone felt that way. I heard the woman behind me say to her partner, 'Now *that's* chemistry'."

I winced. "The kiss."

The smile left Russell's face. "Yeah. That looked pretty real."

"It's part of the choreography to make it look so realistic. I was acting."

"That's all?" He looked unconvinced.

"I love dancing with Vincent. He's a great onstage partner. But that's all he is to me now."

"So... how do you do it? How can you kiss someone and fake it for so long, and make it look so real?"

My warm cheeks grew downright hot. He noticed.

"I'm sorry," he said. "Fiona's always telling me I overstep boundaries socially. This is too personal."

"No, it's all right." I reached over and touched his arm. "You and I have known each other a long time. And I've confided in you a lot since I moved out here. The truth is, it *was* a real kiss, one that I neither expected nor asked for." I shook my head, less angry about it now. "It was inappropriate, and I told him so. He apologized. Sort of."

"Oh." He looked uncertain. I could tell he wanted to ask more questions, but good manners, or the lack of skills in navigating such tricky terrain, kept him silent.

One intimate question deserved another, I decided. "All right, my turn," I said.

"Yes?" He looked wary.

"You and Nicola."

His shoulders relaxed. "Over. We ended things last weekend."

"Oh, no. I'm sorry."

"Don't be."

"How did she take it?"

"Not great. She thinks I'm an unfeeling bastard with communication issues."

"Well." I eyed him appreciatively. "You can tell her that hasn't been my experience. Or, wait. Maybe she doesn't want to hear that, huh?"

"I think not."

We both laughed. Emboldened, I continued. "What about you? How do you feel now?"

He considered this. "Am I a villain that my strongest feeling is relief?"

"No."

"I just didn't have the time for a relationship on top of my work." He studied his glass as he spoke. "What a drain, all that 'we need to talk' and 'you need to listen to what I'm saying' and half the time not understanding what she was getting at." He gave a great exhale and looked up at me. "I'm free again. Free to be married to my work without guilt."

I saw Russell's expression change and glanced over my shoulder to see Fiona approaching with Vincent. "Anders loves the couple's appeal of you two," Fiona told me. "He wants you to spend more time together." Russell directed a scowl toward his sister, but Fiona ignored him.

Vincent squinted at Russell. "Hey, wait. Did I meet you last week? Fiona's brother?"

Russell cast Vincent a skeptical look. "You don't remember?"

"You were dressed differently."

"So were you."

"Sorry." Vincent's smile was both apologetic and confident. "It's a celebrity thing. I'm recognized a lot more than I myself recognize people."

"Keep an eye on that." Russell echoed Vincent's easy tone. "That's also a sign of early-onset Alzheimer's."

Fiona looked horrified. "Russell! Don't be rude."

"It wasn't rude, Fiona," I said as I took Russell's arm. "It was humor. Right, Vincent?"

"Of course."

I gave Russell's arm a squeeze and met his eye. "Good one," I murmured, and when he smiled back at me, his gaze made me feel like we were the only two people in the room.

"Forgive my brother," Fiona was saying to Vincent. "He's got a mathematician's social skills."

"The world needs mathematicians, too," I heard Vincent reply in a soothing voice.

"Twenty minutes," I murmured to Russell. "Then I tell my boss I'm off the clock."

Russell nodded. "I'll go hunt down Roger again. Come find me when you're free."

"April!" Vincent sounded aggrieved. "Stop ignoring me. It looks bad."

"All right, all right!" With reluctance I stepped away from Russell and took Vincent's arm. "Let's go be Anders' golden couple."

An hour later, Russell and I left the party. Fiona had opted to stay longer, with Lexie. It was well past midnight, and the streets had emptied, so the drive took only minutes. He found parking close to my building and insisted on walking me to the door.

"You don't have to," I said as I got out of the car. An absurd, unexpected shyness had crept over me, and I wondered desperately how I'd make conversation.

"I insist. I want to be seen walking this beautiful, famous woman to her door."

Now we both grew tongue-tied. Once inside the building, I was achingly aware of his presence behind me as I led the way up the two flights of stairs. Clever words rose to mind and wilted on my tongue before I could get them out.

I stopped outside my door and turned to smile at him. "Do you want to come in?"

"Me? Oh, no. No thanks. I mean, thanks, but no thanks." Russell sounded terrified.

We stood in an agony of electric hesitation.

"Things are about to get busy," I blurted out. "Nutcracker rehearsals."

"Oh, busy for me too. Crazy busy."

"And it's already November. Thanksgiving is just three weeks away."

"It is."

"Will you go back to Omaha for Thanksgiving?"

He shook his head. "Not a chance. Never have. Just too busy."

"That's exactly how it is for a dancer, too. Prepping for Nut. And the insanity goes through December."

"I'm right there with you. We have a release on December 27th. It's going to be brutal until then."

I began to breathe easier. This was less complicated terrain. Careers were safer than relationships. All that heartache and second-guessing and nervous, high emotion the latter required. Tonight, I'd felt like Cinderella at the ball. But the clock had struck midnight and my glass slippers had turned back into pointe shoes.

"It's getting late," I said.

"It is," he agreed.

He didn't move. Neither did I.

"Good night, then." My heart began to thump against my chest like I was a teen girl. Ironically, it was precisely like the mood I'd faked onstage just a few hours earlier.

"Good night." His eyes searched my face. "Thank you for inviting me. It was amazing. You are amazing."

"Thank you for being my date," I said.

"Anytime." He took a sudden step back, and pivoted ninety degrees, like a soldier being given marching orders. "See you around," he said, and sped off.

Deflated, I waited till he'd rounded the corner and disappeared from sight before I stepped into my apartment. I locked the door and slumped against it. Suddenly I felt so stupidly bereft, as if I'd made a choice to which we'd forever adhere. How noble and elevated I'd felt, voicing my pronouncement of how busy I was. And Russell—the light in those blue eyes had dimmed even as he'd agreed with me. Or perhaps that had been my imagination. For all I knew, he'd hurried away, thinking, *whew, that was a close one.*

He'd been kind and polite, a perfect gentleman all evening. Now we could each go to our respective empty beds, and lie there, noble and restless. That, and wonder, *what if?*

I'd made a mistake.

You fool, I berated myself. *Afraid to take the risk.*

A knock on the door had me leaping away in shock. I hadn't heard footsteps. I hastily undid the lock and flung open the door.

Russell stood there, looking flustered. "I'm sorry to bother you again. I was wondering if I could—"

His words were cut short as I pulled him in. I shut the door behind him and did the thing I'd been wanting to do all evening. I touched his face, felt its smooth warmth, inhaling the aching good smell of his aftershave, before I latched my lips onto his. There was something crazed and desperate about it, as if he'd disappear if I didn't act fast.

We'd bumped up against the wall. My arms looped around his neck. His hands went around me, pulling me close, and the way they moved up and down my back told me he felt the same hunger.

After we separated, we stared at each other. He looked incredulous. I found my breath, my wits, finally. "Now *that* would be a kiss that I asked for." My voice shook. I didn't sound witty, I realized; I sounded vulnerable.

It didn't matter. Not with Russell.

"Wow," he said softly. "April."

As if in a trance, his hands reached out and clasped my forearms. From there his hands moved slowly up my arms, stopping at my shoulders. His fingers slid under the spaghetti straps of my evening gown and caressed the skin beneath them. My breath caught. Goosebumps appeared up and down my arm. I gestured to them and he smiled.

"It's a reflex, you know. The muscles attached to the base of each hair follicle contract, which creates a shallow depression on the skin surface, which causes the surrounding area to protrude."

"Thank you for that factoid," I teased.

He chuckled. "Let's see if warm pressure applied to the neck produces the same reflex." Before I could respond, he took a step closer and ran his lips along my neck, stopping at a pulsing spot to nibble.

Pleasurable sensations exploded within me. I felt faint. My knees shook.

He glanced down. "Will you look at that? Goosebumps."

He inclined his head a notch and now our lips were mere inches apart. We remained in that combustible space, unmoving. His hands had landed on my hips and my hands had gravitated to his back, beneath his jacket, where I felt the warmth of his skin through the fine, silken cotton of his shirt.

His lips brushed mine with a butterfly touch, more a suggestion than a kiss. His pupils had grown so dark, they'd changed the color of his eyes.

"This is a terrible idea," I said, our lips a quarter inch apart.

"The worst."

"Our jobs."

"I know."

"No free time," I said. "None."

"Impossible situation."

He kissed me again. Time passed, amid a dizzying kaleidoscope of sensations.

"Don't go," I murmured against his mouth. "But wait. You have to go."

"Do I?"

"Fiona could be here any minute."

This did the trick.

He pulled away from me, his expression aggrieved even at the mention of his sister. "I don't want to see her. Not right now."

"No," I admitted. "I don't either."

"I'm going," he said, but he didn't move.

"Go," I said. I leaned in and gave him one last kiss. "And don't call me."

He hesitated.

"I'm serious," I said. "This isn't a romance starting."

"Then what is it?"

I looked at him and exhaled softly. "Something absolutely unexpected and wonderful. And tomorrow, reality returns."

He looked at his watch. "It's tomorrow already."

This made me laugh. "Go." I gave him a soft nudge. He responded by pulling me in for one last, lingering kiss.

"Okay, I'm leaving," he said afterward. He opened the door and slipped out, glancing right and left, as if Fiona might have crept up to ambush us. Seeing no one, he relaxed. He looked at me and his expression grew soft.

"Good night, my Juliet. Sweet dreams."

I lay awake in bed, long after his departure, long after Fiona's return, replaying the evening over and over in my mind, returning to those last five life-changing minutes by the door. So unexpected. And yet, somehow not. Predestined. Which presented a situation too complicated to consider outside the realm of daily life and my work.

My earlier onstage bedazzlement, after Romeo's kiss. I understood it better now.

He kissed me.

Russell Garvey kissed me.

Chapter 15

December

I'd just finished up my Christmas purchases in Union Square and was heading back to the apartment when a sudden rainstorm changed my plans. I'd brought no umbrella, so I darted into a nearby diner to wait out the worst of the rain. My concern was for the scarves. Three of them, delicate, diaphanous and silky, Christmas gifts for the three aunts. Buying them had been a bittersweet experience, accentuating my mom's absence in my life. My aunts would like the scarves, I knew, although they'd tsk-tsk the price if they knew it. I'd bought a few cheaper scarves in Chinatown, soft pashminas of such rich colors, I hadn't been able to resist. The shop had offered one scarf for $12, two for $20 and three for $25. I'd bought three: one for Fiona, one for me, and a spare that I'd find a home for later.

The diner was one of those anonymous, instantly forgettable places with linoleum floors, Formica tabletops and a counter with stools facing the grill. As I shook the raindrops off my jacket, away from the scarves, I looked around, and froze.

Jana. Wearing a waitress uniform, a polyester-blend dress that had an apron that tied in back. Her hair was tucked into an untidy ponytail and a pen was stuck behind her ear, which she pulled out to take a customer's order at a table in back.

There was no etiquette tip on how to deal with the situation of a former peer now serving you at a diner. Like the last time I saw Jana, I could only feel guilt, as though I'd taken the job she'd lost. Never mind that Jana had left on her own terms. I wanted to apologize. I wanted to creep back out without being seen.

Before I could decide what to do, Jana looked up and spied me. A trapped look came over her face, but as she approached me, she smiled.

To my surprise, she gave me a hug. "I'm so happy to see you."

"Thanks. Likewise!" I lied.

Jana took a plastic-covered menu from the side rack of the reception counter. "I've got the perfect table for you. And lunch is on me. I insist."

I didn't feel like eating, but there was no polite way to extract myself from the situation. I followed Jana to a corner spot by the window. That part, at least, suited me. I smiled at Jana in gratitude.

"Coffee? Tea?" she asked.

"Iced tea would be great." I arranged myself on the booth seat. The spring beneath felt broken; the tabletop came up to my chest. Jana noticed.

"There's a spot if you move dead center that doesn't sag quite so much."

I shifted and found the spot.

"We get some heavy-set customers," Jana said with a wry smile. "This is the best table. They've worked that seat to death."

"This spot is good." I patted the vinyl beside me. "It's like getting the middle spot in the back of a car with bucket seats. I can see the world from here."

Jana left and I relaxed into the seat, deciding that thirty minutes of do-nothing-ness was, in truth, a good thing. December had been a frenzy of rehearsing and performing. Here was a chance to relax and process, as the rain drummed against the windows, forcing pedestrians to scatter and scurry.

It was the second week of *Nutcracker,* Nut for short. I knew Jana had to be following the dates as well. Nut dominated your life as a dancer, from your earliest years of training. Just because you ceased dancing didn't mean it left your heart, even though, ironically, you got so sick of the music, the slog, the thirty to forty performances of it squeezed into three weeks of December. A love-hate relationship by the end.

I studied Jana furtively as she prepared my tea. She looked heavier. I might not have even recognized her from behind. There was a dullness to her movements that made her seem heartbreakingly woeful and vulnerable.

Jana delivered my tea and stayed to chat. As expected, talk revolved around Nut. I told her about castings of Sugar Plum Fairy, Snow Queen and Rosebud—the soloist in "Waltz of the Flowers." Jana wanted to know which roles Carrie and Renata were dancing, and how the three of us split up the lead performances, which of the lower-ranked dancers had the Act II divertissement soloist roles, which corps dancers were being given that rare opportunity to dance a bigger role. I explained the impact Katrina and Javier's arrival had made, upping everyone's game, particularly the soloists, who'd watched in dismay as Anders gave Katrina two performances of Rosebud.

Behind Jana, someone called out an impatient, "Oh, miss!"

"Excuse me." Jana gestured to the customer. "I should go check on him. But first, what would you like?"

"Um, something that's not too big. What do you recommend?"

"People really like the club sandwich."

"Perfect. I'll take that."

Jana returned ten minutes later with the sandwich. She seemed eager to continue with dance talk while I ate. "It sounds like the gala went great."

I nodded, mouth full.

"I read all the reviews. You and Vincent Neumann wowed everyone."

I felt my cheeks go warm with pleasure. "Thanks," I said after swallowing my bite. "I think everyone did a brilliant job. Which, as you know, has an element of just plain good luck in it. Nothing went wrong."

"I especially liked the *Chronicle* review."

"Me too."

"I was so impressed that I cut it out and saved it," Jana said. "It's tacked onto my bulletin board. I think I've memorized it!"

I laughed, but Jana paused, shut her eyes, and recited. "'Guest artist Vincent Neumann and new company principal April Manning delivered a show-stealer in MacMillan's *Romeo and Juliet* balcony pas de deux scene.' And there was the bit about you. 'Manning's attitude turns and the airiness of her pointe work perfectly conjured a young girl's energy and infatuation. Her initial shy-girl body language was a brilliant contrast to the uninhibited abandon she later displayed as she leapt backward into Neumann's waiting arms.'" Jana opened her eyes. "Something like that."

My jaw had gone slack. "Wow! You *did* memorize it. Word for word."

Jana shrugged modestly. "It's a skill, memorizing. Dancers are good at that."

"Very true."

"That Vincent guy. Word around town is that he might dance with the company again."

I regarded Jana curiously. "Where do you get your information from, if you're not spending time with the dancers?"

"The Security guys are still my friends. And the ladies in Wardrobe. I sometimes slip in and visit, bring them cookies, or if there's something to celebrate, a cake. Reginald in Security will look the other way if I've got goodies and share them with him."

"Thanks again for bringing us those cookies in Santa Rosa. They were delicious."

"You're welcome."

"Anyway, the word around town is correct. Vincent will be back for two programs. In *The Sleeping Beauty*, he'll be Prince Desiré to my Aurora."

"Wow, what a prince. Lucky you." Jana sighed and her eyes took on a faraway look. "You know, I've got this picture of him from years back. I clipped it out of *Dance Magazine*, one of those issues where they did a feature on him."

I chuckled. "I did the same thing, actually. Probably it was the same article. I was still a student, and had such a crush on him."

"So did I!" Jana's eyes shone with delight.

"But we can never tell him. His ego is huge."

"Are you two, like, involved? I heard you looked absolutely like a couple, during the *Romeo and Juliet* pas de deux."

"Back in New York, we were, for a while. Now it's just friends."

It was the question the other females in the company asked, some casually, some simply with their eyes, trying to figure out if Vincent was available. Even Russell kept asking, as if I might have changed my mind.

Russell.

Suddenly I had the urge to share my secret with someone. "Want to know how I'm sure we'll remain just friends? I have a desperate crush on someone else."

Jana's eyes widened. "Tell me more!"

Just then, the cook pinged a bell and two plates of food appeared on the service counter. Jana signaled for me to wait as she sped off to deliver the plates to her customers. It gave me a minute to let the thoughts and feelings flow over me, something I restricted by day, allowing myself mere sips at a time, the sensations as potent as any drug. I could say nothing to Fiona, because Fiona remained critical of her brother. She wanted me to work harder at reeling in Vincent, so that he would make the move Anders most wanted—leave the ABT permanently for a contract with the WCBT. She wanted me to agree with her that Russell was a pain in the ass, and unrelatable. Fiona was sure Nicola had been the best thing to happen to Russell, and kept trying to persuade him to give the relationship a second chance.

It had made Thanksgiving Day rather hilarious. Fiona had organized a big dinner at Anders' house, inviting a half dozen of the dancers and staff. Fiona had invited Russell, as well, concurring, not without some reluctance, that real family should be part of the scenario too.

There'd been an adorable tension between Russell and me, given that the last time I'd seen him had been the night of that kiss. My mandate that he not call had worked in our favor; there was no way I could have successfully conducted a neutral-sounding conversation on the phone at the apartment, hyper-aware of Fiona's presence nearby. Instead I called him at work by day, sliding quarters into the payphone in the hallway of the WCBT, caressing the nubbled edge of the next quarter as we talked. It was classic infatuation-speak: voices lowered an octave, both of us chuckling over things that weren't particularly funny, talking about anything and nothing, both reluctant to hang up. On Thanksgiving Day, he'd come to our apartment to pick us up and transport us and the bags of food to Anders' house. A jolt of electricity had come over me when we'd locked eyes. It was a full-fledged crush. I hadn't felt this since the early days of Vincent.

His eyes, following me everywhere at Anders' place, told me he felt the same. When the two of us snuck away at one point to meet in a vacant upstairs room, his hands confirmed it. They slid under my blouse and around my waist to clasp my back. His lips covered mine, as my mouth opened to his, amid a dizzying hunger for more, more.

Jana's return to the table brought me back to the present with a jolt.

"So, tell me all about your new guy," she demanded, and I happily shared the details. Afterward, I took a reflective sip of my iced tea.

"We both know this is crazy and that we shouldn't even be trying. But that's just the thing. It's not 'trying.' The hard work is staying apart. Once Nut is over, and his big release has come out—and they land on the same week—we're going to throw caution to the wind. Five whole days together, free of obligation."

Spending it together was our Christmas gift to each other, we'd decided. I couldn't wait. Just thinking about it made me feel drunk with happiness.

I realized how self-absorbed I was acting. "But what about you? Do you have holiday plans?" I asked Jana.

"No."

"No close friends or family nearby, to meet up with?"

"No."

Of course. Too late, I remembered Alice's story, how Jana had been living on her own at age fifteen, no family support at all. For all I knew, she was an orphan, too.

"I don't hear from Carrie," Jana said. "Or Dmitri. Or any of the dancers. They've dropped me like I'm contagious."

A vicarious pang of sorrow shot through me. "Why Carrie?" I asked gently. "You were so close."

"She blames me for what happened to Sid. Said I distracted him and that's why he fell."

It shocked me, how casually Jana stated what everyone else had avoided discussing. "What happened?" I asked.

"We were at his house. I was feeling out of sorts. I decided to leave. Everyone was acting mad at me. Sid took me by the arm, and I shook it free."

A pleading expression came over her face, even though she wasn't looking at me. Outside, the rain increased. Two women darted into the diner, laughing, shaking the rain off their jackets. Jana seemed to not notice them, even when they looked around for someone to seat them or tell them where to sit.

"I loved Sid so much," Jana said, as if to herself. "I don't know how it happened, but he fell, and they blame me. As if I'd wanted to hurt him. I'd have sooner kicked a puppy than hurt Sid."

She gazed at me with agony. My throat tightened.

"Jana!" The owner strode toward her. "You have more than this one customer!"

In a blink, the agonized expression disappeared. She smiled at her boss. "Right away."

"Sorry!" I sang out to the owner, as Jana cheerfully greeted the arriving customers. She sat them at a booth, handed out menus, joked with them as she took drink orders.

It disoriented me, how quickly she could change moods, even personalities. I wasn't sure anymore which one was the real Jana.

Her other customers kept her busy. Once I'd finished eating, I slid a twenty-dollar bill under my iced tea glass and reclaimed my shopping bags from the floor. At the top, poking out, was one of the Chinatown scarves. The spare one.

I hesitated. Anders had told me to avoid interaction with the former dancers, the ones who'd walked out on their own volition. "Work on friendships within the company," he'd said. "Your peers." By which he meant Carrie. How to explain to Anders that Carrie had erected a wall between us? A glass wall, invisible to all others, yet one I bumped up against constantly.

And yet this was Christmas, the season of giving. Jana and I had formed a connection. We both understood the pain of having no family.

My aunts' scarves had been boxed, with gift ribbon bows. I confiscated one of the boxes and replaced the aunt's scarf with the spare, retying the bow. I left it on the table and rose to leave. Jana, confused by the sight of the box, approached.

"What's that?" She gestured to the box.

"A gift. For you."

"But why?"

"It's nothing big," I said, feeling awkward now.

"Can I open it?"

"Of course!"

Jana opened it cautiously, but when she saw the scarf, she gasped in delight.

"Something to make your holiday a little brighter," I said.

Jana stroked it in wonder. "Oh my gosh. Thank you so much!" Her eyes filled with tears, which she dashed away impatiently with the back of her hand.

"I'm glad it's finding a good home," I said. "It matches your eyes."

"I'll treasure it."

"Merry Christmas. Something to dress up your outfit when you go out with friends."

Jana looked ashamed. "I don't have friends anymore."

I spoke before thinking. "Well, I'm here," I said firmly. "And here's what I propose. Let's meet up in January. I'll come back when you're getting off your shift, and we can grab our own coffee."

Good Lord. What had I just suggested?

But when Jana nodded, eyes brimming with gratitude, I knew I'd done the right thing.

On the final performance of the run, three days after Christmas, I stayed by Anders' side backstage to watch the Act II variations.

Renata, Jacob and Fiona had already left for the break, so it gave me the chance to reclaim some of my earlier closeness with Anders. I'd danced Snow Queen with Holt in Act I, donning sweats beneath my tutu afterward and trading pointe shoes for the comfort of plush, padded slippers, which felt like heaven against my throbbing, wrecked feet.

Anders and I exchanged murmured comments through Spanish, Arabian, Chinese, Russian and Mirlitons. "I liked how these two danced together," Anders commented as James, the Royal Ballet new hire, and Alice took their bows after Mirlitons.

"I did too."

"James has been very solid through this whole run. Everything I'd hoped when I brought him on board. And Holt looked excellent earlier as your Snow King. How did it feel?"

"It was a lot of fun." While Holt couldn't match Dmitri's technique and charisma, his pedigree as a SAB-trained dancer was impeccable. He was a good, conscientious dancer and I appreciated his respect and deference, the solicitous nature of his partnering. We needed each other to succeed, to stand out as "dancers to watch" within the company, and tonight we had. He'd been so relieved over the performance's success, that backstage, he'd kissed me fiercely on the lips, before blushing and apologizing.

Alice and James hurried offstage and glanced anxiously over at Anders and me. I smiled at them and flashed two thumbs up. They relaxed and smiled back before the milling dancers obscured them.

We took a step further back to allow the next variation's dancers to assemble. "What do you think of young Javier?" Anders asked.

"He's amazing. He's got the skills of a soloist already."

"Agreed. I'll watch and wait, but I'm thinking I'll promote him and James to soloist at season's end. Their potential is enormous, and that should nicely make up for what we lost in August."

"What about the females?" I asked.

"Not so dire. Maybe move one up at the same time. Helena, perhaps. Or Grete."

"What's your strategy on Katrina?"

She and I had grown close recently, bonding when her parents canceled their Christmas Eve visit. I'd insisted to the inconsolable Katrina that she spend the night at my place, complete with hot cocoa, PJs and fuzzy slippers, and her first ever viewing of *It's a Wonderful Life*. Initially, we'd both been nervous, that uncomfortable, first-date, "what will we talk about?" feeling. But when I'd spied Katrina furtively wipe a tear from her eye, my mixed feelings had dissolved into something decidedly maternal. Supporting a young, homesick teen who hadn't seen her parents in over a year was easy, in the end. I knew all about missing one's parents. Any sense of unspoken competition—on my end, never on hers—evaporated, and like that, the evening had become relaxed, fun, a comfort to us both.

Anders sighed, a happy sound. "Katrina's is the kind of talent every artistic director dreams of nurturing. But she's young. I don't want to rush anything and risk spoiling what's flowering in her so naturally."

He stopped talking in order to watch the Mother Ginger dance. It was a curious one, with children spilling out from beneath Mother Ginger's oversized skirt onstage, like circus clowns emerging from a Volkswagen Beetle. More and more appeared, until they numbered a dozen. Mother Ginger was supposed to be an *en travesti* role, which meant a man dressing like a woman. But WCBT tradition dictated that the role belonged to Yelena, which made the variation even more clever and hilarious. Yelena, whose ugliness, girth and aggressive nature made her seem like a man already, was a brilliant mime, uncanny at imitating a man imitating a woman. She made broad, sweeping gestures, both flowery and garish, as her constructed skirt, the size of a boardroom table, swayed and billowed with every move.

Anders laughed out loud at one particularly overblown gesture. "What will I ever do without her?" he murmured, with a catch in his voice that surprised me. "She is such an original. She's a glimpse of the past, that will go missing once she retires."

"Is she talking about retiring?" I tried to keep the hope out of my voice.

"Two or three more years, she's saying."

Damn. "That's a long time," I said faintly.

He glanced at me in amusement. "You're not above learning from her, you know."

"I'm not of the school that advocates cruelty as a form of motivation."

"When you're the ballet master, you can enforce your own method of motivation."

"I'll keep that in mind."

The children finished their prancing and tumbling, and returned to their hidden places beneath her skirt, like baby quails seeking shelter. To the music's noisy climax, Mother Ginger lumbered her way offstage in a sideways, crablike gait. It always produced a moment of maximum chaos backstage, the too-big skirt, the overwhelmed children, the frantic parent chaperones who tried to corral their charges into orderly lines as quickly as possible. Meanwhile, the Waltz of the Flowers dancers jostled their way toward the front of each wing, preparing for their cue. Phil's amplified voice filled the backstage. "Ginger dancers, clear the way. Flowers, places. Twenty seconds to music. Ginger dancers *clear the way.*"

Anders and I watched everyone assemble. I felt a flutter of vicarious nervousness for Katrina, who made her way over to Anders and me in her jeweled, rose-hued tutu. It was her second performance of Rosebud in Waltz of the Flowers. The first time, she'd danced it beautifully. Her test now was to perform it just as well, at the end of a thirty-performance run where she'd been challenged like she'd never been as a trainee.

I reached over to give Katrina's hand a squeeze. It was icy cold. "Nervous?" I asked.

"No," Katrina squeaked.

I leaned closer. "It's okay to be nervous, you know. It doesn't make you a lesser dancer. I'm terrified before any lead role."

Some of the fear receded from Katrina's eyes. "All right. Yes. I am nervous."

"Good. It means you'll work harder to dance your absolute best." I gave her hand one more squeeze. "Go take your place. *Merde.*"

"You'll stay right there? You'll keep watching?"

"I won't move."

She hurried to take her place center stage, tucked away from view by six of the fourteen corps dancers, the rest of whom remained backstage.

"Quiet backstage," came Phil's voice over the speakers. "Cue music."

The opening melody line sounded, followed by a response from the harp. Two dancers appeared from the wings with a pique arabesque. Same melody line, four counts later, producing two more dancers. Each time a new dancer appeared, the ones already onstage bourréed over to the center stage pack of dancers. When they were all gathered in one center-stage huddle, they unfurled, like petals. As the harp music peaked, the dancers' arms dropped down to low fifth just as Katrina popped up into view, the bud of the group's flower.

Lights beamed down on Katrina in her sous-sus en pointe, legs pressed together as one, arms in high fifth. The transition from nervous teen dancer to professional was instantaneous. The stage makeup that had looked so exaggerated up close played wonderfully to the audience. She lowered her arms and began her first solo passage, all elegant long arms and legs, creating pure classical lines that made me sigh in satisfaction. I knew the audience was drinking it in, as well. Katrina seemed to have an instinctive knowledge of how to play to them, engage and delight them, employ her strengths, and tackle her few weaknesses with surplus effort.

In spite of my best intentions, that competitive feeling crept up. I was ten years Katrina's senior and her superior in the company hierarchy. But in three years' time, she'd be sharper, more seasoned and a formidable force. I was watching a Sonya/Natalia in training. Except a shy one with a pure heart. Katrina didn't even seem to understand how extraordinary she was. I knew, however, and it complicated things. My humanitarian instincts told me to support, with an open heart, the underling who might one day surpass me. This, even as my dancer's instincts were telling me to dance better than her, be better, rise higher.

If I had to choose to act on one instinct or the other, which would it be?

I prayed no choice would ever be required.

At the post-production celebration at L'Orange, Anders spied Russell. He turned to me, frowning. "I don't seem to recall extending an invitation to Fiona's brother. Was he at the performance? I assume he paid for his ticket this time. Because we already saw him on opening night, courtesy of your comp ticket."

I couldn't help but laugh. "Do you see who he's with? Roger, from your board of trustees. That's who Russell was sitting with during the performance. Roger had a spare ticket because his wife is out of town. Seems to me you should be thanking Russell for getting Roger here to L'Orange."

His frown deepened. "All right, don't push your luck."

"If you'll excuse me, I think I'll go join them."

"Keep it respectful with Roger. He's a big influencer."

"Anders." I eyed him in mock-reproof. "Have I ever let you down?"

"No," he admitted.

I worked my way through the crowd. When Roger saw me, his face broke into a smile. "Another excellent performance, April! Although that was no surprise to me."

"Thank you so much. It's good to see you again." I turned to Russell. "How did you like Roger's seats? They're good ones, I imagine. Better than my comp ticket seats?"

He nodded. "Great seat, great company."

"We were discussing the success of Russell's company's latest release. Well done, sir." Roger clapped a hand on Russell's shoulder. "And what are your plans, now that you have an actual holiday break?"

"Since April is off as well, I'm hoping to take her to explore north of the Bay Area."

"Hmmm." Roger looked interested. "Out of curiosity, are you thinking daytrip distance, or are overnights involved?"

Russell and I exchanged looks and shrugged. "I guess we haven't decided," Russell said.

"The reason I'm asking is because we have a vacation rental that we can't use. My wife and two kids went back to her family in Atlanta for Christmas. The plan was for them to return for our own getaway, but now she's asking that I join them there instead." He rolled his eyes. "A different kind of vacation entirely. But it's good for the kids to spend time with extended family, so I'll do it. Meanwhile, there's a charming vacation home just outside of Mendocino that will be going unused. Five nights in the Mendocino area. Nice little romantic getaway. Interested?"

"Yes!" Russell blurted out before I could process it all.

"But... we're not a couple," I told Roger.

"Yet," Russell quickly added.

I turned and met his gaze. He looked pleading. "Let's take it, April."

The thought made my head spin. We hadn't even been on a date or spent more than a few hours together. Five nights together would bring with it certain... expectations.

Roger seemed to intuit my concern. "It's a two-bedroom house, with ample living room space. I'm sure young Mr. Garvey would be a gentleman about giving you the space you need, should his attention and intention not be wholly reciprocated."

Still I hesitated.

"It would cost absolutely nothing," Roger added. "The arrangement was a thank-you for a favor I did for an acquaintance. No payment involved. And the owner is in Barcelona for the holidays, so the house will remain empty if you choose to pass."

"April." Russell seized my hand. "We have to do this. It's so perfect."

I eyed him, indecisive. "You'll behave?"

Russell nodded, excitement building in his eyes.

Roger, seeing it as well, smiled. "Go have fun. Both of you. You two are so young, yet so serious about your lives and your work. Which is excellent. But the down time is equally important. That's how we become whole human beings. Balance. Although it strikes me as rather hilarious that I'm telling a ballet dancer to make sure to have balance in her life."

"The irony is that professional ballet dancers *aren't* balanced about their lives," I admitted.

"Those who rise to the highest ranks rarely are. I myself am a mere beginner in learning about finding balance, as my wife is always telling me."

He looked from me to Russell and back to me. "So, we have a deal?"

What the hell. Anders would be having his good time with Sabine, who was arriving the next day and staying for a week. Why shouldn't I have my own fun?

"All right," I relented. "But, Roger, don't tell Anders I'm doing something hedonistic. He's not looking for me to become better acquainted with that kind of balance."

We all laughed, and suddenly I felt giddy as a child.

Work hard, play hard.

Fair trade.

Chapter 16

Mendocino

Russell drove me home. This time he accepted my invitation to come in; we had a trip to plan, after all. Fiona was gone, her first Christmas with her family in three years. Her plan was to fly to Denver a few days later and meet up with William and his family. After New Year's Day, the two of them would drive back to California, where William would claim his new apartment and commence the long-awaited job in San Francisco.

It was a very different environment with Fiona out of town. No imminent chaperone presence. The two of us sat side by side on the couch, newly awkward and insecure. Or perhaps I was the only one feeling that way. Russell, meanwhile, was off on one of his stream-of-consciousness rambles.

"We should plan to bring both heavy jackets and light jackets. And good socks. Do you have good hiking shoes? I'd like to hike lots. And eat at Café Provence and Johnny Burger. Mendocino is great. They have a fantastic bookstore. You told me you love to hang out in bookstores. You'll love theirs. It's a good time of the year for whale watching. We'll want to bring binoculars. And we'll have to shop for food stuff for the rental. We can do that as we get closer. Well, except there are only small grocery stores once you get past Santa Rosa and Petaluma. Small-town stuff. We should start a list."

The clinical nature of the discussion made the earlier excitement drizzle out of me, replaced by unease. Five days was a very long time. I felt a sudden, desperate urge to back out of the whole thing. I was robbing myself of personal time, coveted reading time. What if we started bickering, like he and Fiona always did? What if the fault lay inherently with Russell and his personality, as Fiona was always claiming?

Russell finally seemed to sense my unease. He fell silent. A moment later, he took my hand. "Hey. I just want you to know, this isn't about trying to get laid. I swear. I wouldn't disrespect you in that way. We can just go as friends, each with our own room. I mean, we haven't even been on a real date yet, have we?"

"No, we haven't." The tight feeling in my chest eased.

He shifted around so that his back came to rest against the arm of the couch. He gave my hand a gentle tug. "Come here. Let me just hold you. I'll stop talking."

Good. I let him draw me gently closer, until I was draped over his semi-reclining body.

Pelvis to pelvis.

Nice.

Electric.

In spite of his erection now pressing against my lower abdomen, he didn't rush to take it any further. He gently stroked my back and I began to relax into him, my clenched muscles releasing their grip. Tension left. The joy rushed back in.

I raised my head, my chest, propping myself up by my elbows. My hair hung down like a curtain, framing my face, spilling onto his chest. He reached up, cupped my face in his hands, brought my face closer and kissed me. In an instant, all thoughts subsided, leaving behind a heady understanding that everything between us made sense, this foray into deeper involvement. It was relaxed, natural, really quite uncomplicated.

We proceeded slowly. Russell now seemed hyper-aware of how I was reacting. Our hands had slipped under the other's shirts to roam bare skin, but the shirts themselves remained intact until I cast mine boldly aside, prompting him to do the same. The decision to stay on the couch—safety zone—held another thirty minutes, until I rose, took him by the hand, and led him to the bedroom. I slid off my slacks, climbed into the bed and held out my arms to him. He hastily shucked his jeans before joining me. His body was shaking as he slowly lowered himself over mine. I found it utterly disarming.

No rushing. Instead we continued to neck like teenagers. A half-hour passed before the last bastion of safety, my underwear, came off, in a graceful little shimmy. He watched, eyes round, mute with something that seemed to straddle the line between gratitude and awe.

And finally, there we were, two naked bodies, and nothing on earth could compare with the sensation. As a ballet dancer, I'd had ample experience of skin being pressed against bare skin. The contemporary ballets gravitated to the skimpiest of costumes, sometimes without tights, where your partner, in order to lift you, grabbed at your bare inner thigh, your armpit, your waist, holding tight wherever the hands landed, and the physical intimacy was easy because it was never sexual.

But this was a world apart. Feeling Russell's private parts match up against my own felt as intimate and mind-blowing as the actual act of penetration. Better, even. Penetration was still something to delay here, as we continued on our journey of getting to know each other's bodies. Vincent had never mastered the art of foreplay and pleasing the woman; he'd assumed I'd wanted what he wanted, to have him inside me as soon as possible.

Russell wasn't Vincent, in a dozen different ways, all of them surprising and gratifying. Even now, he'd made no assumptions as to where the action might go. At one point he propped himself up on his elbows and whispered, "April, I have no condoms. I didn't think that—I mean, I could only dream this might happen. ... That is, if this happens."

He was so adorable.

"I keep some in the bathroom," I whispered. "I kind of didn't see this coming so soon either. Wait here."

I eased myself out from under his embrace and skittered, limbs and hands shaking, to the bathroom, the medicine cabinet. I pulled out the box, ripped it open hastily and yanked out a ribbon of six. I raced back to the bedroom, holding them up like a prize kill.

"Tell me I'm not pressuring you," he said. He sounded anxious.

"You're not pressuring me. I want this. Here. Now. It feels right."

"Good." He gave a great exhale of relief as he pulled back the covers for me.

I climbed back in and we held each other, now both of us practically fibrillating with excitement, yet going no further, not yet, because sometimes when you're handed the biggest gift in the world, you want to slow down and savor it.

Mendocino was paradise. It was ocean, scenery, pleasurable diversions, amid a charming, picturesque little town. One day, the fog hovered, creating a dreamy, insular world, and it was perfect. Another day was sunny and cloudless with a brisk ocean breeze and it was perfect. Another day it rained, and it was perfect. We ate out and it was sublime. We bought food and made our own meals and they were sublime. We talked and it was as if we could keep talking forever. We basked in long, companionable silence and it felt equally natural, without a hint of awkwardness. We held hands whenever we could. We slept pressed close against each other, limbs overlapping, shoulders touching, hands reaching out to pat the other through the night, an unconscious, mostly asleep gesture, as if to confirm that, no, this wasn't a dream. It was really happening.

We walked along trails on the headlands, rising high above the crashing surf, and inhaled the fresh ocean air. Mid-mornings, we wandered in and out of shops. Mendocino was small and could be navigated wholly in a day's visit, which left ample time for us to return to the house, make love and take a long, luxurious nap, arising for a late afternoon walk and a sunset view over the Pacific Ocean. Half the meals, we ate out, and I was so impressed by Russell's first-choice restaurant, we ate there twice more.

We whale-watched. We hiked. With no television, we put music on the stereo and read the books we'd bought at the local bookstore, a charming three-room structure, cozy as a house, with a silky long-haired cat who wandered around as though she owned the place, deigning to accept the pets and caresses of the store's patrons.

One morning we stepped into a jewelry store, where Russell gave me an impromptu lesson on metallurgy and the alchemy of gold, silver, what made white gold still gold if it wasn't gold-colored. "What style are you?" he asked me as we passed by the designer ring display counter. "Ornate or plain?"

"I don't wear jewelry much," I admitted. "Some of these just look so busy."

"So. Plain?"

"Not boring-plain." My eyes roamed the display. "There." I pointed to a diamond ring that stood out from the rest. A big stone, a cathedral setting in gold. "Elegant, simple, tasteful. And probably ungodly expensive."

"Good thing looking is free." He took my hand. "I'm hungry. Ready for lunch?"

"I am. Lead the way."

The vacation house had an enormous back yard, surrounded by dense, high hedges on one side and nature on the other two sides. Within the cloistered space was a wooden deck, table and chairs, and, curiously, an outdoor shower area with an adjacent, wholly exposed, enormous claw-foot bathtub. "Who's going to use *that?*" Russell had asked, laughing, when we first spied it, the night of our arrival.

"A dancer," I'd exclaimed, hurrying right over to fiddle with the faucets and test the water's temperature. When it began to gush out hot water, I'd squealed in pleasure.

A hot outdoor bath for me became part of our nightly routine. Russell would put on music and light a dozen tea candles, strategically placing them throughout the yard and on the deck table. I'd soak in the steaming bath, suds collecting on my shoulder, my chest, as I sipped a glass of wine and we talked. I felt so enamored by it all. By Northern California, with its contradictions—chilly, dark, winter nights, made mysterious by nearby growing palms, olive trees interspersed with firs, the scent of jasmine filling the night air from the crisscrossing vines on the wooden trellises that flanked the back door. It was wintertime but not. It was an unlikely, unexpected slice of heaven.

We went to bed early but stayed awake into the early morning hours. Post-lovemaking, we exchanged confidences, childhood stories, spooned up side-by-side in the bed.

"And so Fiona stuck her mint gum into the tuna noodle casserole when it was just us kids eating," Russell said. "When I started to complain, my mom told me to stop attacking my little sister. She refused to listen to what I had to say. The meal was just for us kids; she and my dad would eat out later, but this night, she decided to sit and have a serving with us. Alison's eyes were bulging—she saw my mom take the section that had the mint gum—but she didn't say a thing. Fi looked terrified. We all ate it very quietly, and only at the end did my mom say, 'Hmm, that tuna tasted minty.' None of us said a thing in reply. So, see? I could have ratted out Fiona and she would have gotten into trouble, but I kept my mouth shut."

"Mint tuna casserole. Man. The things I missed, being an only child."

"Truly."

"Do you see yourself as ever having a family?" I asked.

"Family, as in, kids?"

I nodded.

"Sure. In a vague, hypothetical way. Like needing to get reading glasses at some point, or going all grey. I imagine they'll happen."

"I'm sort of surprised," I said.

"Why?"

"You're a math and technology guy to the core. It's your world, like physics was for my dad. A lot of childless bachelors in your line of work."

"You may have a point."

"I'm certain my dad would have gone childless, had there not been the surprise of my mom appearing in his life when he was fifty-two. I think she was just as surprised."

"How old was she?"

"Forty."

"How'd they meet?"

"At the library where she worked. It's a very cute story."

"Tell me."

"He was on his way to a group dinner, but had this manic urge, en route, to obtain a copy of some scholarly article, to share with his colleagues. Normally he would have just used the university library, but instead he dropped by the library closest to the restaurant. He approached my mom at the reference desk and told her what he was looking for. It took a half-hour for her to find it, mostly because they kept wandering off topic, sharing bits about themselves to each other. My mom told him stuff about herself, thoughts and concepts, that she hadn't realized were inside her. And for his part, he opened up to her in an entirely different way for him. They shared discovery after discovery. This whole new world, unfolding before them. He, a confirmed bachelor for life, she a spinster librarian. Neither of them had even considered marriage in their respective past relationships.

"Think of it." I shifted around until my head settled against that perfect spot, between his shoulder and neck. "I'll bet they thought for sure that they'd already figured out life and how the rest of it would unfold for them. And one chance encounter in a library forever changed that."

"The group dinner?"

"He missed it. He likely never gave it a thought once the two of them started confiding in each other. You know my dad. Once he'd locked in on a fascinating concept, it was tunnel vision. My mom was that fascinating concept. It's really touching to consider. She'd never seen herself as a beauty, a catch. Lois and Sally were the beauties, Aunt Irma the vivacious one. My mom thought of herself as a mere afterthought. Until my dad appeared." I fell silent, sad yet comforted by the memories.

"My mom forever divided her life into two segments," I said. "Before that meeting, and after. She told me that she woke the following morning as a different person. Someone had found her special, attractive, interesting. Singular. She said they both knew, by the end of that week, that they'd marry. They'd found each other, and now they'd walk through life side by side, through everything. And they remained in love. They'd gaze at each other from across the breakfast table every morning and there'd be these goofy smiles on their faces, which drove me nuts around adolescence. I was embarrassed to be around them in public when they got that way, holding hands, murmuring endearments to each other. I told them it was disgusting. It wasn't. It's the most beautiful thing to consider now."

Hot tears worked their way up and out, rolling down my face. "Now that it's been over a year since I lost Mom, I can almost be glad that she didn't have to suffer his absence for decades. She was enough of her own person to find personal happiness after he died, but I know it was hugely diminished, and that she never stopped loving him, missing him."

Russell's warm hand stroked my back. My tears were dripping onto him, which made me laugh through them. "Sorry about the puddle." I dabbed at it ineffectively.

"No problem." He reached over for a Kleenex and handed it to me. "Your parents were lucky."

"They were."

"Maybe there's hope for someone like me some day, after all."

"My dad is up there in heaven nodding emphatically."

"Nicola seemed to think dancers didn't marry, didn't have kids."

"What Nicola doesn't know about dancers is a lot," I said.

"Does that mean you don't agree?"

"I do not."

His hands tightened around me. "Good to know."

On the morning we were to leave Mendocino, we took a long walk along the headlands. It was chilly and foggy, and both of us were deep in our own thoughts. On the return he stopped suddenly and looked at me. "I don't want this to end," he said.

"This getaway?"

"No. This. Us. I know things are too busy with work for us both, but I want to try."

Euphoria battled with reason. The luxury of it, after all. The warmth and security.

But reason spoke first.

"There's a dozen reasons why it won't work, Russell."

"Name one."

"I work days and nights."

"I do too."

"You said yourself you're far too busy and involved in your work to have a girlfriend."

"That was different. I didn't want to make time for Nicola. I know that sounds awful, but that's how it is. I was never in love with her."

"And now?"

His steady gaze met mine. "I'm in love with you."

My breath caught. So it could happen that fast. Be that unequivocal. Vincent had never once spoken those words—it was a mind game that had left me forever insecure.

"Russell. It would be crazy."

"So was leaping into a startup."

"What if it doesn't work?"

"What if it does?"

Elation hovered outside the conversation, politely tapping at the window to be let in.

Russell and I stared at each other in silence. The tapping grew insistent. Hammering.

If you don't try, you'll never know.

"I want to try too," I heard myself say.

"Oh, April." Russell pulled me close and enfolded me in his arms. I could feel the warmth of his body, hear the thump of his heart. "I'm so glad. We won't regret this."

I sincerely hoped we wouldn't.

January 1991

Chapter 17

Back to Work

January and the return from layoff revealed a new West Coast Ballet Theatre. I myself felt like a completely different person. Sex did that to you. Falling in love did that to you. It created an altered existence, a double life, built on the stolen moments and evenings Russell and I could squeeze in. But what became paramount in importance, once I entered the front double glass doors of the WCBT each day amid a growing, unspoken sense of urgency, was this: the repertory season was about to start up, and everything mattered.

Everyone at the WCBT took their jobs seriously. Every last person worked harder. Choreographers and their stagers returned to assess the progress the dancers had made. Loretta from PR appeared more frequently, with teams of journalists and photographers in tow. Another day, she escorted a group composed of major donors and sponsors, those giving tens—and even hundreds—of thousands of dollars in support, and in turn getting a coveted peek "behind the scene." Anders seemed to be everywhere at once, chatting up the donors he himself had reeled in, murmuring with Charlie Stanton, both of them in suits and ties, a startling daytime change in Anders. Larry and Phil showed up constantly, talking to Jacob and Anders about this and that. Fiona did her best to keep up with Anders, dashing around with dozens of small tasks every hour. Wardrobe went into overdrive, preoccupied with fittings and costumes for all the productions, particularly *The Sleeping Beauty,* the season's fourth program.

And there was conflict. Because that, too, seemed an incontrovertible facet of the WCBT.

My conflict with Dmitri intensified during rehearsals for a ballet in Program III called *Havana Nights,* where he was my partner. Bob was the ballet master in charge today, where it seemed Dmitri and I couldn't agree on anything—the pacing, the musicality of certain passages, the distinct salsa flavor that tinted everything, even as the pointe work remained precise and classical.

"It should be smoother before and after the lift passages. Your hips shouldn't bump mine there," Dmitri said.

"But that's the salsa section," I pointed out. "It's all about the hips."

"Who's done this ballet before? Three different seasons in the past eight years."

I watched the archive footage of this, I wanted to retort. *Not once but four times.* But I sensed the ensemble dancers' irritation, so I shut my mouth, gritted my teeth, and did it the way Dmitri mandated.

Worst was the ballet's third movement, a distinctly sexy adagio. Midway, Bob stopped us and instructed me to "go more boneless" against Dmitri's body. I was all but splayed against his chest, like a just-cracked egg that spreads in every direction at once. Dmitri's back was arched, supporting my body at an incline. My back rested against his chest, my head and shoulders arched as if in sexual ecstasy. His hands reached around to caress my waist, my chest. Never mind that I had a flat chest and thus little concern about his hands roaming too high. The problem was that it now felt so blatantly sexual in a way it hadn't, back in the fall.

It was Russell. My continued deep sexual attraction to him—the stolen hours with him since Mendocino had revealed an animal hunger in us both—had made me approach this passage from a different physical place. It felt as though my sexuality were now something wafting off me, in a way Dmitri couldn't miss. I knew I was right a few minutes later, in the way he regarded me once Bob paused us to consult the accompanist on tempo. "Dear, virginal April," Dmitri murmured in my ear, "I do believe you're sleeping with someone."

I hated the way I blushed almost as much as I hated his smirk. "That's no business of yours," I snapped.

"It's plenty of my business. You are my dance partner here and this is a very physical ballet. You're moving differently against me. I'm a little embarrassed for you."

He wasn't embarrassed in the least. But I was. Which had been the point.

"Let's take that passage again, please," Bob called out.

It was a dreadful rehearsal.

Vincent's inclusion in Anders' new ballet, scheduled for late spring, was a big relief for me, not just because I enjoyed partnering up with him, but also he was a buffer against Dmitri's intensity. Lexie, who covered the role when Vincent was in New York, would never contradict or challenge Dmitri. In truth, none of the dancers would.

Anders remained noncommittal about which of the two couples—Vincent and me, Dmitri and Renata—would be first cast. I sensed Anders was doing it simply to keep Dmitri on guard.

Vincent returned in mid-January, with a few days to spare. The number of ABT roles he had for their season had been reduced, ironically because Sonya and Kirill were faring so well there. "I can't believe it," he griped to me. "They've come from the paltry WCBT and he's stealing roles from *me?*"

"How's Natalia doing, next to Sonya?"

"Oh, she's holding her own." He sounded aggrieved. "Being a damned show-off, if you ask me. Drawing all this attention to her. And just toying with the men. It's disgusting."

"Really? I never noticed." I hoped I didn't sound too bitchy.

Vincent looked quizzically over at me. "Seriously?"

"That was sarcasm, Vincent."

Vincent's gaze turned woeful, puppy-eyed. "She broke things off with me. In December."

"I'm sorry. My condolences."

"It was her coming on to me last year, April. It wasn't the other way around. I was loyal to you, to the end."

I rolled my eyes. "I'm sure you fought valiantly."

Anders approached Vincent with a broad smile. "Good to have you here," he said, clapping him on the shoulder. I knew Anders would love for Vincent to be a permanent member of the WCBT. The snag was that Vincent could and would command an enormous salary, and Anders didn't have a big enough budget. One Vincent equaled two soloists with the potential to become principals in their own right, in a few years' time. But finding the money was yet one more miracle Anders vowed to make happen.

Our rehearsal for Anders' ballet reminded me what a supremely good partner Vincent was: intuitive, strong, efficient, trustworthy. Lexie was there too; Anders supported his efforts as an aspiring choreographer, and he welcomed Lexie's ideas and feedback. Lexie had been the one to suggest the toss, gleeful and prosaic, as though I were a bagful of laundry. From center stage, four male corps dancers launched me, and Vincent caught me from three feet away. He kept a sure grip on me as he spun me around his body and lifted me overhead. He dropped one hand as I balanced on his other, keeping my core as rigid as possible, so it looked as if he were balancing a plank of wood on the palm of his upraised hand.

"How do I get her down?" Vincent cried to Anders, his voice high with the strain of holding me. "You haven't shown us."

"I'm still not sure," Anders said. "You tell me. Do what's fun."

"Let me grab my feet," I gasped out. "Like a bow." I arched back and grabbed both ankles to become a human hula-hoop. Vincent, caught by surprise, managed through impeccably timed grabbing and sinuous body waves to rotate me safely to the ground. Once back on my feet, I took his proffered hand and leapt back into his arms, as Anders had earlier choreographed. My arms were looped around his neck, which struck me as too traditional and helpless for someone who'd just hula-hooped her way to the earth, so I released my arms, arched back. From this inverted place, I caught his leg from behind as my own legs cartwheeled out of the pose. I finished in a triumphant standing pose, hands on hips. Vincent stared at me, dumfounded by all my elusive wriggling, and I thrust out my hand impulsively for him to shake.

Our eyes met as we shook hands, a firm grip that seemed to represent an arm-wrestling battle of wills. *I've changed,* my eyes told him. *The impressionable girl is gone.*

His expression was easier to read. *What the hell?!*

By this time, everyone else was whooping with laughter and clapping.

"I love it," Anders called out, still laughing. "That handshake ending, especially. Please tell me you can duplicate the whole thing."

"You're kidding," Dmitri burst out from behind us. "You would actually keep that in?"

"I would."

Renata looked pleased. "I hope she can duplicate it. It looks fun."

"Let's try." Vincent cast a flickered glance at me, as if to say, "you don't have it in you to be that spirited, twice. ... Or do you?"

I did. We ran it again, and again. The passage was lightning-fast, a mere eight counts of music from the time the four corps men launched me, a human cannon ball, to the moment Vincent and I shook hands. Anders refined it all from there, adding emphasis to certain held poses in order to expand the moment.

"And that handshake," Anders said. "Both of you should have your feet firmly planted. Have your shoulders be facing one another. It's a meeting of equals."

Both Vincent and Dmitri snorted at Anders' words. Renata and I exchanged grins.

"Our turn." Renata gave Dmitri a nudge.

Vincent cleared the center area and ambled over to flirt with the girls gathered at the door, watching. I retreated to the sidelines to watch Anders run the passage with Dmitri and Renata. It worked.

Dmitri seemed to be in a private sulk about it. "I don't like it," he said in a haughty voice.

"That's a shame," Anders said. "Because I do."

"You decided to use April's idea just because you want to aggravate me."

"No, I did it because I am both the choreographer and the artistic director."

The mood shifted abruptly.

"I have more power here than you think," Dmitri said in a low, menacing voice.

"Is that so?"

It became a stare-down. Vincent was now chatting with one of the soloists, and together they walked over to the accompanist at the piano. I stood there, frozen, like Renata, both of us watching Dmitri and Anders. A shiver of fear came over me. I'd thought we were done with this kind of hostility.

Illogically, I wanted to run to Vincent, tug him back over. He was always telling me Anders would be fine, that Dmitri's toughness was an act, and I was overreacting. I wasn't. This was proof.

"Anders," Vincent called out, seemingly oblivious to the dynamics. "Remember that ballet we did together six years ago, with Larisa and Marie-Claire? I'm blanking out on the music."

"Tchaikovsky," Anders replied, his eyes still on Dmitri. "One of his string quartets."

"Which one?"

Anders sighed in impatience and glanced over at Vincent. "Can this wait?"

"No! We need your wisdom. Come over here—give us twenty seconds."

"Twenty seconds, no more," Anders warned, as he walked over. "I'm paying you to rehearse, not chit-chat."

And like that, the mood broke. I drew a shaky breath and sat myself down, taking the opportunity to untie my right pointe shoe and readjust the cushion layer between my tights and the shoe box. Rewrapping the spongy panty-hose knee-high around my toes, I heard Dmitri grumble something to Renata, his voice low and angry.

"But he's *not* Sid," I heard her say in response. "And Jacob is second in command, not you."

"Who's third in command?" Dmitri challenged.

She chuckled. "Why, that would be me."

"You're on his side. You're supporting him over me, your longtime colleague. With whom you have such a history."

"I am." Renata sounded unruffled. "It's the wisest, most logical thing to do. I'm puzzled that you've yet to implement this thinking. Drop the politics, my friend. I have. I'm just here to dance. There will be no dramas, no accidents on my watch."

I'd been sliding my pointe shoe back on, but at Renata's words, my hand froze.

She was referring to Sid's accident.

I saw, out of the corner of my eye, the way Dmitri had nervously glanced my way.

"What?" Renata asked. "She knows the story, right?"

Dmitri said nothing. Instead, he took Renata's hand and led her into a dance, something waltz-y and whimsical. He dipped her, nuzzled her neck, which made her laugh and bat at him. "You're changing the subject. And it's cruel of you to go teasing a divorced woman like that."

"Do forgive me, *carissima*," he murmured, smiling, as he straightened her and spun her in a half-circle. She planted a kiss on his cheek before reversing the spin. They stood there for a moment and exchanged a look of affection that surprised me. It made me grateful to have Renata in the company with us. She seemed to be the bearer of keys that unlocked mysteries.

Except for the story she thought I knew.

Chapter 18

Jana Again

"What is this about your meeting up with Jana?" Fiona asked me when I walked into the apartment that evening after a long day of rehearsals.

I eased down my bulging dance bag onto the hall table and regarded Fiona in confusion. "I have no idea what you're talking about."

Fiona gestured to the kitchen, where the answering machine was stationed. Still baffled, I followed her into the kitchen and pressed the machine's play button.

"Hi April!" Jana's bright voice filled the kitchen. "I know the plan was for you to contact me when you had the chance in January, but I'm kind of worrying now that maybe you lost my number, and I know the end of January is Program 1's opening night, so I thought I'd just ring you."

Shit. I'd forgotten all about the promise, made that long-ago December day.

I stared at the answering machine in dismay as Jana chattered on.

"I know Monday afternoons tend to be light for dancers, what with no performances on Monday nights. I work weekends and so Monday is like my Saturday. That would be a great time to meet up. So, call me back. I'm excited to get together again!"

"Tell me that's not Jana who left the company," Fiona said.

"It is."

"Haven't I heard Anders say he didn't want you befriending the dancers who walked out?" Fiona crossed her arms and regarded me in disapproval.

"It's not what you think," I said. "I saw her last December and I felt sorry for her. Her friends from the company have all dropped her. True, she was the one to walk out on a contract. But she seemed so sad and alone, the day I saw her. The invite just slipped out. I'd all but forgotten about it."

"Then do forget about it. Don't call her back."

I opened the refrigerator and pulled out a Diet Coke. "That's not very charitable of you."

"I know how Anders feels. This is about supporting him."

Over supporting your friend, I felt like saying, but we were on more tentative terms these days, tiptoeing around the new reality that I was having a sexual relationship with the brother she didn't get along with. It had been made worse because Anders had been the one to break the news to Fiona a week earlier. He'd been peeved at me for some reason, as if sensing how my loyalties had shifted, and when Fiona, more devoted to him with every passing week, said, "I don't know what's with you lately, April," Anders had replied with, "You know she's sleeping with your brother, right?" A wave of terrible heat had come over me, making me feel momentarily faint. There'd been a plan, not yet implemented, for Russell and me to break the news more gently, discreetly. It was as if Anders grabbed this and used the announcement to show me who was boss.

Fiona, to her credit, had cast Anders a cool, amused smile and said, "How could you think I wouldn't know that? She's my roommate." And Anders had nodded, as if in deference that he had underestimated Fiona's fine instincts. I was furious with Anders over it, but kept the same amused expression on my face, and when Fiona met my eyes with a *ha, ha, Anders doesn't know women and their intuition so well,* I felt a closeness with her that had been seeping away since her return to California with William.

"I made a promise to Jana," I said now as I poured my Diet Coke into a glass. "Maybe I regret having done that now, but it's done, and I keep my promises. She has no family, no support system. I just want to help in this small way."

I watched impatience and frustration crease Fiona's brow before finally she shrugged. "It's your life," she said. "I'm going to be heading out here shortly to meet William for dinner. We're going out for Thai. Want to join us?"

I was secretly relieved to have the place to myself. "Thanks for the offer, but I think I'll stay put and make myself a little pasta. See you later tonight?"

The casual question. Would Fiona and William stay over here, or would Fiona join William overnight at his place? If the latter, I would be on the phone to Russell in an instant, telling him the coast was clear and, yes, come up after work to spend the night.

"Yes, you'll see us here." Fiona smiled back at me. "Want to watch a movie together?"

I swallowed my disappointment. "Sure. Thanks for including me. William's great."

Just the mention of William's name made Fiona's expression grow dopey with infatuation. "He is, isn't he?" A sigh slipped out and in a happy reverie, she returned to her bedroom to dress for her date.

At least the issue of Jana had been quickly forgotten.

Thank you, William.

On Monday afternoon I met Jana outside the café she'd chosen. She was waiting for me, an eager smile on her face. The tables inside were all occupied, so we took our coffees to go. We walked along Market Street, wrapping our jackets tighter against the chilly January breeze. We talked about odds and ends, mostly dance-related topics. Jana liked to talk, in particular, about *The Sleeping Beauty* and its rehearsals. The fiendishly difficult Rose Adagio. The dreamy nature in the Act II Vision pas de deux versus the "mature" Aurora in the third act Wedding pas de deux. Costumes. Sets. The other dancers. It was easier, this generic dancer-to-dancer shop talk, than to try and broach the mysteries of the past.

We were approaching the terminus for the Powell Street cable car, where Market met the beginning of Powell. It was, for some reason, devoid of its long, snaking line of people waiting to get on. "Omigosh, let's ride it!" Jana broke into a run. "Hurry!" she cried over her shoulder. And in a laughing rush we bought tickets and hopped on board just as the conductor was sounding the bell. We clung to the pole between us, hanging out the side, letting the air slap our faces, and laughing. It was such a reversal from the way Jana had been the last two times. Suddenly she seemed more like Fiona, the less disapproving one from last fall.

"See that guy?" Jana gestured to the man operating the car. "He's the gripman. My first love here in San Francisco was a gripman. I would hop on board and just stare at him, watching him work. I was so in love!"

"What does a gripman do?"

"He's the one who connects the car to the cable underneath the street. It runs all the time, and he can start and slow down the car just by grabbing or releasing the cable. It sounds easy but it's harder than you'd think. My sweetie had been doing it for years. It showed. He was a distinctive bell-ringer, too. He let me ring his bell a few times." Here she broke into giggles. "That sounded obscene."

"You mean, like that disco song from the 70s?"

She pointed a finger at me in delight. "Yes! 'Ring My Bell.' That was it." She began to hum the song, then, to my embarrassment, sing it, loudly.

"*You can ring my be-e-e-e-l-l-l. Ring my bell. Ding dong ding,*" she sang, off key.

Others on the cable car were now glancing over at us. Jana seemed to be in her own world, not noticing. She rotated her pelvis and shimmied her hips and snapped her fingers like she was in a 70's disco. I felt a distinct prickle of unease. Was Jana just utterly unself-conscious, or was she a little ... off?

Abruptly the singing cut off. "What about you?" Jana asked. "Have you had your bell rung by that guy you were crushing on, last time I saw you?"

I found myself nodding, a smile breaking across my face.

Jana's eyes brightened. "Tell me! Tell me everything!"

I shared some of the details about our Mendocino trip, reveling in the fact that, not only was I free to divulge all the details, but that Jana wasn't frowning in disapproval. The cable car trundled up Powell and Nob Hill as I shared choice bits that made her expression come alive. I found I wanted to make her smile, hear her laugh. Make her feel as though someone cared. She had no family, no support system anymore, after all. In that, she and I shared something the others couldn't understand.

After a left turn, then a right on Hyde, the cable car traveled along the crest of one of the city's biggest hills, and we cooed with admiration over the view of the bay and the hills beyond. We gaped and gestured, like everyone did, at Lombard Street, that famed crooked street that seemed absurd, almost fake, particularly considering people lived in those houses, with driveways and garages and cars parked all along the freakishly curving street. We were both in good moods as the cable car route terminated down by the waterfront. For our return, Jana suggested we take something different, the F Line trolley. "It's as cute as the cable cars, actually, and very historic," Jana said. "It'll make a nice loop and we'll see different things."

"You're the boss," I told her. "You know much more about this city than I do."

Jana seemed to like this. She smiled as we boarded but grew quiet as the trolley headed back toward Market Street. The animation fizzled out of her. Her shoulders sagged. I could feel the air around us growing heavy, negative.

"Hey," I said. "You okay?"

She shrugged. "Yeah, sure. Just another day in paradise. Thank you, Anders Gunst."

This was so not what I was expecting her to say, I almost asked her to repeat herself.

"What does Anders have to do with things right now?" I asked warily.

She shot me a look of scorn, reminiscent of the Jana I'd first met. "You're kidding, right?"

I didn't know what kind of reply she was expecting.

"The way he ran me off," she prompted.

"Like, back in August?"

"Of course. When else?"

"Anders didn't 'run you off,' Jana." I tried to sound gentle. "You left. If anyone, it's Dmitri you should be blaming. He persuaded the group of you to leave, and then tricked you all by not walking out. It was a terrible thing for him to do."

She shook her head. "You're wrong. Dmitri loves me and supports me. Anders tricked him, too. It wasn't Dmitri's fault things turned out the way they did."

I stared at her in disbelief and decided right then to let it drop.

An awkward silence settled between us. I didn't know what to say next. It was complicated, the way Jana acted so normal sometimes and so... off, the other times. Like the transients you saw on Market Street, a disloyal thought I banished from my head the moment it arose. Jana was nothing like those people. Nothing like the guy standing near me in the bookstore the other day, who began softly murmuring to someone—or so I thought. Polite, thoughtful dialogue. When I glanced his way, I realized he was alone, and had been the whole time. He was schizophrenic, all the sadder because he otherwise seemed so normal, like someone's brother or cousin, with family who cared. His gaze darted around a moment later. "Let's get out of here," he murmured. "The CIA has received word." He began rubbing his hands vigorously together as if he were washing them under hot water. "Are you up for this?" he asked the air in a low, conspiratorial voice. "They might try to make us talk. Use the probe." The experience had horrified yet fascinated me.

I felt terrible for comparing Jana to that guy. I looked over at her, this discouraged, once-rising star ballerina. She was slouched, her body no longer ballerina-slim but fleshy, although not as heavyset as when I last saw her. I thought back to Alice's speculation that Jana suffered from hypothyroidism. Jana's medication seemed to be doing a better job now than it had in the fall. Surely a bittersweet irony to her, now, when being thin didn't matter so much.

"You've lost weight since December," I offered, to cheer her up.

It worked. "You think?" she asked, her eyes lit with hope.

"Definitely. More like a ballet dancer again."

The last bit had been an exaggeration, but it made her smile in pure delight.

"Aurora, here I come," she sang out. "Guess I'll go buy some pointe shoes!"

I laughed, even as confusion swept over me. Her eyes had taken on the same determined glint as when she'd accused Anders of derailing her career. Surely she understood her ballet career was over. Surely she was joking now. "I'll clear out space in the dressing room for you!" I joked back.

"Perfect!"

"Yeah!" I faked a heartiness in my voice and shifted my gaze to the passing scenery.

To my relief, she followed my cue, looking out her own window. For the rest of the ride, neither of us spoke.

Back on Market and Powell Street, we disembarked. "Thanks," I said. "That was a lot of fun." I refrained from saying, "Let's do it again." I understood it needed to stop here, this friendship-but-not, for a variety of reasons. She seemed to understand this too.

She seemed like a lesser person now, all bravado and good cheer gone. I sized her up in sympathy and a sense of growing concern. "You okay?"

"Sure."

"Do you need to take a taxi to get home?"

"No thanks."

"I'll pay for it," I added.

Jana hesitated. "No thank you. I'm fine."

No, you're not, I wanted to say, but we were back to being strangers. With an ache in my heart, I watched her walk down the street until she turned a corner and disappeared.

Chapter 19

Katrina & Yelena

Katrina and her prodigious talent had emerged as a threat. I saw it sweep over the company's females like a bad case of the flu. As a principal, I was safe, and could afford to befriend her, even champion her. I'd earlier harbored this illusion that I could pair up Katrina and Alice and we could be this chummy trio, with me serving as wise mentor and the two younger girls united by their status as corps dancers. But the skeptical look Alice shot me while we were all in rehearsal for the contemporary ballet, *Almost Sunday*, where Katrina effortlessly tossed off a soloist's passage that was new to her, told me it wasn't going to happen. Alice knew she wasn't Katrina's equal; none of the corps females were.

Katrina was a new addition to *Beauty* rehearsals, having recently been made third-cast Aurora, replacing Marilyn, who was now forth-cast Aurora (read: understudy). She was furious about the demotion. If looks could burn, her glare at Katrina's back would have singed her.

Today we were rehearsing the Act III Wedding grand pas de deux. Like in most of the rehearsals, Yelena simply ignored the third cast, leaving them to stand in back and mimic all the moves. As the two-hour rehearsal ticked on, Yelena maintained her focus on the second-cast leads, Dmitri and Carrie. Katrina had confided to me her concern about never having received any instruction or attention beyond the trickle-down nature of watching from the rear, so at a pause, I asked Yelena if she might consider running a passage or two with the third cast. She stared at me, incredulous. "Because, well, you've never watched Katrina and Lexie together," I said, willing myself not to shrink under her gaze. "She's new to the role; it would help."

She said nothing, letting her withering glare speak in place of words.

I ducked my head. "Or not," I mumbled.

"We continue," Yelena snapped. And yet, less than two minutes later, she stopped Dmitri and Carrie. "You two, go to the back. And you"—she pointed and curled a finger at Katrina and Lexie—"come here. Same passage."

We were rehearsing the passage where Aurora ran to Prince Desiré, who'd descended to one knee, and she stepped into a penché arabesque, leaning into him until their faces were close as could be without kissing. From there it led up to a dramatic passage on the diagonal, the music thundering, with fish dives. When done well, the passage was one of the most unforgettable moments of the pas de deux and when it was done poorly, it looked awkward.

Lexie and Katrina ran it. It looked awkward.

They ran it again. It looked even worse.

"No!" Yelena said to Katrina each time. "You must hold your core."

"I'm sorry. I'm sorry," Katrina said. She looked miserable. The other dancers were growing restless. Dmitri cast me dark, accusing looks. Holt, Vincent's proxy, sighed and dropped to sitting.

Again. Lexie swept Katrina off her feet a millisecond too soon and it looked sloppy. Her shoulders bobbed when he locked her in the fish dive. When he hoisted her back onto one foot, en pointe, the other leg in an attitude devant, it looked like work, as though she weighed 150 pounds, rather than ninety.

"Stop, stop!" Yelena screeched. "This is mess, all of it. Fish dive pose. It must be solid like rock, foolish young girl."

She had Katrina and Lexie hold the pose—no easy feat, as they were both at a downward incline. He gripped her around the waist to keep her from falling, as she, in a face-down diagonal, held on precariously with her core muscles and her back leg. Yelena slapped at Katrina's shoulders and she visibly flinched.

"No! Like rock!" She slapped Katrina again, and Lexie nearly lost his hold on her.

Yelena had them take the passage from the start again. It looked, if anything, worse. "No!" *Smack.* "Not that!" *Smack.* "Stupid girl, are you doing this on purpose?"

The words burst out of me. "Maybe she'd do better if you stopped slapping her."

Yelena spun around to face me, enraged. "You know all the answers? Then *you* be ballet mistress. You with all your answers." She whirled around and stalked toward the door, where she paused, as if awaiting my cringing apology.

The tension that had been building in me of late exploded like an overinflated balloon. "Fine," I shouted back. "I will."

She stared at me, thunderstruck.

"I am leaving," she announced theatrically, and swept out of the room.

A stunned silence followed. I turned to Lexie. "Has she ever done that before?"

He slowly shook his head.

"Good job, April," Dmitri called out from his place next to Carrie. "Because those of us not in cast one were really hoping for more attention from Yelena today. So, thank you."

I decided I was just as sick of him, too. To hell with my detractors. I could be the ballet master. If it hadn't been for Yelena's rage, I might have even been pleased. "Fine. Let's start back up." I strode to the front of the room and faced the other dancers. "Hurry it up," I snapped when they only gaped at me in confusion. "Lexie and Katrina, places. Now."

"You are so out of line here," Dmitri told me, his voice rich with amusement.

I marched over to him and gave him a hard push on the chest. "Shut up and move. You heard Yelena. I'm in charge."

"She wasn't serious," Dmitri retorted.

"Yeah? Well, I am. Now move."

He sneered and mumbled under his breath in Russian, but he moved.

I drew a deep breath and when I next spoke, I made sure to sound calm, reasonable. "Let's slow down and see what isn't working on the fish dive passage," I told Katrina and Lexie. I cued the accompanist—the likeable Herbert today, not Chess—and Lexie and Katrina ran it through.

The same problem occurred. Katrina lowered her head. "I am so sorry," she murmured. "This is my fault."

But I didn't buy that. Much as I liked Lexie—who was nodding at Katrina's words—he was green as a partner here. This was his first year of taking on the ballet's lead role. This passage, the success of *The Sleeping Beauty* as a whole, required that the two lead dancers work in perfect synch. When I had them run it again and the same clunky outcome occurred, I decided I was on to something. "Dmitri," I called out.

Dmitri, from his spot with Carrie and Marilyn on the side of the room, eyed me peevishly. "You said you didn't want me there."

"I changed my mind." Observing his set face, I realized, with distaste, it would require some kowtowing. "I think it's no overstatement to say you're the best Prince Desiré in the room, if not the whole company. Would you do me a favor and run the passage with Katrina while Lexie watches and observes how it is best executed?"

I watched suspicion battle with self-righteous pride as he debated my request. "All right," he said, as he released a theatrical sigh. "I was supposed to be rehearsing anyway, after all."

Lexie conceded with an easygoing shrug and stepped to the sidelines.

"Take it from the spot when you meet center," I instructed, and cued Herbert at the piano.

Dmitri and Katrina took their places. To the music, they met and she shot into a perfect penché arabesque. They separated, danced their way back to center, where he promenaded her in a back attitude en pointe, one arm in high fifth. After a full circle, she released his hand and perfectly held her pose, unsupported. The music crescendoed, cueing high drama; time for the tricky fish dive passage.

It was amazing. I watched how Katrina set herself up perfectly, using his arm as a bar to wind herself up and spin, a clean inside double pirouette, after which he grabbed her waist, scooping her off her feet the instant she tilted forward. Her left leg shot into arabesque, the right leg following, artfully angled behind, as he dipped her, and before you could fully analyze the pose's perfection, why it worked so well this time around, he'd pulled her up and into a regal attitude devant, and they repeated it all. And a third time, holding the final pose a beat longer, both of them unmoving, perfectly positioned, they became a living statue. The dazzling effect achieved made everything in me go silent in awe. It was night and day from how she'd danced it with Lexie. It was as if Katrina were made for this—dancing with a senior principal, holding her own while even as, paradoxically, she gave in to his energy, his propulsion.

"Keep going," I called out, because I didn't want them to stop. I wanted to keep watching the exquisite ballerina Katrina had become. Everyone else did, too. I could feel it in the air. We were all witnessing something remarkable.

They stopped, finally, and I found my voice. "That went well," I said.

Understatement of the year.

"It did," Dmitri said, and I could tell that he, too, had been taken by surprise.

I turned to Lexie. "Did you see the way he had his arm around Katrina's waist, but waited until she angled her body forward, a hint off balance, before he pulled her off her feet?" He nodded. "And after that, when you've got her deepest in the dive, try not to give into the momentum, which is the thing that's making her head and her shoulders bobble around."

"Got it," he said, with a decisive nod.

Dmitri grandly accepted my thanks, and returned to Carrie and Marilyn, as I worked with Katrina and Lexie on the next section. A sense of well-being and calm spread through me. I found a curious psychic relief in not being the dancer but instead being the one with knowledge and objectivity and a visual image of the end product that, together, we could work toward.

A few minutes later, Fiona appeared at the door with Yelena by her side. "April?" she called out. "Anders is hoping you might have a minute."

Judging by the triumphant look on Yelena's face, I likely had more than a minute. My newfound confidence evaporated. Did Yelena have the power to pull me from my first-cast role? Heart hammering, I kept my expression perfectly neutral, ignoring Yelena, ignoring Dmitri. I felt like apologizing to Katrina.

Instead I slid my feet into my bootie slippers, grabbed my
sweater and left.

Anders, to my surprise, didn't seem angry with me. Inside his office,
he invited me to step around to his side of the desk. There, he
gestured to a poster board that held costume design sketches. "This
was just dropped off," he said, and I bent closer to study the detailed
illustrations. They were beautiful: jeweled gowns and elaborate tutus.
Royal robes of deep red velvet and ermine, finely detailed costumes
for the princes and the courtiers.

"Costumes for *The Sleeping Beauty!*"

"Yes."

"They're absolutely gorgeous. But... how? There's no money, no
time, to create these for the spring production."

"One can only dream. We'll be repeating the production next
season. I want potential donors and underwriters to know this is
something I really want, and really value, and they should, as well.
Better costumes mean a better production. It has to start now, if only
the dialogue about how we plan to pay for changes like these."

"Anders, that's wonderful!"

"It is. And it's all about networking, increasing awareness, being
proactive."

I sensed he was about to spring something on me, like how this
all came around to the fact that I was on Yelena's hate list and how I
planned to remedy it. I was all set with a craven (if not honest)
admission of guilt over my unspeakable rudeness in reacting to
Yelena, but he surprised me.

"So. Have you spent time outside work with Carrie and Curtis?"

I stared at him, baffled. "Um, excuse me?"

"Have you made any efforts to increase your circle of friends
within the company?"

"Of course I have," I sputtered. "There's… There's Alice. And Katrina. And…"

He cast me a skeptical look. My hands, making circles, fell to my sides. "No," I admitted.

"But you have found time, apparently, to meet with Jana."

His words, the expectant expression on his face, shocked me. So Fiona was a snitch, a spy. Or had someone seen us? Maybe Carrie found out and told Anders.

I explained about the chance encounter at Marshalls. The one at the diner. How it had absolutely nothing to do with Jana following me or displaying any malicious behavior. The coffee and cable car ride had been following up on a promise. End of story.

Anders studied me solemnly. "Stay away from her. She's a wild card. Maybe she's got a sad story to tell, or she struggles with health issues. The life of a dancer is hard, period. Why would you go befriending an ex-dancer when there are thirty-five other dancers here that you could be better friends with? Carrie, and now Renata. These are fine women, impeccable role models. Renata, in particular, is amazing. Intelligent, principled, witty, well-read. She shares your love of books. She's got a music theorist's knowledge of classical music. She loves fine wines."

And you've clearly gotten very friendly with Renata, I thought.

"It staggers me that you don't work harder to cultivate those kinds of relationships," he continued. "Instead, you run out at the first available opportunity to spend time with company outsiders." His lips pinched together in distaste as if the last two words had been bitter.

Company outsiders. A clever way to group both Russell and Jana into one category.

"I get it." I smiled politely at him. "I am to be best friends with Carrie and or Renata and resume my affair with Vincent, because

you want Vincent to sign a contract with the company, and there's
no better lure than sex."

This was new for us, and not in a good way. Anders' eyes went
cold, but only for a moment. He offered me the same polite smile.
"Please stop by HR during one of your breaks and share with Megann
what you've told me about your meet-ups with Jana."

"I will."

"And let Fiona in. She's eager to support my efforts, not hinder
them."

"How am I hindering your efforts?" I protested.

"Never mind. Just let her in. I'm sure she's right there."

Sure enough, Fiona darted right in the moment I opened the
door, like a cat inadvertently left in a closet. She ignored the scowl I
shot her way. The two of them began murmuring about an event he
planned to attend the following night. I started to leave until I
realized we hadn't discussed Yelena. I hesitated.

"Anders? The issue with Yelena?"

His eyes took on the irritated look I'd expected all along. "Do we
really need to have this discussion? Are you going to try and defend
your actions in any way?"

"No. Except..." My voice trailed off.

"No. No 'except' about it. It's her show. She runs it the way she
sees fit. She's been doing a fine job for the company for forty years
and I am not about to run her off with demands that she change her
style."

"But she was being so cruel toward Katrina."

"Katrina was trained by some of the toughest women in the
business. She can handle it. Yelena's style is more shocking to you
than it is to Katrina. Trust me."

"All right. Look, I'm sorry about the disruption. I was just...
tense. Things have been eventful, of late."

"There's something you can do about that, as well."

Stop dating a ballet outsider.

I smiled brightly. "I'll bear that in mind," I trilled. "But in the meantime, I think my time is best served going back to rehearsal. Focusing on my dance during work hours."

"Excellent idea. Carry on, then."

Chapter 20

The Big Stumble

"I knew we could make this work," Russell said whenever we successfully spent time together. The first time he'd declared this had been back in early January. It was my layoff still, and I'd spent two nights and three days at his place, a continuation of Mendocino's hedonism. I'd slept in, enjoyed a long, relaxing workout at his gym, made us elegant, multi-course dinners. At the time, I hadn't bothered to bring up how that kind of routine could only be my life during layoff weeks, with the other forty-two weeks proving much more tricky.

"We're still making it work," he said after opening night of Program I, and the night, the following week, where I managed to rehearse all day, perform at night, and still spend the night with him.

"We are," I agreed, opting not to mention that I didn't sleep well on his mattress, and that being newly in love, however glorious, exhausted me.

But glorious, it was. It filled the room we were in. It filled the apartment, the city, the whole universe. I'd look at him, beside me in the kitchen, quietly peeling carrots or scrubbing at a pot I'd dirtied, and my heart would swell to a point where it almost hurt. Other times, he'd smile at me from across the room and I'd feel a rush of such heady delight, it was as if I'd won the lottery. Sometimes at night I'd dream that he wasn't a presence in my life, and in the dream, I'd feel such an ache, an existential sense of loss and emptiness. I'd wake to find Russell lying there next to me, and I'd almost weep with gratitude. I'd thump up against him and wrap my arms and legs around him. In his sleep, he'd give a little wriggle that allowed me to fit next to him even more tightly, and he'd tuck my hand closer to his chest. I'd lie there awake, feeling no need to fall back asleep quickly, because being awake to this reality in my life, the staggering good fortune of true love, was a gift.

It was a tentative gift, however, fragile and vulnerable as a newborn. It could be snatched away, just like that.

January rolled into February. The physical stress, the adrenaline of performing, the upheaval of being newly in love, began to take its toll. On the positive side, I told myself, mid-month on a Wednesday, the season's second program would finish on Saturday night and focus would return, for two weeks, to rehearsing by day and regenerating by night.

After Friday's performance, Russell picked me up and we went to his place so we could sleep together without worrying about Fiona and her judgmental scowl. But Russell's cheap, old mattress had lumps, and the result was that I woke up Saturday morning with a knotted muscle under my shoulder blade. Within an hour, the knot had summoned all the neighboring muscles into a cramp-fest. It hurt to breathe. It felt like the time I'd broken a rib, except in my back. Russell was horrified by the way I winced and the fact that his bed had done this to me. And shocked to hear that, even though I couldn't raise my right arm without pain, along with my other issues, I still planned to dance that evening.

It was all typical performing-season pain, I assured him. True, my right knee was killing me. Joint inflammation that flared up for no reason, had me double-dosing on ibuprofen and putting a bag of frozen peas on my knee in twenty-minute doses. This, on top of a throbbing sacroiliac joint. It was Russell's first view of how professional dancers powered through, while their bodies were in continual pain, one spot or another. When I was unlucky, it was four spots at once. But to stop dancing every time something ached was inconceivable. The WCBT, like most generous-sized professional companies, had a physical therapist, massage therapist and an on-call orthopedist day in, day out.

"I'll be fine," I assured him. "I'll get in to see the massage therapist two hours before curtain. She knows how to tackle exactly the right spots. In the meantime, let's go to your gym. An hour of stretching will do me good."

The gym visit didn't help, and Russell eyed me worriedly over lunch. "This isn't good. Your body needs a break."

"I'll be fine," I repeated. "I've got two hours to rest."

"You need more than that. You need days. Weeks."

"So do you."

"No time."

"Ditto."

"April, I can walk without limping."

"I can dance without limping."

"This is insane." He didn't look happy.

"Russell." I laid a hand on his arm. "This is not your problem. It's mine. I don't need your suggestions. I don't want them. You can't understand the world I inhabit. Don't try."

At his insistence, we stopped at a Walgreens and he bought a heating pad, and from a nearby store, a therapeutic mattress pad to roll over his crappy mattress. "I'll buy a better mattress soon, I promise," he said.

When we returned to his place, I looked at my watch. "I've got that massage at six o'clock. If I'm going to rest, I should do it in the city, at my place. That way I won't have to rush."

"You won't have to rush anyway. It's Saturday. No rush hour."

I hesitated and he stepped closer. His eyes took on that look, the one that told me he was planning to run his lips down my neck, the base of my throat, that little hollow above my clavicle that he knew made me faint with desire. I laughed and held up one hand. "Promise me you can get me back to the city by five-thirty."

"I promise."

His mouth found my neck. His hands slipped under my shirt and found my back. I emitted a little groan, half desire and half defeat. He chuckled, a vibration I felt against my neck, before he lifted me up and carried me to his bed.

Half an hour later, both of us spent and relaxed, I glanced sleepily at the clock. "Time for me to move."

"No." His grip around me tightened. "Not yet. You feel so good."

"Promise you'll get me up to the city on time?"

"Of course. Just lie with me for a little longer."

"Okay."

I fell asleep. I half-woke when I felt him move, rise from the bed. "Wake me in twenty minutes," I murmured.

"Okay. I'll be right back. Got to write down some things while they're in my head."

But when I opened my eyes again, the afternoon light was gone, and I saw to my horror that it was almost six o'clock.

"Russell!" I cried out. "What happened?"

He came running back into the room, looking as distraught as I felt.

"Oh, love. I'm so, so sorry. I got swept up in work and forgot all about the time."

We tore out of the apartment. A car, double-parked, blocked his car and it took ten minutes of honking and shouting to find its owner. An accident on northbound Hwy 101 slowed traffic to a stop-and-go crawl for mile after mile. Traffic jammed as we approached the city, people seeking Saturday night fun. I began to emit panicked gasps, all but crying. At a gridlock on Ninth Street well before Market, the most gridlocked of all San Francisco streets, I flung myself out of the car in order to sprint the mile to the theater. Call for dancers was seven o'clock. It was now 7:45pm, and as luck would have it, tonight I was in the first ballet.

I made it in under ten minutes, panting, dashing down the backstage corridor, where shocked faces met mine. Undisguised contempt on some of them, delight on others (no surprise, Dmitri). Relief on my understudy's face, a corps girl not yet ready for the big leap. I dressed right there backstage with the help of two dressers as the makeup artist gripped my face in his beefy hand and expertly applied the makeup needed. I put on my pointe shoes and tied the laces with shaking hands, fingers numb and clumsy. There were only seconds to spare as the dancers warming up cleared the stage. I myself could only do a few desperate pliés, tendus, rondes de jamb, développé a leg and grip my heel, pivoting the hip around to stretch anything that would be at risk during the killer workout to come. Phil's ever-steady voice said, "Dancers, places," and "thirty seconds to curtain" and four of us leapt out once the music began.

It was an impeccable performance. Which went to show you how capricious the fates were, because if ever there were a night to deserve a bad performance, this was it. I almost wanted it to happen, have a fall or something, to atone for my ghastly transgression. Instead, the reckless way I pushed myself through each movement translated into something marvelous: the pirouettes endlessly precise, quadruples where normally there were triples; leaps that stayed sky-bound for an extra millisecond, adrenaline from the two-hour commute nightmare now spilling out into my movements. I saw Anders watching from the wings and could almost feel his rage. But each time I leapt offstage, he kept his distance, likely recognizing that to interrupt the trance I'd placed myself in might jeopardize the rest of the performance.

The ballet ended, to wild applause. Curtain call didn't last long enough, even though we were all called back for a second bow. Finally the heavy velvet curtain descended for the last time. Sweat-soaked, utterly spent, my limbs shaking—they hadn't stopped shaking since I'd leapt up from Russell's bed—I limped offstage, within the safety of the other dozen dancers. But Anders appeared, and nobody wanted to be around him when he was clearly enraged. My people-shield evaporated in seconds.

Anders sized me up. He radiated pure contempt. "If you're done performing for the night, feel free to leave. You seem to have less and less interest in being here to support the others. All the dancers who were here on time, all the backstage personnel, all the people who invest all into every performance."

"Anders—" I began.

He cut me off with one hand.

"Plan to come over to my place Sunday night, at which time you and I will talk. Right now, I'm so pissed off with you, I know I'll regret anything I say on the matter."

It was worse, somehow, his controlled rage, the awareness that I'd have to wait twenty hours to attack this issue. He'd already walked away, leaving me to stew in my flimsy explanations, my craven apologies.

I walked down the brightly lit hallway. I ignored the people I passed, dancers who seemed amused, if not downright entertained, that tonight's high drama revolved around silly April and how she'd been sleeping at her boyfriend's, in a post-coital daze, uncaring of the hour. The thought made me feel physically ill. This wasn't me. I didn't like this April with the lowered standards. My craft felt tarnished.

I finished taking off my makeup, the room fortunately free of Renata and Carrie. I opened the messages that had been tacked to the bulletin board outside our door, one from Fiona and two from Russell. Reading them, a groan of despair slipped out. They were both waiting for me at the apartment. I had no appetite for what was to come.

It was bad. I heard them shouting even before I entered the apartment. These two people I loved so much—I hated seeing them in this ugly, unforgiving light. "Get along!" I screamed at them, instantly as unhinged as they were. "Solve your differences once and for all! Or at least be mature and rational about agreeing to disagree. You're family. You're supposed to be on each other's side."

To my surprise, Fiona turned on me in a fury. "Guess what, April? This *is* family. The arguing, the fighting, the getting under each other's skin. You think being family is all comfort and warmth. Well, I'm here to tell you, it's not. I'd trade places with you in a heartbeat. *You* have the overachieving siblings. I'll be the only child."

Her words enraged me. "Yes! Let's switch, Fiona! So I can have living parents again! And to have a brother, a sister, someone to call family when those living parents drop dead too early."

"You see?" Russell said to me. "Even here, Fiona's just thinking about herself and not the fact that you've lost both your parents and don't have family."

"Don't act like you're guilt-free here, Russell! She's your sister."
"Too bad for me!"
Russell's words sent Fiona rushing to the phone. She called William, asking him in a shaky voice if she could come over. Right

then. She'd take a taxi. She hung up and within minutes was gone. Meanwhile, unbelievably, Russell seemed satisfied that, with his sister gone, all was fine again with us.

I thought of Anders' reaction, the rage and disgust on his face. What the hell had I done?

This would never have happened if I were dating a dancer. My anger at myself for putting work second was as strong as my anger toward Russell. Stronger, in fact. He could have sweet-talked me out of anger directed toward him. He couldn't, however, over anger toward myself. The more stubbornly he tried, the angrier I got. This was not a thorny line of code he needed to modify to produce the result he wanted. This was not an equation to be worked to death.

"Please go," I told him. "Leave. Now."

"April." He tried to seize my hands and I pulled them back, wrapped my arms around myself as if I were cold. Which I was. Shaking, icy cold. Like my voice.

"Hear me out. If you value our relationship—that is to say, if this is a relationship we plan to continue, because right now, that's a big 'if' to me—you will go home and stop trying to pressure me. You have put my career at risk tonight because you deemed your own agenda a greater priority. No. I stand corrected. *I've* put my career at great risk tonight. I'm not ready to forgive myself. And there's nothing you can do to change that."

If I hadn't been so angry with myself, so adamant, the woeful look in his blue eyes might have made me change my mind.

But there it was.

He left.

Chapter 21

Dinner with Anders

On Sunday night, Anders greeted me at his door with a smile that offered no clues as to what was brewing beneath the surface. "I thought we'd cook," he said as I stepped in.

"Sure," I said. "Sounds great!" Because that alone was what you said to your angry boss.

"Pad thai," Anders called over his shoulder as I followed him into the kitchen. On his gleaming forest-green granite counters, I saw the ingredients, in their ordered places. Rice noodles were soaking in a large bowl. A quartet of tiny glass containers each held ingredients, like tamarind pulp, fish sauce, chili pepper flakes, sugar. A clutch of green onions were stacked next to limes to be quartered, shallots to be peeled and chopped, peanuts to be crushed and sprinkled atop the finished product. In the kitchen sink I saw shrimp thawing in a colander, dripping from the water he'd run over them.

"Wine?" he asked.

"Yes, thank you."

"Red or white?"

"Definitely white, with pad thai."

"Agreed." He poured me a glass of wine and topped off his glass.

I gestured to the assembled ingredients. "Where should I start?"

"There's a chicken breast in the refrigerator," he said. "I think we'll scramble two eggs to add to it, as well. But for now, let's chop. Shallots?"

"Sure. Minced?"

"Yes, please."

"Done." I seized one of the cutting boards and butcher knives from nearby and set to work.

At first, we didn't speak, which served to relax something tight in me since, in truth, the return from layoff. It had been too long since the two of us had done something like this. Then again, the easy equanimity of our early days here—myself newly arrived, Anders the only one I could call a friend—was gone. Who knew if it was a permanent thing? Had it been avoidable, or just how these things went? Like Fiona and myself. A pang of grief shot through me. Back in August I'd seen such a different trajectory. Old friends, working together in the same dance company, a dream-come-true scenario. Both of us helping Anders, the charismatic, driven new boss we both admired and believed in.

We talked about work. It seemed to be the safest topic.

"What's your take on the status of *Havana Nights?*" he asked.

I loved it when he asked my opinion. "I think it's coming along nicely. During that onstage run-through on Wednesday, everything fell into place. I think Dmitri and I have finally worked out our differences."

"I agree, and it shows. The second cast still has a few bumps to iron out. I might have Bob focus on just them this coming week."

"Good idea."

"I'm going to give Javier a performance as the male lead, with Renata, one night. See how he runs with it."

"Wow." I eyed him with interest. "That'll be big."

"Agreed. But I think he's up to a big challenge." He tossed shallots into the pan, where they sizzled and shimmered in the hot oil.

An easier silence settled between us. He pulled out a shredded green papaya salad and set it on the counter. He reached for the wine and gestured to my half-empty glass. I nodded. A pleasant buzz had settled over me. It didn't cross my mind that he'd waited for that moment on purpose.

"About last night," he said, in that same chatty tone, as he poured, capped the wine and returned it to the refrigerator. The words hung in the air. He smiled at me, which seemed cruel, unlike him, more like Dmitri.

"Yes?" My heart began to pound against my chest, so loud I wondered if he could hear it.

"You do that again, I'll put you on probation. You do it a third time, I'll fire you."

We stood there, looking at each other, the only sound in the room the hiss of frying shallots. "Do I make myself clear?" he asked.

"It won't happen again." I forced the words out through numb lips.

"I asked you a question."

It was like being a kid again, my father towering over me, his normally placid, friendly face replaced by anger, such a rare occurrence, it would terrify me that much more.

"Yes," I whispered. I cleared my throat and tried again. "You made yourself clear. And it won't happen again."

He studied me coolly, not releasing that piercing gaze of his. My knees shook. I reached for my glass of wine and thought better of it. I'd only spill it, with the way my hands were trembling.

Would he follow through on his threat and fire me? Could I really lose the position I'd spent twenty years reaching for? Was it really that perilous for me?

Apparently it was.

"Good," he said, and turned his attention to the sizzling pan. I gripped the counter so hard my knuckles turned white. I coached myself to breathe, breathe.

But that was it. He said no more. Not that I trusted him for the next twenty minutes, as we continued to prepare the food. He knew how to effectively attack and disarm. I'd been on the receiving end of it so infrequently. It was an excruciating place to be.

We took our food to the table and ate. Even in my stressed-out state, I found it delicious. Toward the end of our meal, the phone rang, and Anders excused himself to take the call. I could hear the warmth in his voice that he reserved for Sabine. I smiled, relaxed, knowing that he, too, would return to the table more relaxed.

And yet, something didn't match up. The conversation was too closely linked to San Francisco and the WCBT studios. I heard him say, "I need to get back to April and dinner. Why don't we hash this out tomorrow, in my office?"

I strained my ears to catch what he said next. Silence, as he listened. Then, unfathomably, he switched to German. He chuckled over something his caller said, before concluding with an *"Einverstanden. Tschüss dann, bis Morgan."*

Sabine never spoke German with him. Sabine couldn't be in the WCBT studios tomorrow; she was in Brussels. I realized, with a sense of shock, that he'd been talking with Renata. In that intimate tone.

Renata and Anders were close. Dangerously close. Did Sabine know? Was I getting it wrong? When Anders returned to the table, I focused on my pad thai, trying to pretend I hadn't heard what I'd heard. He, too, seemed more interested in eating than talking.

Something rebellious rose in me. He'd threatened me, my job. He'd done the alpha male thing that he was entitled, as my artistic director, to do. And yet, I decided, that shouldn't make him above reproach.

My indignation built. I planned my attack much in the way he'd planned his, waiting for the moment where he seemed off guard. "So, how was Renata?" I asked.

I'd been hoping for a dropped jaw, alarm in his eyes, or simply a grudging nod of respect that I'd guessed his caller's identity. I got nothing.

He met my eyes. "She's fine. Shop talk."

That was the baffling part.

"Gosh," I tried. "You two have become so friendly."

No reply.

I cleared my throat nervously. "May I pose a question in candor without the risk of your ripping my head off?"

He regarded me warily. "You can try."

"Okay. What would Sabine say?"

He gave a snort, devoid of any mirth. "She'd likely be glad."

This was not at all what I'd expected. "Why?" I asked.

"She knows I'm lonely." He started to say more, but stopped.

"Anders." I waited till he looked up from his food before I continued. "There's something big here that I'm not following. Could you please elaborate?"

He sighed and waited a long moment, probably in the hopes that I'd get bored with his non-response and change the subject. I didn't.

"Sabine won't be joining me here in San Francisco."

I stared at him in confusion. "You mean during the dance season. Too busy, and all. Right?"

"I mean, my stupid, hopeful, naïve plan that I stupidly, hopefully invested in."

A memory came to mind, the dream he'd confided at their housewarming party, this yearning to share the artistic directorship with Sabine someday. "Anders. Please tell me more."

He set his fork down. "She has no interest in moving out here. Visiting, yes. Changing jobs? A decisive no."

"So… where does that leave things between you two?"

"I don't think one can call it a 'separation' when one is already separated by 5000 miles."

The two of them were *separating*?

He met my eyes and nodded. "She actually asked me if I wanted a divorce."

"Anders, no!"

A child's terror crept up in me. Anders and Sabine *had* to stay together. Their relationship was my North Star, proof that you could be a professional ballet dancer and still find love, have a happy marriage. I couldn't bear to consider them going their separate ways.

I thought of Renata. "You don't want a divorce, do you?" I asked, and instantly regretted it.

Anders slapped his hands down on the table so hard the dishes rattled. The wine in the glasses sloshed. "What do you think?" he shouted. "That I would have suddenly, overnight, lost my love for her? My hunger? My longing?" His voice broke.

It was as if only now I was seeing the real Anders, the one with uncontrolled, messy emotions. He terrified me. Not because he seemed threatening, but because his pain was so raw, so huge and feral.

"That's it for the co-artistic directorship of my dreams," he said grimly. "And the bitter irony is that I'd successfully floated the idea past the board of trustees, just last week. All the subtle building up to it, and now I have to find a way to back out of all of it. It makes me look weak, indecisive, like I don't yet have a full grasp on what I'm doing, where things are going."

"What about a different co-artistic director?"

"Absolutely not. It was to be Sabine, or no one."

"When did you and Sabine have this conversation?"

"Saturday morning. It was stupid timing. Her mind was on their performance that night."

And on Saturday evening, his new principal, his key supporter, almost no-showed for the performance. I felt sick with the shame of it all over again.

"I'm so sorry, Anders. For everything."

He abruptly rose from the table. "Doesn't change a thing," he said, and began stacking platters and dishes on top of his half-finished plate. Before I could say anything more, he strode to the kitchen where, a moment later, I heard the hiss of water running.

Dinner was over.

Cleaning up helped calm him. Together we worked, in silence, until the room was clean.

"Renata brought me a chocolate torte yesterday," he said, gesturing to a white bakery box on the side counter. "Would you like a slice?"

"Yes, please."

I sliced and plated two pieces as he made coffee. This time we ate in the kitchen, on sleek bar stools he'd acquired since I'd last been here. The torte was good, one of those dense flourless kind, rich texture, pure cocoa, butter, and not too much sugar. I chose my words, my conversation topics carefully. I didn't want him to blow up again. At one point, though, he eyed me irritably.

"I'll be fine," he snapped. "Quit tiptoeing around every subject."

"It just that I care," I said.

His eyes met mine. He didn't speak, but his frown dissolved. "Thank you. And see that you continue to care."

He said no more, but I got it.

Care about the things that matter. Not people. People are expendable. Unreliable.

Dance. Only the dance mattered.

Chapter 22

Dmitri's Move

Dmitri had seemed highly entertained by my fall from grace. On the positive side, he didn't act as snippy and critical as he had in the past. It dawned on me, by Thursday, that maybe it wasn't about the previous week's drama. He was acting differently toward everyone. Authoritative. But benignly so, particularly to the younger dancers. As if he'd put himself in charge.

One afternoon, we were in the smaller rehearsal room, waiting for Bob to arrive and rehearse ten of us for a Program V ballet. The others were chatting among themselves. I was sitting apart, massaging my aching quads over a tennis ball, which hurt, but broke up the fascia. Dmitri came over and sat down next to me.

"I have something to tell you," he announced grandly.

"Yes?" I smiled politely.

"I have submitted my name for the co-artistic director position."

I froze. I felt my jaw drop.

How did he know?

"How pleased I was to hear that, finally, Anders came around to my idea," he said. "I'm so glad he's open to sharing the directorship, after all."

"How did you find out?"

"An ally of mine on the board of trustees told me about Anders' suggestion. I've told you countless times, April. I am not without my friends."

"You can't force Anders out," I said faintly. "He has a five-year contract."

"Oh, I don't want him to leave. Curiously, they like the havoc he's wreaked and its shaky end result. And this way I can both dance the lead roles and co-direct. I'd call that a win-win."

It was too horrible to consider. Did Dmitri know it was to have been for Sabine alone? But what if Anders had been so subtle in planting his idea, that he'd underemphasized that?

"He doesn't need someone in the position, after all," I told him.

"I beg to differ. And the board likes what I can bring to the table."

"What?"

He stretched himself out luxuriously, perching himself on his elbow to face me, and smiled like the Cheshire Cat. "Why, I can bring back Sonya and Kirill. The return of the WCBT's star couple—won't *that* be nice? And guest artists? Try Natalia on for size."

"You're lying."

"I'm not."

"You're just trying to get a reaction out of me."

"No." Jubilance filled his eyes. He looked ready to burst into laughter. "But it appears, regardless, that I have."

Natalia. She and Sonya would steal every lead. Even Anders wouldn't be able to resist their allure. They were money-makers.

This is so unfair! I wanted to scream. If Dmitri were allowed a voice in the artistic directorship, he would systematically break down everything that was not 100 percent in his best interests. It would be catastrophic. For Anders and myself both.

And here I'd thought my shaky, unhappy-but-good-enough existence of trying to live without Russell was as bad as it was going to get for a while.

Bob's arrival seemed to break Dmitri's dark spell. As he rose, he smiled at me. "It's something for you to think about, April. You're so young. So is Anders. It's time for the adults to step in and readjust things. Don't worry, I won't touch your contract. I do see the potential in you. I simply think you need a few seasons of watching the masters, before you replace them in lead roles. You'll learn from them, and three years from now, you'll be a better dancer for it."

"I'd like to start with the second section today," Bob called out. "Find your places, please. Where's my lead couple?"

Dmitri waved and gestured, before he turned back to me. "Be sure and let me know if you have any further questions on the issue." He managed to sound warm, solicitous. "Know that I am here to advise you in any way that helps."

I drew in a slow breath so that I could sound unhurried, unrattled. "I'm pleased to see how consideration toward me has become part of your repertoire, Dmitri. That's new. It's good to see that you, too, are learning how to stretch beyond your comfort zone, in considering the new, the untried. Consideration hasn't been in your skill set, has it?"

He frowned, but there was a certain look of admiration in his eyes. He didn't hate me, I realized. He merely wanted me to know my place and acknowledge him as the boss.

Like hell, Dmitri.

We walked over to join the others. I kept a cool, unconcerned look on my face.

This was a catastrophe. I had to tell Anders.

Except, nope. I had to dance.

The two-hour rehearsal dragged on and on. The moment it was over, I slipped out and hurried to Anders' office. To my unutterable relief, he was there, working alone. Without asking his permission, I stepped in and shut the door. Anders looked up from his paperwork and frowned. Although he hadn't treated me with hostility or contempt since our dinner together, neither had we returned to a convivial place. Deprived of my secret joy over Russell and our romance, Anders' chilliness hurt.

"I can't imagine how it's escaping your notice that I am very busy right now," he said.

"You'll want to hear this." I took a seat across from him.

He regarded me in irritation, but curiosity got the best of him.

"Speak, then. Make it fast."

"Dmitri caught wind of your plans for a co-artistic director position."

His forehead creased in confusion.

"He's put in his name for consideration," I said.

His eyes grew wide with outrage. And then, a flicker of fear. "Tell me what you know," he said tersely.

I relayed the whole conversation. Afterward, we sat there for a long, miserable moment, taking in all the dreadful implications.

"This can't happen," he said.

"I know."

"What do we do?" Despair had crept into my voice.

"We don't act hastily. We don't show alarm. It isn't going to happen, of course. But we need to handle it right." He sighed and rubbed his face. "Let's keep this conversation to ourselves. Don't engage any further with Dmitri over this issue. He's just looking for a chink in our armor. We won't give him that."

"All right. But… beyond that?"

He sighed, a sad, defeated sound. "I'll have to figure something out."

Throughout the following week, Anders was moodier, more mercurial, snarling at everyone, nitpicking over the dancers' form.

Curiously, the dancers responded positively to it all. The old-timers, Dmitri aside, had never treated him with more deference and respect.

Anders reached his limit one morning during company class. "Can you please inject more energy into your playing?" he called out to Chess for the grand allegro.

Chess got that snippy, disdainful look. "Haven't we had this discussion before? I think you know what I have to say." He sounded almost mocking.

"I beg your pardon?" A coldness had crept into Anders' voice. A warning, that made my limbs instantly go rigid with tension.

Chess rose, his face pinched with anger. "Unless you can play it any better," he shrilled, "leave me to do my job."

Chess had picked the wrong time to escalate his defiance.

I watched Anders, the way his body seemed to inflate with rage and fire. My gaze swung to Chess, whose proud stance began to falter as Anders began to stride toward him and the piano, with an energy that terrified me. Alice, nearby, scurried close to me.

"Is this a fight? Should we call Security?" she whispered, which made me laugh in spite of the tension.

"He's not going to hit Chess," I murmured. "Just watch."

Chess tried to back away from the charging Anders. He gave a girlish squeal of terror and threw his arms up, scuttling out of the way like a cockroach seeking a dark corner.

Anders ignored him. He strode up to the piano, where he reached over to the music rack and sifted through the sheet music. Not finding what he wanted, he slapped the pages impatiently aside, where they went flying, fluttering to the floor. He sat himself down on the bench, gave it a few angry shoves so that he was seated in the proper space. He raised his hands high and for a millisecond, paused. Then his hands came down to a crashing, unforgettable, searing cascade of notes. A dense, driving Chopin composition, an étude.

The sound filled the room. The piano had most decidedly never been played like that before.

I looked around and watched in amusement as Chess and the dancers took it all in with open jaws. Every last person, aside from those of us who'd already heard him play, was stunned into silence.

While Anders' fingers raced over the keyboard and his feet worked the petals, his whole body leaned into his efforts. He looked up, eyes full of fire. "Dancers, move!" he roared. "Why the hell are you standing there like sheep? Where are my groups of four? Across the floor, now!"

We all scrambled, terrified to aggravate him further. Even Dmitri seemed unnerved. The females scurried to upstage-left corner of the room; we always went first. Renata and Carrie and two senior soloists readied themselves and shot across the diagonal. Three other soloists and I prepared behind them to go the moment first group had completed the sixteen-count passage.

It was terrifying.

It was eye-opening.

It was actually pretty amazing.

The energy kicked in, the adrenaline, the way it does in great fear, but also when you're really in the groove, having a great performance, onstage or not. It was as if Anders had infused us all with an electric shock and now we were galvanized, jet-propelled, on top of the music, body in the air more than on the ground. Leaps became higher, turns more daring.

Right side, whole group. Left side, whole group. Repeat.

Anders kept playing; by now he was standing, watching us, shouting at us, to be more airborne, to attack the turns, to bring fire to the first développé devant, and *move*, dammit. It got all of us dancing better than we ever had. It was amazing. After the second time, both sides, Carrie cried out, "again, again! Once more!"

Everyone laughed and agreed. All of the first-group dancers ran to get in place, and when Anders didn't stop, they launched themselves out there. I followed suit, with the three others in my group. Every last dancer did. We all repeated it on the left, even though by now, it was brutally hard to catch our breath, and my legs were burning, shaking. It was like a Balanchine ballet, one of those where you're running and moving for a full twenty minutes straight, your lungs screaming for air, your quads burning, but it was too glorious not to dance it to the end.

It even made me forget about Russell for a full ten minutes.

When the last dancers had gone from the second side for the last time, Anders finally stopped playing. We broke into applause and cries of *bravo!* He tried to brush it off impatiently, but he couldn't keep the smile from appearing on his face.

He turned to Chess. "There. That's how I'd like it played. Think you can manage?"

"Yes." Chess's voice was faint.

"Thank you. Then I'll leave you to your job."

Vincent called me that night. He was in a cheerful mood, eager to talk, unaware of my low spirits. Which was fine; I wasn't about to confide in Vincent how being in love like this hurt. Nor could I tell him about Dmitri's latest threat. Instead I told him about the piano story and he cackled with laughter. He then shared the latest ABT gossip, who Natalia was now hitting on (scandalously, it was Kirill), which dancer had finally come out of the closet, what choreographer was being amazing, what stager was being a pain in the ass.

He asked me how *Beauty* rehearsals were coming along and I told him about my run-in with Yelena, my fifteen minutes as a substitute ballet master, and Katrina's dazzling display of technique. I mentioned my recent fitting for the Aurora costume, which Jana had worn, and how she'd told me she'd secretly stitched a smiley face inside the bodice, which turned out to be true.

"Wait," Vincent said. "Who?"

"Jana. One of the dancers who walked out on Anders in August. You've never met her."

"Whoa, whoa," he said. "Not psycho Jana?"

"What is that supposed to mean?" I demanded. "That's cruel."

"April. Her nickname is Psycho Jana. And for a reason. She's prone to psychotic episodes."

"You're lying! Or it's pure, malicious gossip."

"Honey, it's not. And it's serious. Haven't you been told to steer clear of her?"

"Well... yes. But I've also been told Carrie should be my close friend. It's not happening."

"Carrie should be the least of your worries here. Jana's dangerous."

"Just tell me what you know."

"Okay, so, I hit it off with one of the senior soloists during my last visit there. She and I got... very friendly."

"Imagine that," I said, dryly.

"She told me this story that's otherwise hush-hush. Five years ago, Jana hit Sid on the back of the head with something heavy, like cast-iron. It sent him tumbling down a flight of stairs and gave him a skull fracture. Big, big drama that they managed to cover up, but a dozen of the dancers know the truth."

I couldn't believe what Vincent was telling me. "That's impossible! Are you going to tell me that Anders knows this?"

"He knows he is to avoid any interaction with Jana."

"This stuff you're saying is preposterous. And that *you* of all people are telling me this."

"They don't say a word about it, do they? I told you from the start, April, the company has got some real problems. Not in their dancing, but in what they've glossed over."

"Who told you this?" I demanded. "I want to know."

He chuckled. "I never divulge my sources. I want her to sleep with me again."

"God. You are such a slut."

"A slut with integrity."

"I still say it can't be true," I said.

"Ask Dmitri. Tell him I said so."

"Dmitri doesn't like me. He'll tell me something false just to get a rise out of me."

"He does that to everyone. Liking them or not liking them doesn't play into the equation."

"He won't tell me anything," I insisted.

"Fine, Renata. Or Curtis. They're both straight shooters. Find a time where it's the group of you. Then ask."

I hesitated.

"Do it, April." He sounded strangely urgent. "I'm not kidding."

"Fine, fine! I'll do it."

Chapter 23

The Real Story

I would have brushed off the urgency of Vincent's suggestion, had it not been for the letter in my mailbox the very next day. From Jana. Even though I'd never given her my address.

Dearest April,

My life has changed so much for the better and I wanted to tell you because you are my good friend who cares about me. I have a new therapist. A new therapy. A new discovery of all that is in this world.

432hz is the Universal frequency. We are fractal to that ... so it reconnects as ... as in 144 x 3 = 432 (radius of our sun) and 1440 minutes in 24 hours. It is an incredibly healing number. It works, I've learned, if I expose myself to 432hz for an hour at a time, three hours a day, I don't have to take the medication that is making me sick and gain weight.

I am so much happier and so much better, and I can't wait till I'm well enough to be a ballet dancer again. I think that time is approaching.

Thank you for caring about me.

Love,

Jana

I felt sick. If Vincent hadn't told me what he had, I might have been able to brush this off as just another San Francisco alternative-healing therapy. But I couldn't unhear what he'd said.

It was, therefore, an easy decision the next day when I saw Curtis and Carrie chatting with Renata during lunch break. I told them I needed a minute of their time, in private, with Dmitri included. Once Renata had fetched Dmitri and the five of us had gone to a quiet area, they stood there, regarding me expectantly. I drew a deep breath.

"Vincent said to tell you that I need to know 'the real story' about Jana." I saw alarm flare up in the back of Dmitri's eyes, but he said nothing. Neither did Curtis or Carrie.

Renata looked incredulous as she turned to the others. "Does this mean none of you have told April, and she had to find out through Vincent? Why? How does this help her acclimate to the dynamics here?"

"We decided, back then." Carrie kept her gaze to the floor. "It was Sid's call. Just because he's gone doesn't change anything. My loyalties on this issue are still in place."

"Your loyalties. And yet, here is April, spending time with Jana. And all of you are mute about what happened. I'm so disappointed." She crossed her arms and frowned at them. "I'm more than disappointed; I'm angry. This is precisely why I chose to leave. This is so unhealthy."

"She's right." Curtis cast the others a sorrowful look before turning to me. "It's time you knew. Are you free this evening to come over to our place?"

"Curtis?" Carrie sounded guarded.

"Carrie. It's time."

Carrie sighed, a slow hiss of sound that seemed to deflate her.

"Yes, I'm free," I said.

"Come over tonight, after seven." Curtis looked around. "All of you. We'll talk."

At their apartment that evening, Carrie answered my knock. "I can't believe we haven't had you over before this." She held open the door for me to pass through. "I'm so sorry. This is a strange situation. I've mishandled it."

"It's okay," I said, except that it wasn't. Nothing felt okay. Dmitri wanted to take over the company. Jana was sending me scary letters. Russell's absence in my life felt like a missing limb. Anders wasn't my friend anymore and neither was Fiona.

Carrie led me into the living room as Curtis called out a hello from the kitchen. There was another knock at the door and Carrie excused herself. Taking a seat on the couch, I looked around. Judging by the tan and turquoise colors, the matching artwork and accessories, Curtis and Carrie liked the Southwest. A trio of Kachina dolls, exquisitely detailed, were positioned on the side table next to me. It was a pretty apartment, neat, clean and orderly.

Voices in the hallway confirmed Renata and Dmitri's arrival, and a moment later they joined me in the living room. Renata smiled as she greeted me, but Dmitri seemed uncharacteristically subdued. They settled themselves in the plush armchairs across from me. Curtis joined us in the living room, bringing out a bottle of Chianti and glasses.

I sat there facing the woman who was probably having an affair with Anders. Next to him, the scheming dancer who planned to barge his way into a co-artistic directorship. Taking a seat on the other end of the couch, the smiling, polite, unknowable Carrie.

"Where do we begin?" Carrie asked, once Curtis had poured us all a glass of wine and taken his own seat.

"Let's hear what April knows," Dmitri proposed.

Everyone regarded me expectantly.

I drew a deep breath, feeling like an idiot for even repeating Vincent's preposterous claim. "I was told Jana took something heavy, like cast-iron, to Sid's head one night, that made him fall down a flight of stairs and gave him a skull fracture. That she'd gone psychotic." I waited for their eyes to light up with laughter, sputter how Vincent had gotten it so wrong.

No one spoke. No one laughed.

It was not a good sign.

"Who told Vincent this?" Dmitri asked curtly.

"I don't know. He wouldn't say. It was a 'she,' though."

"Marilyn," Dmitri said to himself and shook his head.

"Maybe Grete," Carrie admitted in a small voice.

Dmitri looked fierce. "We weren't supposed to tell anyone!"

"Oh, come on, Dmitri," Curtis said. "I *heard* you telling Marilyn. Besides, Sid's goal was to keep it among ourselves. Meaning the Ballet Theatre dancers. And we did."

"That evening," Renata said. "Sid's house. Let's just come out with it."

No one seemed to be in any hurry to speak.

"Jana had a bit of a breakdown," Carrie said finally.

Renata snorted, and Carrie's nervous gaze slid her way. "Okay, more than a bit," she admitted. "But we were all feeling edgy and stressed. It was the end of the Nut run, where you're utterly spent but then it's over and you feel out of sorts. Especially if you don't have family or someone special to spend the holidays with. I'd done something shitty, in retrospect, just before Sid's gathering. Back at our apartment, I'd told Jana she'd need to start looking for a new roommate, that Curtis and I wanted to move in together. She told me no, that it would be impossible. Too hard on her. I said, too bad, we'd already made the decision. In the taxi over to Sid's house, she wouldn't speak to me. I didn't care by that point. I was as tired and run down as she was. And not just from the Nut run. For months, I'd been tiptoeing around her and her issues—everything too loud, too bright, her believing PG&E had a personal vendetta against her and that PacBell was tapping our phone line. I was worried about her career; the declining quality of her dancing. The night was a train wreck I could have seen coming. I *should* have seen it. I let my friend down."

"No you didn't," Curtis cut in. "Jana took as you gave and gave. She's a taker. The truth of the matter is that the blame should be cast on *me*. I took you from her. At least in her mind. She refused to talk to me that night."

"I'm culpable, too," Renata admitted. "I saw the toxicity brewing in her that night and thought, 'I'm not going there.' Sid, bless his heart, was extra kind to her, I remember. He didn't seem offended when she ignored him in return."

I considered all this and my heart sank. It made sense. "But how did it get from her being angry and hurt, not talking to anyone, to hitting Sid on the back of the head?"

In the silence that followed, I glanced from one person to the next. They were all watching Dmitri.

"She doesn't need to know," he said to the others.

Renata shook her head. "Wrong. April needs to know it all. She can be trusted. She has to be trusted. She's part of the family now."

Dmitri glared at Renata, who seemed unperturbed. "Fine," he snapped. He exhaled heavily, looking like he'd rather be anywhere else besides in this room, telling me this story.

"Jana was coming onto me in a big way. Even though she knew I was in a relationship with Carlos. She'd made this connection in her mind, end of Nut run, that she and I would finally consummate this love affair she saw us having. She beckoned me upstairs, to Sid's guest room. I don't know why I followed her into the room, except thinking that I could let her down privately. It was a mistake. Instead she started doing this horrible dance, a strip tease. It disgusted me; I don't know why she'd thought to try it on me. I think it was locked in her mind that time in the bedroom with her would change my mind. Off came her top. Her jeans. It was so wrong, I was embarrassed for her. I took her by the shoulders and spelled it out, telling her there was zero chance I'd see her in that way. But she wouldn't listen. She turned and grabbed something out of her shoulder bag, and I used the distraction to try and get out of there. But somehow she got to the door first, flattening her back against it. When I tried to push her out of the way, I heard a little *click*. It was a knife. This switchblade she carried around in her bag. I couldn't believe it. What a dirty little *putana* trick.

"She managed to trip me, straddle me, undo my belt, my fly, reach in there, pull out my member. All with that knife held to my neck and her weight pinning me down. Then she proceeded to rub her body against mine. Of course I got hard—I'm not a eunuch. My own body, betraying me."

His eyes had taken on a hypnotized look, like he was reliving it out loud, unaware he was revealing to me this most vulnerable of stories. I shrank into my seat, fearful of the moment his gaze would land on me, wake him up, and make him realize what he'd told me.

"She was going to use my body to punish me. Show me who held the power. If she hadn't gotten distracted over how to take off her panties, she might have succeeded. Instead, I knocked the knife out of her hand and scrambled away from her, got the hell out of there."

He abruptly fell silent, eyes flinty, his gaze fixed on the coffee table.

"We heard the scuffle from downstairs." Curtis took over the story. "We all ran up to see what was going on. The door burst open and Dmitri ran out, clothing all askew, and Jana, in her panties, following in pursuit. And then *you* tried to step in." He gestured to Carrie.

She looked sad enough to cry. "I thought I could help. I was so sure I could calm her down. But she came at me with her knife like she didn't even recognize me. I remember looking in those crazed eyes and thinking that was it, she was going to kill me. Instead she went for my hair. She grabbed a fistful of it, wound it up in her hand, and slashed it off."

"Sid was shouting at Jana by this time," Curtis said. "If anyone could talk sense to her, it was him. But she was too far gone. Sid said something like, 'That's it, I'm getting help,' and started back down the stairs. 'Help' to him was probably just a bucket of cold water, but Jana panicked like he'd vowed to call the cops on her. She ran and grabbed this cast-iron sculpture on a nearby stand and swung it at him like it was a discus. Sid never saw it coming."

Their story stole my breath away. I sat there numbly, at a complete loss for words.

"The irony is that Sid, tumbling down the stairs, landing there at the bottom, silent, did what none of us could," Carrie told me. "It stopped her cold. She stood there, dead quiet, and slid down the wall to a seated position. By that time, we were so freaked out about Sid that we hardly even cared about her. He came to, and sat up, but we had no idea how badly he'd been injured. Turns out it was a skull fracture. He was confused, couldn't tell us why he was on the floor, or what we were doing there. But when we told him what Jana had done, how she'd threatened Carrie as well, he said, 'No police. No ambulance. I'll take a taxi. Keep Jana safe.'"

"The group split up," Curtis said. "Carrie and I took Sid to the emergency room. Dmitri and Renata stayed with Jana."

They all looked at each other somberly. "What to do for Jana was tricky," Renata said. "She was dazed, and completely foggy about what she'd done. She wanted to know where Carrie had gone, and why everyone was angry with her. She claimed to remember nothing beyond asking Dmitri to join her upstairs. To 'talk.' That was where her memory stopped. I knew the safest thing for Jana was to be brought in on a 5150—that's a mandatory 72-hour hold for those proven at risk of hurting themselves or others. Jana certainly qualified. But Sid had been adamant that we alone were to protect her. Just before they got him into Curtis's car, he pointed a finger at me and said, 'I'm holding you responsible. You hurt my Jana and I'll fire you.'"

I couldn't believe it. Sid would have risked losing *Renata*? And how must that have felt for Renata? And Carrie. That Sid should have valued Jana and protecting her over Carrie's legitimate trauma made me ache with sympathy for Carrie, and chastise myself for ever thinking poorly of her.

Renata still felt the sting of it—I could tell by the way her lips had compressed so tightly they'd turned pale. "So we protected her," she said. "Even though we were afraid of her."

"Petrified," Dmitri said. "I don't think I've ever been in a room alone with her since that night. That she claimed to remember none of her assault on me—she'd held the knife to my *throat* and told me to cooperate, or else—made me all the more afraid of her."

Which explained a lot. Those half-dozen times I'd seen them interact my first week: his distinct unease over Jana's presence, coupled with something akin to respect for her. To be a gay man, held at knifepoint by a woman intent on having sex with him, must have been awful.

He looked up and met my eyes. Fury blazed in his. "Don't you dare pity me."

"I don't pity you," I lied. I chose my next words carefully. "I'm just sorry about what you had to suffer."

It worked. He nodded, mollified.

I turned back to the others. "So how did the rest of it unfold?"

"Sid spent two nights in the hospital," Renata said. "The story he gave them was that he'd stumbled going down the stairs, and hit his head on the marble floor. He would say no more, and we knew better than to cross him. But when he came home, I confronted him. Told him he couldn't hide from the fact that Jana was psychotic, never mind that the episode had passed and she was acting subdued. There was no way to call it 'just overtired' or 'too much to drink and got emotional.' I told him Jana needed real help. I was furious, frankly, that he refused to see Carrie as a traumatized victim of Jana's instability."

"Jacob made the difference," Curtis said, and they all nodded.

"We told Jacob everything," Renata said. "Sid always listened to him, so we sent in Jacob to talk sense into him. It worked, and Sid finally agreed. More importantly, Sid got Jana to agree. He paid for a four-week residential program at a rehab center for her to get the professional help that she needed. He told her to think of it as a vacation, a time to relax. She checked herself in; no one could force her to go. She did it for Sid."

I reached for my glass of wine and took a too-big gulp. The burning warmth of it calmed me. Renata poured the last of the wine into hers and Carrie's glasses.

Dmitri looked around. "Where did you put that wine I brought?"

"In the kitchen," Carrie said.

"We need it." He rose abruptly.

"Sit, sit." Curtis rose as well. "We'll get it."

"I need to move," he snapped. "Besides, I'm done with this story."

"Then help me in the kitchen," Curtis said. "We have snacks."

"Fine."

"I'll join you two," Carrie said, and the three of them left the living room.

"What was Jana's diagnosis, finally?" I asked Renata.

"They're calling it schizoaffective disorder." Renata took a sip of her wine. "With therapy and medications, she can keep it under control. But the medications make her gain weight. No dancer likes that."

Here I'd been thinking it was hypothyroidism. That a heavy body meant unwell and thin meant the medication was working. "That's why Carrie was concerned, the night in Santa Rosa when Jana brought me cookies," I said. "Because Jana looked thin."

Renata nodded.

"Wow. I called that wrong."

Renata leaned back into her chair with a sigh. "Anyway. Now you know. And we are going to keep everything in the open, from here on out." She seemed so composed as she smiled at me. "Do you have any other questions for me?"

"No," I started to say, until something unhinged came over me. "Yes I do," I blurted out, and Renata's untroubled eyes rested on me again. "Are you sleeping with Anders?"

The air between us grew charged, but Renata's expression didn't change. No drama or evasion in her eyes.

"No, April. Anders is a married man. He's also a conscientious, principled one, who's in love with his wife. As well as being my boss. But I'm curious to know why you'd think so."

All the angry bits inside me seemed to come together, sucked into a vortex like a tornado, roaring through me. Anders and Renata. How she could do no wrong these days, and I could do no right, after that one, lone, grand, mistake of mine.

"I heard him talking to you on the phone, when I was having dinner with him that Sunday night."

She blinked at me, perplexed. "And?"

Now I felt like an idiot. "He sounded so comfortable with you. Intimate. I'd thought he was talking to Sabine."

"And in your mind, he is not allowed any platonic intimacy with others? Say it had been Curtis or Jacob."

The idiot feeling deepened. "All right, I get your point."

"I'm eight years his senior with eighteen years of experience with this company. Anders' interest in me stems from that equation." She frowned at me. "Were you really thinking he was the type to sleep with his dancers? Or that I was the type to cross that line?"

I felt my face grow hot. "No," I said, feeling alternately defensive and ashamed. "But I heard what I heard. And in the next breath, he told me Sabine had asked him if he wanted space in their marriage."

Renata's expression softened. "Poor Anders. He *doesn't* want space. He wants her. She's the one who wants space." She shook her head. "Marriages are minefields. Business relationships are so much more rational."

"Not all marriages are minefields." I thought of my parents and my throat grew tight. "A good marriage can be the greatest blessing in a person's life. Two people who'd felt so alone, coming together to create something powerful and eternal."

Renata pondered this. Before she could reply, the others returned, bearing snacks and more wine, and my anger toward her faded. What was the point? She was the company's alpha female, and for good reason. I saw, grudgingly, what Anders saw in her, liked about her. She was a rock of strength and stability. Tonight proved it.

I turned to Carrie as Curtis poured. "Can I ask you another question about Jana?"

"Of course."

"So if all that was five years ago, how was she in the interim?"

"Up and down. Three years back, things got scary again, and she spent two weeks at a different inpatient facility. She stabilized, which was great to see. All that time, I treated Jana like a fragile thing. I'm embarrassed to say that years passed like that. It was only once Jana left the company, that I realized I was done. I just couldn't do it any longer. Except now, I don't feel relieved by the lack of contact with her. I'm worried."

The letter.

How could I have forgotten?

"I should let you guys know," I began. "She thinks she's fine but I don't think she is."

I pulled out the letter and read it to the others.

Afterward, no one spoke. Everyone looked appalled.

Renata asked to see the letter. "*I can't wait till I'm well enough to be a ballet dancer again,*" she read out loud. "*I think that time is approaching.* Oh, Lord, this is so delusional." She set the letter down; Dmitri grabbed it and reread it, his expression grim.

"What happens now?" I asked.

"We look for her," Curtis said. "And at the same time, we steer clear of her."

"I should be the one to hunt her down," Renata said. "Try and talk to her. I'm neutral ground for her. The rest of you aren't."

"That could be hard," Carrie said. "She's left her job. She's moved out of her apartment. She could be anywhere. She stopped returning my calls last fall."

"She told me back in December that you'd dropped her as a friend," I said.

Carrie shook her head in disgust. "Well, now you know that Jana lives in The World of Jana, and believes whatever suits her story, versus reality. She's still in denial about what happened that night, after all."

"That's what makes me the angriest," Curtis said. "Carrie was sister and mother to Jana. She put so much energy into keeping Jana stable, on her meds, going to her psychiatrist appointments, her therapy sessions. She's kept Carrie in this constant state of anxiety and dread. I have sympathy for all that Jana is going through and that she feels alone right now. But I don't miss her presence in our lives. I don't feel affection for her. I feel a sense of duty, nothing more."

"All right." Renata looked around the room at all of us. "We all know what's up, and whatever happens, we'll tackle it together. Agreed?"

"Agreed," we all chimed back.

Around midnight we disbanded. Renata had her car, and she gave both Dmitri and me a ride. When I stepped out of the car at my apartment, to my surprise, Dmitri got out too, and gripped my arm. "Hear me out. If she calls you and proposes a meet-up, do not go somewhere where you'll be in a room alone with her. Do not trust her. She should scare the shit out of you. She does me."

I wanted to protest, explain how she now saw me as a friend. But this wasn't about following a stage directive he was insisting on.

He was warning me.

Jana was a walking time bomb.

Chapter 24

Program III

During Program III's opening night performance of *Havana Nights*, I screwed up. It was the cha-cha passage that Dmitri and I repeated twice in the ballet, the first time to the right, the second time to the left. I mixed up the two and nearly smashed into Dmitri. He instinctively grabbed at my elbow to steady us both. It was quick, a blink-and-you-missed-it thing, and a second later we were fine, continuing beyond the passage as if nothing had happened. Tonight Anders wasn't backstage watching but I knew he was sitting in the theater, in the box seats reserved for artistic staff, and that he'd seen my mistake.

Lights shone in my eyes, rose-hued from the red gels that matched lighting to costumes. Our unitards of red and yellow, splashed with fern-like swaths of emerald green, clung, hiding nothing. Body imperfections, stupid missteps—all were visible. It was just as well Russell wasn't in the audience tonight.

The two demi-soloist couples joined us onstage, and I held a bright, insouciant smile for three minutes longer, until Dmitri and I exited stage right. Panting, furious with myself, I grabbed my towel, longing to bury my face in it so no one could see the tears that rose up, unwelcome and unavoidable. I could only dab at my face, however, because anything more would wreck my stage makeup. I dabbed at my leaking eyes, pretending it was just sweat. I could feel Dmitri's presence nearby and knew he was just waiting for the chance to berate me. "Get out of my way," I growled and pushed past him to stand at the upstage wing to await our next cue.

I heard him approach from behind. "Relax," he commanded. "It's not the end of the world." He took a step closer and began to massage my tight shoulders. "I said relax," he snapped.

I let my shoulders drop into an exaggerated slump.

"Better." He kneaded and rubbed.

"I'm sorry I screwed up." I forced the words out.

"It happens. And when it does, you need to trust your partner."

Which was an ironic thing for him to say, in so many ways.

"It was fine," he added. "I saved us from looking awful."

"You did." The admission left a bitter taste in my mouth. "Thank you."

He briskly rubbed my arms. "Drop it. All of it. We have to focus here."

His response surprised me. He could have chastised me like he had in the past, and been in the right. This more diplomatic touch both comforted me and chilled me.

It was the kind of attitude a dancer planning on being a co-artistic director would take.

Onstage, the eight ensemble dancers executed their final pirouettes and with a sauté arabesque, they exited the stage. Dmitri gripped my hips and on our musical cue, I leapt up as he carried me onstage, high overhead, my back arched and my eyes focused upward on those rose-hued gel lights.

The night's dancing improved for me in Balanchine's *Theme and Variations*, the program's third ballet. I had a smaller role, and partnered with Holt in the ensemble sections. Both of us, as students of the School of American Ballet, had danced a lot of Balanchine repertoire—no surprise as the SAB was Balanchine's feeder school for the New York City Ballet. Holt and I could have danced *Theme and Variations* in our sleep.

The music, the final movement of Tchaikovsky's Suite No. 3, was grand and glorious. The dancing, too, was old-school classicism, Balanchine paying homage to Imperial Russian classicism and Marius Petipa. Alice danced in it as well, in the corps ensemble. Our costumes were classical: for the females, white pancake tutus with blue satin bodices, and for the males, white tights and elegant, Imperial style teal jackets. The ballet had a total of twenty-four dancers, and when the full ensemble filled the stage, it felt hilariously packed. Balanchine had wanted his dancers to move ever faster, and when you threw in the little quirky moves he loved, so speedy and precise, it was organized chaos.

Dancing it tonight was infinitely easier than *Havana Nights*. All I had to do was lock my focus on staying on top of the music, the moves, doing my part to mesh with the other dancers. Alice's inclusive smile, her pleasure at my nearness, made it that much easier. Holt, too, met my eye with a broad smile, and I felt my spirits lift. At least some of the WCBT members loved dancing with me.

After curtain call, Fiona met me backstage and presented me with a bouquet of yellow roses. I'd given her one of my two comp tickets and offered Russell the other one, during one of our brief, infrequent (and miserably unsatisfying) phone conversations. He'd asked if he could take a rain check on opening night, attend closing night instead. Disappointed, I'd told him sure, any night that better suited his schedule was fine.

I fingered one of the rose's velvety softness, pausing to inhale its rich scent. "Thank you. These are incredible."

"Oh, they're not from me. They're from Russell. I'm just the delivery girl."

"You mean he came tonight?" My heart leapt. Maybe he was waiting for me upstairs, by the security desk, and we could go out for a drink, celebrate opening night, and then…

Fiona's head shake put an end to my fantasy. "He ordered them and I picked them up from the florist."

"Thank you." I tried to smile. "They're gorgeous."

"Fiona! April!" Lexie called out. "Just the ladies we wanted to see." He and Holt made their way over to us. "Join us. There's a band playing live music at the Arts Center. Fiona—are you ready for this?—it's a West African band. A huge one, apparently."

Fiona gasped as her hand flew to her heart. "Are you serious? Playing right now?"

"Yes to both." He grinned. "When Giorgio told me, I said, 'Fiona's gotta hear this.' Holt, Giorgio and I are going in twenty minutes, once we've cleaned up. You two *have* to come with us."

"We do!" Fiona bounced up and down, excited as a kid.

I didn't want to go out and sit in a crowded place where you had to shout over the music. I wanted to go home and sleep. Fiona took one look at my expression and her own excitement dimmed. "April, you'll go with me, right?"

"I just don't know," I said, mentally searching for an excuse.

"Oh, April, please?" Fiona begged.

Holt, too, gave me a pleading look. "I know you're tired, but it'll be more fun if you're there, April. Say you'll come."

Seeing the raw yearning on Fiona's face, my resistance melted. Fiona loved all things African since her Peace Corps days there. This was a gift I could give her, a step toward reconciliation. And here was Holt, being so sweet, his eyes fixed on me as I debated.

"All right," I relented, and the delight on both their faces made me feel like a hero.

The band was indeed amazing, with singers and musicians filling the stage. Horns, three kinds of drums, bass guitars, the works. A quartet of female backup singers moved in tandem with the music. The way they swayed and danced was nothing I could imitate.

Fiona could. She and Giorgio, a corps dancer with dusky good looks, hit the floor, stepping right into the African dance groove, which seemed to be everything ballet was not. Gone, the careful control, holding the core steady as arms and legs worked. Fiona had almost a rag doll-like ability to fling her arms, her head, her whole body around. It was art in motion. Watching her, you'd think she'd lived in Africa all her life and never studied ballet.

Lexie found us a table, and once Fiona and Giorgio returned and squeezed in, Holt asked her about her time in Africa. "I taught high school English to African teenagers," she replied. "I was one of a handful of white people in a town of 6000. By the end of two years, being the only white person in the room was what felt normal. Can you imagine what it was like to leave all that and return to Omaha?"

"Rough," I said.

"Seriously," she agreed.

"I think I know the feeling," Giorgio said. "Do visits to North Africa count? I've been there several times, once for the whole summer. My grandmother is Moroccan."

"Really?" Fiona regarded him in delight. "That explains your beautiful looks."

This made Holt and Lexie hoot with laughter. "Pretty boy Giorgio!" Lexie crowed.

"It's true! That perfect skin tone, and look at his gorgeous eyes," Fiona said. "Not quite blue, not quite green—they're mesmerizing. It all reminds me of my friend in Gabon, Christophe. He was three-quarters Gabonese, a quarter French, and 100 percent gorgeous."

"Just a 'friend'?" I raised a skeptical eyebrow. "Seems to me he was something much more, judging by your letters to me that first year."

Fiona looked abashed. "Guilty as charged. I was head over heels. Boy, was I in bad shape those first several months. What a hold he had over me. It's hard to fathom right now."

"Tell us more about living in Africa," Lexie urged.

"Oh, boy. It was heat and sweat and this jarring sense of unfamiliarity. It was a mystical, mysterious place, where people worked hard and struggled and mostly lost, but kept on going, and still found time for dance, for music-making. I met incredible people. Suffice to say, it was two years of my life I'll never forget." She gestured around the venue. "This is great. Thank you so much, guys, for inviting us."

"You have Holt to thank," Lexie said. "He insisted you and April join us."

"I love you, Holt," Fiona said. Holt grinned and ducked his head.

I was glad Holt was there. With his sweetly handsome, freckled face, he was down to earth and less flamboyant than Lexie and Giorgio. I welcomed his lack of drama. When more friends of Lexie's arrived, everyone squeezed in to make room for the newcomers. I had Lexie on one side of me, Holt on the other, our thighs pressing close, a comforting group-hug kind of feeling.

Once the band had finished its final set, recorded salsa music came on, and Lexie grabbed Fiona to dance. Holt, his thigh still pressing into mine, even though we now had more space, asked me to dance. I agreed.

The salsa music was easy to move to. Holt and I laughed, because *Havana Nights* was so salsa-flavored. We danced and joked with each other through a second song as well. When that song ended and a slower, distinctly romantic song followed, I started to head back to the table. Holt grabbed at my hand and tugged. "Aw, c'mon, April. Stay. This is fun."

"All right," I conceded. "One last song."

He was right; it *was* fun. It felt good to sway and relax. His grip around my waist was strong, just like in rehearsals, and I let my weight settle against his. Which was nice. Until his hands began to caress my back in a distinctly un-platonic way.

An alarm sounded in my head, a dozen thoughts springing to mind at once.

This didn't feel right.

This was what Anders preferred. Something lightly romantic with one of my own kind.

This was not Russell.

This was what made sense.

Something in me went passive and wordless. More like giving up than making a choice.

Our movements slowed. I let his hands caress my arms. I let him move closer against me, his erection brushing against my pelvis in a way that felt more troubling than arousing.

I couldn't. I couldn't do this.

I pulled back to tell him enough already, only I hesitated, frozen in place. His eyes, dark with intent, locked onto mine.

He was going to kiss me. I had a sense of my earlier dream playing out, this more sensible realm, no Russell in my life, and it sent a stab of pain through my heart, along with a dull acceptance.

Maybe this was what I needed to settle for.

The instant the thought came out, I rejected it. The instant Holt's lips landed on mine, I rejected them.

I lunged back. All the sensible thoughts I'd been thinking crashed and burned. Instinct roared through me.

You couldn't order romance and a relationship like a takeout pizza.

We regarded each other, stricken. "I'm sorry," we both said, and it would have been otherwise funny, except that it was so agonizing just then, so awkward and jarring.

"I can't," I said. "I'm not available."

"Oh," he said. His brow furrowed. "Are you sure?"

I gaped at him, unsure of how to respond.

"It's just," he began, "well, you've seemed so sad lately, and so happy here tonight. Happy to be with me."

"I am," I assured him.

"No, I mean, happy to 'be' with me. Like…" He made a swirling movement with his hands, and I finally caught on.

Like we were a couple. Like this was a date. I mentally replayed the entire evening through the lens of this different perspective. My smiles, my comfortable intimacy with him. Pressing against him, even laying my head on his shoulder at one point, something I easily did with Lexie.

But Lexie was gay. Holt wasn't.

I could feel my face grow hot with chagrin. "I am so sorry. I didn't mean to lead you on."

"It's okay," he said, only it wasn't. It felt catastrophic and awkward. We stood there, not moving, jostled from time to time by the other couples on the dance floor.

"Is it the other guy?" he asked. "Fiona's brother?"

Russell. I missed him so badly right then, I wanted to cry. "It is," I said.

He exhaled heavily and looked down. "I guess there's some comfort in that, and it's not because you think I'm an unattractive toad."

This made me laugh. "Stop it! You're gorgeous. All the women here are eyeing me in envy. Possibly some of the men, too." We both glanced to the side where, hilariously, a slim, attractive Latino male was indeed speculatively eyeing him. This time both of us laughed.

Holt was a genuinely nice guy. I allowed him to draw me back up against him as we recommenced dancing, both of us now trying to ignore the awkward presence of his erection. But we knew each other physically well enough. Even erections—it was one of the reasons male dancers wore dance belts onstage, with their thick, protective cup. To hide things. Gradually we relaxed.

"Friends still?" he asked.

"Yes. Please." I heard a note of despairing urgency creep into the second word. He must have heard it too, because he gave my hips a reassuring squeeze, the kind your partner gives you when you stumble a tiny bit onstage while you're performing together.

"Hey," he said a moment later. "For the record, I'm really glad you're here. In San Francisco. With the company, and all."

I stopped dancing to study his kind face. "Thank you. That makes me feel better than you can possibly imagine."

Fiona asked me about what had transpired once we were back in the apartment. I told her as we shrugged out of our coats and hung them in the hall closet.

"I had a hunch," she said. "I certainly noticed the way he leapt out of the car to hug you, and hold onto your hand an extra second. I could tell giving me a hug was an afterthought. I saw the sadness in his eyes, too."

I felt sad just hearing it. "Yeah. Super awkward moment on the dance floor. I like him so much, I hated to hurt him. But there was no point in leading him on."

"This thing with Russell. It's the real deal, isn't it?"

"I think it is."

"I'm sorry," she said. "I've been an obstructionist. I've seen you down in the dumps every evening since that night, and I realized I played some part in it, and I'm so sorry, April." She met my eyes;

hers were bright with unshed tears. "I think, deep down, I'm jealous of you both. Thinking you were both gifted with such incredible talents and potential, and that it was only fair that someone ordinary like me should have her own special thing—this relationship with William. That life handed some of us a perfect relationship, and others, a perfect talent. And that would be that. My brother—I'm ashamed of my competitiveness toward him. My belief that he doesn't feel and hurt the way I do, because he just stays locked in the unemotional side of his brain."

"Oh, he hurts, Fi."

"I know. We had a long talk last Sunday."

"You did?!"

She nodded. "He said he wants us to try harder in getting along. Which is funny, because the way he phrased it immediately put me on the defensive, as though we were a team and I was the one lagging, slowing down my partner. But when I pointed that out—calmly, mind you—he rephrased it. Said he wanted to be friends with me. It was touching, actually. He and I are going to meet up for dinner one night next week."

"Omigosh. Fi. That's wonderful."

A frown knitted her brows and I hastened to add, "For me, I mean. You two are the people I love the most in the world. Literally. I don't have the luxury of a big family. I'm jealous as hell over what you have. I know what you said, that night, about how being in a family means the ugly stuff as well as the good. But… I envy you."

Fiona sighed, kicked off her shoes, and wandered over to the couch. "Well, aren't we a pair? Quietly envying the other's life."

I hobbled over to the couch; my hips and feet were aching. So was my sacroiliac joint. So were the joints in my knees. I gestured to my body as I dropped onto the couch next to her. "You'd want this? Really? This bony, overworked body that I will continue to overwork and max out on a daily basis until season's end in May? A career that won't last much beyond my thirties?"

She grinned. "Point made. I guess I like my life, my job, well enough to keep them."

We sat there in silence, relaxing into the couch's softness, while outside, an occasional car on the street below was the only noise in otherwise early-morning peace.

"So, I have to ask," I said finally. "Your African friend, Christophe, the one who had you suffering through such a terrible crush, before you got wise and chose William. Was he an analogy of sorts for me? A cautionary tale, that maybe Russell was my Christophe?"

Fiona didn't reply immediately, which, I decided, was better than a quick protestation. I looked over her way. Her eyes had taken on a faraway look. "No," she said finally. "Christophe was amazing and exotic and unusual, and I'll never regret having him in my life. But he was selfish, self-indulgent, used to getting his way. I think he was shocked that I ultimately got over him and hooked up with William. That's not Russell in any way. I see that now. Just like I can see now, in retrospect, that night when we were arguing, that he was fighting because he was in love with you. Not in a selfish 'she's mine and you can't have her' sort of way. More in a desperate sort of way. Because he was terrified he'd lose you."

I mulled over this and nodded.

Fiona yawned. "Yikes, it's late," she said as she rose from the couch. "I'm beat."

"Me too." I watched her pad down the hallway. "Fiona?" I called, and she turned. "Thank you. For everything."

"You're welcome." She grinned at me, and for a moment, in the dim light, she looked like the mischievous Fi from our childhood, plotting with me against her grumpy big brother. "And for the record, my brother's a very lucky guy. Think I'll call him tomorrow and tell him so."

"Tell him to call me."

Her smile grew soft. "I will. He'll be glad."

Chapter 25

Roger and Russell

Russell called me the following Tuesday morning before I left for company class. At the sound of his voice, my heart leapt and began to bang around in my chest.

"I'm meeting Roger in the city for lunch today," he said. "I just talked to him and he asked about you. Wondered, since you're local, if you'd like to join us."

Speechless, I drew a deep breath, thoughts whirling. Closing night, which he was planning to attend, was a week away. I'd told myself I could last that long without seeing him, but now, the thought of being with him in a matter of hours was a siren call I couldn't resist.

"This would be your chance, too," he added. "You told me about how you wanted to help Anders with a tricky problem. Roger's your man. He's got the influence, and he likes you."

He was right. This was my lone chance. "I think that's an excellent idea," I told him, and heard him exhale in relief. He was nervous, too, I realized.

I worked my way through company class in a fog of distraction. By a stroke of luck, I had the day's first rehearsal slot free, plus the lunch hour. Perfect timing. Post-class, I hastily brushed out my hair, switched to street clothes, and once outside, hailed a taxi.

It was one of those cloudless, blue-sky, winter-but-not days that made you fall in love with San Francisco all over again. The restaurant, located near Fort Mason, was a long, elegantly appointed room with large north-facing windows, offering views of the bay and the Golden Gate Bridge. I spied Roger by one of the window tables. He was smiling, his eyes bright with interest, his attention directed toward his dining partner.

Russell.

The sight of him made heat rush to my face and the rest of me constrict with longing. Russell turned around, as if intuiting my arrival. Our eyes met. In his, I saw the same mix of longing and trepidation. Then he smiled.

A hostess led me to their table where both men shot to their feet, an adorable old-fashioned courtesy. We sat, and after the waiter took my drink order, I gestured for them to continue their conversation. It gave me the chance to regain my bearings, adjust to being next to Russell again. My eyes greedily took in his handsome, even-featured face, his articulate hands, the way smiling made the corner of his eyes turn up. He was wearing a pressed button-down shirt and looked impossibly good. A hint of cologne wafting off his neck hit me along with a jolt of desire. I sternly reminded myself that this was a business lunch.

The waiter returned with my drink and took our food orders. "Enough business talk," Roger said once he left. "How are you, April? I saw you just Saturday night, in fact. You and Dmitri Petrenko in *Havana Nights.* The two of you were pretty amazing."

Thank goodness it hadn't been the night I'd messed up. "Thank you," I told Roger. "Dancing with Dmitri is both a privilege and a challenge. He's a very good dancer, but with very exacting standards."

"My wife liked it too, but what she's really eager for is the *Sleeping Beauty* production. Between you and me, I think she's more than a little enamored with Vincent Neumann."

Russell snorted with ill-disguised mirth, which he tried to turn into a cough. Ignoring him, I smiled sweetly at Roger.

Time to plant the first seed.

"She's not the only one, trust me! We're thrilled he's agreed to perform with us. You might know that Anders has spoken to him about joining the company on a permanent basis. And I have to be honest, it would be doubly valuable right now. Curtis, unfortunately, is still sidelined. That puts us one male principal down. Thank goodness for Dmitri—he's never before played such a crucial part of the Ballet Theatre roster."

"Can Vincent Neumann be persuaded to join the West Coast Ballet Theatre?"

"Unfortunately, it might all come down to price. A principal from the American Ballet Theatre can command a high salary. As things stand right now, it might be too tight a fit, particularly since we need to redirect any budget surpluses into costume renovation. Have you seen the color sketches for the proposed *Sleeping Beauty* costumes?"

"I haven't."

Second seed planted.

"They're just incredible. Thrilling to consider. I imagine Anders will show all of you at the next board of trustees meeting. He'll be looking for underwriting. You can assure any interested party that it is well worth the investment."

"Anders brought forth a different issue for our consideration last month," Roger said. "Taking on another administrator in a co-artistic director capacity. Which, I have to be honest, strikes me as a little problematic."

Thank you, Roger. Thank you, thank you, thank you.

"I think Anders has come around to that way of thinking too, particularly since it's clear Curtis isn't going to rebound as quickly as we'd hoped. But there's a positive side," I added. "While Curtis is sidelined, he's working in a ballet master capacity. He's enjoying it; he told me so. And it's freed Jacob to take on greater responsibilities as associate artistic director. Anders has a good personal assistant— Russell's sister, Fiona, in fact—who's becoming an ever stronger support. Who needs more on the administrative side with that kind of setup?"

"Apparently Dmitri Petrenko has expressed interest," Roger said.

I pretended to look stricken. "No! We can't risk that. He's our most important male principal. We desperately need him to stay on the performance side and not shift to administration."

"He felt he could do both."

"Well." I made a face. "How often does *that* work, pulling top talent in order to split their work hours into two very different jobs that will both demand his all?"

Roger and Russell looked at each other. "Never," they said at the same time, and we all burst into laughter. Mine carried a hysterical edge.

"If Anders could have two wishes granted," I said, "it would be for new costumes for next season, and to get Vincent Neumann on board. Then there's the need for better sets, and funding for more prestigious tours, in the bigger cities and venues. Anything beyond that is now a low priority."

"Anders will concur with all of this?" he asked.

"He will."

Roger nodded. "It's a good shifting of priorities."

"I agree. I hope the rest of the board sees it that way, too."

"I'll bring it up at our next meeting. It's coming up."

"That would be great. But, a small request—I'd rather Anders didn't know that you and I talked today. He'd just get irritable with me and tell me I should have minded my own business. And yet… this *is* my business. I care deeply about him and his success." I thought about the way he'd sagged in discouragement when I'd brought in Dmitri's news two weeks earlier. "He's worked so very hard this past year," I said softly. "The odds have been stacked against him at every turn."

"He took a tough job," Roger said. "But he's proving himself. The board of trustees and the big donors see this. It bodes well for the future."

"I wish major donors could underwrite dancers' salaries in the way they can for costumes and big productions," I said wistfully. "Or maybe that's a silly idea."

"For what it's worth, you're sharing the silly idea with the right person." He smiled at me and my heart soared.

I hadn't made a mistake, saying what I had.

My clenched toes uncurled. My tensed quads relaxed. When the waiter showed up with our food, setting down the plates in front of us, I looked at the grilled salmon atop a bed of spring greens, suddenly ravenous.

Conversation grew breezier, but fell short of relaxed. Roger, I could tell, was curious about the dynamics between Russell and me. He'd seen us together, at a post-performance party following opening night of Program I. We'd been holding hands, our intimacy and happiness palpable, as we chatted with Roger, thanking him profusely for the Mendocino cabin rental. Today, none of that. It was easy to focus on ballet alone when I was at the studios, hounded by the fear that I might screw up again. But here was Russell, now, and all the longing I'd held in for eighteen days spilled out. I wanted him in my life. I wanted to be with him, touch him, sleep with him, wake with him by my side. I just didn't know how to make it all work.

Roger didn't bring up the issue until we'd finished eating.

"So, you two, how are... things?" He looked from Russell to me.

"Oh... good!" I said. "But busy."

"Busy, busy!" Russell agreed, studying the tablecloth.

"Busy is good," Roger said. "But so is having a personal life. I myself know how tricky that can be, balancing the two. Liz and the kids sometimes don't see me for days at a time. Most weeknights I'll get home after they've gone to bed and be out the door the next morning before they've gotten up. It's not ideal. Liz is adamant that two or three times a year I take at least three days in a row off. We tack on a weekend and go away somewhere, off the busy circuit, where the four of us look at each other in surprise, as if we'd forgotten how to do this family thing."

I hesitated. "Is it worth it? The tug of war between work and personal life?"

He looked astonished. "They're my family. They're the most important thing in my life. I know it might not sound like it, based on what I said about my long working hours, but they are." He glanced at the two of us and his furrowed brow relaxed. "I'm going to tell you kids something I don't normally share. Liz is my second wife. I blew the first marriage, in my early thirties, in my hunger to get as far as I could, earn as much as I could, casting aside the gentler things in life. My wife left me after five years. I deserved it. I blocked off any pain and increased my work hours, traveling, staying on the road as much as possible. I was making ridiculous sums of money. I told myself it was a good enough life, that I didn't need kids, didn't need a home, a family. What an idiot I was. I practically killed myself through a decade of self-neglect. Liz saved me. She literally saved my life. Made me see what mattered in the world. My kids—sometimes

I look at them, all they represent, this miracle I almost missed, and I just want to bawl."

He stopped talking, but the impact of his words hovered, powerful and profound. "My parents would so agree with you," I heard myself blurt out. "They married late in life and I think they forever had the sense of it all being a miracle. From two lonely individuals to a family of three."

Roger smiled at me, a look of fatherly warmth that pierced my heart. "And how proud they must be of you. Where are they now?"

Even though I knew the question was coming—I'd brought it on, myself, in bringing them up—it was impossible to speak immediately. Impossible not to feel the tears rise in my throat at the thought of them. I felt Russell's hand cover mine and give it a gentle squeeze.

I met Roger's eyes. "My parents are dead, Roger." To my relief, my voice was strong and clear. "My father, nearly four years ago, and my mother a year and a half ago."

There. You said it. You survived.

Roger looked stricken. "Oh my dear, I am so, so sorry."

"Thank you." I could feel Russell's thumb caress the top of my hand, soothing and steadying. I looked at it, his larger hand atop mine, and felt such a wave of powerful feeling for him, it made the tears I'd tamped down threaten to rise again. "You're right. Family is everything. But fortunately life gives us opportunities to try again, create family anew."

"I couldn't agree more," Roger said. "And we are so much richer for seizing those opportunities."

The waiter's approach dissipated the charged mood. I reached for my water glass with a shaky hand, and drank in grateful gulps as Roger declined a dessert menu and asked for the check. He and Russell murmured about a mutual business acquaintance, conversation I only half registered as my pulse gradually returned to normal.

When the check arrived, Roger waved away Russell's offer to help pay. "Save your money to take this lovely young lady out for a nice dinner. See to it that she has fun once in a while. Both of you." He gave us a stern look. "Remember what I told you before. Balance. Find it, and life will reward you."

As the three of us left the restaurant, my hand found Russell's. We walked Roger to his car, said our thank-yous, our goodbyes, and watched him drive off. The moment he was out of sight, Russell turned and wrapped his arms tightly around me. People passed us, laughing and chatting. Seagulls shrieked overhead. Bicycle bells jingled. I sagged into him, utterly at peace.

Finally we separated. I looked around us, as if noticing the scenery for the first time, the soft blue of the bay that mirrored the blue sky. Together we watched ferries, from here the size of Hot Wheels toy cars, chug silently to and from Sausalito and Alcatraz. The cheery conversations around us, the coo of pigeons rooting for flung bits of bread, the gentle slosh of water, all served to relax me further.

A soft sigh escaped from me. "I wish I could stay right here, in this place, forever."

"Me too." Russell looked pensive. "Can you delay your return?"

"No, I have to be back by two-thirty. I have an Aurora rehearsal at three."

"How's that going?" he asked.

"Knock on wood, I'm still on track for an opening-night debut."

"Congratulations. I know what that means to you."

"Thank you." I smiled at him, suddenly feeling shy, awkward. What were the rules here, after all? Being in love with him felt as emotionally perilous as balancing on a tightrope. The glory of being so high; the risk of no safety net.

"Can I drive you to the studio?" he asked.

I lowered my gaze. "It's best that I take a taxi."

"Why?" he asked.

I studied the ground, not sure how to reply.

"April," he said, and this made me look up, which I'd been trying to avoid, because when our gaze met, everything locked into place between us and the world felt deceptively uncomplicated. "Why?" he repeated.

"Because I need to stay in that space, that workplace mentality. I can't screw up again. My career is everything; it has to be. It's why I'm here in San Francisco."

"But what if Roger is right? What if it's a matter of balance?"

"You and Roger are males. You can have it all."

"What if I told you that you could have it all, too? That I would make it a goal to make sure you had all the support you needed to be successful there."

A giddy, euphoric feeling rose in me, which my sterner side tried to squelch.

"Russell. You're building a company. You can't be a support provider; you're the one who needs a partner who supports *you* unequivocally, so work can be your life, your world."

He shook his head stubbornly. "No. That's not what Roger was saying. 'Find the balance,' he said. Besides. I'm not looking for a partner who will support me unequivocally. Actually, I was never looking for a partner. Neither were you. But it happened."

"It did," I admitted in a small voice.

"I love you," he said. "I want what's best for you. I made a stupid mistake that afternoon you were over, and I understand I need to keep paying for it. But the time apart, as well as seeing you today, listening to Roger, has brought me something. Perspective. An awareness of what I want from my life."

He'd been examining his hands as he spoke, as if the answers lay there, amid the whorls and creases. Or maybe they did, because when he next looked up, his eyes had taken on that genius glow. "I'm certain I can be the support you need. How can I prove it?"

Before I could answer—and, really, what kind of answer could I give such a broad, dramatic question?—his eyes lit from within. Surprise washed over his features. He drew in a deep breath and exhaled sharply. "That's it," he said to himself, and when he next met my eyes, all the query and insecurity were gone.

"I need to take care of some business before I head back to the office." He glanced down at his watch. "Perfect. I have time."

His expression had gone opaque, unreadable. I could only stand there, bemused and oddly insecure over what had just stolen his attention away, made him now move with such purpose. He strode out into the road and hailed an approaching taxi. It screeched to a stop and Russell flung open the door for me, as if now he couldn't shoo me away fast enough. "You go rehearse," he said. "Good idea to take a taxi. Keep your mind on your work, where it belongs."

"But…" I stopped short of entering the taxi. This abrupt end to our time together made my mind whirl in confusion. Had I just chased him away?

"Miss?" I heard the taxi driver ask in an impatient voice. I ignored him and focused on Russell's face. He didn't look awkward or uneasy, which I took as a positive sign.

"Sorry about dashing," he said. "I'll call you."

"That would be good."

"Miss!" The taxi driver sounded irritable. I sighed and slid into the seat. Russell shut the door, smiled at me, and tore off in the direction of his car, giving me no idea what was on his mind, except that clearly it wasn't me.

"Where to?" the taxi driver asked me.

I sighed again. "Civic Center. The West Coast Ballet Theatre."

Afternoon rehearsal passed without incident. After a bite of dinner at the apartment, I returned to the theater, even though I wasn't performing, to watch Renata dance *Havana Nights* with Javier for a single performance. I wasn't the only one eager to watch them; backstage was crowded with other dancers. It had been a risk for Anders, trusting a teenager to fling around this precious company dancer, hoist her overhead, spin her, catch her. She was twenty years Javier's senior. But the risk was paying off.

They worked beautifully together, with palpable onstage chemistry. Renata's propulsive energy, along with her supple extensions and airy leaps, made her seem like a dancer in her twenties. Meanwhile Javier, in his delivery of flawless pirouettes, powerful leaps and double tours en l'air, exuded a confidence and authority that made him appear older. Only at one point did I see his youth, when the two leapt offstage for their final exit. Javier turned to Renata, eyes wide with astonishment, and burst into tears, clutching at her like she was his mother. Renata stroked his back and murmured something into his ear. He nodded and his eyes flickered shut, a blissed out smile on his face.

It choked me up. I think all of us watching felt the same.

William and Fiona were at the apartment when I returned home. They were standing around the answering machine and laughing over something they'd just heard.

"What is it?" I asked.

"Wrong number," Fiona said. "Or a prank call. But it's hilarious. Listen." She pressed play.

"He was right," a high, agitated voice said. "You can listen to all these frequencies all day but they do nothing if you still believe what the enemies are telling them. You have to do your own experiments to find real ones. Discover what you know is possible in your own mind's eye."

My heart sank. I recognized the voice.

It was Jana.

"Beneath the streets, under the asphalt, are all these clues. It's like, it's like, an Easter egg hunt but invisible. Even my thoughts, these thoughts, could be based on what they have *told* them to do, and now I see it so clearly, what I am to do, to take power back, before it's too late."

"Crazy, huh?" Fiona said with a chuckle, once it had ended. I reached over to play it again, but Fiona, closer, had pressed the "delete" button.

"Wait!" I cried. Fiona looked at me curiously. She hadn't recognized the caller, which, I realized, might have been for the best.

"It's just that"—I improvised swiftly—"if someone is pranking us, we should keep track of calls like that, to compare the callers and their messages."

"Good point. Next time I will. But for now, come and join us for a movie on the couch. Some nice horror, perhaps?" She waved a VHS cassette tape at me.

"Ugh." I mock-recoiled. "No blood for me, thanks. I'm off to bed. Good night, you two."

"Good night," they chorused back.

I lay there in bed, unable to sleep. Thinking about Russell, seeing him. Thinking about Renata and Javier and their breakthrough performance. But mostly, thinking about Jana.

She was in trouble.

Which meant the rest of us might be, too.

Chapter 26

Jana's Party

On closing night for Program III, all the dancers crowded into our dressing room to drink champagne. Carrie's visiting friend had brought her a magnum and she was sharing. Dmitri had returned with his own two bottles, which meant seconds for all.

"Can you pour me some more?" Alice grinned and held up her Dixie Cup.

"Sure." I grabbed the bottle and tilted it into her cup. "Anyone else?" I raised the bottle and a dozen hands shot in the air.

"Looks like I came to the right dressing room," a familiar voice called out. I looked over the dozen people to the door and saw Vincent, holding up another bottle of champagne.

"You're here!" I exclaimed. "I thought you weren't coming until tomorrow."

"I decided to come a day early and adjust to the time zone."

He draped his free arm over a smiling corps girl, one of three who laughingly pressed close to him, and I had the sense that adjusting to the time zone would include staying up late, boozing and flirting. What the hell, I decided happily. He could have his fun. I would be seeing Russell within the hour. Maybe it was time I resumed a little of my own fun.

Casting was official; Vincent and I had opening night of *The*

Sleeping Beauty, a dream-come-true scenario I still had trouble believing. Carrie seemed good-natured about being second cast, and Katrina was thrilled to get a matinee performance with Lexie, late in the run. Tomorrow we would begin rehearsing in earnest, this final lap, fine tuning and polishing every last detail.

I glanced at the wall clock and saw it was getting late. I had plans to meet Russell and Fiona for a late dinner. "Okay, out please," I shouted, shooing everyone away. "Take your party elsewhere."

"Who's up for a drink at Murphy's?" Vincent called out.

"Me! Me!" A half-dozen hands shot in the air—unsurprisingly, all female—and in seconds they'd all dispersed.

Alone finally with just Carrie, I hurriedly slathered my face with cold cream and wiped off my makeup. Carrie, a step ahead of me, combed out her hair and changed into sweats and a T-shirt that made her look like a young girl.

"I'm out of here," she announced. "See you tomorrow and get ready to become Aurora!"

I caught Carrie's reflection in the mirror and grinned back. "Okay! G'nite, twin Aurora!"

The hallway grew quiet as the other dancers headed home. I slowed down, wanting to look my best for this night with Russell. No, it wouldn't be a date, with Fiona there too. It would be something equally precious. Three people who loved each other in different ways, working together to forge a caring, nurturing bond.

The door creaked open and I smiled to myself. It was Fiona, I guessed. Maybe she'd found a way to sneak Russell to my dressing room, in spite of the fact that he wasn't allowed back here without a security escort.

Except it wasn't Fiona. It was Jana. Which surprised me so much, I could only sit there, mute with confusion, as she slipped in and shut the door behind her. Locked it. She turned and faced me. There was a white bakery box in her hands and clothing slung over one arm.

Jana was smiling, a look of pure delight on her face. Aside from that, however, she didn't look good. She was gaunt, disheveled, wearing the scarf I'd given her in December, except it didn't look dressy anymore. In truth, it was a macabre sight, with oil stains, dirt, pilled-up wool bits, frayed ends and sides.

Do not let her in, Dmitri had warned me. *Do not be in an enclosed place with her.*

Too late.

I decided the best thing I could do was remain calm and soothing. Maybe that was all she wanted, in the end. "Carrie will be glad to hear I saw you," I told her in a gentle voice. "Promise me you'll call her. She's so worried. She loves you."

"Oh, *Carrie.*" Jana gave a dismissive sniff. "I don't care about her. Look what I brought you and me!" She held the white box.

"Ooh," I exclaimed. "What's that about?"

She set it down and opened it to reveal a store-bought cake, frosted in white with garish sprinkles cluttering the top and the sides.

"It's my birthday."

"Omigosh. Happy Birthday, Jana!"

Was it her birthday? Who knew?

"It's my birthday, and I wanted to share it with my new best friend at Ballet Theatre. The others, they can go to hell. But you. You alone see me. Understand my pain. My loss. You're the only person I want to share this cake with. That's why I waited till Carrie was gone."

Jana released her armful of clothing onto the couch and tenderly shifted the items around. I saw a battered tutu and bodice, like something Wardrobe had pronounced too dingy to keep.

"And now, the cake!" she announced. She took it out of the box, but then paused, perplexed.

"Uh, oh. We need something to cut it with," I said, impatience rising in me.

"Oh." Jana paused to consider this.

"I'll just go out and find us a—" I started, eager to leave the room.

"No." Jana interrupted, and her eyes brightened. "I've got something right here." She rifled through her shoulder bag and pulled out a pearl-handled switchblade that she opened with a flick of her thumb. "I always keep it my bag," she explained, "because it's very, very dangerous out there and a girl has to protect herself against would-be attackers."

A prickle raced down my back. The switchblade from Dmitri's story.

I had to get the hell out.

Except that I couldn't believe Jana would actually turn on me. She was cutting the cake, a serene look on her face. This wasn't Dmitri's attack happening again, I assured myself.

"Ready for a slice?" she sang out.

"Okay. Just a small one, though, and then I've got to run. I've got people waiting for me."

"I know." Jana looked apologetic but a giggle slipped out. "He was there. It's your guy, isn't it? I heard Reginald, our security guard, tell him he couldn't come down. I just slipped on past with a wave and let the two of them talk."

Our security guard.

I took a piece of cake, practically choking on it in my efforts to finish and get out of there. I tried to come up with unthreatening things to say. "What's that tutu you brought in?" I gestured to the clothing items on the couch.

"What do you think?" Jana chuckled, eyes crinkled in mirth, a *you can't pull that one over me* expression. "It's my Aurora costume."

"Your... Aurora costume?"

"Because my old one won't fit anymore."

In this, she had a point. She'd gotten so thin, but not in a good way. Particularly since I now knew what it meant: she was off her meds. She was emaciated, her eyes sunken in, jaw more prominent. What had once surely been a dazzling smile now looked strangely macabre.

She looked psychotic.

She *was* psychotic.

It was time for me to get out of there.

I made a great display of glancing at my watch and widening my eyes. "Look at the time! Thank you for the cake, this was lovely, but now I really need to go."

"No, you can't. I haven't gotten in my costume yet. And if we wait long enough, Larry and Phil will have gone home and we can turn on the stage lights and do our performance. So you have to wait."

"I can't. I have people waiting."

"Nothing's more important than this." Jana began to pace, agitated now.

"Tell you what." I improvised swiftly. "I'll just go upstairs and let Russell know that I'm going to be a few minutes longer, while you change. And then I'll come back down. Sound like a plan?"

Jana might have been psychotic, but she wasn't stupid. "No. I have a better idea. You stay here and *eat my cake*"—here she lifted it up and waved it menacingly at me—"and I'll go tell them you'll be a little longer."

My heart began beating double-time, but I managed a smile that I hoped looked apologetic. "I'm sorry, Jana. That doesn't work for me. None of this does."

I rose and strode to the door, but Jana caught my arm and hung on. I hadn't expected her to fight me. Nor had she expected me to resist her.

Tugs. Body slams. There was almost a sexual nature to it, the way she backed me against the door, and pressed her body into mine. I tried to push her away and she punched me in the stomach, twice, two rapid thrusts that hurt. I shoved her harder and this time, she stumbled back. I hastily unlocked the door and darted out.

Jana was behind me in an instant. I ran down the hall as she struggled to catch up with me, pulling at my blouse to slow me down. "Help!" I screamed. "Help me!"

Jana maintained her grip on me as she alternately pushed and pulled, trying to knock me off balance. It was like a human tug of war. I slapped at her, tried to anchor my feet to the ground. "Help me!" I screamed again.

Nobody. And then people, running our way. Jana finally released her grip on me. I caught sight of her hands; unfathomably, they were stained red. Had some of the cake frosting been red? I couldn't remember. It was the adrenaline, I told myself. It was making me lightheaded and forgetful. My ears began to ring. Everything felt vaguely off.

Dmitri reached us first, his eyes wild. I was about to apologize, tell him I was sorry, I was so sorry, he'd told me to not let Jana in, and I had, and all hell had broken loose. And still there was this red stuff, and it was blood. Had Jana cut herself?

It was the cake knife, in her hand, and when Dmitri seized Jana's wrist, it clanked to the ground. Bright with blood.

People now encircled us. Alice, my sweet Alice, cried my name over and over, a cry that turned into a scream when she looked closer at my throbbing midriff, aching from where Jana punched me.

"April!" she cried. "You're bleeding!"

I looked down in incomprehension. Punches bruised; they didn't bleed. I couldn't understand what had happened. But my blue-patterned shirt was growing dark and wet in the center.

Jana hadn't punched me. She'd stabbed me. With the cake switchblade.

The realization washed over me and I swayed. Reginald from Security rushed up with two other guys behind him and they grabbed Jana. I stood there and realized I was about to tip over. Dmitri scooped me up a millisecond before my knees gave out. In the strangest of ways, it felt like a dramatic story-ballet we were performing together. The difference was the blood, flowing heavily now, and that I was having a harder time focusing. Thinking became a challenge, explaining, an impossibility.

The overhead lights became too bright and I shut my eyes, jostled about as Dmitri raced me up the stairs to the main level.

Fiona's half-screamed "April! Oh, God!" made me open my eyes. Alice was sobbing. Everyone was talking at once. I heard the sound of running feet and more voices. Faces came close to mine and recoiled in horror.

"Bring her over here."

"Quick, get a towel. Press it against the wound, fast."

Finally I heard Russell, except he didn't quite sound like himself. Too out-of-control and panicked. "There's so much blood!" he cried. I reached out to clutch his hand, but only found air.

"What happened?" people kept asking over and over. I wanted to tell them Jana hurt me, but I found that the less I attempted to speak, the less the pain consumed me. I hadn't felt anything more than a throb until someone told me that I'd been stabbed. Now the pain was roaring through me, like a fire. Dmitri laid me down on a cot— who knew they had these things in Security? From outside came the thin wail of an ambulance growing louder.

"April," I heard someone ask. "Do you know what happened?"

"Don't make her talk," someone else said. "She's in shock."

Russell squatted down next to me and took my hand. He looked terrified.

"Ssssokay," I tried to tell him.

"April. Love. Don't die. Please, please, oh God."

The sirens screamed closer and abruptly cut off. There was a new commotion. New faces. Hands, capable and firm, were wrapping and clasping, doing things that were beyond my understanding, particularly after the sting of a needle was followed by a fog of soothing warmth that softened the pain.

The new faces moved me onto a stretcher as my eyes flickered shut—it was all easier to tolerate that way. Someone was holding my hand as they wheeled me. Russell. I knew it was him, but my eyelids were now too heavy and wouldn't stay open. Attempts to say "Russell" produced only a *rrrss* sound, but he understood.

"I'm right here, love. I'm by your side."

The paramedics wheeled me down the corridor, out into the dark night and into the ambulance. Russell was there, his voice shaking as he said, "I love you, April. Please hang in there. I love you so much."

My eyes opened. "Russell."

His face was close to mine. Those beautiful Garvey eyes.

"You are the most precious thing in my life. Please don't leave. Stay with me forever."

"Nnnkay," I managed, eyes flickering shut.

Stay with me, April.

I wasn't sure if he said it again or if it was echoing around in my mind, self-replicating.

I felt his hand curl around mine.

Stay.

Chapter 27

Aftermath

Anders likely thought he'd be my first visitor that next morning in my hospital room. He wasn't. Or maybe he qualified, since Russell had spent the night, making a bed out of two chairs that only someone like Russell could find comfortable enough to sleep on.

Russell had left to hunt down a cup of coffee. Anders stood in the doorway to my room, unspeaking, frowning. I was in bed, in a half-reclining position, sleepy and mildly doped up.

What could I say? What could either of us say? This was the end of the world. For *Beauty*, at least. There would be no Aurora for me. Six weeks, minimum, for healing, the doctors had informed me. Three nights, minimum, in the hospital, under surveillance. An abdominal stab wound, it turned out, was serious business.

Anders knew this. Apparently he'd been in the waiting room last night, alongside Fiona and Russell, awaiting the surgeon's report. Once I'd been transferred to a regular room, the visitors were told to go away. Russell, being Russell, had ignored the mandate and returned ten minutes later, stationing himself in a chair by my bed. After they kicked him out a second time and he returned a second time, the night nurses sighed and told him to at least keep out of the way.

He didn't do that either. I woke holding his hand, his face inches from mine. His hair was adorably tousled. His intense blue eyes blinked and refocused. "Good morning, April," he'd said, instantly lucid. "I love you so much."

"You're awake," Anders said to me now. "Are you up for talking?"

"Yes. I think."

I could almost see his mind working, considering the consequences of what had happened, wondering if he could strong-arm me into getting better in two weeks' time for opening night.

"Oops," I offered weakly.

Anders' expression hadn't changed. "That's it," he said. "You're fired."

His words were so unexpected, they made me laugh. The movement sent a shard of pain through my abs and made me think I needed more painkillers, or maybe less, because the situation, the black humor of it all, seemed uproariously funny.

The corners of his mouth turned up. "You think I'm funny."

"I do." Unless he were serious. I hesitated.

"Glad we can find something to laugh about here."

He glanced around the room, frowning at the sight of Russell's jacket thrown over the armchair, his backpack on the table, work papers strewn about.

"You have another visitor."

"I do."

"Let me guess."

"It would be an easy guess."

He sighed heavily. You'd have thought I'd told him I was pregnant.

"He's a persistent one."

Russell appeared at the door and stopped when he saw Anders.

Anders shot him a wrathful look.

Russell didn't shrink. "You're not going to try and pin *this* one on me, are you?" he asked, sounding amused.

"She was to have had no visitors overnight!"

Russell dipped his head in acknowledgement. "True enough."

Anders took a step closer to my bed as if to close out Russell. "I spoke with Vincent a half-hour ago," he told me. "He knows you're out. Thankfully, he says he's still in. We need him for opening night; he's a huge draw."

"What about Aurora?" I felt sick. It hurt to say the words. It hurt to think.

"Look," Russell interrupted, "can this wait? April's in the early stages of recovering from a severe trauma, both physical and emotional."

Anders glared at him. "Excuse me," he snapped, "we have a production to get into shape that has suffered a devastating eleventh-hour blow. What will hinder April is *your* presence here, not my words or my questions."

Russell smiled pleasantly. "I'm not leaving, if that's your hope."

"Fine. I'm not dropping my role of artistic director, just because April is laid up." Anders folded his arms. "We as ballet professionals inhabit a physically and emotionally challenging world. The higher the level, the higher the stress. Dancers perform with torn ligaments, sprained ankles—never at my approval, mind you. But it's the mindset. This is our life." He swung around to face me. "Is this upsetting you, April? Shall I tiptoe out and keep my concerns to myself, so that you can heal in peace?"

"No." I beckoned Russell over and took his hand. "He's right. I promise you I won't try and dance in the production. But the company needs any other help I can provide."

Anders looked victorious.

"And *you* stop needling Russell," I told him. "He belongs in my life just as much. I'm not chasing him out of the picture, Anders. Not anymore. There's a way to make it all work out."

"No, there isn't." His gaze grew dark.

"That's your personal situation. It is not the scenario here."

Russell kept quiet. I saw out of the corner of my eye that he wanted to speak, but thought better of it.

Good for him. He was learning.

"Sabine is flying out," Anders told me.

If he was trying to divert my attention from Russell, he was successful. "What?" I gasped.

Anders smiled at my reaction. "I called her last night and apprised her of the situation. They're between productions and she insisted on being here for all of us."

"That's really good news. Right?"

"Yes. I suppose it is." But his expression grew less certain.

"When will she arrive?"

"Three o'clock." He looked around the room, assessing. "If they're keeping you here for three days, at least they gave you a room that can fit a lot of people."

"I don't like the sound of this," Russell said.

"Consider yourself fortunate," Anders said. "Number one, we won't try so hard to spring April out of here early. And number two, you don't have to be one of those people, here discussing our production this afternoon. Aren't you supposed to be immersed in a startup business venture, anyway? There at work, day and night?"

Russell didn't take the bait. "April and her well-being come first. Period."

In lieu of response, Anders frowned at Russell. "Where did you find that cup of coffee? I'm in dire need of some myself. I trust I'm not stepping beyond my bounds if I insist you tell me where I can buy a cup?"

Russell laughed. "Two levels down, make a right out of the

elevator, go about 500 feet, and follow the smell."

"Thank you. I shall take my temporary leave."

After he left, Russell stroked my hand softly, staring at it as if in a trance. "They're all going to be in here," he said mournfully. "Your friends and colleagues."

"Anders is right. We have to make decisions. I'd rather be in on them, even if it hurts."

Russell rose abruptly and began to pace. He drew in a heavy breath, followed by a second one, the kind a kid does before they jump off the high dive at the pool. "I don't know if this is the right time," he murmured, as if to himself. "But if I don't say it, I'll be furious at myself."

"What are you talking about?"

The nurse came in, interrupting us. She bustled around, checked my vitals, gave me pills and adjusted the dressing on my wound. The whole time, Russell paced, looking downright spooked.

"Russell, what is it?" I exclaimed as soon as the nurse was out of the room. "What's wrong?"

"I only have a few more minutes before Anders comes back."

"That's probably true."

He stared at me, helpless, until a resolute look came over his face. "All right," he said, sounding firm. "We do it."

He went to his backpack and fished out a small white paper bag, the kind a pharmacy might give you if you bought a trinket at their shop. He pulled up the chair to the bed's edge. Taking my hand, he enfolded it in his. His eyes locked with mine.

"I love you," I said. Those three simple little words that encompassed so much.

He lowered his head and softly kissed my hand. "Marry me," he said.

I stared at him in shock. "What did you just say?"

320

"You heard me right."

"Can you please repeat it so I know it's what I heard?"

"April Manning." His gaze was so intent. "Will you marry me?"

He released my hand in order to pull something from the paper bag. It was a box. A ring box. And inside, a ring. A gold band, sturdy and eternal, that ramped up in a cathedral setting, on which was perched a diamond. A nice one.

I could hear myself gasping, unable to find words. My mind was whirring uselessly, unprepared for this kind of stimulus. Did the pharmacy sell rings? Did he break into a jewelry store under the pretext of getting his morning cup of coffee?

"Where did you get this?" I finally managed.

"San Francisco."

"But when?"

"The day you joined Roger and me for lunch."

Now I remembered. "This was the thing you had to do, right then, that made you dash off?"

He nodded.

"Oh, Russell," I began, and stopped short, still trying to process it all.

His expression creased in concern. "That's not an 'Oh, Russell, but…' kind of 'Oh, Russell,' is it? Tell me this isn't going to be one of those horrible situations that I misread in the biggest of ways and you're going to tell me no." His face had grown pale.

I managed to grab his hand before he pulled it away. I clung to it. He looked scared enough to bolt from the room.

"Don't leave," I said. "Please don't ever leave. I want to be with you, forever."

The panic receded from his eyes. "Okay. Sorry. I'm not too good at this. I've never asked a girl to marry me before."

"Neither am I." My voice shook. "But I'm game to try."

"Okay. Cool." He exhaled sharply. "This is where you try on the ring."

"Could you pull it out for me? My hands are shaking."

"Mine too."

"We're kind of making a mess of this," I admitted.

He'd wrested the ring from its satin bed and held it up. I took it with trembling fingers and studied it in amazement. This cool, hard golden circle with the diamond—good Lord, it was huge, all glittery, almost glowing with incandescence. It meant so much. Putting it on forever changed your life.

I put it on. It fit perfectly.

We heard Anders approach. He was talking to someone, a nurse, likely. My eyes met Russell's.

"Do I keep the ring on?" I whispered.

"Do what feels right," he said. "But wait!" Alarm flared up in his eyes. "You didn't say whether you'd marry me or not. I don't think it works unless you say 'yes.'"

"Yes." I assured him. "Yes, yes and yes."

I kept the ring on.

Carrie and Curtis showed up just as Anders was sputtering over the ring and my decision. Russell saw them first. "Nope," he said. "April doesn't talk shop until this afternoon, at the earliest. I'm protecting her."

"It's okay," I murmured. "These two are good. They'll understand. Carrie especially."

Introductions were made. As Curtis and Anders stepped to the side of the room to discuss a matter going on at the studios, Carrie approached me. It was interesting, observing Carrie and Russell interact. I watched him give her a visual sweep, her long blond hair in a low ponytail, the sorrow in her china-doll blue eyes. I watched her study him in the same way. Her gaze shifted and she caught sight of the ring on my finger. Her eyes bulged, and she began to sputter with laughter.

Anders turned around to regard us at the sound and Carrie gestured to my hand. "Really?" he said to Carrie. "You can't appreciate how inappropriate their timing is? Did this ring have to come now? Did one more thing have to complicate the situation?"

"I don't see this complicating the situation, Anders," Carrie said in that gentle way of hers.

"Absolutely it does. He's taking her away. Taking charge of her future."

"He's doing no such thing. Provided he understands he will have to move up to San Francisco so April can continue to live close to the theater and the studios. And provided he learns to live with tights dangling from the shower curtain rod and erratic meal hours." She cast him a querying look and he nodded.

Anders shook his head in disgust. "Here I was thinking you'd side with me. And Sabine—she'll think it's charming. Mark my word."

"It *is* charming, Anders," Carrie said.

Russell consulted his watch furtively. I could tell he was torn about something work-related. "If you need to go, go," I told him. "I know that look. You have something important."

"It's a meeting I can call into. There's a payphone downstairs."

"Go," I urged. "There'll be plenty of people to keep me company."

"That's my concern." He gestured with his head toward the others. "The minute I leave, they'll try to get you back in work mode. It's not the end of the world if I don't call in."

"Go take your phone call," Carrie told him. "I'll make sure she's safe with this group."

He looked from me to Carrie and back to me. "All right," he relented.

323

Once he left, Carrie shooed out Anders and Curtis as well, so she and I could talk in confidence. Because we had a lot to talk about. A lot in common.

Jana.

"I don't know who I'm sadder about right now," I said as Carrie settled into a chair. "Me being sidelined and losing Aurora, or her. She's gotten herself into such a terrible mess."

"Agreed. And this time she can't just walk away."

"Where is she right now?"

"She's in the county jail."

"Oh, God." Everything in me clenched, which sent a stab of pain through my stitched-up abdomen. "Not a hospital psych unit?"

"No. She committed a crime."

"But... she was unaware of what she was doing. It wasn't premeditated—I would have seen it in her eyes."

"It doesn't matter." Carrie sighed. "Trust me, I feel just as awful."

"What's going to happen to her?"

"It's time her family steps in. Enough of Jana's grudge against them. I called them. It's their job to get her released from custody, get the best legal help, and reach an agreement with the courts."

Carrie's words were slow to sink in.

Jana had *family*?

"They asked me to stand in as their proxy," Carrie was saying, "and I told them no. Last time, I thought I could help. Even 'fix' Jana. This time, I know better."

"A family?" I still couldn't believe it. "I thought she was all alone in the world. The story of Sid discovering her when she was only fifteen, out on her own in the city—was that true?"

"It was," Carrie admitted. "Her family disowned her. Well. That was her side of the story, and we now know how unreliable she can be. Jana told me they lived down south, some rural California desert town. Bible thumpers, very conservative, thought the arts world was a path to depravity and sin and so on. So she left. But the part about them disowning her, I don't buy anymore. One year when we were roommates, they sent her a Christmas card, which Jana threw out without opening. I fished it out of the trash and read it. All it said was, 'Merry Christmas from Mother and Dad,' but it was a kind gesture. For all I know, they've tried to keep in touch with her all along. I saved the envelope for the family's home address. It's like I knew that someday I'd need it. That she'd need them."

"Does she have siblings?" I asked faintly.

Carrie nodded. "Three brothers."

Not just a family, then, but a big one.

"The oldest one is driving up here to attend to matters," Carrie added. "They've gotten her an attorney, one she needs immediately. If the police extract a confession from her, even if she doesn't really remember what happened, or isn't lucid now, whatever she says will hold up in court."

"But that's terrible—this is mental illness! She needs help more than punishment."

"I know. That's just how the law goes. An assault with a deadly weapon, in public, with witnesses, puts it all into the hands of the police and the prosecutor's office. They'll make the decision to file charges, decide what the charges will be."

Jana was screwed. My head spun with all the implications. My stomach churned. "This is all my fault. If I'd only taken Dmitri's advice and instantly left the room—"

Carrie's raised hand stopped my words. "Don't," she said sharply. "Do not go there. Trust me, I took that route last time, and I'm here to tell you, it'll get you nowhere. This is all about Jana and what she chose to do."

She glared at me—who knew Carrie could look so mean?

I lowered my gaze. "Okay. I get it."

"April." She waited until I looked up. "There's nothing we can do to change any of this. There's release in that, though. There is nothing we *need* to do. Jana's brother will be here for the arraignment, day after tomorrow. I'll meet with him beforehand. I think you should stay completely out of the loop. This is a criminal offense, not a civil one. Unless you want to go that route. That one's in your power, to press charges in a civil trial."

"Not a chance." I shook my head.

"Then you're free, April. Free to let any obligation drop."

I exhaled softly. Carrie reached over and took my hand.

We both knew it would be a while before I felt any freedom over the situation.

Russell and Anders had negotiated an agreement: I was to have rest and peace until four o'clock, and in return, Russell would leave for two hours to give our group the time and space to talk shop. It was now approaching that meeting time. Anders had gone to the airport to pick up Sabine and I was taking a slow, encumbered walk, complete with hovering aide and portable IV hookup. But it was exercise, which felt good. Returning with the aide now, I spied Anders and Sabine up ahead of us.

They were walking hand in hand, and just before they entered my room, Anders stopped, tugging at Sabine's hand. When she glanced back at him in query, he pulled her close and kissed her. Deeply, passionately, while they were still hidden—or so he thought—from my scrutiny. She stepped away first, with an easy smile, caressed his face with a lover's lingering touch, and walked into the room without him. His shoulders sagged. He stood there an instant longer, a moment as poignant and real as anything I'd ever seen from him. Their problem became crystal clear: although Sabine loved him, it was not with the same intensity. I remembered the night Anders shouted at me over dinner, the despair in his eyes when he talked about his love for her, the fire of it, his yearning to always be with her.

Sabine was not suffering with the current setup. That was a vibrant, independent, happy woman striding into my room just now. She was thriving as artistic director of her own company. It made me ache for Anders, who wanted so much more.

I loved Sabine with all my heart. She was, at once, friend, mentor and mother figure. But if I had to choose loyalties, I would go, unhesitatingly, with Anders. The thought wrenched my heart. I hoped I'd never be forced to choose.

The two of them were standing by the window, looking out, when the aide and I entered the room. Sabine turned at the sound of my clumsy arrival.

"April, *ma pauvre petite*. I've been so worried!" She approached with open arms but stopped short as the aide bustled around, setting me back up in the bed. It gave me the chance to observe her, marvel at how amazing she looked, beautiful and alert, like someone who'd spent the past twelve hours at a spa, not in airports and on a transatlantic flight.

"You look good," I told her. "Well rested."

"I had the good fortune of an upgrade to first class, thanks to one of our donors who was on the same flight." She offered me a mischievous smile. "Friends in high places, if you will. It was heaven at 30,000 feet."

Voices in the hallway grew closer as the aide angled my bed to a sitting position. Moments later, my visitor count doubled, then tripled: Vincent, flamboyant and energized, crushing Sabine in a bear hug; Jacob, bringing me a bouquet of flowers; Carrie and Renata, with Dmitri and Curtis behind them, lugging folding chairs.

Everyone made a fuss over my injury and my ring. Vincent seemed equally horrified by both. Sabine and Renata, like Carrie, were utterly beguiled. Anders was impatient; he wanted to talk shop.

I let the others do the talking, a spirited discussion over how to spin the substitution (in positive terms), how much of the real story to share (none), how to keep me in the loop (media spots highlighting my ABT past, a potential *Dance Magazine* feature). Finally Anders raised the subject of opening-night Aurora. "Sabine has a partial solution," he said, and gestured for her to speak.

"Françoise from our company can slip right into the role and all it requires," Sabine said. "She's a strong Aurora, very familiar with the Petipa staging, and Anders, you and Vincent both know her as a dancer. She can cover two of the performances. But not opening night."

Dmitri spoke up. "Anders, I think it's absurd beyond measure that you're not simply giving Carrie and me opening night. It's far and away the most problem-free situation."

"Face it, old boy," Vincent said. "You two are a familiar product. Anders needs the splash of the newer face of the WCBT."

"What are you talking about?" Dmitri demanded. "You're not even a member of this company. You're an outsider, brought in to add glitter."

"Glitter sells. New York City dancers sell."

This made me smile, at least on the inside. It was good to have Vincent here.

"Did you know we've got the *New York Times* coming to review opening night of the production?" Vincent continued. "Do you know how we've got the *New York Times*? Because they caught wind that an ABT principal was dancing the lead."

"I agree," Renata said. "It needs to be an Aurora that creates a buzz."

"You?" Vincent asked, and everyone glanced her way.

She chuckled and shook her head.

Katrina had been promoted from understudy to third cast for a reason. Why had no one brought her up? I hesitated, my thoughts going back and forth. The selfish voice spoke first.

Say nothing. Because Katrina could be such a hit that Anders might want to keep trying her out in the big principal roles. I saw Katrina's potential; she'd likely take the opportunity and flourish, just like Javier was doing. And like that, within two years, she might replace me as Anders' next prima ballerina. It was like taking your biggest, most precious dream, the one you'd devoted your life to attaining, ripping it out along with your heart and handing it to someone else, saying, "Here, you take it instead."

If I remained silent, Katrina's name might never come up, and that would be that.

Then I thought of the Katrina on Christmas Eve, at my apartment, her face lit up with animation while we sipped our hot cocoa in front of the TV. The sweet girl, shaking with nervousness backstage, before her Rosebud debut, regarding me with such trust in her eyes. I'd grown to love her with a mother's protective intensity. Where did that put me now?

"Marilyn?" Carrie suggested, and the others recoiled. Being a solid back-up dancer was not the right qualification. "Okay, okay," she said, laughing, her face pinkening.

"Who's free at the ABT?" Dmitri asked Vincent. "Why not Natalia? Or Sonya?"

"No." Anders spoke before my brain could fully process the dreadful suggestion. "This is not an ABT production. Vincent is all the ABT the stage can handle."

"I'll take that as a compliment," Vincent said.

"I don't think it was one," Dmitri told him. "What Anders wants is *us*. The West Coast Ballet Theatre."

I drew a deep breath. "Katrina."

There. I'd made my choice.

No one recoiled, but no one leapt to their feet to shout, "Yes!"

"I mean, she actually *is* sixteen," I said. "It's Aurora's sixteenth birthday party they're celebrating in Act I, after all."

"Too green," Sabine said. "Too risky."

"Sabine, you haven't seen the way she's blossomed since you brought her and Javier over," I said.

Anders said nothing, but he looked thoughtful.

"Vincent," I said. "What do you think? She'd be your partner. Remember how impressive she was with Javier in the Don Quixote pas de deux in November?"

"That's right, the gala. She was amazing," he admitted. "But Sabine has a point, April. She's so green. I have my reputation to uphold."

"It's not *your* reputation you should be thinking about here," Dmitri burst out. "You see? You're not a team player for us. You are here for you alone. Meanwhile, the rest of us, we make choices based on what is best for the company."

It was quite the speech from Dmitri. Right then, I almost liked him. I certainly liked what he was saying. And I had to admit, he'd been heroic last night, in helping me. "So, you'd support Katrina taking the role?" I asked him.

He hesitated, then nodded.

"Anders?" I asked.

He looked up. I could tell he, too, was undecided.

"It's too risky," Sabine repeated.

"But you are not the final decision-maker here, are you?" Anders smiled as he said it, but his voice carried an edge, one that everyone heard. I saw Carrie, Curtis and Jacob exchange bewildered glances. Renata met my eye; we alone knew that Sabine had rejected Anders' offer to share the directorship with him.

"Of course I'm not." Sabine looked startled. "My role here is simply to support you and the company. Which is why I'm here." *Why I just flew thousands of miles at a moment's notice to help you,* her eyes said, even as she smiled broadly.

"Thank you for coming here." Anders sounded oddly formal. "Your help is beyond invaluable. But April might be on to something. Dmitri, too."

We all fell silent. This was, in the end, Anders' decision.

"I don't think Katrina is too green," he said finally. "And she's one of us."

I released the breath I'd been holding. Renata gave a private, decisive nod. Dmitri smiled.

"If that's your decision, I support it wholly," Sabine said, giving Anders a bright smile.

"Thank you," Anders said, warmer now. "I appreciate that support." He turned to Vincent. "I'd like to rehearse Katrina and you on Monday after company class," he said. "We'll see how you two look in the third act. That pas de deux will be her greatest challenge."

He turned next to Jacob. "See that Yelena and Bob are there as well. And Jimbo, Larry and Phil. And Charlie Stanton. Tell him to bring a few board of trustee members."

"That's going to be intimidating for her," I said in a smaller voice.

"Good." Anders looked impassive. "That's my goal."

Sabine gave a nod of approval. I saw how Anders noticed, even though he acted like he hadn't. He still wanted and needed her support, her approval. He wanted much more, of course, but life didn't always work out that way.

Their problem to figure out.

Chapter 28

Returning

Anders gave Katrina the opening night role and promptly handed me a new role too. "I want you to assist Yelena in coaching Katrina," he told me in his office. It was my first day back and one week since the stabbing. Russell had implored me to take two more weeks of sick leave, but I'd only patted his hand affectionately and told him not a chance. Not with opening night of *Beauty* one week away. "And for as much as you're up for it," Anders continued, "observe Yelena running other rehearsals. I'll make sure there's a chair in each studio for you." He bit into his bagel, densely slathered with cream cheese. A genial expression covered his face, as if he were extending an offer sure to please me.

I regarded him in dismay. "Yelena and I don't get along. Why would you do that to me?"

"It's not just 'to you.' I'm doing this for Yelena, too. Come get yourself one of these bagels. They're quite good—almost New York-good. A donor brought them in." He gestured to a tray on the nearby credenza.

"Thanks, I'll stick to business first."

He took another bite and chewed thoughtfully. "Back to you and Yelena. What I see is that the two of you could profit from each other."

"How so?"

"You see, you intimidate her."

"What? How is that possible?"

"She sees in you the future. You and the younger dancers. A newer generation. Smarter, more informed, more personal investment in the whole process. Someone who is willing to go against the word of the ballet mistress. Shout back. She told me no dancer had ever shouted back at her in the way you had. Not that it was in any way appropriate, mind you. It was not."

"And so this is my punishment. A mandate that I cringingly follow behind her, murmur that I'm sorry I was a bad girl that one day, and pay the price by sitting behind her, watching without being allowed to speak." Agitated, I half-rose in my seat, until a twinge in my still-healing abdomen forced me to sit back down.

"This is not a mandate." He calmly took another bite of his bagel. "Nor is it a punishment. Moving Katrina to opening night was your idea, after all, and even Yelena agrees that Katrina responds well to your guidance."

I eyed him curiously and he smiled. A dot of cream cheese on his cheek made him look like an innocent boy, which made it harder to feel anger toward him. "She reported back to me that day. She told me Katrina had made a leap in understanding. She credited Dmitri, who said he'd run the passage with Katrina a few times in order to help her and Lexie out, but I have a hunch who made the suggestion to Dmitri."

I relaxed into my seat. "Do you now?"

He took another bite of his bagel. "You really should try one of these," he mumbled through the mouthful. "They are sublime."

"I think I'm ready for one now."

The perk: the delight and affection in Katrina's eyes when I showed up in the rehearsal studio. Relief suffused her face when Yelena announced to those assembled that I would serve as her assistant, focusing on Aurora rehearsals in particular. Yelena herself hadn't greeted me with a hug or concern or even much sympathy. She'd gestured to the chair beside hers and I sat.

Today was Aurora and the four princes, suitors for her hand in the Rose Adagio. I watched Katrina listen to Yelena's feedback. "You must not be too dependent on them," she insisted. "Is your choice. Do I wish for this prince, or the next? The roses, they are gifts, but they are flung down later."

As Katrina moved, Yelena watched closely, frowning, but not slapping. I sat there, all awkwardness gone, newly fascinated by this coaching business. Aurora's grip. Aurora's sense of wonder. The way the Kirov—called the Imperial Russian Ballet in its pre-revolution days— had remained faithful to Marius Petipa's 1890 choreography, through a century, passing it down to Yelena's own teachers. How this ballet should maintain the essence of that era. "Ten-minute break," Yelena announced finally, and I saw to my surprise that an hour had passed.

A group of dancers descended on me during break. I braced myself for the questions. *Why were you with Jana? Why did you let her attack you? How does it feel to lose your debut role? How does it feel to watch us dance and know you can't?*

They surprised me. "Can they see your ring?" Alice asked. She'd already seen it, having visited me at the hospital.

Bemused, I showed it to them, and they all cooed in pleasure. When new female faces appeared at the door, one of the girls turned and beckoned. "It wasn't just a rumor. She really is engaged!"

Marilyn came in, scrutinized the ring and shook her head. "Honey, you made it to principal and got a ring before age thirty. My dream scenario, which doesn't look like it'll happen. If I didn't feel so bad for you, that stabbing business and you losing Aurora, I'd hate you."

"Thank you," I laughed. "I think."

Dmitri appeared at the doorway. Spying me, he made his way over, shooing away the others as he took a seat next to me. "Welcome back," he said. "I have a question for you. Please tell me why the board of trustees has ceased discussion about a co-artistic director?"

This was news to me. Good news.

"How would I know?" I tried to sound innocent.

He studied me suspiciously. "Anders says he knows nothing. And somehow, I believe him. He gave me that look, where he doesn't know the answer himself but gets blustery anyway."

I shrugged. "I can't help you, Dmitri. Sorry."

His frown deepened. "I don't trust you anymore."

This made me laugh. "That makes us even."

"Nonsense. I'm very trustworthy. Ask anyone who's known me for years."

"Glad to know."

"How soon will you return to rehearsing?"

"I was told to take six weeks off. That's nonsense. At the three-week mark, I'll start to see what I can do."

"I don't want to dance *Almost Sunday* with Marilyn," he fretted. "Her interpretation is too vanilla for me. She lacks all that spirit you bring to the role. You really need to see about speeding up your recovery."

I made a mental note to tell Russell about "all that spirit" I brought to the role—we could crack up together. "I'll let my body know that," I told Dmitri. "And my doctor."

He rose to leave.

"Hey," I said, more gently, and he stopped to regard me in query. "I haven't gotten the chance to thank you for your help that night. When you caught me as I was falling. Things were getting foggy, but I remember that."

"Why did you let her in that night?" His expression turned thunderous. "I told you not to. I can't believe you didn't listen to me. And look what happened."

"I know, I know." Chastened, I lowered my gaze, wishing I'd kept my mouth shut. "It was a terrible mistake, one that I'm paying for. But I'm trying to move forward." I raised my gaze and met his eyes. "I also wanted to thank you for the way you supported my idea to use Katrina for opening night."

"I didn't do it for you. I did it for the company."

"Um, I think it's safe to say that's why I did it too." Annoyed now, I echoed his sharp tone. "And why I'm here now."

He acknowledged this with a nod. "You did. It was noble of you."

It was the kindest thing he'd ever said to me.

"Just don't go thinking it gets you off the hook," he added. "I have no intention of working with a dancer who's less than top-notch. So don't spoil yourself with this break for too long."

He didn't wait for my sputtered reply, but instead strode over to Yelena. I saw them talking, Dmitri gesturing back to me. A moment later, Yelena looked at her watch.

"Dancers, break is over," she called out. "We must work."

As Dmitri left and the others assembled, Yelena approached me. Her expression seemed more complicated now. Wary. Grave. "Dmitri, he tells me you had become friends with Januschka," she said. "That this was your connection and why she targeted you."

"Yes," I admitted.

"Why?" She gave me an accusing look, which rankled me.

"Why? Because I try to be a kind person. When I see someone hurting, I want to offer my support. She was in pain. I mistakenly thought I could help."

She said nothing, but merely nodded, as if I'd shared some complicated theorem that required time for the brain to digest. To my surprise, she reached out and patted my hand. "We work now. Talk later. You and I, we eat lunch together."

"No, thank you—" I started to say, but she raised one hand in that imperious way of hers.

"You are not full-fledged company principal until you've had lunch with Yelena," she boomed. "You stop protesting and we return to work."

Resigned, I gave her a little nod.

Some forces were too strong to resist.

Back at the apartment that evening, I told Fiona all about the lunch. "She took me to this tiny restaurant two blocks away that I'd never noticed before. Apparently it's where the ballet masters and senior principals go when they don't want to run into the dancers. Jacob and Renata showed up, in fact, and Yelena invited them to join our table. I was so relieved. No matter how pleasant she was acting, she terrifies me."

"She was actually acting pleasant?" Fiona asked.

"She was! Can you believe it? And want to hear something crazy? When she asked about the wedding and I told her it would take place in June, her expression got all soft and she said that she, too, had been a June bride. Forty-five years ago. I was floored."

"Holy cow. Is the guy still alive?"

"Apparently not. A heart attack took him, ten years ago. She told me he was a weak man, petty and small, and that the one time he tried to hit her, she gave him an even bigger thrashing."

Fiona snorted with laughter. "So you're buddies with Yelena now?"

"Hardly."

"Do you think she'll shout at you less now?" Fiona asked.

"Absolutely not."

Which made us both laugh.

We were sitting at the kitchen table, chopping and shredding ingredients for a salad. Russell's chili, his specialty, simmered on a back burner. On Tuesdays he came home mid-afternoon, set himself up in his office—formerly Fiona's bedroom—and continued to work. During a break, he'd make his chili. Fiona and I, home later, supplied the salad and garlic bread. Tuesday nights, we'd decided, would be our group dinner night.

These were some of the new arrangements we'd all agreed upon. Russell had taken over Fiona's rent and Fiona, for all intents and purposes, had moved in with William. Three of Russell's young employees had jumped on his offer to sublet his apartment, so close to Pegasus Systems. He still had to work long hours, but I had no problem with his bringing work home and starting back up after dinner. I was a night owl and an avid reader, after all. I'd make myself comfortable on the couch, pluck a book from my stack, immersing myself in it. When possible, he'd bring his work out to the living room and we'd intertwine legs from our opposite ends of the couch. We'd look up and exchange glances from time to time, and the quiet elation on his face seemed to mirror what was in my heart.

Russell came out of the office now, rubbing his face tiredly, but the fatigue disappeared when he saw me. I hurried over to him, relishing in that moment when he put his arms around me and the rest of the world went all quiet. How good it felt, such a joy to come home to a beloved. Finally he released me (after Fiona noisily cleared her throat), stirred his soup, and poured himself a glass of the wine Fiona had opened.

I explained to Russell how I'd seen a different side of Yelena.

"It was freaky," I said. "It reminds me of when I was nine and had to spend a week with my Aunt Irma while my parents traveled. I didn't want to go; you'd have thought it was the end of the world.

But it turned out fine, and I got to see her softer side."

"What does she think of your getting married?" Fiona asked.

"I haven't told her yet."

"What?!" Fiona protested.

Russell, surprisingly, was on Fiona's side. "April, why not?" he asked.

"I was going to send the news in a letter. With my mom gone, I just don't have much of a relationship with my aunts. Phone calls are awkward. I'm unrelatable to them."

"Getting married is relatable," Russell said, and Fiona nodded.

"You should call at least one of them right now," she said.

"No thanks. I mean, what would I say?"

"Just be honest," Russell replied. "Be yourself."

"So I tell them hi, it's been a while, and things are fine, except a psychotic ex-dancer I'd befriended stabbed me and put me in the hospital for three days?"

Russell and Fiona chuckled. "You call and say, 'Hi, guess what, I'm getting married in Omaha,'" Russell said.

"Do it right now," Fiona said. "I dare you." She and Russell exchanged mischievous grins.

I regarded them in dismay. "You know, right now I'm kind of missing the days where at least one of you would side with me."

"Those days are over, I guess," Fiona announced cheerfully. "All thanks to you."

"Okay, don't rub it in," I grumbled. "And just for the record—I will call, but only to stop you two from hounding me."

I went to hunt down Aunt Irma's phone number, ignoring their mirth. They didn't know about awkward family phone calls. There was no awkwardness in the Garvey family.

I dialed Aunt Irma's number, half hoping for a busy signal. No such luck. She answered on the second ring.

"Aunt Irma? Hi. This is April." I drew a nervous breath before adding, "Mary Frances' daughter."

"April!" She sounded as startled as I'd expected. "What a surprise."

"Is this too late to call?"

"No, actually, we're just saying goodbye to Sally and Homer. The four of us had dinner together."

"Tell Aunt Sally not to leave just yet. I've got news."

"Not… bad news?"

"Good news," I assured her.

"All right. Let me tell Sally."

I could hear her set down the phone and approach her sister. "It's April on the phone," I heard, and steeled myself for an "April *who?*" Instead I heard pleasure in Aunt Sally's voice as she said "Mary Frances' April?"

"Yes! She said she has news."

Aunt Irma returned, with Aunt Sally in tow.

"So, anyway, hi!" I said, feeling foolish and clumsy. "I called because… You see, the reason I'm calling, is that, well, I'm getting married."

Silence.

"In Omaha." I clutched the phone tighter, fighting an impulse to just hang up.

"Honey!" Aunt Irma spluttered, and suddenly the dreadful silence was over, with the two of them interrupting each other in their excitement. "Who? When?"

"His name is Russell Garvey. And we were thinking the second Saturday in June."

"My word!" Aunt Sally exclaimed. "What news!"

"You said in Omaha?" Aunt Irma asked.

"Yes."

"Honey, we wouldn't miss it for the world."

"He's from Omaha, too, then?"

"He is. An Omaha native, like me."

"All the better!"

"Do you want to say hi to Russell?" I cast a wicked glance at him. He was waving his hands in protest, but I'd taken my dare, and now it was his turn. "He's standing right here."

"Yes!"

I put him on, relishing his trepidation. But he surprised me by relaxing into the conversation. He smiled as he listened. "I am so in love with your niece, Aunt Irma—I can call you that, right?—that I can hardly see straight." His eyes met mine and the now-familiar sensation of dizzying pleasure crashed through me.

Fiona caught sight of my goofy lovestruck expression and gave a faux-weary shake of the head. "Just don't say I didn't tell you, April. Being a member of the Garvey family can be a challenge. No backing out. Families are for life."

She had no idea how much I wanted precisely that.

"We'll be sisters," I said.

A broad smile spread across her face. "I've been waiting fifteen years for that wish to come true."

"No backing out," I teased.

"Nope. It's for life," she agreed, and we raised our glasses in a toast.

Family, again.

And proof, on the phone with Russell, that I'd never fully lost it.

Chapter 29

Opening Night

Opening night. This was it.

I stood there next to Katrina on a high, rickety mount in the upstage right wing, which connected to the grand staircase onstage, from which Katrina would make her entrance. A stagehand was there to cue her—and upright her if she tripped. None of us spoke. Katrina was awash in nerves, having been forced to wait downstairs through the ballet's prologue scene. It was particularly nerve-wracking for the prospective Aurora, having nothing to do besides wait for thirty minutes. She'd thrown up fifteen minutes earlier, from sheer terror, and asked me, in the politest of ways, if she smelled like vomit. I rubbed her tense shoulders and assured her that, number one, she didn't, and that number two, it wouldn't matter in the least. All dancers understood nerves, the very human smells of body odor, vomit, fear, adrenaline, sweat. We were all reduced to the same primal state just before we danced. Some suffered nerves more than others. Katrina, so young, was only now discovering who she was, in dancing a huge lead role on opening night.

This opening-night lead role I myself had spent months dreaming of and working toward.

It was like grief, the impact of it coming and going, at unexpected times. I'd been proactive and can-do all week long, but last night, back home, I'd had a good cry. Russell had rubbed my back and let it pour out of me until I was spent, empty of grief, accepting of reality. He'd poured us a brandy, we'd cuddled and found things to laugh about, before retiring to our—*our!*—bedroom, where I decided that reality, in the end, had a whole lot going for it.

Katrina was calm now, rolling up en pointe and down in a quiet, focused fashion. Below, onstage, sixteen ensemble dancers were performing the Garland Dance, to Tchaikovsky's lovely, sweeping waltz music. We couldn't see any of it from our perch; the point was to remain hidden. Below, in the downstage right wing, monitors displayed what was going on onstage, but up here, we could only listen and wait.

The Garland Dance ended and we heard applause. When the music started up again, more stately and thoughtful, I could visualize what was going on: the four princes who'd come seeking Aurora's hand in marriage were being introduced to the king and the queen.

The music changed, alerting Katrina to her imminent cue. For the briefest moment, fear cut across her pretty, made-up face. Then it was gone, replaced by a professional smile, a split-second transformation to Aurora, the sixteen-year-old princess, her delight at celebrating this pivotal birthday event that marked her entry into the adult world. The stagehand gave Katrina a nod and off she went, down the stairs, girlish and effervescent.

As I descended carefully down the back way, Vincent met me and took my hand. He was costumed and all set to go, even though he didn't dance until the second act. The backstage area was crowded; everyone wanted to watch how Katrina did. There was hardly any room for us, except that since I was The Dancer Who Got Stabbed, escorted by Vincent, the ABT star, dancers parted to make room for us. In this fashion, we made our way to the downstage right wing to watch.

Katrina was bounding around with sprightly pas de chats, piqué attitudes devant, alive with energy. Gleefully she approached her parents, the king and queen, eliciting a kiss from her mother, and from the king, a kindly cupping of her face in his hands, a "my, how you've grown!" gesture, before he pointed to the ring finger and gestured to the four princes.

And so came the fiendishly difficult Rose Adagio.

As Vincent and I watched, I could feel my quads and gluts clenching in vicarious tension. First, a passage of partnered développés á la second, with a little soutenu turn connecting them. Second, maintaining a set of attitude balances unsupported, as one suitor stepped away and the next prince stepped forward to offer his hand.

Katrina held her unsupported balance each time, with perfect confidence, as if she were too young to realize how hard it could be. In this way, she perfectly fit the teen Aurora personality. The way Jana had, in the archived performance I'd watched, all those months back.

Jana. A dagger of pain tore through my heart at the thought. Ex-dancer, ex-Aurora, ex-friend. What had I been thinking, befriending her? And yet, it had all seemed logical at the time. I'd seen someone hurting and alone, so much like I'd felt. I'd created a story that suited my interests. She'd done the same. The only difference between us was that her psychosis took the narrative and ran, made it more real than reality. Last week, I'd joined Carrie at a support group she'd attended for years, since her own attack. She'd invited me and I'd thought, "no big deal," until I'd taken my turn in the circle, explaining my situation, and out of nowhere, I'd lost it, sobbing and incoherent, in front of all those strangers. Everyone had been kind about it, and Carrie and her friend had taken me out for a milkshake afterwards, both patting my shoulder, assuring me they'd had similar breakdowns, and that was what they loved about the support group. We were all in the same boat, victims of a loved one—or not—with a mental illness. "Know that I'm here for you," Carrie had said, which had warmed my heart.

Vincent and I watched Katrina now as she bourréed and spun, a breather before the next set of even harder balances.

"I'm still gutted over the fact that I can't dance this tonight with you," he said.

The noble feeling in me faltered. The sorrow clamored to be let back in. "Yeah." I tried to smile. "A crappy situation. But that's show biz."

"It is." He took my hand and gave it a squeeze. "I made Anders promise he'd consider us for first cast when the company performs it again next year."

I glanced at him in surprise. "So you've committed to next year's run already?"

"I have." He kept his eyes fixed to the action onstage.

"That's comforting to know."

"You like dancing with me, huh?"

"You know I do."

"Well, then, I have good news for you. I'm joining the company next season."

I turned to gape at him in astonishment. "Tell me you're not kidding here."

"I'm not kidding."

"You're dead serious."

"I am."

Joy unfurled within me. Vincent, here all the time—my favorite advocate and partner.

"*How?*" I protested. "How did Anders convince you?"

"I'd assumed he couldn't give me the salary I was asking, but somehow he struck oil. Even he sounded amazed by his good fortune. My place on the roster is being underwritten by a Mr. and Mrs. Douglas Clapton Finke. I think I have to meet them and smile broadly and let them throw parties in my honor at their Nob Hill penthouse apartment. It sounds manageable."

My idea.

Roger had made it work.

There was no time to consider it further. The music built; the hardest part of the Rose Adagio was approaching. Katrina had to sustain a picture-perfect back attitude en pointe in promenade, four times, each with a different suitor, each with another unsupported hold.

This grueling test of strength and fortitude, after seven minutes of high-octane work.

I held my breath as she took her pose.

First one, impeccable. Hand transfer relaxed and solid. Second one, ditto.

Third one, best yet.

I exhaled, feeling lightheaded, as she completed the fourth promenade with Holt as her suitor. She released her grip on his hand and held the final unsupported pose one, two, three extra seconds, to prove she could, which made the audience burst into ecstatic applause. She stepped down, and amid a great rumbling of drums and triumphant horns, prepped for the final pirouette. I watched Holt's hands busily spin her waist, four perfectly clean revolutions, to conclude the adagio.

Done. Beautifully done.

My heart exploded with happiness.

Katrina was going to be Anders' golden dancer one day. A star above stars. And I would make my biggest mark at the West Coast Ballet Theatre within administration, as a ballet master. The moment these twin thoughts arose, I felt their rightness, deep in my bones. I could continue to support Katrina without the bite of competition. I could keep dancing at my personal best until the urge to coach grew bigger. Anders needed a strong, trustworthy support team; he always would. My career with the West Coast Ballet Theatre could extend decades beyond my performing years. The realization filled me with power and joy.

Anders approached us from behind. I could tell he was as euphoric as I, by the way he inserted himself between Vincent and me and slung his arms over our shoulders. For an instant, it felt like that night, last spring, when we'd successfully premiered his ballet in New York.

We listened to the audience go wild. Katrina's smile was rapturous as she curtseyed and made her exit downstage left.

"I'm so glad you two are both here," he told us.

"My friend, we are here to stay," Vincent told him.

We exchanged smiles, the three of us, and I had the reassuring sense that finally we'd arrived at the place where it could all begin.

THE END

Acknowledgements

Writing a novel is a journey, a long and frequently lonely one, rife with detours and road blocks and, fortunately, fellow travelers. Thank you to my writer buddies and supportive friends and family all across the country. Particular thanks to Kelly Mustian, Tara Staley and Carolyn Burns Bass and our North Carolina writers' retreat that proved fruitful and nourishing to me, in so many ways. Heaps of thanks to editor Sandra Kring, who studied the story closely and told me what worked, what didn't, in the wisest and most effective of ways. Thank you, early readers Kathleen Hermes and Grace Harstad, as well as Grier Cooper, who offered her own fascinating perspective of life backstage during a professional ballet career.

Books that educated me and enriched my writing include *Private View: Inside Baryshnikov's American Ballet Theatre,* by John Fraser; Steven Manes' *Where Snowflakes Dance and Swear: Inside the Land of Ballet;* Christine Temin's *Behind the Scenes at Boston Ballet.* Michael A. Hiltzik's *Dealers of Lightning: Xerox PARC and The Dawn of the Computer Age,* was a fun and engrossing education for me in the world of pre-internet, pre-laptop high tech. I gobbled down Clive Thompson's *Coders: The Making of a New Tribe and the Remaking of the World.* I thoroughly enjoyed the article about "What it Was Like to Surf the Web in 1989," by Brian Merchant at Vice.com. Wow. What an eye-opener.

Thank you to my husband, Peter, who shared his own experiences as the co-founder of a Silicon Valley tech startup in the late 80's and early 90's, and who was endlessly patient as I posed all sorts of stupid questions about the high-tech sector and the history of Silicon Valley.

Big thanks to Guy Crucianelli for excellent copyediting. For gorgeous cover art, a fourth time in a row, I'm indebted to James T. Egan of Bookfly Design. Thank you, to all the beautiful dancers of the San Francisco Ballet, Smuin Contemporary Ballet and Diablo Ballet, whose performances it has been a privilege to watch and write about, over the past eight years, as a reviewer. While my own characters are wholly fictionalized and none specifically resemble those I watch onstage, I draw so much inspiration from watching these supremely talented and devoted professionals.

No story with "Orphans" in the title can leave out the most important part of my life, particularly since my dad, my last living parent, left the world 10 days ago. So. To my family: the one I was born into, and the one I went on to create. To my parents, Tom and Mary Mertes, and my siblings—Kathleen, MarySue, Mark, Annette, Greg, Maureen and Laura. And to my husband Peter and son Jonathan, for celebrating every milestone with me, and tolerating my bouts of both artistic fervor and writerly angst. I love you all so much.

Glossary of Ballet Terms

This is a sampling taken from "Ballet Terms Made Simple" © 2016 The Classical Girl. For the more comprehensive list, go to http://www.theclassicalgirl.com/ballet-terms-made-simple/

A

Adagio – slow, sustained movement. A section in a ballet, or in the center during class. Pretty to watch. Can also be called an adage.

Attitude (devant or derrière) – one leg goes up at an angle, preferably with the knee way high and the foot just a little lower and nothing dangling downward like a bird's broken wing.

Arabesque – the non-standing leg lifts in back and holds, nice and straight, somewhere between a ninety and 120 degree angle.

À la seconde – refers to a body and leg position, which here would be to the side.

Assemblé – a jump movement where one foot/leg sort of swings out to the side and then both feet/legs "assemble" midair just before you land in fifth position. Commonly linked to a glissade.

B

Barre – that wooden railing affixed to the wall that you see in every ballet studio. Also the term for the first part of ballet class, which takes place—you guessed it—at the barre.

Battement – "beat." Petit battements are these little foot beats at the ankle you do midway through barre, and grand battements are these big, leg-swinging kicks you do to the front, side and back, at the end of barre.

Ballet master – the guy (or female, who is sometimes called a ballet mistress) who does things like supervise rehearsals, teach class, serve as the dude in charge when the artistic director is not around.

Ballon – wow, I could write an essay on this one. Translated as "bounce," this coveted trait, most commonly noted in male dancers (mostly because they tend to be the big jumpers), refers to a sense of lightness and ease when doing jumps. A dancer with great ballon will seem to sort of linger in the air, defying gravity for an instant. To use it in a sentence, and thus impress others with your newfound ballet acumen, you might say, "wow, did that guy have great ballon, or what?"

Bourré – a busy little foot skitter en pointe that makes it look like the dancer (always female—males *totally* don't bourré) is skimming across the stage. Used to great effect in the "Wili" scene in *Giselle*. Also part of a pas de bourré.

C

Cambré – an arch back with one arm overhead. Usually done while at the barre, during a port de bras. A very iconic movement in *La Bayadère's* "Kingdom of the Shades."

Chaîné turns – a moving "chain" of quick revolutions, usually en pointe.

Choreographer – the person (usually a male; why is that?) who created the ballet, although if he's busy and/or quite established (or dead), he'll send out his representatives, called stagers, to teach the ballet to the dancers.

Corps de ballet – the entry level rank into a ballet company, above apprentice, below soloist and principal. Not the most coveted place to spend your whole dance performance career.

Chassé – a movement step, from fifth position, where one foot sort of "chases" the other while doing this little baby leap/hop. Ideally the feet sort of slap together midair. Commonly paired up for a chassé sauté.

D

Dégagé – a movement at the barre where your foot goes out, like in a tendu, but "disengages" from the ground, a few inches, before returning to a closed first or fifth position.

Demi-plié – demi means half and plié means "bent." At the barre, the plié exercise you begin class with usually includes a few demi-pliés tossed in. All jumps begin with a demi-plié preparation.

Devant – "front." It's a floor position, a body position, that gets tacked on to other terms, such as in "attitude devant" where your attitude leg is in its pretty shape in front of you, not back.

Derrière – "back." Otherwise, pretty much the same definition as the one above.

Développé à la seconde – tell me you don't need me to translate the French here. A leg lift, where the toe traces a path from ankle, to knee, before developing out to the side and up. Some dancers can développé their leg way high, like close to 180 degrees. Pretty crazy to watch.

Downstage – back in the day, stages were raised in back, or "raked," which meant downstage, closest to the audience, was literally down from the back part of the stage.

E

Échappé – this jumpy thing where your feet are in first/fifth position and they "escape," while you're in the air, out to second position. And then in the next jump, the feet go back to first/fifth.

En l'air – "in the air," and it's usually paired with something like rond de jambe, which means your leg's in the air as it does the rond de jambe.

En pointe – on full point, when you're wearing pointe shoes.

Entrechat – a jump from fifth position, where the feet switch positions, and there's a sort of midair meeting of the feet before they land in their new spot. An entrechat quatre (French for "four") means you double up the midair action, so the feet go back and then front before landing. An entrechat six (pronounced CEES) means there's yet one more meet-up happening, before the feet land. Guys with great jumps can do entrechats huit ("eight") and story has it Rudolf Nureyev could do entrechats dix ("ten"). Whoa!

F

First [position] – when your heels are together, toes turned out, usually 150 to 180 degrees, depending on how turned out your hips are. (See Turnout)

Fifth [position] – a foot position where the hips are doing the turned-out thing (see Turnout) so that the right heel fits snugly up against the left big toe and the left heel is behind the right toes.

First cast – the casting everyone craves. You are the top dog. You will likely perform on opening night, which is when most of the critics come to review, so you are lucky and fabulous, but likely you already know it, and so does your artistic director.

G

Giselle – the classic 1841 story ballet about Giselle, this village girl betrayed by love, who dies and becomes a Wili, one of a band of vengeful maiden spirits, but nonetheless tries to protect her beloved from being killed by them. The story motif of "bereaved, betrayed, innocent maiden sent to the spirit world" would make its way in several more story ballets (see *La Bayadère*).

Glissade – translated as "glide," it's this movement that starts in demi-plié, fifth position, and, well, *glides,* with a teeny, weeny leap-but-not, into another fifth position. A common prep step for glissade assemblé.

Grand allegro – the big run combination across the diagonal at the end of a ballet class. Big fun. Classical Girl's favorite part of class.

Grand battement – a big giant beat (see Battement). Basically, big kicks at the end of barre, that you do to the front, side and back.

Grand jeté – a big-assed leap. Comes at the end of a few prep steps, most commonly a tombé, pas de bourré, glissade, and voilà. I don't know a single dancer who doesn't *love* doing this combination. It's what dance is all about. All dancers, regardless of age and/or physical condition, secretly long to do this every time we walk down a long, wide, empty hallway. Kudos to those who actually do.

Grand jeté lift – when the guy lifts his partner, either waist-high or overhead, and she does the leap in the air. Overhead is the most common. Cool to watch. This is why male dancers must be very, very strong. It's a HUGE myth that male dancers are wimpy. Couldn't be further from the truth. Basically, they bench press girls. And they do it without those grunts or face contortions you see on some guys at the gym. But I digress. Sorry.

Interested in seeing more? Visit here:

http://www.theclassicalgirl.com/ballet-terms-made-simple/

Be sure to visit The Classical Girl (www.theclassicalgirl.com) for more articles and fun facts about the ballet world, its history and its repertoire.

About the Author

Terez Mertes Rose is a writer and former ballet dancer whose work has appeared in the *Crab Orchard Review, Women Who Eat* (Seal Press), *A Woman's Europe* (Travelers' Tales), the *Philadelphia Inquirer* and the *San Jose Mercury News*. She is also the author of *Off Balance* (2015) and *Outside the Limelight* (2016), Books 1 and 2 of the Ballet Theatre Chronicles, and *A Dancer's Guide to Africa* (2018). She reviews dance performances for Bachtrack.com and blogs about ballet and classical music at The Classical Girl (www.theclassicalgirl.com). She makes her home in the Santa Cruz Mountains with her husband and son.

More Books by Terez Mertes Rose

Off Balance
Outside the Limelight
A Dancer's Guide to Africa

Off Balance, Book 1 of the Ballet Theatre Chronicles

Alice thinks she's accepted the loss of her ballet career, injury having forced her to trade in pointe shoes onstage for spreadsheets upstairs. That is, until the day Alice's boss asks her to befriend Lana, a pretty new company member he's got his eye on. Lana represents all Alice has lost, not just as a ballet dancer, but as a motherless daughter. It's pain she's kept hidden, even from herself, as every good ballet dancer knows to do.

Lana, lonely and unmoored, desperately needs some help, and her mother, back home, vows eternal support. But when Lana begins to profit from Alice's advice and help, her mother's constant attention curdles into something more sinister.

Together, both women must embark on a journey of painful rediscoveries, not just about career opportunities won and lost, but the mothers they thought they knew.

OFF BALANCE takes the reader beyond the glitter of the stage to expose the sweat and struggle, amid the mandate to sustain the illusion at all cost.

Praise for *Off Balance*

"A refreshing and gritty story about friendships, dreams, and life. The reason why this story works on so many levels is the author's ability to create characters that ring true. Terez Mertes Rose delves deep into her characters' back story to show how they really are: human and flawed. While her characters are off balance, Rose has balanced her novel perfectly."
— Self-Publishing Review, 5 Stars

"Terez Mertes Rose writes with an urgency that keeps us reading long past our bedtimes."
— Dance Advantage

"Any readers who have ever grappled to find the courage to strengthen or to soften, to embrace a dream or to let go of one, will find themselves rooting for the two willful, yet wounded, protagonists in Terez Mertes Rose's edgy debut, *Off Balance*. I loved this exquisitely written, fast-paced novel from the first page to the last."
— Sandra Kring, bestselling author of *The Book of Bright Ideas*

Outside the Limelight, Book 2 of the Ballet Theatre Chronicles

A Kirkus Indie Books of the Month pick and a Kirkus Top 100 Books of 2017 selection.

Ballet star Dena Lindgren's dream career is knocked off its axis when a puzzling onstage fall results in a crushing diagnosis: a brain tumor. Looming surgery and its long recovery period prompt the company's artistic director, Anders Gunst, to shift his attention to an overshadowed company dancer: Dena's older sister, Rebecca, with whom Anders once shared a special relationship.

Under the heady glow of Anders' attention, Rebecca thrives, even as her recuperating sister, hobbled and unnoticed, languishes on the sidelines of a world that demands beauty and perfection. Rebecca ultimately faces a painful choice: play by the artistic director's rules and profit, or take shocking action to help her sister.

Exposing the glamorous onstage world of professional ballet, as well as its shadowed wings and dark underbelly, OUTSIDE THE LIMELIGHT examines loyalty, beauty, artistic passion, and asks what might be worth losing in order to help the ones you love.

Praise for *Outside the Limelight*

"A lovely and engaging tale of sibling rivalry in the high-stakes dance world."

    – *Kirkus Reviews* (Starred review)

A Dancer's Guide to Africa

Fiona Garvey, ballet dancer and new college graduate, is desperate to escape her sister's betrayal and a failed relationship. Vowing to restart as far from home as possible, she accepts a two-year teaching position with the Peace Corps in Africa. It's a role she's sure she can perform. But in no time, Fiona realizes she's traded her problems in Omaha for bigger ones in Gabon, a country as beautiful as it is filled with contradictions.

Emotionally derailed by Christophe, a charismatic and privileged Gabonese man who can teach her to let go of her inhibitions but can't commit to anything more, threatened by an overly familiar student with a menacing fixation on her, and drawn into the compelling but potentially dangerous local dance ceremonies, Fiona finds herself at increasing risk. And when matters come to a shocking head, she must reach inside herself, find her dancer's power, and fight back.

Blending humor and pathos, A DANCER'S GUIDE TO AFRICA takes the reader along on a suspense-laden, sensual journey through Africa's complex beauty, mystery and mysticism.

Praise for *A Dancer's Guide to Africa*

"Vivid prose and rapt evocations of the African surroundings make the story come alive."
— *Kirkus Reviews*

"Hilarious and poignant, with a frank, observant narrator who seems forever on the outside looking in, and all the more lovable and relatable for that."

— Sarah Bird, bestselling author of *The Yokota Officers Club* and *Daughter of a Daughter of a Queen*

"Terez Mertes Rose knows dancing. She can make us feel its soulful allure. And in *A Dancer's Guide To Africa* she captures the wonder, the culture divide, the longing and loneliness of being an outsider in the nation of Gabon. Better still, she delivers a cast of characters and a story that holds our attention from beginning to end. With this novel, Terez Mertes Rose, a savvy, insightful and entertaining writer, has come into her own."

— John Dalton, award-winning author of *Heaven Lake*

"Rich with the smells, sounds, sights and culture of Africa, this novel takes us on an exquisite journey, through the eyes of a ballet dancer turned Peace Corps volunteer. *A Dancer's Guide to Africa* is at once funny and dark, and superbly nuanced."

— Marika Brussel, choreographer and former dancer

"Terez Mertes Rose has drawn on her considerable passions—dance, music, and storytelling—to take readers on a sometimes mystical and often suspenseful journey. The spiritual, visceral, and sensory-laden beauty of Gabon was a believable and riveting backdrop for this touching story of a women discovering her truth and power. *A Dancer's Guide to Africa* commanded my attention from the first page to the last sentence."

— Jennifer Haupt, author of *In the Shadow of 10,000 Hills*